THE CURIOUS CASE OF THE MISSING HEAD

Jack Rogan Mysteries Book 5

GABRIEL FARAGO

This book is brought to you by Bear & King Publishing.

Publishing & Marketing Consultant: Lama Jabr
Website: https://xanapublishingandmarketing.com
Sydney, Australia

Cover Design by Giovanni Banfi

Signup for the author's New Releases mailing list and get a free copy of *The Forgotten Painting** novella and find out where it all began ...

https://gabrielfarago.com.au/free-download-forgotten-painting/

* I'm delighted to tell you that *The Forgotten Painting* has received two major literary awards in the US. It was awarded the Gold Medal by Readers' Favorite in the Short Stories and Novellas category and was named the 'Outstanding Novella' of 2018 by the IAN Book of the Year Awards.

'Life would be tragic if it weren't funny.'
Stephen Hawking

INTRODUCTION

Westminster Abbey. Iconic final resting place of kings and queens, composers, statesmen, explorers and scientists, where every stone has a story to tell about the journey of man. Not only is it a spectacular reminder of extraordinary people and great achievements, but at the same time, every stone whispers of mortality and the certainty of death. As a repository of history, Westminster Abbey is unparalleled.

I will never forget 15 June 2018. On that day, one of the greatest minds of our time, Stephen Hawking – who died in March that year after decades suffering from motor neurone disease – had his ashes interred close to the graves of Newton and Darwin in the Scientists' Corner of the Abbey.

And how appropriate it was, I thought. Hawking was born exactly three hundred years after Newton. It was Newton who formulated the laws of motion and universal gravitation, and it was Hawking's genius that took astrophysics to new heights. The inscription on his memorial stone is a translation of the Latin text on Newton's gravestone: 'Here lies what was mortal of Stephen Hawking 1942–2018'. In addition, the stone is inscribed with one of Hawking's most famous equations:

$$T = \frac{hc3}{8\ PiGMk}$$

But that wasn't all. The Greek composer Vangelis set Hawking's inspirational message to the world, to music, which according to Hawking's daughter was beamed into space that day from a European Space Agency satellite dish, aimed at the nearest black hole, 1A 0620-00.

I have followed Hawking and his inspired, groundbreaking ideas for over thirty years. A keen interest in mathematics and physics inspired me to read all his books, especially *A Brief History of Time* (1988 Bantam London), which explains complex, revolutionary ideas in ways a layman like me can relate to and understand.

The service was attended by luminaries from around the world. Martin Rees, the Astronomer Royal, made a moving speech; actor Benedict Cumberbatch, who played Hawking in a BBC drama, delivered a reading; and Nobel laureate Kip Thorne paid tribute to his remarkable colleague and friend.

As the sound of Richard Wagner's stirring 'Ride of the Valkyries' rose, heralding the end of the service, and the bells of the Abbey began to toll, conjuring up images of man's futile quest for immortality, my mind began to wander ...

How tragic, I thought, that such a gifted mind capable of solving some of the greatest and most challenging mysteries of the cosmos, was cut down by a terrible disease in the middle, if not at the very beginning, of what he might have been capable of, thereby preventing him from reaching his full potential, and depriving mankind of precious knowledge.

However, was this any more regrettable than Beethoven going deaf and unable to hear some of his greatest works, or Mozart dying as a young man of only thirty-five? One can only speculate what might have been possible if these gifted minds could have stayed around for longer, allowing their creative genius to blossom and reach new heights.

And then something occurred to me. What if we could somehow change all that and *make* it possible? Turn a vision into reality today, right now? Recent groundbreaking advances in medical research and technology – especially in surgery and surgical techniques and procedures – have led to some breathtaking discoveries and results, placing some concepts that only a few short years ago would have been considered science fiction, into the realm of realistic possibilities. What if a gifted mind like that of Stephen Hawking's could somehow be liberated from a terribly disabled body, and manage to live on for some more time, allowing it to continue its groundbreaking work and reach for the stars, literally? What if ...?

That was the thought I took away with me from this moving service. It was a thought inspired by optimism and hope for the future that stayed with me and became the inspiration for this book.

Gabriel Farago
Leura, Blue Mountains, Australia
November 2019

THE CURIOUS CASE OF THE MISSING HEAD

GABRIEL FARAGO

Contents

Introduction i
Part I. Operation Libertad 1
Part II. Babu 139
Part III. The Theory of Everything 293
Afterword 484
A Parting Note from the Author 486
More Books by the Author 489
About the Author 503
Author's Note 505
Connect with the Author 507

PART I

OPERATION LIBERTAD

Prologue

Arizona State Prison Complex, Florence, Arizona:
Friday 13 July 2018, 9:00 am

Alonso Cordoba was preparing himself to die. The son of Hernando Cordoba – the notorious Colombian drug lord and head of the Huitzilopochtli, or H Cartel as it was generally known – he was by far the most famous prisoner in Arizona State Prison Complex, Florence.

Convicted of the murder of two undercover police officers while resisting arrest in Tombstone during a major drug deal, he had been languishing on death row for more than two years. After his conviction, a lengthy appeals process had slowly dragged itself through the court system until, with the final appeal dismissed and nowhere else to go, an execution date was set. Not even the ingenuity of the expensive New York legal team engaged by his father to delay the execution could stop the relentless progress of the death penalty juggernaut hurtling towards him.

Arizona was determined to execute the drug baron responsible for importing tonnes of cocaine from Colombia via the 'Aztec Highway' through Mexico into the United States, and killing two of their finest law enforcement officers in the process. Death by lethal injection seemed only fair, and a proper punishment for such heinous crimes. And besides, the governor was under enormous pressure from Washington to expedite the execution as a clear signal that America meant business and was determined to do something about the huge drug problem plaguing the country. If nothing was done, voter backlash was predicted to be swift and brutal. The slippery bribery tentacles greased by a seemingly inexhaustible money supply controlled by South American drug lords reached into the highest places and had spread scandal and corruption not only throughout Mexico, but in the United States as well.

Not being a religious man, Alonso had refused to see the priest who had tried to visit him in his cell that morning. Instead, arrogant and defiant to the end, he ate his final meal – a huge steak – with gusto under the watchful eyes of the prison guards, who must have wondered how a man about to die a horrible death could devour such a meal.

At nine am sharp, Alonso was taken from his cell to Housing Unit 9, a small, freestanding building with a gruesome reputation. This was the place where all the executions in the Arizona Prison Complex – Florence were carried out.

Separated by a large window from the stark lethal-injection chamber, spectators who were about to witness the execution in the small viewing room had a clear view of the gurney. Apart from prison officials and several journalists, family members of the two murdered police officers were already seated, their eyes fixed in morbid fascination on the operating table-like gurney with leather straps that would shortly be used to restrain the condemned prisoner, to allow the lethal injection to take its course. The spectators watched in silence as the prisoner entered the tiny room.

Dressed in an orange jumpsuit, Alonso – a short, stocky man in his mid-forties – was escorted to the gurney where prison medical staff were preparing the intravenous lines about to be inserted into his arms. Remembering the botched execution of Joseph Wood, who took almost two hours to die – his repulsive convulsions on the table causing horror and panic among the spectators – the medical officer in charge of the lines was determined to get it right this time. The drugs – a combination of midazolam and hydromorphone – had been improved since that execution fiasco, but they were difficult to obtain, as reputable drug companies refused to sell the drugs to the United States knowing that they would be used for executions. Alternative sources were notoriously unreliable, and the drug quality questionable.

As soon as Alonso set eyes on the gurney with the leather straps, a wave of uncertainty and fear washed over him. For the first time that day, his unwavering belief that he would somehow be spared at the last minute began to fade. Raul Rodrigo, his father's personal lawyer who had handled all legal matters since his arrest, had visited him just two days earlier, assuring him that all would be fine. He had told Alonso that a last-minute application to have the execution stayed was about to be heard by the US Supreme Court. He had also told Alonso that he was very confident it would succeed because it was based on solid constitutional arguments. When questioned further by Alonso about what would happen if it didn't, a smiling Raul had sidestepped the question and refused to provide further details. Instead, he had urged Alonso to have faith, trust his father, and be strong.

As Alonso lay down on the gurney, he glanced at the clock above the door. *I hope Raul knows what he's doing*, he thought. *Because very soon, it will be too late.*

Bogota, Colombia

Rodrigo looked at his client, who was staring out of one of the bulletproof windows. Ignoring the armed guards patrolling the grounds and the tall razor-wire fences behind the exotic, manicured gardens surrounding the compound, it was a beautiful, peaceful view down to Bogota, covered in morning mist. Protected by thick concrete walls, state-of-the-art security systems and massive steel gates, most of the large fortified building was underground. The Cordoba compound on the outskirts of Bogota was more like a fortress than a villa. In Colombia this wasn't unusual, but to be expected of the headquarters of the notorious H Cartel, one of the most powerful and ruthless cartels in the country.

Named after Huitzilopochtli, the bloody Aztec god of war, sun and human sacrifice, the Cartel had the Xiuhcoatl, the fire serpent that the god wielded as a weapon, as its emblem. With influence, money and power came powerful enemies. As head of the H Cartel, Hernando Cordoba was still alive only because he understood that very well.

Cordoba rarely left the compound and conducted most of his business from his 'observation room' as he liked to call it, overlooking his beloved garden and the city in the distance below. When he did leave – usually to inspect secret drug manufacturing sites hidden deep in the jungle – he did so by helicopter, which was more like a gunship than a civilian aircraft. Sourced from the Venezuelan Air Force and modified to suit his needs, it was equipped with the latest weapons systems, which gave it awesome firepower. Cordoba lived in a constant state of war and he liked it that way. It kept him sharp and alert, and a step or two ahead of his enemies and competitors.

'We are cutting it fine,' said Cordoba, turning to face his lawyer sitting at a desk behind him. 'If the execution goes to plan, the boy will be dead in less than forty-five minutes.'

For some reason that hadn't been explained, the Arizona authorities had suddenly accelerated the execution and set a date. This had caught the Cordoba legal team by surprise, and an appeal had been lodged immediately to have the execution stayed on constitutional grounds.

Rodrigo glanced at his watch. 'I know,' he said. 'But we should hear any—' He was interrupted by his mobile ringing in his breast pocket. Rodrigo sat up straight as if poked by a hot needle, bit his lip, and answered the call he had so anxiously been waiting for. 'I see; thank you,' he said after a while, and slipped the phone back into his pocket.

Cordoba watched his lawyer carefully. The look on Rodrigo's face told him all he had to know.

Rodrigo shook his head and stood up. 'Only one dissenting judge agreed with our arguments. It's a disgrace. Constitutional matters no longer seem to count. The execution is to go ahead. The US Government has the court in its pocket.'

Cordoba stood up as well. Feeling relieved because the excruciating waiting was over, he was ready to act. And that was what he liked most of all and was good at. 'Then you better hurry; the chopper is standing by and the ambassador is waiting. It's all arranged.'

Rodrigo picked up the briefcase on the table in front of him and hurried to the door. He was used to working under pressure, but the pressure at that moment was about as much as a man could take. He realised what he and Cordoba had been feverishly working on for several months to save Alonso, was hanging in the balance. The next forty minutes were crucial.

Rodrigo stopped at the door and turned around. 'We'll make it, you'll see,' he said.

'I hope so,' replied Cordoba, staring out of the window. 'If not, it will destroy Rahima,' he added quietly to himself. 'She already lost a son; losing another would be unthinkable.'

The chopper landed in a deserted car park close to the US embassy. This was of course totally illegal, but in Bogota, Cordoba made his own rules. A black Land Rover was standing by and took Rodrigo to the front gate of the embassy a few hundred metres away.

The US ambassador was waiting in his office with his aide. An urgent appointment had been arranged the day before by Cordoba himself. He had advised the ambassador that he had vital information concerning US national security, and that his lawyer would come to see him and explain everything the next day. He had also asked the ambassador to arrange a direct line of communication with the White House, as matters of great importance and urgency were likely to arise. Having dealt with Cordoba before, the ambassador knew better than to refuse or ask for an explanation or, God forbid, dismiss the entire matter as a meaningless nuisance. In Bogota you did what Cordoba asked, or you left the country – if you could.

'I'm intrigued, Mr Rodrigo,' said the ambassador, extending his hand. 'I was told that the timing of our meeting had something to do with Alonso Cordoba's execution scheduled for, well, just about now.'

'Correct, Mr Ambassador,' said Rodrigo. 'There isn't much time, so let me cut to the chase if I may.'

'Please do.'

'Everything I've been instructed to say is in this short video, Mr Ambassador. It will explain everything.'

Rodrigo placed a DVD on the table in front of him. The ambassador motioned towards his aide. The aide walked over to the table, picked up the DVD and slipped it into a hard drive connected to a large monitor behind the ambassador's desk.

For the next five minutes, the three men in the room watched the video in stunned silence, the atmosphere in the room electric.

After the video stopped, the ambassador was the first to speak. 'Are you suggesting, Mr Rodrigo, that all of this is *real*?'

'I am; very real.'

'In that case, I must make an urgent phone call,' said the ambassador and stood up.

'I was hoping you would say that, Mr Ambassador,' said Rodrigo and stood up as well.

'Please wait outside, Mr Rodrigo. My aide will show you ...'

The ambassador waited until Rodrigo and his aide had left the room, before unlocking one of the drawers of his desk. He took out an encrypted satellite phone and speed-dialled a number at the White House.

**Arizona State Prison Complex,
lethal-injection chamber: 10:15 am**

Alonso was lying on the gurney with his eyes closed, unable to move, the tight leather restraining straps cutting into his chest, arms and legs. Because the medical officer couldn't find any veins he considered suitable, he had to – much to the horror of the spectators – surgically insert a catheter into Alonso's groin to allow the lethal drugs to enter his bloodstream. This had delayed the execution by a few minutes, but the medical officer wasn't prepared to take any chances. The humiliating Wood fiasco would not be repeated on his watch! The prisoner would die, and quickly.

The medical officer stepped away from the gurney and looked at the governor standing in the corner, watching. 'Ready, sir,' he said.

The governor nodded.

The medical officer was about to turn on the lethal drip, when the door opened and a young woman holding a mobile phone burst into the chamber. The governor turned and gave her a withering look. '*Not now*, for heaven's sake!' he hissed.

Looking embarrassed, the young woman hurried over to the governor. 'It's the president ... for you, sir,' she stammered and handed the phone to the governor, her hand shaking.

The medical officer, and the spectators on the other side of the window, stared at the governor, stunned. After what seemed like an eternity, the governor handed the phone back to the young woman and turned to face the window.

'Ladies and gentlemen,' he began, speaking softly. 'I just spoke with the President of the United States. The execution has been stayed indefinitely.'

Kosovo, near the Albanian border: 25 October 1999

The vicious, bloody war may have been finally over, but the suffering and atrocities continued underground. When the rule of law disintegrates and is replaced by the arbitrary rule of violence and the gun, old feuds and grudges come out of the shadows and rub shoulders with more sinister urges that are allowed to run riot, leaving the vulnerable and weak exposed and at the mercy of the ruthless.

Two dark-green, mud-covered, military-style vehicles turned off the road and followed a rutted dirt track into the forest. 'How much further?' asked the man sitting next to the driver of the first vehicle.

'A few kilometres; it's quite remote,' replied the man sitting behind him.

'Good. A couple with two girls, you say?'

'Yes.'

'Just what we want. Mirko will be pleased!'

'Mirko?'

'The man who owns the place where we do all the ... you know.'

'He likes young girls?'

'Oh yes, he does!'

After the armed conflict had ended, many Kosovo Albanians hadn't laid down their arms, but had melted into the forests and continued their dirty work – aimed mainly at ethnic Serbs. Old grudges rarely die. They just go to ground and simmer – often for years – until, suddenly liberated, they erupt more violently than ever, spreading their poison and terror.

Bogodan Petrovic looked affectionately at his twins, Nadia and Teodora, sitting opposite him at the kitchen table. At fourteen, they were almost impossible to tell apart and it took a mother's love and intuition to do so. His wife, Anya, busied herself at the stove, preparing dinner. Bogodan, a strong man in his late thirties, had lived on the land all his life, eking out a modest living on the small family farm, just like his father before him. A simple life of hard, honest work. The dreadful war had taken its toll, but Bogodan had somehow managed to stay out of the conflict and protect his family and his property, and most important of all, keep them all alive. This had a lot to do with the remote location of the farm near the Albanian border, and the fact that he kept to himself and got on with his neighbours. Or so he thought. But no-one can hide from the world around them forever.

For years, one of his neighbours – a wealthy landowner with influence in the village – had tried to buy Bogodan's farm, claiming an agreement had been reached a long time ago between their grandfathers. Bogodan had laughed this off as nonsense, as there was no evidence to support this, and he refused to sell. This had created serious bad blood between them, which had turned increasingly acrimonious and bitter over the years.

'There it is,' said the man in the back seat and pointed to a small house at the end of the track.

'You stay here and leave the rest to us,' replied the man in the front.

The man in the back tapped him on the shoulder and handed him a large bundle of bank notes. 'As agreed,' he said. 'What will you do with the family?'

'Not your concern,' replied the man and slipped the notes into his pocket. 'But I can tell you, Mirko will have fun with the girls, that's for sure,' he added, laughing. 'Enjoy your new farm. We'll drop you off on our way back.' Then he pulled a black balaclava over his head and reached for his gun.

Anya had just put a pot of soup on the table and was about to fill the bowls, when she heard a vehicle pull up in the yard outside. This was most unusual because they rarely had visitors, and almost never after dark. 'Who could that be?' she said looking at Bogodan, a flash of uncertainty and fear in her eyes.

Bogodan stood up and walked to the front door to have a look. That's when he heard a second vehicle approach, its bright headlights shining through the window. Then someone started banging on the door. As soon as Bogodan opened the door, four men – their faces hidden behind balaclavas – burst into the room, guns drawn and shouting.

Sitting awkwardly on the floor in the back of a small van with their hands tied behind their backs and duct tape covering their mouths, Bogodan, Anya and the two girls lurched from side to side every time the van took a turn. Terrified, bruised and finding it difficult to breathe, they could only communicate with their eyes. The terrified look in Anya's eyes said it all.

The two vehicles crossed the border, drove through the sleeping Albanian town of Burrel and then turned off the road. 'Here we are,' said the man in the front seat and pointed to a dilapidated farmhouse with stables at the back. Several cars were parked in front of the house, and two armed men sat on a wooden bench by the front door, smoking. They stood up as the vehicles approached.

As soon as his car stopped, the man in the front seat got out, walked to the back of the van stopped behind him and opened the door. 'Get out; you two first,' he barked, pointing to the girls. Then he turned towards the two armed men watching him.

'Where's Mirko?' he asked, obviously used to being in command.

'In the stables, getting drunk as usual,' replied one of the men, a former KLA fighter called Janko.

'Tell him I've a present for him.'

'Oh?'

'These two here. Take them to him. Tell him it's rent for two weeks. But first, take off the tape and handcuffs. We want them to look pretty.'

'Will do. Girls this time? Lucky bastard,' said Janko, laughing. He had taken women to Mirko before but never girls this young.

'Is everything ready?'

'Yes. They are all waiting inside.'

'Good. The other two here are a present for the doctor; take them inside. I need a drink!'

Janko pushed the stable door open with his shoulder and looked inside.

Mirko, a man in his fifties, was lying on a bale of hay clutching a half-empty bottle of vodka to his chest. His eyes were closed and he appeared to be asleep.

'You,' said Janko, pointing to Teodora standing next to him, 'go inside, take off your clothes and wait for me; understood?' Teodora nodded – her eyes wide with terror – and stumbled inside, shaking. 'While your sister and I are having a little fun right here,' continued Janko, smacking his lips. He turned around, pulled Nadia roughly towards him, undid his belt and then put his sweaty hand up her skirt.

Dr Dritan Shehu, a former KLA commander, was carefully laying out his instruments on a makeshift operating table set up in another of the stables behind the house. The conditions were primitive, but adequate as long as certain procedures were followed meticulously. And Dr Shehu was a meticulous man, bordering on pedantic when it came to his work.

The only child of a prominent doctor from Pec, Shehu had been exposed to things medical from an early age, and it soon became apparent to his doting parents that young Dritan would follow in his father's footsteps. Inquisitive and exceptionally bright, he had devoured books on medical subjects in his father's extensive library even before he had left primary school, and he had often sat in on consultations and small procedures performed in his father's surgery. By the time he was eighteen he spoke fluent English and German, and his parents sent him to England to study medicine.

An incredibly gifted student, he soon came to the attention of professors, who took a special interest in him and encouraged his fascination with surgery. After his graduation, he returned to Pec to begin an internship. That was just before the brutal Kosovo war broke out in 1998, and then everything changed.

As Kosovar Albanians, the Shehu family became embroiled in the bitter conflict between the KLA – the Kosovo Liberation Army – and Yugoslav forces targeting KLA sympathisers and political opponents. Shehu's father – thought to be a sympathiser because he often treated wounded KLA fighters – was detained for questioning by Serb paramilitary forces, who broke into his house one night looking for KLA fighters. He was executed in the kitchen in front of his wife and son. The next day, Shehu joined the KLA.

'So, what have we got here?' asked Shehu, looking at Bogodan and his wife – both handcuffed – standing in a circle of light next to the operating table. 'Take off his shirt.'

The armed man standing behind Bogodan undid the handcuffs and ordered Bogodan to take off his shirt. Shehu nodded appreciatively. *A strong healthy male, late thirties, obviously used to hard work; excellent*, he thought and turned to Anya. 'His wife?' he asked.

The armed man nodded.

'Good. We'll begin with him. Take them outside. You know what to do; back of the head as I showed you. Then bring him in here and put him on the table.'

Ignoring Bogodan's and Anya's shrill questions and protests as they were being dragged outside, Shehu put on a pair of plastic gloves and checked his scalpels.

In the stable next to the makeshift surgery, Mirko had woken up after Janko had kicked him in the shins. He stared at the two naked girls standing in front of him, shaking.

'Present from the commander,' said Janko, pushing the girls towards Mirko, who was rubbing his eyes in disbelief. That's when two shots shattered the stillness of the night.

'Ah,' said Janko, 'I'm needed outside. I'm sure you can think of something to do with these two cuties for a while,' he added, pinching Teodora on her bottom.

Aroused, Mirko sat up, took another swig of vodka, burped and then pulled Nadia roughly towards him.

'Careful,' said Shehu, as two men lifted the green plastic sheet with Bogodan's body onto the operating table. The entry wound at the back of the head was neat, but the face had almost entirely been blown away and was still bleeding.

'Perfect,' continued Shehu. He reached for his scalpel and made the first long incision, opening the chest as he had done many times before. He knew he would reach the heart within a few minutes, extract it and then place it into the state-of-the art storage container with inflatable cushions and eutectoid cooling. The container would provide the precisely controlled environmental temperature needed to ensure safe transport of the harvested organ to its destination in the Middle East. But first, it would be driven to a nearby airport and flown to Istanbul. The small plane was standing by, but as always time was of the essence.

The sophisticated organ-harvesting operation consisted of many complex stages but it had been perfected by Shehu, who was known as 'Dr Death'. Healthy organs fetched huge amounts of money on the black market, and ready cash was in short supply after the war. Run with military precision, what had begun as an experiment had soon turned into a thriving business.

Teodora watched her struggling sister being savagely raped by Mirko, who was clearly enjoying himself. Unable to watch any longer, she let her eyes wander until they came to rest on something leaning against the wooden wall in a corner. A pitchfork. Teodora had always been the more strong-willed and impulsive of the twins. She was also the more adventurous and courageous, prepared to reach out and have a go, however dangerous or foolhardy it may at first appear.

When Mirko turned Nadia around and began to do something unthinkable to her, Teodora made a spontaneous decision. Slowly, she began to move towards the pitchfork in the corner without taking her eyes off Mirko. He seemed to be having some difficulty controlling Nadia, who was crying hysterically and struggling violently in a desperate attempt to resist. When Nadia lashed out and scratched Mirko's face, drawing blood, and Mirko responded by hitting her hard with a fist clenched in anger, Teodora knew it was time.

She made a dash for the pitchfork, picked it up and holding it firmly with both hands, she ran towards Mirko, who had his back turned towards her. Fear and loathing gave her strength. She lifted the fork and plunged it deep into Mirko's back, piercing his heart. She pulled out the fork and stabbed him again until Mirko let go of Nadia and, pressing his hands against his chest, he fell forward and died, blood gushing from the deep wounds and turning the straw crimson.

'Get dressed quickly!' hissed Teodora, picking up her own clothes. 'We have to get out of here *now!*'

As they ran towards the door, Teodora stopped. She could hear animated voices coming from the stable next door. For some reason she couldn't explain, she walked over to a large crack in one of the rough wooden planks forming part of the wall separating the two stables, pressed her cheek against the plank, and looked into the brightly lit chamber. What she saw made her gasp and tremble with revulsion and fear.

At first, she didn't recognise the mutilated corpse on a blood-covered green plastic sheet lying on the ground a couple of metres from the wall. But when she saw the trousers and the shoes, recognition dawned and a wave of nausea overcame her, making her retch. But worse was to come. Lying on a table next to her father's body was a woman. Her face was unrecognisable, and her chest had been opened wide. A man was cutting something inside the chest cavity with what looked like a pair of large scissors. The face of the man was illuminated by a strong light from above, accentuating his features. His image was etched into Teodora's memory, never to be erased.

'M-mother!' stammered Teodora, as tears began to stream down her wan cheeks, her lips trembling.

'What is it?' asked Nadia, standing next to her. She was about to take a look through another crack in the wall when Teodora grabbed her from behind.

'*No!*' she cried, pulling her sister away. '*You mustn't!* Let's get out of here!'

Teodora opened the stable door and looked outside. The yard looked deserted. Everyone appeared to be inside. 'Come, quickly!' she said, taking Nadia by the hand, and began to walk slowly along the wall of the stable, trying to stay in the shadows. They had almost reached the corner when they heard voices. Teodora froze and pressed herself against the wall. Nadia did the same. Two men came out of the adjoining stable. Each one was carrying what looked like a large, shiny box. They hurried over to one of the cars, opened the boot and carefully placed the boxes inside. Then they got into the car, reversed and drove away.

'Over there,' said Teodora, pointing to the dark forest behind some rusty farm machinery. 'Now! Let's run!'

The girls ran across the deserted yard and reached the forest without being seen, and then disappeared into the night.

1

International Space Station: 14 March 2018

Orbiting earth at an altitude of four hundred and five kilometres and at a speed of 27,600 km/h, the International Space Station had just passed over the Pacific and was approaching Australia. Launched into orbit in 1998 and inhabited without interruption since that date, it was the largest man-made object in low earth orbit visible with the naked eye from our planet. A marvel of cutting-edge technology, it was a symbol of human ingenuity and international cooperation. During the next twenty-four hours, it would complete 15.54 orbits and send valuable data back to the Goddard Space Flight Center in Greenbelt, Maryland. As a microgravity and space environment research laboratory, it had no equal. In a way, it was an outpost of humankind, preparing to leave earth and explore space.

In a state of near-weightlessness, Professor Zachariah Stolzfus rested on his back in the cupola, a unique seven-window observatory, and stared down at the blue planet as it slowly drifted past the eighty-centimetre round window, the largest on the space station. This was his favourite place on the station; the place where he did his best thinking. The planet looked so peaceful, so serene, so timeless from above, yet this marvellous view could not calm the emotional turmoil boiling within him. Stolzfus had just received news that Steven Hawking, his hero and idol, had passed away in Cambridge.

In a way, Stolzfus owed everything to Hawking. It was Hawking's groundbreaking work back in the 1980s that had ignited the spark of curiosity about the universe and its origin in the young man working on the family farm with his father and brothers in Pennsylvania. Growing up in a strict Amish home without electricity or any kind of modern appliance or convenience – not even a motor car; transport was by horse and buggy – had been stifling, and it was by sheer accident that he had come across Hawking's book *A Brief History of Time* in 1988. It was an event that changed his life.

An accident during a barn raising – he slipped and fell from a roof – had left Stolzfus with a permanent injury to his spine. He spent several months in a Philadelphia hospital under the care of an eminent orthopaedic surgeon. The surgeon and his young patient struck up a friendship and it was during his lengthy, painful rehabilitation that Stolzfus's extraordinary, inquisitive mind attracted attention. As the surgeon got to know his young patient better, he realised he was dealing with an exceptionally gifted human being with an insatiable hunger for knowledge.

He lent the boy books on history, mathematics and philosophy, and they spent hours discussing Nietzsche, Aristotle and Hume. However, it soon became apparent that young Zachariah's real interest was the cosmos and how it worked, but most of all, how it began. He devoured books about Copernicus, Galileo, Kepler and Newton, and it was then that Zachariah came across Hawking's *A Brief History of Time*, which changed everything.

A crooked little smile creased the corners of Stolzfus's mouth as he remembered the first time he read about the Big Bang and black holes, general relativity and quantum mechanics, all subjects that would fascinate him later and dominate his life. After that, there was no going back. He realised then exactly what he wanted to do, and why. And he was still doing it as he tried to come to terms with the fact that Hawking, his inspiration, was no more.

'You look troubled, my friend,' said Sergei, a fellow physicist from Russia, as he settled into the seat next to Zachariah. 'Hawking?'

Stolzfus nodded. 'You know me too well. His death is affecting me more than I thought possible.'

'Understandable.'

Living in the tight confines of the space station for months with little or no privacy had brought the tightly knit group of four scientists closer together. So much so, they could not only read each other's moods, but intuitively know their thoughts as well.

'For the first time, I wish I was down there and not up here. I feel so confined, so helpless. *So alone.* For some reason, I want to reach out, talk about him and his work. Tell the world what he ... I want *to do* something!'

Sergei put his hand on his friend's arm. 'Then why don't you?' he asked quietly.

'What do you mean?'

'Talk about him. From up here, right now. Send a message to the world down there, from up here. Can you think of a more fitting place for a tribute? After all, that's what you have in mind, don't you?'

'Do it from here? That hadn't occurred to me. What a great idea! Do you think they'll go for this?'

Sergei floated out of his seat and turned to face his friend. 'I'll contact the control centre right now. Leave it to me.'

Feeling better, Stolzfus stared out the window as the familiar shapes of the continents drifted past, and contemplated what he would say about Hawking should NASA agree to such a broadcast.

The idea of a tribute to Hawking made from space, expressed by the very man who had for some time been considered his most likely successor, was a publicist's dream. It raced from Maryland to Washington, right up to the president himself, who thought it was an excellent suggestion. Not only would it be a fitting tribute to a genius, it would also create huge publicity and awareness of the United States space program, and enhance the reputation and prestige of the International Space Station and the scientists working there. Permission for a short video broadcast by Stolzfus was given within the hour.

Stolzfus settled back in his seat in the cupola and then turned to face the camera. *Three minutes are better than nothing*, he thought, and cleared his throat.

'I am Professor Zachariah Stolzfus, talking to you from the International Space Station high above our wonderful blue planet,' he began slowly. 'Today, one of the most remarkable minds of our time has faded into eternity, leaving behind some extraordinary insights and challenges. Professor Stephen Hawking has taken his place next to Copernicus, Galileo, Kepler and Einstein, who paved the way. Yet it was his genius as a theoretical physicist and cosmologist that gave us the second law of black hole dynamics, and the prediction that black holes emit radiation – now called Hawking radiation – that will change the way we look at how the universe works, how it began, and where it is heading.

'But it wasn't only the big scientific questions that occupied his exceptional mind. He looked closely at the future of the human race and pointed out the great dangers of climate change and how artificial intelligence could help us deal with the challenges that lie ahead. He was convinced, as I am, that our planet cannot indefinitely support the human race, and that to survive we would have to travel into space and find new places to colonise,' Stolzfus paused and pointed to the window above him, 'out there.

'Professor Hawking wasn't just a theoretical physicist; he was also a philosopher. One particular sentence taken from his book *A Brief History of Time* has stayed with me all these years: "If we discover a complete theory, it would be the ultimate triumph of human reason – for then we should know the mind of God." I believe that this is the challenge Professor Hawking has left behind for us to take up. The laws of physics are eternal, and so are the ideas that help us discover them. Professor Hawking had many such ideas and they are out there, somewhere, forever. And that is as close as we can get to immortality. I will miss you, Stephen, but every time I look up at the stars, I can see you, and I can hear you.'

Sitting in his office in New York, Raul Rodrigo watched Stolzfus's extraordinary tribute to the late Professor Hawking from space with great interest. As he listened to these stirring words, an idea began to take shape in his mind. At first he almost dismissed it as ridiculous and absurd, but it wouldn't go away. In fact, it became even stronger and clearer when the NASA commentator spoke about Professor

Zachariah Stolzfus and explained who he was, what he did, and what his work meant to the international space program, science, the United States, and the world.

At the end of the broadcast, which had been watched by millions and went viral on social media later that day, Professor Stolzfus, who until then had only been known in science circles, became an overnight celebrity as one of the leading theoretical physicists and cosmologists on the planet, and Stephen Hawking's most likely successor.

Rodrigo turned off the television and walked over to the large window overlooking Central Park. Holding his hands behind his back, he stared out the window and began formulating a plan so daring, it made him smile and tremble with excitement. It was the kind of plan he thrived on because he knew there were perhaps only a handful of people who could come up with something like this, and fewer still who could even think of implementing it. However, he did know of one man who would not only embrace the idea, he would love it.

Rodrigo turned around, walked over to his desk and called his client in Bogota.

2

Cordoba compound, Bogota: 30 March

Rahima knelt in front of the altar of the small chapel in the garden, praying. Built by Jesuit missionaries in the early eighteenth century, the chapel had survived the destruction of the monastery that had stood next to it. It was also the reason Hernando Cordoba had purchased the dilapidated property on the outskirts of Bogota in the nineties and built his home there, which later became the fortified headquarters of the notorious H Cartel. He considered the presence of the little chapel a good omen. Having grown up in the slums of Bogota, the church had always played an important part in his life.

Rahima had been praying in the chapel since early that morning. She had to find a way to come to terms with the devastating news that her son's final appeal had been dismissed, and he was now on death row in Arizona, awaiting execution. The only way she knew she could do that, was to go into the little chapel and pray. It was her place of solace and comfort. It was the only place in the fortified compound full of armed men where she could go in private to cry, and to find some peace.

The man who had rescued her all those years ago and with whom she had fallen in love, was a different man today. Hernando, the carefree, loving father of her beloved son, had turned into a feared, ruthless, all-powerful billionaire, head of the notorious H Cartel. Over the years he had become increasingly distant and withdrawn, obsessed with only two things: his empire, and his wars. He thrived on danger and taking risks. Alonso adored his father and wanted to be just like him. What Rahima had dreaded most, had just happened. Despite all her efforts and pleading, Alonso had followed his father into the Cartel, taking on more and more responsibilities for the running of the complex and dangerous drug business, with investments all over the globe.

All the riches came from cocaine, and keeping competitors out of the market. The craving for cocaine, especially in the United States and Europe, had grown exponentially over the years, consuming everyone and everything standing in its path, and delivering rivers of gold to the suppliers who found more and more ingenious ways to smuggle the addictive poison into the country and build sophisticated distribution networks.

Alonso was the reason Rahima had stayed with Hernando all these years. She adored her son, and to lose him now in such a brutal way was unthinkable. All the money and power in the world came to nothing if she couldn't somehow save him. Rahima, an incredibly strong-willed and resourceful woman, was determined to do just that, whatever it took. She crossed herself, leant forward and kissed the Russian icon on the altar in front of her. Then she stood up resolutely, wiped away the tears and hurried back to the compound to find her husband.

Hernando was sitting on a couch in his observation room overlooking the garden, as usual. He appeared locked deep in conversation with Raul Rodrigo, his lawyer and right-hand man, when the door opened. Hernando looked up, surprised. His wife rarely entered his inner sanctum, and never unannounced. Rahima walked over to her husband, sat down next to him, and took his hands in hers. She knew that the terrible news had hit him hard as well, but Hernando rarely showed his emotions.

'I'm sure you will agree with me that I haven't asked for much over the years,' began Rahima softly.

Hernando wondered where this was heading.

Rodrigo, always tactful and polite, stood up. 'I will wait outside if you like,' he said, sensing that something very personal and private was about to take place.

'No, please stay,' said Rahima. 'I would like you to hear this.'

'As you wish,' said Rodrigo, his curiosity aroused, and sat down again.

For a while Rahima just looked at her husband, collecting her thoughts. 'This morning, I have been mortally wounded. I think both of us have been mortally wounded. Our son is on death row awaiting execution in the US. Hernando, how could we have let it come to this?'

Hernando squeezed his wife's hands in silent reply and looked at her sadly.

'I would like you to promise me something; here, right now,' continued Rahima, tears glistening in her eyes. Even now, in her seventies, she was a beautiful woman, radiating intelligence and grace. Her short, silver-grey hair accentuated her prominent cheekbones and large, cornflower-blue eyes, just as her lush, curly, white-blonde hair had done in her youth. Her bearing was almost regal and her movements athletic and full of purpose, hinting at a life lived mainly outdoors and close to nature.

'What's on your mind?' asked Hernando, his voice sounding hoarse.

'I want your promise that you will do everything in your power, leave no stone unturned, use everything we have to save our son, regardless of the consequences. I don't care how you do it, as long as you do. I need this promise, Hernando, because I cannot go on without it. It would give me something to hold onto. I know how strong and resourceful you are once you set your mind to something. You and Raul are a formidable team. I have seen you two in action many times. I've seen you turn the impossible into possible and make it work. I believe that together you can do it. What do you say?'

Hernando turned to Rodrigo sitting opposite. 'Would you please tell Rahima what we've been discussing just before she came in?'

'Certainly.'

Rahima looked expectantly at Rodrigo.

'We've been exploring possible avenues to get Alonso out of jail.'

'*You have?*' said Rahima, surprised. 'Tell me!'

Rodrigo looked at Cordoba, the question on his face obvious.

'Please tell Rahima,' said Cordoba. 'There are no secrets between us.' Cordoba turned to face his wife. 'We've been discussing one particular possibility, quite a daring and ingenious one Raul has just come up with,' he continued. 'Go on Raul, please ...'

'Before you do,' interrupted Rahima, looking intently at her husband, '*the promise*?'

'I promise,' replied Hernando, squeezing Rahima's hands again. 'On our son's life.'

'And you?' said Rahima, turning to Rodrigo. 'Are you prepared to promise as well? Because Hernando can only do this with your help, of that I'm sure.'

Rodrigo nodded. 'I promise; on our friendship.'

Feeling better, a hesitant little smile crept across Rahima's troubled face, as the heavy hand pressing against her heart began to loosen its grip.

'Thank you. Thank you both. I can't tell you what this means to me,' whispered Rahima, close to tears. 'Now, please tell me. What is this plan of yours?'

For the next hour, Rahima listened in silence as Cordoba took her step by step through a plan so daring that she had to bite her bottom lip several times until it almost bled, to make sure she wasn't dreaming. It began with the recent death of a great man in Cambridge ...

'But we've been talking about London just now. I don't understand ...' said Rahima.

'Tell her,' said Cordoba.

Rodrigo held up his hand. 'That's the best bit, and it only happened just recently,' he said, smiling.

Rahima looked at him and frowned.

'A couple of days ago – on the twenty-eighth, to be precise – it was announced that a memorial service will be held in Westminster Abbey on June fifteen to honour and lay to rest—'

'But how is this connected to this genius scientist?' interrupted Rahima, frustrated.

'Because it has also been announced,' continued Rodrigo calmly, 'that the "genius scientist" as you call him, is due to return from space in two weeks and will therefore be able to attend the memorial service to which he has been specifically invited.'

'And this is good news because ...?' asked Rahima.

'Because the memorial service that will be held in Westminster Abbey in London is the perfect occasion for what we have in mind ...'

3

Amsterdam: 3 April

Rodrigo knew Amsterdam very well. He always stayed at the exclusive Hotel De L'Europe near Munttoren. It was his preferred hotel in Amsterdam and he had even secured his favourite room overlooking the Amstel River. Rodrigo had reserved a table in the Hoofdstad Brasserie that evening and had requested a table well away from prying eyes and curious ears. The person he was about to meet, and the reason behind the meeting, definitely warranted such caution.

A veteran of countless bruising legal battles – many of them fought for notorious, high-profile clients – Rodrigo had acquired an almost uncanny ability to read people and situations. His stellar rise during a highly successful twenty-year legal career in New York had come to a sudden, embarrassing end the day he brought his partner – a young man – to the firm Christmas party. That's when the whispers and sideways looks had started, the office staff had begun to gossip and giggle when he walked past, and the partners had begun to snub him during meetings. Discreetly gay, and a flamboyant dresser with flair and style, he had always moved in the right circles, or so he thought, until it became clear that being openly gay in the conservative New York legal establishment was definitely a disadvantage as far as career advancement and client relations were concerned.

Disillusioned and disappointed, Rodrigo had left the prestigious law firm he had been with for years and set up his own practice. This was when he came to Cordoba's notice. That had been ten years ago. Cordoba had been embroiled in a bitter commercial dispute involving a hotel he owned with a partner in Brooklyn. A last-minute change of legal representation had left Cordoba vulnerable and exposed. Someone referred him to Rodrigo, who stepped in and won the case in a dramatic showdown in court. Impressed, Cordoba continued to engage Rodrigo until a friendship had developed between two outcasts who understood what it meant to be different. Rodrigo rearranged his practice in New York and began to work exclusively for Cordoba on a multimillion-dollar retainer that would have been the envy of his former senior partners. He divided his time between New York and Bogota, and any other place his instructions demanded.

Rodrigo looked at his watch and frowned; his guest was late. The meeting with Alessandro Giordano, second son of Riccardo Giordano, the notorious head of a powerful Mafia family in Florence, had been arranged quite recently by Cordoba himself.

Since the assassination of his main rival Salvatore Gambio in 2016, Riccardo Giordano had attempted to expand his drug distribution network in Italy and beyond. What was holding him back was a reliable drug supplier he could count on. It was for that reason Giordano had reached out to Cordoba on several occasions in the hope of establishing a new business relationship he could trust. The bloody Mafia turf wars in Florence during 2016 were well known, which had begun with the assassination of Giordano's eldest son, Mario. It was rumoured that Gambio was behind the hit and that this was the reason for Gambio's own very public assassination during Mario's funeral, which had dominated the headlines all over Europe for weeks. As a result, the lucrative business interests of the two remaining Mafia families – the Giordanos and the Lombardos – were rearranged and 'Gambio turf' was divided between them during an uneasy truce.

Riccardo Giordano had been delighted when Cordoba had contacted him unexpectedly a few days earlier, suggesting a meeting in Amsterdam. What Giordano didn't know was that the proposed meeting had nothing whatsoever to do with drug distribution, but an entirely different purpose altogether.

In fact, Rodrigo had suggested contacting Giordano as the first step in implementing the daring plan to free Alonso. Cordoba had even given it a name: 'Operation Libertad'. It was the first move in a risky chess-like game where the stakes were about as high as they came – and losing wasn't an option.

Rodrigo, a master tactician, always tried to be a step ahead of the game. Just like a champion chess player, he carefully planned his moves well in advance, and his opponents rarely knew where he was coming from, or why, until it was too late.

Rodrigo was about to order his second martini when his guest walked into the brasserie. Apologising profusely, he sat down facing Rodrigo. Shortish, in his early thirties with classic Italian good looks, Alessandro was exactly as Rodrigo had imagined. He was a messenger, a trusted representative of his powerful father who made all the decisions. Like Cordoba, Alessandro's father rarely travelled, preferring the familiarity and safety of Florence. And like all traditional Mafia families, Riccardo Giordano felt more comfortable doing business through family members, preferably his sons. Tradition. Rodrigo had no doubt that Alessandro would deliver his proposal promptly and accurately. It was a solid first step, but any decision would be made by his father. The detail would follow later. However, self-interest and the possibility of huge profits would focus Giordano's attention; Rodrigo was sure of it. And where money was concerned, the Mafia always paid attention and understood the game perfectly.

After exchanging pleasantries, Rodrigo introduced the real subject of interest.

'We understand you are looking for a new supply line ...' began Rodrigo, steering the conversation in the desired direction. Alessandro wiped his mouth with his serviette, took another sip of wine and then launched into a detailed account of the family's drug business, providing quantities, territories and connections. He explained how, with Gambio's death, a main rival had been removed, allowing the family to dramatically expand its influence, territory and reach, as far as drug supply was concerned. He pointed out that the family's business interests now extended deep into Central and Eastern Europe, with extensive new interests in the United States as well, especially in Chicago.

Making sure he looked suitably impressed, Rodrigo listened patiently. 'If I understand you correctly, you are looking to us for an exclusive drug supply line, possibly through Naples or Marseilles; is that correct?' he asked.

Alessandro nodded. 'Could you deliver the quantities I mentioned?'

Rodrigo began to laugh. 'You know we can,' he said. He was intentionally a little curt, to put Alessandro off balance. 'The real question here is, *do we want to*?' he continued. 'Do we want to restrict ourselves to an exclusive arrangement with you, or do we continue to do business with our existing partners as usual?'

'Yes, I suppose that's the real question here,' conceded Alessandro. He realised he was no match for Rodrigo when it came to negotiating a deal of this magnitude and complexity, and almost regretted having come alone. Rodrigo saw a flicker of uncertainty on Alessandro's face, and a hint of dejection in his body language. It only lasted for an instant, but being a practised observer of human behaviour, he had noticed it. At that moment, he knew he had his opponent exactly where he wanted him to be: vulnerable and exposed. It was time to throw him a lifeline. Yet, what that lifeline entailed was the very thing Rodrigo needed himself, desperately. It was the very reason for the meeting itself. But of course, Alessandro wasn't to know this.

'As an experienced businessman, you will understand that a deal like this is only possible if there is something in it for both parties,' said Rodrigo.

'Obviously.'

Rodrigo sat back in his chair and watched Alessandro carefully. 'As it happens, there is something we need; something you could provide that may persuade us to consider your proposal,' he said. 'And it isn't money,' he added quietly.

Alessandro sat up. Perhaps not all was lost. 'What might that be?' he asked hoarsely.

'Your expertise and your connections.'

Alessandro looked puzzled. 'I don't understand. Would you care to elaborate?'

'Of course. Your family has all the right connections, experience and expertise to carry out something we need, but we wouldn't be confident to do ourselves.'

'Forgive me, you speak in riddles. What is it you need?'

'An abduction.'

'A what?'

'You heard right; we want you to abduct someone and deliver him to us.'

'Who?'

'Later.'

'Where?'

'London.'

'When?'

'Soon.'

'High-profile target?'

'Absolutely.'

'Public place?'

'Definitely.'

'Security?'

'Huge.'

'Difficult then,' said Alessandro, draining the last of his wine.

'What do you think? The stakes are high here, but so are the profits,' said Rodrigo, lowering his voice. 'If it were simple, I wouldn't be talking to you. In our world, Alessandro, nothing is free. I'm sure you know that.'

Alessandro nodded, feeling more confident. This was the kind of language he understood. 'To be perfectly clear, what you are telling me is this,' he said. 'If we carry out the abduction successfully and deliver the target to you, you will enter into an exclusive supply arrangement with us?'

'That's about it.'

'I will have to discuss this with my father. In our family ... you know ... he—'

'I understand perfectly,' interrupted Rodrigo, smiling. He knew he was on the home stretch now. 'I will need a decision.'

'When?'

'By Friday.'

'You got it.'

'Let's drink to that.' Rodrigo reached for the bottle and refilled their glasses, secure in the knowledge that *Operation Libertad* had just taken a huge step forward; it had moved from probable to possible.

'Good idea. Salute!' said Alessandro, and held up his glass.

4

Giordano villa, Florence: 5 April

Florence airport was bustling as usual. Because he had no luggage, Rodrigo walked straight past the baggage carousel and headed for the exit. Dressed in a pair of khaki pants, white shirt, blue linen jacket and wearing a panama hat, he looked like one of the many tourists who had just arrived from London.

When he gave the taxi driver the address, the driver looked at him, surprised. 'Are you sure this is the right place, sir?' he asked.

'Quite sure,' replied Rodrigo.

The driver shrugged as he pulled his taxi away from the kerb.

Rodrigo put on his dark sunglasses, settled back into his seat, and prepared himself for the meeting he had so hoped would eventuate. Used to dealing with the ruthless mega-rich and powerful, he wasn't fazed by what he was heading towards. However, it wasn't every day that he went to meet one of the most notorious Mafia bosses in Italy. An experienced negotiator, Rodrigo knew that preparation was always the key to a successful outcome.

So far, everything had gone exactly as he had planned. After their meeting in Amsterdam, Alessandro had gone back to Florence to talk to his father, and Rodrigo had gone to London to wait for the invitation he was almost certain would come soon. It did. He had received a phone call from Alessandro the night before, inviting him to come to Florence to meet with his father to discuss the proposal raised during their meeting.

The baited hook had been thrown into the lake of temptation; it was now up to Rodrigo to make sure it was swallowed as well. And that, Rodrigo knew, would be far more difficult to achieve because what he was about to ask in return for the juicy bait, was so daring and audacious that only a handful of 'specialists' in Europe were capable of carrying out what he had in mind. Most, he knew, wouldn't even consider it at any price and dismiss the whole idea as the fantasy of a lunatic. Rodrigo was hoping that greed, ego and ambition – his main negotiating tools – would be strong enough to tip the scales in his favour, and override caution and good sense. And to get to that point, he had to know how to deal with the man he was about to meet. And to know how to do that, he first had to know as much as possible about him.

Rodrigo had done his homework. His research team in New York had done a marvellous job digging up Giordano's murky past and had come up with a few surprising gems that Rodrigo could use during the negotiations should unexpected obstacles stand in his way.

Rodrigo smiled as soon as the taxi pulled up in front of the massive, wrought-iron gates of the Giordano villa just outside Florence. *Fortified compounds look the same all over the world*, he thought. An armed security guard came over to the taxi and opened the back door. 'Mr Rodrigo?' he asked.

Rodrigo nodded, paid the fare and gave the anxious driver a large tip.

'You are expected, sir. Please come with me,' continued the guard. 'But first I will have to search ... please stand over there. I'm sure you understand.'

'Completely,' replied Rodrigo, smiling, and held up his hands, quite used to the procedure. It was standard practice every time he went to see Cordoba. There were no exceptions when it came to security.

Rodrigo followed the guard up the long gravel driveway to the magnificent seventeenth-century villa overlooking Florence that had once belonged to a wealthy merchant. Alessandro greeted Rodrigo at the front door, thanked him for coming and ushered him inside.

Riccardo Giordano was waiting for his guest in the palatial ballroom on the ground floor, which had been converted into a comfortable living room with large couches facing the tall windows overlooking the gardens. Despite its size the room, with its striking marble floor and two large fireplaces facing each other at either end, was surprisingly intimate.

Giordano, a man of simple tastes, hated ostentation. Unlike his rivals – the Lombardos and the Gambios – he preferred comfort over pretence and didn't believe in spending a fortune on paintings and antiques just to impress. Always aware of his humble childhood in Calabria, where a pair of shoes was a treasure that had to last for years, the women toiled in the fields from sunup to sundown just to put food on the table and the men disappeared, often for weeks, doing what was never discussed around the dinner table, Giordano was a predictable product of his past. Growing up in a traditional Calabrian Mafia family with almost no formal education came at a price.

Barrel-chested, short and stocky, with a tanned face like creased leather that had seen too much sun and violence, he looked more like a peasant from the south used to hard labour than the feared head of one of the most powerful Mafia families in Italy.

'Thank you for coming,' said Giordano, walking towards the door to meet his guest. While perfect, his English had that melodious accent that reminded Rodrigo of Italian celebrity chefs who presented popular cooking shows on TV.

Rodrigo realised at once that the man's appearance was deceptive and disguised a sharp, cunning mind, and he was instantly on guard. He had often met men like Giordano in the course of his career and knew how dangerous and costly underestimating such a man could be. Cordoba, his notorious client, was of the same ilk. Meeting Cordoba for the first time, it had been difficult to imagine that the unassuming, quietly spoken, balding man with the handlebar moustache was a billionaire businessman with a drug empire and a private army that had whole countries living in fear, and presidents and generals doing his bidding at a click of his fingers.

They are well suited to do business together, thought Rodrigo, extending his hand. 'Thank you for inviting me. Like you, I prefer to do business in person,' he said, as they shook hands. As he looked at Giordano, he noticed that the man's most striking feature was his eyes, radiating intelligence and danger.

Giordano pointed to one of the couches. 'Please take a seat. I'm just having a morning snack; would you care to join me?' he continued affably.

'Love to,' replied Rodrigo, recognising the traditional hospitality. In Italy, it was always about food.

Moments later, a little old lady dressed all in black and wearing a headscarf entered the room and placed a large wooden platter stacked high with thinly sliced prosciutto, various salamis, a slab of goat's cheese and handfuls of olives, on the table in front of them.

'My mother,' said Giordano. Rodrigo stood up and smiled at the lady, who smiled back.

'I bring bread and wine,' she said in broken English and hurried out of the room.

'At ninety-two, she still bakes fresh bread every morning,' continued Giordano. 'Come, Alessandro. Sit down and let's eat.'

For a while the three men sat in silence, enjoying the food, and Giordano's mother returned as promised with fresh, warm bread and chilled wine. Rodrigo had decided to let his host take the lead when he was ready as he was clearly used to calling the shots.

'A little more wine?' said Giordano and reached for the bottle of Chianti on the tray.

'Yes, thank you,' said Rodrigo, aware that Giordano was watching him carefully. *He's sizing me up before starting any negotiations,* he thought.

'Alessandro has told me about your proposal,' began Giordano. 'I must say, I was a little surprised.'

'Understandable,' said Rodrigo, instantly on guard. The negotiations had begun.

'Is that why Mr Cordoba got in touch with me and sent you to negotiate? This is more than just about a new supply arrangement, isn't it?'

It was a shrewd opening question and Rodrigo realised at once where this was heading. To sidestep the question or give an evasive answer would be a grave mistake.

'Quite possibly, yes.'

'Why would he do that, you think?'

'Because he obviously considers you the best choice for what we have in mind, and because he believes you are a man we can trust.'

Giordano nodded, seeming satisfied with the answer. 'And why would I be the best choice?'

'Because of your track record.'

'Track record? What on earth do you mean?'

'May I speak frankly?'

'Of course. In my home there is no room for anything else.'

'You have already demonstrated that you have what it takes to carry out a complex, high-risk, high-profile operation similar to the one we have in mind. You have the contacts, the resolve, the courage and the means, and that is exactly what we need.'

'And what makes you say that?'

Rodrigo took his time before replying. He knew he had to choose his words carefully. If he approached this delicate subject the wrong way, the negotiations could quickly turn sour and he could find himself leaving empty-handed. With a man like Giordano there was no second chance. On the other hand, if he chose the correct approach and gained Giordano's confidence, a deal was definitely possible.

'Someone who can arrange the daring assassination of his son's killer in front of a crowded church at a funeral service attended by hundreds, while the chief prosecutor is standing next to him at the time, has all the qualities we are looking for.'

For a while there was silence and Rodrigo could feel his stomach begin to churn as a flicker of sickening doubt raced through him. Perhaps he had chosen the wrong approach? After all, he had just accused his host of having arranged the assassination of a deadly rival, who many believed had ordered the killing of his son two years ago. While there had been much speculation and innuendo in the papers for months about the killing, and accusing fingers had pointed at Giordano, no-one was ever charged. The perpetrator had got away with it. Rodrigo noticed that Alessandro was looking at the floor, but his father was staring straight ahead.

'I like your candour, Mr Rodrigo,' said Giordano, turning towards his guest, 'and your courage.' The ice had been broken. 'In our business, straight-talking men are rare. Yet, I believe it's the best, no, the only way. Now, please tell me about your proposal.'

During the next hour, Rodrigo went through the daring plan in detail. He explained every step, holding nothing back except the identity of the target and the precise date and location of the proposed abduction. That information would be supplied later, once a more formal agreement had been reached. He touched on the obvious risks and dangers without trying to downplay the real possibility of mayhem, even death, should something go wrong. At the same time, he was carefully watching Giordano for signs of hesitation or displeasure or, God forbid, shock. He couldn't see any.

'And in return?' asked Giordano quietly after Rodrigo had finished.

'We enter into a long-term supply arrangement that suits your needs, at a price that will reflect our gratitude and appreciation, after the mission has been successfully completed.'

'And your current arrangements with Lombardo?' asked Giordano, watching his visitor through hooded eyes.

Rodrigo had been expecting this. The Lombardo family was Giordano's main rival in the drug business, and a serious thorn in his side. After the removal of Salvatore Gambio and the collapse of his business empire, the Giordanos and the Lombardos had reached an uneasy truce that had steadily deteriorated as the Lombardos slowly extended their influence and gained the upper hand. To a large extent this had been due to the Lombardos' superior supply arrangements with the H Cartel in Italy and the United States.

A skilled negotiator, Rodrigo realised it was now the right time to play the card that would clinch the deal. It was always prudent to hold something back for just such an opportunity.

'Upon successful delivery of the target, unharmed, to us, we will stop our supply arrangements with the Lombardos and make yours an exclusive one,' said Rodrigo, dropping the bombshell that could drive the Lombardos out of business and establish Giordano as the undisputed master of Florence. This possibility alone was worth millions.

The expression on Giordano's face told Rodrigo everything he needed to know. He had hit the mark.

'In that case, Mr Rodrigo, we have a deal. However, in our circles we seal such a deal with a kiss,' continued Giordano and stood up.

Surprised, Rodrigo stood up as well. Giordano walked over to his visitor, embraced him and kissed him on both cheeks. Rodrigo knew this was an expression of great trust and honour, and to break such trust was unthinkable and would have dire consequences. This gesture alone was worth more than the most watertight contract. His client in Bogota would be pleased. Operation Libertad was on.

'Where are you off to now?' asked Giordano, escorting his guest to the front door.

'Back to London. I have a connecting flight to Colombia leaving tonight.'

'Please tell Mr Cordoba we very much look forward to working with him.'

'I will,' said Rodrigo. He stopped at the front door and turned to face Giordano and his son. It was time to ask the final question. 'There is one more thing I'm sure my client would like to know, if possible, and so would I,' said Rodrigo, 'for peace of mind ...'

'Go ahead.'

'Who would you use to carry out this assignment? You would need a team of experts to work on something like this, right?'

Giordano turned to his son. 'Alessandro, please tell our friend how you will go about this.'

'We have access to a group of highly specialised freelance operators, originally from war-torn Kosovo,' began Alessandro, pleased at finally being asked to contribute. 'With lots of experience; very sophisticated. We have used them before and they have delivered every time. I can assure you; we can supply the necessary boots needed on the ground.'

'So, what's the next step?'

'I will be in touch after we've assembled a suitable team; every day counts now. After that, I expect the operatives will contact you directly for further information and will keep you in the loop. They are very efficient and well connected.' Alessandro paused and opened the door. 'Absolute pros,' he added, 'with an outstanding track record.'

Rodrigo looked impressed. 'Thank you, gentlemen, that's all I needed to hear,' he said, and then shook hands with Giordano and his son, and walked to the waiting car.

5

New York: 9 April

As promised, Alessandro had been in regular contact with Rodrigo since their meeting in Florence and had kept him up to date. Substantial progress appeared to have been made in a few short days, which gave Rodrigo confidence and allayed some of his fears that the project may be too ambitious, or that Giordano might have been carried away and somewhat hasty in agreeing to the deal.

However, it had taken Alessandro less than twenty-four hours to engage a 'team' that was apparently already on the job, gathering vital intelligence about both the target and the venue. Alessandro had called Rodrigo late the night before to tell him that one of the team members would contact him the next day to clarify certain vital matters and to keep him informed of their progress. For the first time, Alessandro also disclosed the name of the team – Spiridon 4 – and indicated that team members would identify themselves by using that name.

An early riser, Rodrigo arrived in his office at seven-thirty as usual. His PA, who had started an hour earlier, prepared his coffee – black and strong – just as he liked it. She was about to take the coffee into her boss's office when her phone rang. It was the security guard downstairs, informing her that a young woman wanted to see Mr Rodrigo. Because the office didn't open until eight-thirty, he would have to activate the lift and send her up to the floor.

'We have no early appointments. Please ask her what she wants,' said the PA, checking Rodrigo's diary again.

The security guard did as he was told and called back.

'That's all she said? How weird,' said the PA. 'Hold on, I won't be a sec.'

The PA put down the receiver and hurried into Rodrigo's office. 'There's a woman downstairs with security, asking for you.'

'Oh? Did she say what it was about?'

'All she said was Spiridon 4 ...'

'*What?*' Rodrigo almost shouted. 'Tell him to send her up straight away. I'll meet her at the lift myself.'

When Alessandro had said that someone from the team would contact him, Rodrigo certainly hadn't expected that to mean in person. Standing at the lift, he watched the indicator light on the panel creep slowly up to the thirty-second floor. For some reason, Rodrigo felt his stomach tighten and a wave of unease wash over him as the lift door opened. From what Alessandro had told him, the team consisted of some of the most deadly and secretive guns for hire on the planet. He was therefore unable to hide his surprise when a young woman of about thirty, a small backpack slung casually over her shoulder and dressed in jeans, a Princeton University sweater and wearing sneakers, stepped out of the lift.

'You must be Raul Rodrigo,' she said, extending her hand. She had noticed the expression on Rodrigo's face and smiled as she recognised the familiar effect she had on people who met her for the first time. 'You look just like your photo on the firm website,' she continued, trying to put Rodrigo at ease. 'I'm Teodora. Can we go somewhere private to talk? The fewer people who see me here, the better.'

Rodrigo ushered his unexpected visitor into the boardroom. He had recovered quickly and was beginning to size up the young woman. *She's so young,* he thought. *Certainly not what I expected.* He found it difficult to imagine that the young woman with the boyish, short black hair and large horn-rimmed glasses, which gave her an endearing, studious look, could possibly be a member of a hit squad hired by the Mafia to carry out treacherous assignments. *She looks like a mature student going to a tutorial,* he thought as he closed the door behind him, but she appeared totally at ease and in control.

'Spiridon 4. What a curious name,' began Rodrigo, trying to take the lead. 'What does it mean?'

'*Spiridon* means spirit in Serbian, and my team has four members.'

Rodrigo raised an eyebrow. '*Your* team?'

Teodora walked over to the large window with an uninterrupted view across the water to the Statue of Liberty, and for a moment glanced at the famous icon that had welcomed thousands of immigrants to the promised land of freedom and opportunity.

'Yes. Is that a problem?' she asked quietly.

Rodrigo wasn't used to being put in his place, and certainly not in his own boardroom. 'That will depend, I suppose,' he replied, a little annoyed, 'on why you're here, and what you are about to tell me. Please take a seat.'

Teodora turned around and gave Rodrigo her best smile. 'Very well,' she said, choosing a chair near the window. 'I can already see we'll get along famously. May I have a glass of water, please?'

Rodrigo walked over to the fridge. 'Still or sparkling?' he asked.

'Sparkling, please. The bottle will do nicely.'

Rodrigo handed her the bottle of water, sat down opposite her, folded his arms in front of his chest and looked at her expectantly.

'Firstly, why am I here? I came to check you out. I do this at the beginning of every assignment,' said Teodora cheerfully, and took a sip of water. 'It's part of our assessment.'

'*Assessment?* Assessment of what?' asked Rodrigo.

'Risk. It helps us decide whether or not to take on the job in the first place, and how much to charge.'

'And did you? Check me out, I mean?'

'Oh yes. I also went to Maryland and Alabama to check out the target.'

'You've been to Marshall Space Flight Center to check out Professor Stolzfus?' Rodrigo looked incredulous.

'I have. What shall we talk about first: you, or the professor?'

'Let's begin with me.'

'Very well.' Teodora sat back in her comfortable chair, and for a moment took in the splendid view as she collected her thoughts.

'In away, we are not all that different from each other,' began Teodora. 'You do in the courtroom and around the negotiating table what we do in the field.'

'And what might that be?' asked Rodrigo.

'We both take on challenging projects that others would find too daunting and risky, and then produce results for our clients and get paid a lot of money for it. This takes courage and imagination. We are also not afraid to think creatively and outside the square.'

Generalities, thought Rodrigo, unimpressed, *bordering on platitudes.*

Teodora read his body language and decided to move up a notch. 'You arrived in this country with your parents and siblings from Mexico when you were six. Penniless and with very little English, your father struggled to find a job. When he finally did, working as a labourer on the wharves, he toiled twelve hours a day for a pittance that could barely keep his family alive.'

Rodrigo stiffened and sat up but didn't interrupt as he remembered those difficult childhood days, brought so unexpectedly alive by the astonishing young woman he had just met.

'Then two years later,' continued Teodora, 'tragedy struck. Your father had a fatal accident ... By the time you were fourteen you already had two jobs, helping your mother who was working in a laundry during the week, and as a cleaner on weekends. This makes your success later at law school even more remarkable, as you continued to work so hard right up to your graduation and bar exams.' Teodora paused, and looked at Rodrigo. 'The only reason I'm telling you all this is to give you an indication of the detail we go into with our initial assessment. We build up a careful profile of our clients and those who are important to our assignments. I'm sure you understand.'

Rodrigo nodded, but didn't reply.

'You live with your partner, a curator at the Metropolitan Museum, in a penthouse overlooking Central Park. You have a bank account in the Cayman Islands with several million dollars on deposit, and another one in Jersey. Tax reasons. After leaving your previous firm where you were a senior partner for many years – under a cloud of scandal because of your homosexuality – you established this practice and are currently working almost exclusively for the H Cartel in Colombia. Hernando Cordoba, to be precise. Do you want me to go on?'

Rodrigo shook his head, completely taken aback. 'No, thank you. That's enough. I get the picture. Very impressive ...'

'And one more thing,' added Teodora. 'You have a luncheon appointment today at twelve-thirty with a prosecutor. The only reason I mention this is that your internet security is seriously defective. It took our hackers just minutes to penetrate your firewall and access your diary ...'

'Remind me never to let your team work against me or my clients,' said Rodrigo, smiling. He found that a little humour was always the best way to hide embarrassment and surprise. 'If I am such an open book, I'm dying to know what you've found out about Professor Stolzfus. Please tell me.'

Teodora took another sip of water and then continued, enjoying herself. Confronting clients with this kind of detailed personal information was always an important part of every assignment; a serious test of personalities and resolve.

'Our enquiries so far have focused on the professor's current position at NASA, not his background and early life as that didn't seem relevant to our assignment. All we know in that regard is that he grew up on a farm in Pennsylvania in a strict Amish family, had a serious accident in his early twenties, then went to Princeton and had a stellar rise in academia as one of the brightest students of his generation. However,' continued Teodora, 'his current position at NASA is interesting ...'

'In what way?' asked Rodrigo.

'Because it has a bearing on likely security arrangements should he be allowed to leave the US and travel to London to attend the Hawking memorial service in June. And that is by no means certain at this stage,' said Teodora, dropping the bombshell.

'What makes you say that?' Rodrigo felt his stomach churn. It was a familiar feeling he experienced every time he faced unexpected bad news.

'First, let me put his current position at NASA into context. Stolzfus is without doubt the brightest, most highly regarded physicist and cosmologist in the US, if not the world today. According to many, including Nobel laureates, he is a genius mathematician and Hawking's likely successor. That makes him an exceedingly valuable asset, a national treasure in fact, who has to be protected. And protected he is, I can tell you. He is surrounded by strict security on all sides. His movements are restricted; his contract with NASA is quite specific about this. He lives in a guarded compound at the Marshall Space Flight Center in Huntsville, Alabama, and outside the compound he's driven around in an armoured car.'

'Why?'

'Because he is part of the "Genius Club", as it is affectionately known in academic circles.'

'Can you elaborate?'

'Apparently, there are currently six members of the Genius Club. Not all of them work at NASA and the space program, but all are somehow connected to national security. They are the brightest of the bright. Mathematicians, physicists like Stolzfus working on artificial intelligence, space programs, missile shields and climate change. Cutting-edge stuff like that. The US military depends on them and their work.'

'Are you suggesting he may not be *allowed* to attend the memorial service?'

'Precisely. Since his return from the space station the other day, he has met with Director Goldberger on several occasions about this. He has created a huge fuss, as the director doesn't want him to go. Strictly speaking, Stolzfus is not allowed to leave the US without permission. It's all in his contract.

'However, he's digging in. He's determined to go. He says this is one occasion in his life he cannot afford to miss. And his recent publicity since that remarkable broadcast from space has given him considerable leverage. But at the same time, it has also given him huge exposure. He's become an overnight celebrity. It will be difficult to stop him. Ultimately, it will be up to the president to make the decision. No-one else is prepared to take responsibility.'

'And you've found all this out in a couple of days?' said Rodrigo.

'We have some of the best hackers in the world working for us. Their ingenuity is surprising ...'

'I can see that. So, where to from here?'

'If you agree, we would like to proceed on the basis that he will be allowed to go. It's the most likely outcome. However, we must already factor something critically important into our planning.'

'What?'

'Extraordinary security arrangements by both the US – CIA most likely and army intelligence – and in the UK, MI5. This will go all the way to the top.'

'Incredible! And you and your team are still interested?'

'Certainly. This will only have a bearing on our fee, but fortunately for you this is not your problem, is it, Mr Rodrigo?' said Teodora, smiling.

'I must say, I didn't quite expect this,' said Rodrigo, shaking his head.

'Assignments like this are never straightforward. That's why we make our assessment first. That way at least, there are no surprises.'

'Do you walk away from many?'

'Some. But most of the time it has nothing to do with difficulties on the ground, so to speak. The real problems are always the clients ...'

'But not this time?'

'It would appear not. We've worked with the Giordanos many times before.'

'So, may I assume that my client and I have passed?'

'With flying colours.'

'Thank God for that!'

'Not that many do.'

'And your fee?' asked Rodrigo, unable to resist the tempting question.

'Not your problem. But it will reflect the huge risks we take.'

Wow! thought Rodrigo. *I can imagine.*

'That's why we can only work every now and then. We have to keep a low profile.'

'Understandable.'

Teodora looked at her watch and stood up. 'But now I really have to go. I have a plane to catch. Thanks for the water,' she added, a sparkle in her eyes. 'There's one more thing ...'

'Oh?'

'Where do you want to take delivery of the target? That may have a bearing on our fee.'

'Morocco.'

'Ah. Makes sense. The H Cartel is using Morocco as an entry point into Europe.'

'You are well informed.'

'Can make the difference between success and failure. Perhaps even life and death.'

'Quite so.'

'I'll be in touch,' said Teodora.

'I'm looking forward to it.'

6

Marshall Space Flight Center, Huntsville, Alabama: 12 April

The think-tank at the Marshall Space Flight Center – MSFC – the brainchild of a US Nobel laureate and jokingly referred to by scientists around the world as the 'Genius Club' – was chaired by Professor Zachariah Stolzfus, the undisputed star. An eccentric genius who lived in almost monastic isolation in a building once occupied by German rocket scientist Wernher von Braun, Stolzfus was a familiar sight at the MSFC, as were his bodyguard, his pushbike and 'Gizmo', a rescue dog who accompanied him everywhere – even to his lectures and meetings. It was rumoured that his dog knew more about rocket science than all the members of the club combined.

It isn't often the case that a man's reputation is closely matched by his appearance. Not only was Stolzfus affectionately known at MSFC as *Little Einstein*, a nickname he had brought with him from Princeton, he looked like him too. Shortish, in his late forties, with a thick beard but no moustache and a bushy head of hair that made him look like the famous German-born theoretical physicist, he walked with a limp and almost always wore a newsboy cap, white shirt, braces, and a bow tie; undoubtedly a throwback to his Amish childhood in Pennsylvania. Yet he was blessed with an exceptional mind and without question was one of the brightest and most gifted theoretical physicists in the United States, if not the world.

At Princeton he had dazzled the professors with his mathematical ability and an inquisitive mind that could grasp complex concepts in an instant, and then turn them upside down and explore ideas and possibilities in ways that were totally original and unique. He could then quickly distil and refine these ideas into concepts he could explain mathematically, and was well known for filling entire blackboards and whiteboards with calculations and long equations only he could understand, and then expressed surprise when others couldn't immediately follow what he was getting at. To him, it all appeared obvious and easy, and he sometimes found it frustrating and tedious having to explain what he was trying to say.

An illustrious career in academia seemed assured and offers came flooding in from various prestigious institutions. That's when he came to the attention of the CIA, who wanted to recruit him. Mathematicians of his calibre only came along once in a generation and were in great demand not only by the CIA, but also by the military.

Stolzfus had declined. With his eyes firmly trained at the heavens, he had bigger things in mind. He wanted to solve the mysteries of the universe, not national security.

Stolzfus left his bike with his bodyguard downstairs at the entrance and walked up the stairs with Gizmo to the meeting room on the first floor. It was the second Thursday of the month, the day the Genius Club met at MSFC. Every other month, it met at the Goddard Space Flight Center in Greenbelt, Maryland, which was Stolzfus's second home. It was the first meeting of the club since Stolzfus had returned after a long stint on the space station. It was also their first meeting since Hawking had died, and Stolzfus had decided to dedicate the meeting to Hawking and his remarkable ideas and achievements. But this was only part of the reason. He also had a plan ...

The other members – two women and three men, all in their thirties – had already arrived by the time Stolzfus entered the room, and were chatting and drinking coffee. Gizmo seemed to know them all and went from one to the other for a pat, his tail wagging, before settling down in his usual corner beside the blackboard.

The first few minutes were spent with good-natured banter as everyone teased Stolzfus about his newfound fame since that extraordinary message from space had gone viral.

'They'll make a movie about him, for sure; you'll see,' said one, 'now that he's a celebrity.'

'If only they could find an actor to do the man justice,' teased another.

'Not easy,' said one of the women, grinning. 'I can't think of anyone.'

Stolzfus held up his hand. 'Enough, guys. Perhaps I'll just have to play myself, should someone be brave enough to ask,' said Stolzfus. 'That should send the box offices around the world into a spin.'

'Well, if they spin fast enough, they could turn into a black hole,' speculated the other woman, 'and no information could then get out. That would solve the problem.'

'And deprive the world of a masterpiece?' said Stolzfus, grinning. 'But seriously, I'm glad you mentioned black holes, because that is precisely what I would like to talk to you about.'

Stolzfus turned to the blackboard behind him, picked up a piece of chalk and quickly wrote down an equation, the chalk making a spine-chilling, screeching noise. It was one of Hawking's most famous equations, the one Hawking had requested be engraved on his tombstone because it embodied his greatest contribution to science:

$$T = \frac{Hc3}{8\ PiGMk}$$

'Hawking radiation,' said Jake, one of the men in the group. 'You want to talk about black holes?'

'Precisely,' replied Stolzfus and turned around to face the others seated in front of him. 'I know this is not what we were going to discuss today, but I would like to raise something a little different if I may, in memory of the great man who just passed away.'

Stolzfus paused and ran his fingers through his bushy hair. 'It's all about the largest objects in the universe, and the smallest particles,' he continued, 'and a tantalising paradox, all embodied in an elegant theory trying to bridge the gap between quantum physics, and physics on a cosmic scale. Simply put, it's about black hole *evaporation.*

'Hawking radiation is a paradox, a conundrum; that's what Hawking left us. He started the conversation, it's now up to us to continue it. But I believe that's not all. He left us much more than that: a challenge. Orbiting in space for a few weeks as I have done just now gives you a lot of time to think, and a different perspective.

'As we know, black holes warp space and time, and until quite recently it was believed that nothing could escape from a black hole, not even light, because it is incredibly dense and gravity would therefore not allow this. Then along came Hawking in 1973 and turned this on its head. "Not so," he said. Why? Because unless they can consume more matter, black holes will leak radiation and particles, shrink over billions of years and eventually explode and disappear. Like hungry beasts they have to be fed. If not, they will fizzle and die.'

'We know all this, Zac,' said one of the men sitting in the front.

'Quite so,' replied Stolzfus. 'In fact, I believe that collectively between all of us in this room, *we know a lot more*, if only we could combine it all, share it, harness it, explore it *together* ...'

'What are you getting at, Zac?' asked one of the women, Barbara, who knew Stolzfus well.

'Hawking believed that we are getting very close to a theory of everything, a unifying theory that would answer all the questions in the universe, including the paradox I was just talking about. In fact, I believe he was getting close but sadly, he ran out of time. One can only speculate what he would have been able to achieve with a little more time up his sleeve ...'

'Sure, it's the holy grail ...' muttered another man at the back, sounding a little impatient.

'It is. Please bear with me. I'm convinced that all the right ideas are here in this very room. But at the moment, they consist of different pieces of information, like a jigsaw puzzle, waiting to be put together to show the whole picture.

'I know your areas of expertise, your talents, your strengths better than anyone. Looking around the room I can see quantum mechanics, thermodynamics, the Big Bang, wormholes and time travel. I can see singularities, event horizons, entropy and space time, to name but a few. You are all intimately acquainted with the work of Laplace,

Planck, Heisenberg and Dirac. What more do we want? If we can bring all those pieces, all that precious knowledge gained together, we just may have the answer right here ...'

'You really believe that?' said Barbara.

'I do.'

'Based on what?' asked Jake, becoming excited. For someone like Stolzfus who was always cautious and reserved, and questioned everything, to say something like this was quite extraordinary.

'On what I know and what I *sense* ... We all know that some of the greatest discoveries begin with gut feeling and asking the right questions. I can point to countless examples and so can you.'

'So, what have you got in mind?' asked Barbara.

'I want to throw you a challenge. We could call it the Hawking Challenge. Apart from everything else we do, we work together on this as a team. Divide the tasks; pool our insights and our knowledge. Six brains, not just one. Just think of the possibilities. Up there in orbit, I could see the big picture. I believe we can do this. I can be the guide, the conductor if you like, but we are all part of the same orchestra, playing in harmony to create an inspired symphony to make the angels listen, and dance to our tune. What do you say?'

'Very poetic, Zac,' said Barbara.

'Exciting stuff. Let's put it to a vote,' said Jake. 'All right. So, who wants to be part of this orchestra?'

Five hands shot up into the air. Stolzfus smiled and then raised his own. 'We'll talk again later, but now let's get down to business and discuss what's on the agenda or we'll get into trouble. Barbara, would you like to begin?'

Barbara was about to open the folder in front of her when someone knocked on the door and then entered. It was the director's secretary.

'Sorry for interrupting, Professor Stolzfus, but the director would like to see you. It's urgent.'

Stolzfus followed the secretary across the courtyard to another building, his bodyguard trailing behind them. 'Do you know what this is about?' asked Stolzfus. To be called into the director's office like this was most unusual.

'No idea,' replied the secretary. 'All I know is some bigwig from Washington and someone from the CIA arrived this morning. Both are with the director right now.'

'Sounds ominous. Could be an arrest warrant; what do you think?' joked Stolzfus.

'Are you a spy, Zac?'

'I'm only spying on the stars.'

'I don't think that's an offence, especially not around here. They are all doing it. Must be something else.'

'We'll soon find out.'

'Ah, Professor Stolzfus,' said Chuck Goldberger, director of the MSFC, as soon as Stolzfus entered his office. 'Apologies for interrupting your meeting, but this couldn't wait. Let me introduce you.'

A man and an attractive young woman in her late thirties who were seated on a couch stood up and introductions were made. The man was from NASA HQ in Washington, the woman, who introduced herself as Major Andersen, was from the CIA.

'This is about your application,' began Goldberger, 'to attend the Hawking memorial service in London.'

'Ah,' said Stolzfus, relieved. 'And here I was thinking I must have unwittingly committed some serious space crime up there and was about to be hauled over the coals …'

Everybody laughed. The ice was broken.

'Nothing like that,' said the man from Washington. 'In fact, it's all good news. Your application has been approved. It went all the way to the top, the president himself.'

'I had no idea this was that important,' said Stolzfus.

'Oh yes, it is. As the coordinator of several highly sensitive, multibillion-dollar projects – many of them defence and national security related – you are one of the most important men in the country, Professor, and therefore a potential target.'

'What do you mean?' asked Stolzfus, frowning.

'There are some governments that would go to great lengths to get their hands on you,' interjected Major Andersen. 'And they'd pay a small fortune for what you know and what you can do. And then of course there are always the terrorists—'

'You can't be serious!' interrupted Stolzfus. 'I'm just a scientist, for God's sake.'

'Precisely, and since your broadcast from space, a very well-known one. You may have been working in the shadows until then, Professor Stolzfus, under a cloak of anonymity, but now you are in the spotlight, like it or not, and that makes you vulnerable,' said the man from Washington.

'Vulnerable? In what way?'

'I will let Major Andersen here explain what will be involved when you travel and leave the country,' said Goldberger, sidestepping the question. 'She will be in charge of security and accompany you on your trip.'

For the next half hour, the major took Stolzfus step by step through the elaborate security arrangements. 'In fact,' she said, coming to the conclusion of the briefing, 'the president ordered that the same level of security is to be provided to you as if he were to travel himself to attend the service. Do I make myself clear?' The major looked sternly at Stolzfus.

'Perfectly.' *She looks so young*, thought Stolzfus, sizing up the CIA agent sitting opposite, but he knew it would be a mistake not to take her seriously. She was obviously used to being in control. *Must be top notch. They wouldn't have sent her otherwise.*

'In London, the Metropolitan Police and MI5 will be in charge of security, obviously in close collaboration with us; CIA mainly ...' continued the major. *Super smart, eccentric; not used to being told what to do*; *a little awkward around women*, thought the major, sizing up the man she would have to protect. *Could be a problem.* He clearly had no idea how important he was. She would have to tread carefully and gain his confidence.

'I don't have to remind you, Professor,' interjected the man from Washington, 'that none of this is to leave this room. You are not to discuss it with anyone. The same secrecy obligations apply to this as to all of your work. I'm sure I don't have to remind you of your obligations in that regard ... and please don't write anything down.'

'I completely understand.'

'That's about it for now,' said Goldberger and stood up. 'We mustn't keep you from your work any longer, Professor. Major Andersen will be in touch and will brief you more fully in due course.'

This is ridiculous and totally unnecessary, thought Stolzfus, shaking his head as he slowly limped back to his meeting. It should have been a simple, straightforward affair, not a full-blown national security exercise. But for some reason, he was suddenly feeling apprehensive about the trip.

7

'Villa Rosa', Lake Como: 14 April

Unlike her twin sister, Nadia, who was still in bed, Teodora was an early riser. She stepped out onto the large terrace of Villa Rosa, a magnificent nineteenth-century estate on the shores of Lake Como, which she had purchased a few years earlier from a profligate young Italian aristocrat who had to sell in a hurry to pay his gambling debts. Teodora looked dreamily across the tranquil water. Still partially hidden by the morning mist hovering above the dark water like a shroud, the brooding lake looked mysterious and calm. It was just after sunrise. For an instant, a strange feeling of doom cast a shadow over the peaceful moment as she looked across to the dark cliffs below the house. Instead of recognising it as a warning, she dismissed the disturbing intrusion and closed her eyes, hoping it would go away.

Teodora loved this time of the day. She loved to feel the cool air caress her face, and the dew-laden moss tickle her toes as she began her morning exercises and prepared herself for what she knew would be a tough day. Today Spiridon 4 would meet to discuss her assessment of the Stolzfus assignment, and vote on whether to go ahead with it.

Over the years, Teodora had emerged as the de facto leader of the group. Her sparkling intelligence, impeccable instincts that always seemed to guide them well, and imaginative resourcefulness to somehow come up with solutions no-one thought possible, had not only contributed to the group's phenomenal success, but was in fact the key to it.

Unless Teodora had assessed an assignment first and recommended it, it couldn't be put to the vote. Even then, the vote to go ahead had to be unanimous. If not, the project was scuttled and Spiridon 4 would walk away from it. This unbreakable discipline had served them well over the years, and was without doubt the reason they were all still alive and in business.

Teodora realised this was by far the most ambitious project Spiridon 4 had ever considered, and could well turn out to be the last they would work on together as a team. She knew it wouldn't be easy to convince the others to go ahead with it. The risks were high, but so were the rewards. She had sensed for some time that there was a certain reluctance to take risks, especially by Silvanus, a Romany gypsy who was the oldest member of Spiridon 4.

His brother, Aladdin, who was the youngest member of the team, had also become more cautious over the years, especially after their spectacularly successful assignment the year before – the assassination of a high-profile politician in Cairo – which had made them a small fortune. With money – lots of money – came caution and the inclination to protect it. Both men were married with families, and lived a life of luxury none of them could have imagined the day they had met the two girls as teenagers in Albania.

As the fog began to lift, allowing the morning sun to break through, Teodora remembered that fateful day. The day she and her sister had run into the woods late at night to escape that evil place of horror, which had devoured their parents in the most brutal way imaginable. Teodora had never told her sister what she had seen through that crack in the barn wall. Nor had they ever spoken about it since. All Nadia knew was that their parents had been killed that night, but she didn't know how, or why.

After walking aimlessly for hours through the dense forest in the dark – their feet bruised and bleeding – they had come to a clearing. Several men, women and children were seated around a campfire, singing, the horse-drawn wagons behind them giving the scene a cheerful, almost theatrical appearance. The girls had stumbled into a gypsy camp. Terrified and exhausted, Teodora realised they couldn't go much further, and decided to make contact and hope for the best. It had been one of the best decisions of her life.

After Teodora told them what had happened, the gypsies gave them shelter and they became part of an extended family. The gypsies had also suffered greatly during the war and understood just too well what the girls had been through. Many gypsies had been hunted down, tortured, raped and murdered by roving Albanian militias, often without any reason – just for fun. It was in that camp that Teodora and Nadia had met Silvanus and Aladdin, the sons of one of the gypsy elders, and a close friendship was forged that turned into a unique bond that was to last for years.

Teodora remembered the time she and her sister had spent travelling with the gypsies as some of the best years of her life. But it was after that carefree period that Spiridon 4 was conceived. Born out of poverty and necessity, Spiridon 4 was based on sheer courage and imagination ignited by the need to survive, after disaster struck when their camp was attacked and virtually wiped out one day in Kosovo. After most of the brothers' family members had been killed, the horses slaughtered and the carts burned to the ground, the four friends, who had escaped the carnage by hiding in a cave nearby, took an oath. Standing on the smouldering ruins of their lives, they swore a blood oath of loyalty, trust, friendship and unconditional support for one another that was to be at the very heart of Spiridon 4, never to be broken.

Silvanus was the first to arrive. He had driven up from Milan early that morning. Two hours later, Aladdin, who lived in Switzerland, arrived by taxi after taking the train to Como station.

'I love this place,' said Silvanus after the maid had served coffee and pastries on the terrace. He looked down to the jetty and the sailing boat. 'You got this for a bargain.'

Nadia smiled. 'Right place, right time; that's all. Remember?'

'And lots of money at our disposal to make it all work,' interjected Teodora, always the realist. 'Without that, no Villa Rosa.'

'True,' said Aladdin. 'Somehow it all comes back to money, doesn't it? But don't we have enough, guys? What we made during the last couple of years is staggering!'

Teodora realised at once where this was heading and decided to nip it in the bud straight away. 'There's more to it than that and you know it,' she said. 'Doing these assignments is our lifeblood. It keeps us together, shows us who we are ... what we can do. They are our identity. *Our destiny*,' she added softly.

'But we have to stop some time,' said Silvanus. 'We are all getting a little too old for this. We are just not hungry enough anymore. Our priorities have changed; families ... remember what almost happened in Cairo?'

'A small mistake, that's all,' said Teodora.

'We were lucky that time. We cannot afford slip-ups like that. It could have been a disaster. We could have lost everything.'

'It won't happen again,' said Nadia, remembering the tiny timing error that had almost got them killed.

Teodora held up her hand. It was time to cut through the hesitation and the doubt. 'All right, guys, I hear you. Loud and clear. I am proposing one more assignment, admittedly our biggest and most ambitious yet. And the most lucrative by far. It would set us up for life—'

'Are you serious?' interrupted Silvanus. 'Are you suggesting this could be our last assignment?'

'I am. It could be our masterpiece and a most fitting way to go out and retire – on our terms.'

'Let's hear it,' said Aladdin, his interest aroused. He could sense that his brother was interested too. He always followed his brother's lead, and Nadia always did what her sister suggested.

'All right. Let me start at the beginning. As you know, we were approached by the Giordanos. Nothing unusual about that. We have done business with them in the past very successfully so that part is sound and the money is safe. We don't have to worry about that.'

'But isn't there another party involved?' asked Silvanus, frowning. 'Doesn't that complicate things?'

'Not really. I met Raul Rodrigo in New York and checked him out. He's a lawyer working for the H Cartel in Colombia, one of the most powerful cartels in South America. I think we can work with him and his client. I don't think his involvement should cause us too much trouble. The nature of the assignment doesn't leave much room for client involvement or interference. It's too complex. In essence, it would all be up to us. The real challenge here is the assignment itself. The logistics, the way we approach the obvious difficulties involved, deal with obstacles and the unexpected. That's what this is all about.'

'May we take it that you have completed your assessment?' said Aladdin. 'And can make a recommendation here, today?'

'Yes, of course, except for one thing. The final bit. The delivery of the "subject" to his destination.'

'And where might that be?'

'Morocco. And before you start, I am meeting with Alessandro Giordano tomorrow to discuss this. I think I can see a solution. So for now, let's ignore this part.'

Always the consummate tactician, Teodora realised it was time for a break. An excellent lunch was about to be served, and the complicated and risky matters she had to raise would look a lot more doable, and less risky and dangerous after a good meal and a glass of wine or two.

'In essence, this assignment is all about an abduction,' began Teodora after the maid had cleared the table and withdrawn. 'In a way, it isn't all that different from what we did with that cleric in Istanbul a few years ago. However, this project is infinitely more complicated and dangerous. Why? Because of who the target is, and who is protecting him.'

'Please continue,' said Aladdin.

Teodora opened a file on the table in front of her, took out a photo and pushed it into the middle of the table. It was a snapshot of a smiling Stolzfus giving a lecture to the CIA in Washington. 'It's all about this man, Professor Zachariah Stolzfus, a theoretical physicist, a genius, and one of the most influential scientists on the planet. He lives at the MSFC campus in Alabama, works for NASA, and is protected around the clock.'

'Interesting guy,' said Nadia. 'Looks like a genius too ...'

'And we are going to abduct him and hand him over to someone in Morocco?' said Silvanus, incredulous.

'Exactly,' replied Teodora. 'But there's a lot more to it than that.'

Silvanus sat back and watched Teodora carefully. For Teodora to make a recommendation in a complex matter like this, he knew she would have done her homework meticulously and had come up with a workable plan.

'Stolzfus is single, lives like a hermit, virtually never travels, and certainly not outside the US. In fact, his contract doesn't allow it.'

'Great,' said Aladdin.

'Except on this one occasion,' continued Teodora, smiling. 'On the fifteenth of June, Professor Stolzfus will travel to London to attend a memorial service for his hero, the late Professor Steven Hawking, in Westminster Abbey together with several hundred illustrious invited guests, including representatives of the British Royal family.'

For a while there was silence as the implications of what Teodora had just said began to sink in.

'You obviously have a plan?' asked Aladdin. 'I can just imagine the security ...'

Teodora gave him her best smile. 'Of course,' she said. 'And it was only possible because of a young hacker working in Ukraine whom we have used before. His fee is exorbitant, but he has been able to hack into all the necessary systems and sites and obtain all the information we need to make this work.'

'Seriously?' said Nadia, who hadn't heard any of this before.

'Thanks to our friend in Ukraine, we know exactly what Professor Stolzfus's movements will be, when and how he will travel to London, the security arrangements, how he will get to Westminster Abbey, how long he will stay there, and how and when he will return to the US.'

'Wow! You have been busy,' said Silvanus. 'Can you tell us more?'

'Of course. Stolzfus will leave Joint Base Andrews, Maryland with his security detail late on the fourteenth of June in a plane provided by the US Air Force specifically for this journey. We'll have the exact times. He will arrive at London Stansted Airport early in the morning on fifteen June, and will then be taken directly from the airport to Westminster Abbey to attend the service. Security will be provided by the Metropolitan Police and MI5. After the service he will return to Stansted, board his plane and fly back to Washington.'

'Does this mean he will only be in the UK for a few hours? asked Aladdin.

'Correct but—'

'And we are going to abduct this man while he's in the UK?' interrupted Aladdin.

'Oh yes and you, my friend, will play a pivotal role in all this.'

'I will?'

'Quite so,' replied Teodora, enjoying herself. She took another photo out of her folder and put it next to the Stolzfus snapshot. It was a photo of an Eastern Orthodox priest with a long beard and wearing a flowing black cassock, a chain around his neck with a large gold cross, and a stiff black hat called a *kamilavka*. 'This is Father Christos Alexopoulos from Athens. He is a prominent astronomer who will be attending the memorial service.'

'And this is relevant because ...?' asked Aladdin.

'You will be taking his place.'

'This is a joke, right?' said Silvanus, shaking his head.

'Far from it,' replied Teodora, becoming serious. She knew it was time to play her trump card that would get everyone over the line. 'We'll have to come up with something ingenious and imaginative to earn the fee I've negotiated ...'

'What kind of fee?' asked Nadia.

'Twenty-five million, US.'

'What!' Silvanus almost shouted. 'Are you serious?'

'Deadly!'

8

Port de Fontvieille, Monaco: 15 April

Teodora left Villa Rosa just after sunrise that morning. She knew the drive to Monaco should take her no more than three hours, traffic permitting. Feeling elated after having persuaded Spiridon 4 to go ahead with the assignment, she was ready to meet with Alessandro on his yacht in Fontvieille harbour to tell him the good news, and to work out the remaining details.

Named after the Greek goddess of speed, strength and victory, *Nike*, the Giordano family motor yacht – a magnificent, thirty-metre customised Majesty 105 superyacht built by Gulf Craft in the United Arab Emirates – was permanently moored at Fontvieille and frequently used by Alessandro and his girlfriends to cruise the Mediterranean. During the summer he lived on the luxurious vessel for weeks and conducted his business from there.

Teodora was on a high. She manoeuvred her powerful sports car – a Lamborghini Centenario roadster – carefully out of the garage and could hardly wait to take the stunning car with its powerful 6.5-litre V12 engine, which could go from zero to one hundred kilometres an hour in 2.8 seconds, through its paces. The winding road down to the coast would be perfect, and she was hoping that so early in the morning there wouldn't be too much traffic to slow her down.

Due to her exceptional driving skills and reflexes, Teodora was Spiridon 4's designated driver. She was also the most accomplished at hand-to-hand combat. Nadia was the best shot by far and knew all about firearms. When it came to explosives and detonators, Silvanus's expertise was second to none. Aladdin was the consummate actor with wonderful people skills, who could turn himself convincingly into another person at a moment's notice, together with appropriate speech patterns, accent, appearance and mannerisms. He was a master of disguise and had also acquired excellent first-aid skills. These were just some of the valuable skills perfected over many years that had allowed Spiridon 4 to take on projects that would have been too daunting by far for others in their business to attempt.

Teodora could still remember the day in 2016 when she'd placed an order with Lamborghini for a Centenario – and paid for it in cash. At that time she already owned an Aventador, another Lamborghini classic, on which the Centenario was based. Only forty Centenarios were built – twenty coupes, and twenty roadsters – to commemorate the one-hundredth birthday of Ferruccio Lamborghini, the famous founder of the company. Teodora preferred the roadster because driving with the roof down was the best way to experience speed, and the car's exceptional performance. Teodora selected 'sport' mode and put her foot down, enjoying the roar and throb of the powerful engine as the car accelerated, heading south.

Just after nine am Teodora turned into Fontvieille harbour and drove slowly along the waterfront, looking for the *Nike*. She had called Alessandro earlier on his mobile and he gave her directions to find the yacht. He also told her that one of the deckhands would be waiting for her on the footpath to park her car, which was apparently always a problem. It didn't take Teodora long to spot the vessel moored in a prominent position along the waterfront.

The deckhand, a wide-eyed young man, watched Teodora in awe as she got out of the car looking like a movie star and handed him the keys to the Centenario, which was already attracting the attention of passers-by, ogling the impressive car with interest.

'Under three hours from Como; not bad,' said Alessandro, helping Teodora to step on board. 'But in that car, hardly surprising.' He kissed her on both cheeks, Italian style, and took her by the hand. 'I have a surprise for you,' he said. 'Come.'

Teodora took off her headscarf and sunglasses, adjusted her hair and followed Alessandro into the mahogany-panelled saloon.

Rodrigo was chatting to two young women seated on the lounge next to him as Teodora walked in. He put down his glass, stood up, and walked towards her. 'Last time a surprise visit to my boring office in New York and now this,' he said, extending his hand. 'I think I prefer this, don't you?'

It took Teodora only a couple of seconds to adjust. She hadn't expected to see Rodrigo that morning, but she suspected this had been carefully arranged by Alessandro, who obviously wanted Rodrigo to hear firsthand what she had to say.

'I completely agree and I must say, this is very fortuitous.'

They shook hands and Teodora let herself sink into the comfortable leather chair opposite. That's when she noticed the two young women. One in particular took her breath away.

'This is Claudia and Izabel,' said Alessandro, pointing to the two women. 'They arrived yesterday from Milan. Claudia just finished a fashion show.' He reached for a bottle of champagne in an ice bucket on the table in front of them and refilled their glasses. 'Victoria's Secret. Claudia is one of their angels. Izabel used to be one too, but is now one of the mentors looking after the younger girls,' he added casually, and turned to face Teodora. 'Champagne?'

'Why not? Thank you. I don't think I'll be doing much more driving today,' replied Teodora, sizing up the two women with interest.

'What a gorgeous car,' said Izabel. 'We saw you arrive. Very impressive; very chic.'

'A little passion of mine,' replied Teodora casually. As she looked at Izabel she felt a shiver of excitement that she hadn't experienced for a long time. So long in fact, that at first she hardly recognised it. It was a ripple of sheer desire triggered by the aura and the voice of the breathtaking woman sitting opposite, barefoot and with her long, tanned legs crossed. Teodora could just imagine Izabel strutting her stuff in front of the cameras in a striking, jewel-encrusted swimsuit.

'Perhaps a little shopping this morning, darling,' said Alessandro, addressing Claudia, 'while Raul, Teodora and I have a little chat?'

Claudia gave Alessandro a knowing smile. Being the girlfriend of a prominent Mafia boss, she was familiar with Cosa Nostra protocol. 'Go shopping,' was Mafia speak for leave us now and let us talk in private.

'What a great idea,' said Claudia and stood up. 'Come, Izabel, let me show you my favourite shoe shop. I know you'll love it.'

'Lunch at twelve-thirty,' said Alessandro as the two women left the saloon. 'Make sure you are back by then.'

Claudia stopped at the door, turned around and blew Alessandro a kiss. 'Sure, darling,' she said and followed Izabel onto the deck outside.

'I invited Raul to join us,' began Alessandro as soon as they were alone, 'because of what you told me the other day ...'

'That we've completed our assessment and were ready to give you our answer?' Teodora cut in.

'Precisely.'

'I'm glad you did, because we have a little problem.'

'Oh? What kind of problem?' asked Alessandro, frowning. He didn't like problems.

'The delivery destination.'

'Morocco?' said Rodrigo, looking concerned. 'Why is that a problem?'

'This is a very complex and high-risk project,' replied Teodora. 'For that reason, we have decided not to involve outsiders. We'll do everything ourselves, and we believe we can, except for one thing: taking the subject to Morocco. To do that, we would need to involve other parties and that, we believe, would be too risky in this case.'

'How come?' asked Alessandro. He didn't like the way this was going.

'Can you imagine what will happen when this high-profile celebrity is abducted while in the care of some of the best security services in the world that are supposed to protect him? MI5, CIA, the Metropolitan Police? In the middle of a much-publicised, world-class event, with live TV coverage reaching millions? Because that is precisely what we are planning to do, right? In this case, the getaway may be even more difficult than the abduction itself, because by then, we will have lost the element of surprise.'

'Makes sense,' said Rodrigo, nodding his head. He liked Teodora's realistic, level-headed approach; she didn't understate problems or brush aside obvious risks and danger. Rather than being disappointed, he found her candour encouraging; it inspired confidence.

'I can tell you, all hell will break loose,' continued Teodora. 'Igniting a security frenzy and a blame game of finger-pointing with everyone running for cover. In a way, that's good for us – we are always counting on chaos; it has served us well in the past. But this will immediately turn into a major political incident and the British Government will pull out all stops to get the good professor back and hunt down the perpetrators: *us*. To save face and avoid embarrassment, if nothing else. Believe me, this will be huge and dangerous.'

'But that's not unusual. Most of your previous assignments, at least those we have been involved in, had such elements,' said Alessandro. 'Istanbul, Cairo, Rome ...'

'True. But in this case, we cannot get the subject out of the country without involving outsiders. The problem here is transport. To fly him out is far too risky. All airports and even small airstrips will be off limits straight away. We would have to get him out by sea. It's the only safe way and to do that, we need a suitable vessel, therefore, outsiders. As you know, Spiridon voted last night—'

'I know,' interjected Alessandro, 'that's why I asked Raul to join us.'

'And I am glad you did. We have decided to take on the project, but only if we can hand over the subject in the UK.'

'That won't work for us,' said Rodrigo, shaking his head and becoming agitated. 'It's Morocco or nothing. For the same reasons you have just outlined, the subject is useless to us in the UK.'

'Understood. But there may be a solution,' said Teodora, watching Alessandro carefully. He was an open book when it came to negotiations. His facial expressions and body language gave him away.

'What kind of solution?' he asked, sitting up like an eager schoolboy looking for answers.

'It's staring us in the face, Alessandro; literally.'

Rodrigo smiled. He could see at once what Teodora was hinting.

'We need the help of the goddess of speed, strength and victory,' continued Teodora.

'*Nike!*' exclaimed Rodrigo.

For a while there was a tense silence in the saloon as the implications of what she had proposed sank in.

'Are you suggesting,' began Alessandro, 'that we use *this* vessel to take the professor out of the UK and then to Morocco?'

'Precisely. If you agree to this, we'll stay involved until he is safely delivered to Morocco as originally planned. For many reasons, *Nike* is the perfect choice. I believe you have a crew of five?' asked Teodora, changing the subject. 'Working for you, I'm sure the crew are most trustworthy, discreet and reliable. In short, the outsider risk goes away and we stay in control. We have already identified a suitable place on the south coast of England where we could rendezvous and take the subject out of the country, quickly. As usual, timing is everything here. We must stay a step ahead of the authorities at all times. That's imperative! He could be on board the *Nike* and safely out to sea within a couple of hours. That's all we would need. After that, we are a needle in a haystack in international waters.'

Rodrigo realised the deal was hanging in the balance and needed a final little push. 'Makes sense to me,' he said, turning to Alessandro. 'I'm sure Mr Cordoba would be most grateful and, on my recommendation,' continued Rodrigo, lowering his voice, 'he will show his gratitude when we negotiate the details of that exclusive supply deal, if you know what I mean ...'

'You think so?' said Alessandro, his face lighting up.

'Oh yes. In the end, the result is all that counts. What do you say?'

'Done!'

'Excellent,' said Teodora. 'In that case, gentlemen, we have a deal!'

After a sumptuous seafood lunch served on deck, washed down with copious quantities of superb French wine, Teodora found herself momentarily alone with Izabel for the first time. They had given each other meaningful looks during lunch, and it was clear there was mutual attraction between them from the start. Teodora had decided to stay overnight on the yacht and return to Como early the next morning.

'Before you arrived, Alessandro told us you are one of the most dangerous women he had ever come across,' began Izabel, feeling relaxed after the splendid meal. 'And the most interesting. What do you think he meant by that?' she added, a sparkle in her eyes.

'He said that? What else did he tell you?'

'Nothing else, actually, and that only added to the mystery and made me curious. Tell me, are you really *that* dangerous?'

Teodora pointed to two deckchairs in the shade. 'Let's go over there,' she said, 'and I will tell you what can *make* someone like me dangerous.'

She's so gorgeous, thought Teodora, watching Izabel slide into the deckchair next to her, her long legs dangling over the edge. *And so unassuming and natural. So elegant!* Teodora felt totally relaxed and at ease in Izabel's company. It was a strange feeling she hadn't experienced for ages, like being with an old friend she had known for years, and could trust implicitly and share secrets with.

For a while the two women sat in silence, enjoying the promise of excitement and adventure floating in the air, and passing from one to the other like a tantalising, carnal temptation.

'I haven't spoken about this to anyone for a long time,' began Teodora. 'Especially not to someone I've just met.' Teodora turned to face Izabel. 'I can't quite explain this, but I feel like I've known you for years. I feel that we were somehow destined to meet; here, today.'

'I feel the same way,' said Izabel and reached for Teodora's hand, her gentle touch sending a wave of excitement tingling across Teodora's blushing neck.

'I can't tell you exactly why I may appear so dangerous to a man like Alessandro,' said Teodora. 'We've had business dealings before – challenging ones. But looking back, he has good reason to think so, I suppose. What I *can* tell you is what *made* me dangerous and why.'

Izabel looked at Teodora, her eyebrows raised. This wasn't the answer she had expected. 'Sounds intriguing,' she said.

'It happened during one night of terror in Albania a long time ago. I was fourteen at the time ... it was a night that changed my life forever.'

Once that secret door had been opened, there was no way back. Teodora told Izabel what had happened that fateful night in graphic detail, leaving nothing out. Izabel listened in silence without letting go of Teodora's hand. Towards the end of the story, Teodora's voice had become a whisper of dark memories and unspeakable pain, exposed for the first time to a stranger she had just met. 'I swore that night that I would not rest until my parents' death had been avenged. I vowed to hunt down that evil man who had so brutally violated their bodies. I can still see his face clearly as if he were standing right here in front of us.'

'And did you? Hunt him down?'

'No. Not yet. Believe me, I've tried, in more ways than you can possibly imagine. But he seems to have vanished like a ghost, leaving behind him an unspeakable trail of suffering.' Teodora paused and wiped away a few tears. 'But one day, I will. Of that I'm sure!'

After Teodora had finished, Izabel leant across to Teodora and kissed her tenderly on the mouth. It was a spontaneous expression of love and affection that sent more tears streaming down Teodora's wan face.

'I too know pain,' said Izabel. She reached for the little jewel-encrusted cross hanging around her neck and stroked it gently. 'I just lost the love of my life ...'

'Want to talk about it?

'She was the most beautiful, gifted, generous and funny person you can imagine, with a talent so big, it had audiences in raptures, and millions of adoring fans around the world buying her records.'

'Who was she?' asked Teodora. She could see that Izabel was beginning to choke and had difficulty in saying the name out loud.

'*Soul,*' she whispered. 'She was Soul, the love of my life ...'

'The jazz singer?'

'Yes.'

'I'm so sorry. I read about it. She—'

'Yes, she died of an overdose on stage in Los Angeles six months ago. I was right there ...'

Teodora squeezed Izabel's hand. 'I'm so sorry.'

'Apart from my memories, this is all I have left,' said Izabel, holding up the beautiful little cross around her neck. 'She used to wear it all the time. It had a special meaning. Her mother gave it to her. It was supposed to protect her, you see. It did so once in Central Park in New York a long time ago, just after we became lovers. I saw it all. I was quite young then. A man who was waiting for us saved her. It was a warning; very frightening. After that, she went into rehab and promised never to touch the stuff again. Unfortunately, the little white devil never quite left her ...' Izabel shrugged. 'That was sixteen years ago. Sadly, this time the little cross couldn't protect her. It's mine now ...'

'How very sad.'

'Let me tell you the story of the little cross and the man who saved her life that time,' said Izabel, feeling better. 'It's quite extraordinary. His name was Jack Rogan, an Australian war correspondent. You might have heard of him. He's quite famous now. A bestselling author and adventurer.'

'Wasn't he in *Time* Magazine a few years ago?'

'Yes, he was. On the cover. I caught up with him again at Soul's funeral. It was all very sad ...'

Somehow the presence of the woman sitting next to her, radiating compassion, understanding and strength, had eased the grief and hurt inside Izabel, and for the first time since her lover's death she felt liberated; a heavy stone of deep sorrow had been lifted from her heart. She told Teodora the story of Jack Rogan and his little cross and how Soul had a copy made of it and sent to him after he returned from the war in Afghanistan, badly injured and alone.

'What a story,' said Teodora, pointing to the little cross. 'That's quite a bond now, between you and him. A special bond of memories ...'

'That's what he said,' replied Izabel dreamily. 'Memories of bitter-sweet love are to be cherished because they can defeat death.'

'Yes, they can,' said Teodora, trying to remember her parents as they were before that dreadful night of horror in Albania all those years ago.

Teodora and Izabel made love that night with a passion and abandon that surprised them both. It was a liberating release of pent-up loneliness, loss and pain that seemed to dissolve in a sea of tenderness and love.

When Izabel woke the next morning and reached sleepily across the bed to caress her new lover, she noticed she wasn't there. Teodora had left at first light and was already halfway to Como.

Disappointed, Izabel turned around to get up. That's when she noticed the little note on her bedside table. It was a phone number with some words scribbled in a tiny, spidery handwriting across the crumpled piece of paper, just below the numbers: *Soon. You promised. I need you!*

9

US Space & Rocket Center, Alabama: 16 April

One of the few connections with the outside world Professor Stolzfus was allowed to foster were his monthly lectures he gave to visiting students at the US Space & Rocket Center, a short internal bus ride from the MSFC where he lived and worked. Stolzfus, an excellent public speaker and communicator, could explain complex ideas and principles without resorting to mathematics and equations, by using easy-to-understand analogies and everyday language. This made his lectures very popular and they were usually sold out weeks, often months in advance.

He never shied away from tackling the big questions. Some of his favourite subjects were the Big Bang, the possibility of time travel, whether there is other intelligent life in the universe, the nature of black holes and the future of artificial intelligence, to name but a few. He particularly enjoyed question time at the end of his lectures and took great care to answer every question, however far-fetched or tedious it may seem, with patience and humour and without patronising or embarrassing his audience. His recently found fame after his tribute to Hawking from space had only added to his popularity.

Major Andersen had an appointment with Stolzfus after his lecture to discuss his London travel and security arrangements, but she arrived early. This was deliberate as she wanted to attend the lecture to get to know the man she had to protect, a little better. She thought that to see him interacting with the public would be a good way to do this.

The major walked in towards the end of the lecture and took a seat at the back of the hall packed full of eager students hanging on Stolzfus's every word. Dressed in his usual eccentric attire – baggy black trousers, red braces, loose white shirt and bowtie – and with

Gizmo sitting next to the lectern, he had wowed his mesmerised audience with stories of time travel, worm holes, black holes and warped space, making these remarkable subjects appear perfectly natural and easy to follow. The exciting Hubble telescope images displayed on the huge screen behind him added extra realism to his eloquent explanations.

Then came question time and things became really interesting. A young woman of about eighteen sitting in the third row stood up and asked: 'Professor Stolzfus, do you believe there is a God?' and then sat down.

Despite the fact Stolzfus had been asked this question many times before, he always found it difficult to answer. He knew he was walking a tightrope when addressing this important and highly emotive topic. He realised that his own Amish background had a lot to do with this; he had wrestled with the question for years himself, as science increasingly answered questions that used to belong exclusively to religion, and blurred the boundaries between the two. Torn between reason and faith, the scientist in him had formed a clear view, which had become stronger over the years as more compelling facts and laws of nature were discovered. However, his Amish upbringing based on strong faith and entrenched beliefs had been difficult to suppress and shake off.

Stolzfus took his time before giving an answer. He took off his small, gold-rimmed glasses and began to polish the lenses with his handkerchief, as he stared at something only he could see. This only heightened the anticipation in the hall as several hundred eyes followed his every move.

Interesting, thought the major. *Is he performing, or just buying a little time and collecting his thoughts?* Whatever it was, he had the spellbound audience eating out of his hands.

After a while, Stolzfus put his glasses back on and turned towards the young woman who had asked the question.

'I think the answer to this can be found in the journey of man,' began Stolzfus quietly. 'It is part of being human to ask this question.

When early man looked up at the stars in wonder, or hid in fright when there was an eclipse or an earthquake, and faced a dangerous and hostile environment down here on earth – just to survive was a daily struggle often between life and death – it was only natural to turn to the supernatural for explanations and help. For thousands of years, man believed the natural world around him was ruled by gods. Gods were responsible for floods, thunder, lightning and storms; they made the sun rise every morning, and the Nile flood every year to ensure a good harvest. Angry gods had to be appeased with sacrifices, and generals and statesmen prayed to the gods for victory and guidance. Priests were in charge and complex rituals and beliefs evolved into religions that ruled the lives of everyone. Those who dared to question this were viewed as heretics, persecuted and burned at the stake.

'Then along came the great thinkers like Aristotle, Aristarchus, Copernicus, Kepler, Galileo, Newton, Einstein, to name but a few, who changed the way we view the natural world. How did they do this? By being inquisitive. They began to ask questions and increasingly they found the answers to those questions through observation and reason, which ultimately resulted in the discovery of laws. Laws of nature that actually explain everything around us in the entire universe. How it all began, where it is heading, how it works, everything. In the past, right now and in the future.

'These great thinkers began to view the universe as a machine governed by physical laws that could be observed and understood by man. Laws that could do this were fixed and eternal.

'This soon begged a question: If that is so, they asked, then where does God fit into this? What is the role of God in a universe governed by fixed and eternal laws that explain everything? They had reached the contradiction between science and religion.'

Stolzfus turned again to face the young woman in the third row. 'You asked me if I believe there is a God,' he said. 'In order to answer this, I would like to use God as a concept, in an impersonal sense like Einstein did, synonymous with the laws of nature. So if we do that, what follows is this: if we know the laws of nature, we know the mind of God. To me, knowing the mind of God is the biggest challenge of science today, and I believe that we are getting very close to achieving just that. A unifying theory of everything will do this. The late Professor Hawking was getting very close and we who are standing on his shoulders will, I believe, achieve it; soon.'

Stolzfus scratched his head.

'However, there are still some great challenges ahead,' he continued. 'One of them has occupied me for years now and is at the very centre of the question you have asked. It's the great mystery of the Big Bang we spoke of earlier: How can *something* materialise out of *nothing*? Today, we are actually getting close to an answer, and the answer is to be found in perhaps one of the strangest facts about the universe you can imagine, a fact predicted and explained by those eternal laws of physics I mentioned before. When we have a close look at those laws we find that they predict, no, *demand* the existence of what we call "negative energy". Remember the three essential building blocks we need to build a universe? What were they? Can someone tell me?'

A young man at the back held up his hand.

'Yes,' said Stolzfus.

'Matter, energy and space,' said the young man.

'Correct. And then along came Einstein with his famous E = mc2, which simply means what? Someone?'

'That mass and energy are in fact the same thing,' said another young man in the back.

'Right. If that is so, we now only need two building blocks to construct a universe: energy and space. Finally, we are getting closer to the ultimate question we asked before. Can someone remember what it was?'

'Where did all that energy and space needed to build a universe come from?' called out a young woman in the first row.

'Precisely. In short, how can energy and space materialise out of nothing? The answer is in that *negative* energy we discussed before. So, what is negative energy? Does anybody know?'

How clever, thought the major. Stolzfus had already explained it all before, but in separate parts, and now he was tying it all together by asking questions of his audience. But now, Stolzfus was only the guide, and they were providing all the answers. *Ingenious!*

Stolzfus looked around the crowded hall, but there were no hands in the air to be seen. 'I thought so,' he said, smiling. 'I will give you the answer first and then try to explain how it can – *must* – be so.' Stolzfus paused to let the anticipation grow before he continued.

'Those eternal, fixed laws of nature we spoke of earlier tell us that the universe in all its spectacular glory, its mind-boggling size and diversity, with its billions of galaxies in all their wonder and their terror, was in fact spontaneously created out of nothing. Yes, out of *nothing*,' repeated Stolzfus. 'And it's all because of negative energy. So, what is negative energy? Professor Hawking explained this very well by using a simple, easy-to-understand analogy, and I'm sure he wouldn't have minded if I now use it to explain what negative energy is to you. It's about a man who wants to create a hill on a flat piece of land. He takes a shovel and begins to dig. He digs a hole and uses the soil to build his hill. But of course he isn't just creating a hill, he is also creating – what? Can someone tell me?'

'A hole,' said someone in the back.

'Precisely. And that hole is the exact negative version of the hill. The removed soil used to create the hill, and the hole left behind by the soil he had dug out balance out perfectly. Simple isn't it? This is exactly what happened at the beginning of the universe during the Big Bang. The huge amount of positive energy that was produced, created the exact same amount of negative energy so that the positive and the negative add up to ... *someone*?'

'Zero!' said a young woman in the front.

'Very good. See? You already know all the answers. We have just described another law of nature.' Stolzfus paused again and pointed to the ceiling. 'But where did all that negative energy go?' he asked, lowering his voice. 'Where is it today? Well, it's all around us. It's in the third building block needed to construct a universe: *space*. Space is an enormous storage device containing negative energy.'

Now Stolzfus became really excited. He explained that the universe had once been smaller than a proton and as such had to obey the laws of quantum mechanics and because of that, it could have spontaneously appeared out of nothing. He then went on to explain something mind-boggling about *time,* one of his favourite subjects and, he said, one of the last frontiers of science to be conquered before a unifying theory of everything was possible.

'Come with me,' said Stolzfus, and took his spellbound audience on a journey back through time, right back to the Big Bang itself until a point was reached where the universe was so tiny and so dense – like the smallest black hole imaginable – where something extraordinary happened: time stopped. Therefore, he argued, time did not *exist* before the Big Bang.

Stolzfus took a deep breath and looked again at the young woman who had asked the question about the existence of God. 'If the laws of nature tell us that it is possible to have something that has no cause because there was no time for a cause to exist, then it must follow that there couldn't have been a creator because there was no time for him to create in. Instead of answering the question for you, I will let you all answer it for yourselves. I think it is the best and fairest way by far. You may not be able to do this right now, but as we move forward and find out more about our universe and the laws of nature, the answer may become clearer and easier to find. Thank you.'

At the end of the lecture, Stolzfus was given a standing ovation by his adoring fans. After that, students crowded around him to get his autograph. With his tail-wagging dog standing patiently beside him, it was clear that Stolzfus was enjoying the moment.

'I had no idea you were such a rocket star, Professor Stolzfus,' said the major, walking up to Stolzfus as the last of the students were leaving. 'This was quite something.'

'A rocket star? I like that. I love giving these lectures,' said Stolzfus, gathering up his notes. 'When I look at these eager faces, I can see the future. And it's looking good. I'm sorry to have kept you; we went a little over time, I'm afraid. I saw you sitting at the back.'

'Don't worry, I enjoyed every moment. You are a charismatic speaker. Can we go somewhere private to talk?'

'Sure. As long as you don't mind Gizmo and my bodyguard over there. Please follow me.'

Stolzfus took the major into a small room next to the lecture hall. 'We could go back to my office, but you said it was urgent.'

'There's never enough time, but I wanted you to hear this from us.'

'Us?'

'The CIA.'

'All right. What is it?'

'We would like you to reconsider.'

Stolzfus looked surprised. 'Reconsider? What exactly?'

'Attending the Hawking service.'

'Why?'

'We've intercepted something ...'

'Oh?'

'Hackers, most likely operating somewhere in the Soviet Union or Eastern Europe, broke into various highly classified sites recently. Nothing unusual about that; it happens. It's a constant problem. But we noticed a disturbing pattern.'

'What kind of pattern?' asked Stolzfus, his curiosity aroused.

'They were obviously looking for something quite specific.'

'And this is relevant because?

'Because what they were looking for was about *you* and your upcoming trip to the UK.'

'Are you serious?'

'Absolutely.'

Stolzfus looked incredulous. 'Why would someone take such interest in my—'

'We have reason to believe that some kind of operation is planned involving you during your visit to the UK,' interrupted Major Andersen, looking concerned.

'What kind of operation? By whom?'

'We are working on that.'

'And this is the reason you want me to reconsider? I suppose you are asking me not to go, is that it?'

'We would like you to think about it.'

'But I haven't been stopped from going?'

'No. Not at this stage. The relevant decision makers have asked for more information.'

'But you are here asking me now?'

'Yes. As the officer responsible for your safety during this trip, I wanted you to hear this from me first. I consider this to be a serious threat and would like you to take this into account when making your decision.'

'Based on what? Some hackers looking for information?'

'You may not know this, Professor, but I have been in the navy for many years and I have extensive combat experience. I was one of the youngest fighter pilots on aircraft carriers before joining the CIA. I know danger. I can sense it; I can feel it,' said the major, raising her voice just a little to make a point. 'And I can feel it now; gut feeling if you like. You too are a man of intuition, following your instincts, right?'

'Yes, but surely this is different.'

'Is it? I don't think so.'

Stolzfus shook his head. 'No, Major Andersen, I will not slink away like a coward because of some vague, perceived threat. You can take it that I will attend Professor Hawking's memorial service unless I am formally forbidden to do so by my superiors.'

For a while the major looked at Stolzfus, the concern on her face remaining. 'I was afraid you would say that, Professor. With that in mind, I have rearranged your travel schedule with MI5 and the Metropolitan Police in London, who will be responsible for your security in the UK.' The major opened her briefcase, pulled out a sheet of paper and placed it on the table in front of Stolzfus.

'These are your travel arrangements,' she said quietly. 'The memorial service is due to start at noon on Friday June fifteen. I would like you to memorise this. You will only be in the UK for a few hours. This is how it will all work ...'

10

London: 14 June

Teodora and Silvanus arrived first and settled into their room in the modest hotel in East London. Nadia and Aladdin were due to arrive a little later to avoid them all being seen together. Looking like a carefree couple on holidays about to enjoy the sights of London, no-one would have suspected that Spiridon 4 was about to launch its most ambitious project ever, which would send London and its security forces into a spin, and send ripples of tension and discord across the Atlantic, right up to the White House.

There was a very good reason why Teodora had chosen this particular hotel. The person who would play a pivotal role in the assignment – Father Christos Alexopoulos – was staying there too. Spiridon 4 had spent the past three weeks in London finalising their preparations. As usual, meticulous planning with painstaking attention to detail was carried out, and checked and rechecked many times to ensure there were no mistakes and nothing had been overlooked. Contingency plans and emergency escape routes – should the unexpected happen – were put in place and a secure line of communication established. As skilful professionals who left nothing to chance, each member of the group had their own tasks and areas of responsibility. At the end of each day, there was a meeting with reports and checklists, and even trial runs of certain parts of the detailed plan, including an inspection of the secure vehicles that had been obtained through trusted third parties without leaving a trail.

The intelligence provided by the hackers in Ukraine had been invaluable and had provided vital information and insights into the official planning and logistics of the high-profile event that would be attended by more than a thousand dignitaries from around the world, and involve an almost equal number of security personnel.

Teodora looked at the diagram spread out on the bed showing Westminster Abbey and its surrounds, and smiled. It was all coming together and best of all, they could do it all themselves. Engaging outsiders had always made her nervous. Most of their problems in the past had been caused by that.

'What do you think?' asked Silvanus, looking over Teodora's shoulder.

'Looks good. Complex, yes, but I think we've got it all covered. All five phases of it. We'll go over everything again tonight as soon as Aladdin and Nadia get here. We have to know this stuff inside out with nothing left to chance.'

'Nothing new about that. Do you really think this will be our last assignment?' asked Silvanus, watching Teodora carefully.

Teodora turned around and faced her friend. 'I do. What you said at Como was right. We are getting too old for this and when that happens, mistakes creep in, and we cannot afford mistakes. Not even small ones. I sense we are just not sharp enough anymore. So, quit while you're ahead, I say.'

'What will you do? After, I mean.'

Teodora stared pensively at the plan in front of her. 'Hunt down that monster ... he will be *my* last assignment.'

'Dr Death from all those years ago?'

'Yes. I promised myself. If he's still alive and out there somewhere, I'll find him and I'll get him, of that I'm sure.'

'War crimes tribunals have tried and failed,' Silvanus reminded Teodora. 'Even the tenacious Carla Del Ponte couldn't find him, remember?'

'I remember. She was the chief prosecutor for the International Criminal Tribunal for the former Yugoslavia – ICTY as they called it. We are better than she could ever be, but her book could be useful. I will use that as my starting point.'

Del Ponte's controversial book – *The Hunt: Me and the War Criminals* published in 2008 – claimed to have seen evidence to support that Kosovo Albanians had carried out widespread organ-harvesting operations after the armed conflict that ended in 1999, involving kidnapped ethnic Serbs. This astonishing accusation had been backed up by several eyewitness statements and by her own visits to various sites where atrocities were supposed to have been committed. There was even a witness who claimed to have made an organ delivery to an Albanian airport from a remote house known as the 'Yellow house' in Albania. After Kosovo's declaration of independence, Del Ponte, a Swiss national, was ordered by her government to stop her investigation and not to discuss the case any further. Pursuing horrendous claims like that was no longer politically desirable and steps were taken to discredit her and her book.

'Doesn't she also talk about a Kosovar doctor from Pec, who eyewitnesses said had removed organs from more than fifty prisoners?'

'Yes. She also mentions the involvement of local villagers. They objected to having graves opened. According to witnesses interviewed by Del Ponte, the bodies of victims were buried in local cemeteries under false Albanian names to hide the evidence. They were all in on it.'

'And didn't she present all this to the UN?'

'She did. But by then, no-one was interested,' said Teodora quietly with sadness in her voice. 'But I am ... even after all these years.'

'Forget the past and move on isn't for you, is it?' said Silvanus.

'Certain things cannot be forgotten. Both of us know that only too well, don't we?'

'We sure do. You would have made an excellent war crimes prosecutor.'

Teodora shook her head. 'Executioner, more likely,' she said and began to trace the outline of Westminster Abbey with the tips of her fingers on the diagram in front of her. 'We'll do it right in here tomorrow,' continued Teodora. 'Sounds almost insane, doesn't it? Are we perhaps a little too ambitious this time?'

Silvanus was taken aback. He had never heard Teodora second-guess a project before. 'Doubts? Cold feet? *You?*' he said.

'Cold feet no, but listen to this: we are staying here in this shabby little hotel because a certain Eastern Orthodox priest, Father Christos

Alexopoulos, is staying here too. Room twelve. Early tomorrow morning, we'll break into his room, drug him, and Aladdin will take his place. No, he will have to do more than that, he will have to *become* Christos Alexopoulos, complete with long beard, flowing black cassock, chain and gold cross and a funny hat called a kamilavka. He will then catch a cab to Westminster Abbey, present his invitation and then enter the Abbey as Father Alexopoulos, the famous astronomer from Athens, making sure that he somehow gets to stand close to Professor Stolzfus, who will also be attending together with several hundred dignitaries protected by one of the most sophisticated security forces on the planet. And this is only phase one. How does this sound to you?'

'Daring and ingenious, and completely in line with our usual modus operandi. In short, classic Spiridon 4,' replied Silvanus without hesitation.

Teodora turned around and gave her friend a hug. 'I was hoping you would say that,' she whispered. 'Now I know we're ready.'

Nadia and Aladdin arrived half an hour later and Spiridon 4 began their final briefing session during which every detail of the complex plan was carefully examined, watches synchronised and encrypted communication channels put in place and tested. As usual, surprise and split-second timing were at the very heart of the project. The briefing took several hours, but by now everyone was running on adrenaline and sleep was out of the question. Instead, each segment of the plan was pulled apart and then put together again to make sure that nothing was forgotten or overlooked.

At six am sharp, Silvanus and Aladdin knocked on the door of room twelve at the end of the dimly lit, deserted corridor on the first floor. When a sleepy Father Alexopoulos finally answered the door and Silvanus and Aladdin burst into his room, Spiridon 4 had begun their final assignment.

A short distance to the north, the US Air Force plane carrying Stolzfus and Major Andersen had just touched down at Stansted Airport and was taxiing towards a small terminal that was off limits to the public. Stolzfus would remain in the terminal until it was time to travel to Westminster Abbey to attend the service scheduled to begin at noon. The major had arranged transport – which would be provided by the Metropolitan Police – to pick them up at eleven am, which should give them ample time to travel from Stansted to the Abbey without cutting it fine. In the meantime, Stolzfus would be served breakfast, given an opportunity to have a shower and get changed, and then relax in a comfortable lounge until it was time to leave.

Until then, the major knew she could relax too. After that, it was game on. Even after the visit had, on her recommendation, been cut down to the bare minimum for security reasons and Stolzfus would only remain in the UK for a few hours, the major was still feeling uneasy about the trip.

The disturbing hacking pattern the CIA had first noticed a few weeks ago had recently become even more pronounced and focused. What was particularly worrying was a recent report received from MI5 during an intelligence exchange, stating that similar hacking incursions had been detected regarding the Stolzfus visit, and security arrangements surrounding the Hawking memorial service generally. To an experienced operator like the major, this could mean only one thing: something was up. Something big!

11

Stansted Airport, London: 15 June

'Don't you look suave,' said Major Andersen as Stolzfus sat down next to her in the exclusive airport lounge reserved for visiting dignitaries. Apart from the security guard standing at the door, the lounge was deserted.

'My only suit,' replied Stolzfus, laughing. 'Can I get you some coffee?'

'Yes please. Let's have some breakfast. I'm starving. We'll be here for a while.'

Stolzfus had just taken a shower and got changed after their night flight from Joint Base Andrews, Maryland. He had slept through most of the flight and felt refreshed and exhilarated. It was just after seven-thirty in the morning and they were not due to leave the airport until eleven. Stolzfus was particularly looking forward to meeting some of his colleagues from around the world he knew would be attending the service. To someone like Stolzfus, who rarely travelled and hadn't been outside the United States for years, the trip was turning into a real adventure, much more so than he had expected.

What a remarkable man, the major thought as she watched Stolzfus put lashings of jam on his second croissant. A mathematics genius who played the cello and dreamed about solving the mysteries of the universe. *Amazing.*

During the flight, Stolzfus had told her about his love of music and how music helped him to focus and transport himself to the far reaches of the universe because it stimulated his imagination. Having spent the past twenty-four hours in his company, she was slowly beginning to glimpse the man behind the carefully erected eccentric scientist facade protecting a sensitive and, she thought, vulnerable genius, torn between his intellect and his Amish family and past.

'That lecture you gave to the students at the Space and Rocket Center was really something,' said the major.

'Oh? It struck a chord then, I take it?' replied Stolzfus, munching happily. 'What did you like about it?'

'The way you approached the question of the existence of God.'

'You mean how I sidestepped the question and let the students find the answer themselves?' asked Stolzfus, a glint in his eyes.

'Yes, I thought that was very clever and respectful. It showed great sensitivity and tact. You didn't use your authority to overwhelm them with a carefully constructed argument, leaving no room for faith or doubt. That's what I thought was very clever.'

'Very perceptive of you, Major. It's a very thorny question. I always have difficulty answering it in public.'

'But in private, you have no such difficulty?'

'Not anymore.'

'May I ask why?'

'The evidence is overwhelming. The facts speak for themselves. The laws of nature we have discovered during the past, say, one hundred years – certainly since Einstein – are irrefutable. I am a scientist. My language is mathematics and reason. And once we speak that language, there is no room or need for faith.'

'But it wasn't always that way, was it?'

'No, it wasn't.' Stolzfus turned to face the major and looked at her pensively. 'It was a struggle. A big one. In a way, it was time travel.'

'What do you mean?'

'I had to leave behind the almost medieval world of my Amish family with its strict, unshakable beliefs, and travel into the present and open my mind.'

'And how did you do that?'

'Through imagination. I began to travel ...'

'How?'

'In my mind. I travelled in my mind and I still do, to the far corners of the universe, observing and looking for answers. And when I find something of interest, I write down what I see using mathematics.'

'All those equations on the blackboard you are so famous for,' said the major, raising an eyebrow. 'That no-one can understand?'

Stolzfus laughed. 'That's a little harsh,' he said. 'I can think of at least half a dozen people who can,' he joked. 'Without mathematics, we can't discover those laws of nature I spoke about. It's through mathematics that we can lift the veil, solve the mystery and find those eternal truths that make it all work. That's the only way we can find *proof* and understanding and that, to me, is one of the greatest achievements of homo sapiens.'

The major smiled. Stolzfus's enthusiasm was infectious.

'I believe man's extraordinary development in what is really quite a short period of time, is to a large extent due to imagination,' continued Stolzfus.

'How come?'

'Well, let's have a closer look at this,' said Stolzfus, warming to one of his favourite subjects. 'Homo sapiens emerged about three hundred thousand years ago in Africa. There were waves of early migration to the Levant and into Europe, but according to recent evidence based on genomics, they died out without leaving a trace in the genome of humans living there today. It wasn't until what is called the "recent dispersal" between seventy and fifty thousand years ago that modern humans began a lasting coastal dispersal and colonisation throughout the world. Now, that's not such a long time ago, is it, when we consider what has been achieved? In fact, I think it's astonishing when we look at how far we've come, where we came from, and where we're at today—'

'Because we are getting very close to a unifying theory of everything?' interjected the major. 'And when that is achieved, we shall know the mind of God?'

Stolzfus was impressed. 'My, my, you have been paying attention. Precisely! And I firmly believe that will only happen because of imagination. And imagination has played a critical role in human evolution and it all began with Mitochondrial Eve.'

The major shook her head. 'You lost me. Please explain.'

'Well, extraordinary advances in human genetics, especially genome sequencing, tell us that all living humans today have one common matrilineal ancestor: Mitochondrial Eve. I hasten to add, this has nothing to do with biblical Eve, but refers to a woman who lived somewhere in Africa approximately one hundred and fifty thousand years ago and all humans living today descend through their mothers and the mothers of those mothers in one unbroken line from one woman. The concept is much more complicated than that and there are many popular misconceptions, but it will do for now.'

'Incredible!'

'But back to God. Mankind has made staggering progress since Mitochondrial Eve walked across the African plains and into the Rift valley. We have discovered the laws of nature that explain and govern almost all that is going on in the universe. However, I believe there is one remaining mystery to solve, one last frontier we have to conquer.'

'And what might that be?'

'It's all about *time.* If we understand the function of time at the very beginning of the universe—'

'The Big Bang, you mean?'

'Yes. If we understand that, we can pull it all together and explain everything.'

'And what do those laws of nature you keep referring to tell us about that?' asked the major.

'They tell us that there *was* no time before the Big Bang.'

'That's mind-boggling! How come?'

'Because of the nature of black holes.'

'I need an explanation.'

'All right. Come with me. Let's travel back in time to the very moment of the Big Bang. As we race back in our imagination to that crucial point in time, the universe becomes smaller and smaller until it turns into a tiny black hole of extraordinary density. With me so far?'

'I think so ...'

'Good, because now comes the really interesting bit and it has to do with those laws of nature we've been talking about.'

'Yes?'

'Those laws tell us, well, they *dictate* that just as with modern-day black holes we know exist and are out there, time must stop inside a black hole wherever, or whenever it may have existed. And that applies to that tiny black hole at the beginning of the universe we just spoke of. What this means is this: there was no time before the Big Bang. Time itself began with the Big Bang. It follows that if there was no time before the Big Bang, the Big Bang didn't have a *cause.*'

'Why?' asked the major, shaking her head 'How does that follow?'

'Isn't it obvious?'

'Not to me it isn't.'

'Come on, fighter pilot ... if there was no time before the Big Bang, it follows that there was *no time for a cause to exist in*; simple!'

'To you perhaps. To me, I think faith and going to church might be simpler,' said the major, laughing.

Stolzfus shook his head. 'I don't think so. Once this irrefutable logic-genie is out of the universe bottle, there's no way back.'

'Conclusion?' asked the major, looking serious.

'Faith and belief are very personal things. We must each make our own decisions in that regard.'

'And have you, if you don't mind me asking?'

Stolzfus looked at the major, a troubled expression on his face, and took his time before replying. 'I'm still struggling,' he said. 'Despite all the science, all the logic ... I'm not explaining this very well, am I?'

'Are you suggesting science isn't enough?'

'It's not that. It's the conclusion that troubles me.'

'In what way?'

'If we follow what we know today to its – some would say – inescapable conclusion, we come up against something disturbing.'

"That pesky logic-genie again?'

'Yes.'

'And what does that logic-genie tell you?'

'That the universe created itself spontaneously out of—'

'What?' interrupted the major.

'Nothing!'

'How?'

'The laws of nature tell us how. But we are still missing a few crucial elements I mentioned before about the role of time at the very beginning. I firmly believe when we solve that, we'll have a unifying theory that will explain it all. And that will be the supreme achievement of mankind since Mitochondrial Eve gave birth and started it all.'

'Because then we shall know the mind of God?'

'Perhaps ...'

'Speaking of time,' said the major, looking at her watch. 'It certainly flies when you talk about the beginning of time, and a time when there wasn't any time. It's almost time to get ready to go, Professor. I could sit here and talk to you for hours, but our car is most likely already waiting downstairs to take us to Westminster Abbey.'

Aladdin looked at his watch. It was almost time to go. Phase one of the assignment had been completed without a hitch. Blissfully comatose, Father Alexopoulos was lying in his bed after having been drugged with a powerful narcotic that would keep him sedated for hours.

Aladdin looked in the mirror for the last time. *Not bad*, he thought, as he examined his long false beard streaked with grey, his flowing black cassock and peculiar stiff hat worn by Eastern Orthodox priests. Then he reached for Father Alexopoulos's wallet and printed invitation on the bedside table, and put them carefully into his pocket. *Now for the final touch*, he thought, and put on a pair of horn-rimmed glasses and then slipped the heavy gold chain with the large cross over his head. *Done. Father Christos Alexopoulos is ready to attend the Hawking memorial service.*

Just before he left the room, Aladdin held up his right hand and adjusted the specially designed ring on his middle finger that was soon to play a vital part in the operation. *Perfect*, he thought. Then he stepped outside, hung the 'Do Not Disturb' sign on the doorknob and locked the door behind him, and walked downstairs to catch a cab. The others had left several hours before to take up their positions and wait for his signal. The second, most critical phase of the assignment had just begun.

12

Westminster Abbey: 15 June, 11:30 am

Aladdin adjusted his earpiece and got out of the cab. Developed in China and little known outside that country, the earpiece was part of a sophisticated, encrypted communications system that worked through the mobile phone network like an app and allowed Spiridon 4 to talk to one another without arousing suspicion or the possibility of being overheard or traced. Anyone noticing Aladdin speaking would assume he was talking to someone using a bluetooth device.

'I have arrived,' said Aladdin as he walked slowly towards the long queue at the Great West Door.

'I can see you,' said Nadia, standing amid a group of spectators on the pavement watching the arrival of the dignitaries about to attend the service. 'I've been here for almost an hour. I don't think he's arrived yet.'

'Good. I was trying to get here before him.'

'You look very convincing.'

'I should hope so. Everyone in position?'

'Yes. The ambulances have arrived and are exactly where we thought they would be – stationed behind the Abbey. There are two of them.'

'Good. I'm about to go in.'

As he approached the entrance, Aladdin could see several stony-faced Metropolitan Police officers wearing body armour and armed with semi-automatic carbine sub-machine guns, watching the crowd. A stark contrast to the solemn service he was about to attend, he thought. He could hear faint organ music, becoming louder. He reached into his pocket, pulled out the printed invitation addressed to Father Christos Alexopoulos and showed it to the security guard.

'This way, Father,' said the guard and pointed to a temporary screening device erected at the entrance just inside the Abbey. 'It works just like the ones at the airport. Please put your phone, wallet and anything with metal into the basket over there, and then walk through.'

Aladdin put his mobile, glasses case and Father Alexopoulos's wallet into the plastic basket, and walked through without a beep. He collected his things and then bowed towards the Dean and Chapter of Westminster, who were receiving members of the Diplomatic Corps. Several uniformed ushers were directing the guests towards their allocated seats in various sections of the Abbey, which was by now beginning to fill up. Aladdin looked at his watch. The service was due to start in twenty minutes.

I hope he isn't late, he thought, walking into the shadows near the entrance. From there, he had a good view of the screening device and could clearly see everyone walking through.

'May I help you, sir?' said a voice from behind.

Aladdin turned slowly around and looked at a little man, obviously an usher, standing in front of him. 'I'm waiting for someone,' said Aladdin. 'We agreed to meet here ...'

'Ah. But please, you must take your seat soon.'

'I will, thank you,' said Aladdin as Richard Wagner's 'Good Friday Music' from *Parsifal* filled the Abbey, giving the solemn occasion an almost festive air.

'He just got out of a car,' said Nadia. 'Andersen is with him, as expected.'

'Perfect,' replied Aladdin and adjusted the ring on his right middle finger, careful not to activate the intricate mechanism operating a retractable spur containing a powerful drug. From recent photographs of Stolzfus, Silvanus had estimated Stolzfus's weight and adjusted the dose accordingly. If all went to plan, the nerve agent should take effect within twenty minutes or so after being administered, which could be done with a tiny pinprick. If the dose was too strong, it could cause instant death. If it was just right, it would cause symptoms that mimicked a heart attack, but caused no permanent damage. It was a fine line with no margin for error, as little was known about the drug, which had been sourced from the Czech Republic. Developed by Russian scientists as part of a Soviet program codenamed 'Foliant', the drug was a by-product of the deadly Novichok, frequently used by Soviet agents in the field.

The traffic around Stansted Airport had been unusually heavy and it took them longer than expected to reach Westminster Abbey. Andersen got out of the car first and opened the back door for Stolzfus.

'I always wanted to visit Westminster Abbey,' said Stolzfus, looking up at the imposing facade, 'but I didn't think it would be on an occasion quite like this.'

'We must hurry; there's little time,' said the major, looking anxiously around and pointing towards the entrance where the Lord-Lieutenant of Greater London and the High Sheriff of Greater London were about to enter the Abbey and go through security. A seasoned agent, she knew that getting out of a car was always a dangerous moment, especially with so many people milling around. She was therefore keen to get Stolzfus into the Abbey as quickly as possible.

Aladdin instantly recognised Stolzfus's distinctive head of unruly hair as he slowly walked through the security device. *Here he is*, he thought and began to walk towards the Great West Door to meet him. Aladdin knew there was only one perfect moment for something so delicate as he was about to attempt, requiring split-second timing. Miss it, and it was all over with no second chance, or worse still, a disaster on his hands.

Aladdin began his breathing exercises to help him focus and keep calm. He reached Stolzfus just as the professor was collecting his things out of the plastic basket, carefully watched by the major who was standing next to him.

'Professor Stolzfus, what a pleasure,' said Aladdin. Stolzfus turned around and looked at the priest with the long beard and strange black hat, standing in front of him looking like some medieval apparition.

'Christos Alexopoulos. We met last year in Chicago,' said Aladdin in a distinctive, Greek accent. As he extended his hand, he activated the mechanism on his ring, which raised a tiny, sharp metal spur. Instinctively, Stolzfus extended his own hand in reply. As they shook hands, the tiny spur on the ring pierced Stolzfus's palm, feeling like a pinprick or little splinter, which Stolzfus didn't even notice. 'Perhaps we can talk later?' said Aladdin, withdrawing his hand.

'I hope so ...' replied Stolzfus politely, trying to remember the meeting and the man.

'We must take our seats,' said the major, pointing to the waiting usher standing in front of her. Aladdin took a bow, stepped back into the shadows and smiled. Phase two had just been successfully completed. He turned around, walked back through the screening device pretending to take an urgent phone call, and left the Abbey.

Stolzfus recognised many familiar faces as he followed the major to his allocated seat almost right at the front and sat down. The service, conducted by The Very Reverend Dr John Hall, Dean of Westminster, was about to begin. Then everyone stood as the Royal Representatives were conducted to their seats and the choir began to sing the Introit.

At first, Stolzfus listened to John Donne's beautiful words: 'Bring us, O Lord God, at our last awakening into the house and gate of heaven, to enter into that gate and dwell in that house, where there shall be no darkness nor dazzling, but one equal light ...'

Then, his mind began to wander. *Longing for a glorious afterlife*, he thought. *How futile. Stardust we are, and to stardust we shall return. There is no afterlife, no last judgement, no heaven and no hell. We only have this life and to be remembered like this, here, is about as good as it gets. This is how we can live on: through our deeds. Stephen, you have been a fortunate man. Perhaps one day, I too—*

Stolzfus's reverie was interrupted by a hymn as all present began to sing 'All Creatures of our God and King, lift up your voice and with us sing. Alleluia, alleluia!' while the procession moved to designated places in the Quire and the Sacrarium. Then the Dean of Westminster began to deliver the Bidding as everyone remained standing.

'We come to celebrate the life and achievements of Stephen Hawking in this holy place where God has been worshipped for over a thousand years,' began the Dean, 'and where kings and queens and the great men and women of our national history and international influence are memorialised ...'

Suddenly, Stolzfus began to feel dizzy. As he looked up, the columns around him began to spin and crazy flashes of light obscured his vision. He had difficulty breathing and pressed his right hand against his chest. The Order of Service booklet fell from his hand and his whole body began to tremble.

Noticing his distress the major, who was standing next to him, looked at Stolzfus. 'Are you all right?' she asked, reaching for his arm to steady him. Before she could grip his arm, Stolzfus lost consciousness, his knees gave way and he fell to the ground, hitting his head on the edge of the chair. The major fell to her knees beside him and reached for his wrist. By now, Stolzfus was lying perfectly still on the stone floor. His eyes were closed, his mouth open.

He isn't breathing, thought the major, assessing the situation. *He's gone into cardiac arrest. Don't panic!*

The major looked up at the worried faces staring down at her. 'Heart attack!' she almost shouted. 'Someone call an ambulance!' Then she loosened Stolzfus's tie and began to administer CPR, first by compressing his chest and then exhaling air into his mouth to keep up the blood supply to his brain to avoid serious damage, or worse. The major knew the next few minutes were critical. Life was hanging in the balance and permanent damage was a real possibility. By now, the Dean of Westminster was kneeling beside the major, holding Stolzfus's hand and quietly praying.

The ambulance crew arrived within minutes with a stretcher. 'We'll take it from here,' said one of the paramedics and helped the major to her feet. 'You did very well ...'

'Heart attack?' asked the major.

The paramedic shook his head. 'Doesn't look like it,' he said. 'He's breathing normally, see? Weird ...'

Within moments, Stolzfus had been lifted onto the stretcher and was being wheeled out of the Abbey past kings and queens and other greats long gone, reminding all who witnessed the distressing incident of the fragility of life and the certainty of death.

As soon as the ambulance crew and the major left the Abbey, the Dean of Westminster said a short prayer for Stolzfus and then resumed the service.

13

London: 15 June, 1:00 pm

Partially concealed from the road, Teodora, Silvanus and Aladdin were sitting in a grey delivery van parked in a driveway with a clear view of the two ambulances stationed behind Westminster Abbey. The carefully chosen driveway was in a rare CCTV surveillance blind spot. Nearby, Nadia waited on a powerful motorbike, also with a clear view of the Abbey. Wearing black leathers and a black full-face helmet, it was impossible to recognise her. The others were also dressed in black leathers and had helmets at the ready that they could put on quickly to conceal their faces.

After walking out of Westminster Abbey just before the service began, Aladdin had made his way to the van to join the others. The fateful handshake with Stolzfus had started an unstoppable chain of events that was about to unfold, and time was racing. The point of no return had arrived. The next phase, the most critical and risky by far, required them all to work together in unison as there was little room for error. It all depended on speed and precision timing.

Aladdin had managed to climb unnoticed into the back of the van and immediately discarded his disguise. Father Alexopoulos became Aladdin again and he was ready to play his part in the ingenious and carefully crafted plan with many moving parts that would require improvisation and split-second decisions to deal with the unexpected. And they always had to count on the unexpected.

Each one of them was armed with a powerful Glock 18 – a semi-automatic machine pistol and the group's preferred firearm, which they had obtained on the thriving black market through a trusted source in London. Reliable, safe, accurate. While Spiridon 4 always tried to avoid unnecessary violence because it could increase the risks, it was often unavoidable and became a necessary element of the assignment. For that reason, none of them shied away from violence as such, but used it carefully and always with a clear purpose in mind. Any casualties were viewed as collateral damage. 'Shit happens,' Teodora always reminded them; the important thing was not to choke on it.

'Here they come, guys,' said Teodora and started the van's engine. Accompanied by two armed police officers, the two paramedics were pushing the ambulance stretcher towards the waiting ambulance. The major was walking beside them with a hand resting on the stretcher. 'She knows something's up,' said Silvanus. 'Just look at her body language. She's looking around all the time, watching ...'

'You're right. I had the same feeling standing close to her in the Abbey,' said Aladdin.

'Don't worry, boys, we can deal with her. Don't forget, she isn't armed. No weapons allowed in the Abbey, remember?' Teodora reminded them. 'The more important question here is, who will travel with her in the ambulance? She will obviously go, but will one of the armed police officers go as well?'

'I don't think so,' said Silvanus, shaking his head. 'Their posts are right here.'

'*What is she doing?*' asked Teodora, pointing towards the ambulance. As the paramedics were lifting the stretcher into the back of the ambulance, the major ran up to a policeman sitting on his motorbike nearby and talked to him briefly.

'Exactly what you would be doing,' said Aladdin. 'She's arranging an escort; watch.'

Moments later, the major hurried back to the ambulance and climbed into the back. The policeman started his motorcycle, pulled out from the kerb and positioned himself in front of the ambulance.

'Did you see that, Nadia?' asked Teodora.

'I did.'

'You know what to do?'

'I do.'

'Can you hear the sirens?' said Teodora, pulling out of the driveway. 'Good luck, guys! Here we go.'

As expected, the London traffic was heavy and despite the ambulance sirens and the motorcycle policeman's best efforts to clear the way, progress towards the nearest hospital was slow. This allowed Nadia and Teodora, who were counting on this, to position themselves directly behind the ambulance. When the ambulance approached a congested intersection and slowed down, Teodora decided it was time to make a move.

'*Now*, Nadia; do it right now!' said Teodora and put on her helmet. The others did the same. Nadia accelerated until her bike almost touched the bumper bar of the ambulance, pulled the Glock with silencer fitted out from her vest, quickly took a shot at each of the vehicle's two rear tyres and then pulled back. Within moments the tyres began to disintegrate, with shredded rubber peeling off the rims. Just before entering the intersection, the ambulance lost control, veered to the left and collided with a parked car. Nadia overtook the stationary ambulance with its siren still going, and accelerated towards the policeman on the motorcycle, who had observed the crash in his rear-view mirror and was slowing down.

The policeman quickly turned his bike around and was now coming towards Nadia. As he was about to pass her, Nadia lifted her gun and shot him twice in the chest. The policeman let go of the handlebars and lost control of his bike, which mounted the footpath, narrowly missed a woman with a pram, and then crashed into a shopfront, the heavy bike coming to rest on his legs. Nadia was certain he was dead and turned her bike around.

'Okay, guys, you know what to do,' said Teodora, carefully watching the chaos unfolding around her. Screaming people on the footpath, broken glass everywhere and the shrill, ear-piercing sound of the siren added to the confusion. Teodora smiled. This was exactly what she had been hoping for. Chaos had always been their best friend.

Silvanus was the first to reach the ambulance. He opened the back doors and pointed his gun at the major. 'Put your hands in the air where I can see them,' he barked. The major did as she was told. She knew this was not the time to make a move, but her eyes kept searching for some kind of weapon nevertheless. By now, Nadia had got off her bike, opened the driver's door of the ambulance and pointed her gun at the two terrified paramedics sitting in the front. She could see they weren't injured. 'You two, get out – *now!* Take the patient on the stretcher out of the back and put him into the van behind us. *Move!*'

Aladdin opened the back doors of the van from the inside just as the two paramedics lifted the stretcher with Stolzfus strapped in, out of the ambulance. 'Have a safe trip back to the States, Major,' said Silvanus. 'Stay right here and don't try anything silly. This will be over in a minute.' Then he climbed out of the back of the ambulance and quickly closed the doors from the outside.

The motorcycle policeman wasn't dead. Under his tunic was body armour he had been specially issued with for security detail around the Abbey that day, which had absorbed the impact of the two bullets at close range, badly bruising his chest and breaking a few ribs. He had briefly lost consciousness when he crashed his bike, but he was coming to as the excruciating pain from his crushed legs, hammered against his brain.

As his eyes began to focus, he surveyed the scene around him. He was only metres from the ambulance and could see the two paramedics wheeling the stretcher with the patient to the back of the van. Nadia was walking along beside them, gun in hand, covering them and looking around.

Slowly, the policeman reached for the Glock he had been issued with for security during Hawking's memorial service. At first, he couldn't release it from its holster because he was pinned down by the heavy bike. But when he turned his body slightly to the left, he managed to free it.

By now the paramedics had reached the back of the van and were about to lift up the stretcher when Nadia moved into the policeman's line of sight. She was now standing directly next to the stretcher with her back towards him. The policeman lifted his gun, his hand shaking, took aim and fired. The bullet hit Nadia in the back and went straight through her heart. With his eyesight fading the policeman fired again, but by now Nadia had fallen forward and collapsed. The second bullet missed her and hit the person on the stretcher instead, embedding itself in Stolzfus's chest just as the paramedics were pushing the stretcher into the back of the van.

'Jesus! *She's been hit!*' shouted Silvanus. He could see the policeman lying on the ground under the bike with his weapon pointing towards him. Silvanus lifted his gun and shot the policeman between his eyes, blowing away the back of his head.

'Put the stretcher inside the van and come over here,' shouted Silvanus, addressing the paramedics. He knelt down beside Nadia and felt her pulse.

'What's going on?' shouted Teodora, adjusting her earpiece. 'Tell me, someone!' She was reluctant to leave the van with the engine running and have a look herself, thereby jeopardising the getaway and putting everyone in danger.

Aladdin secured the stretcher, jumped out of the van and ran across to Nadia, lying on the road. The paramedic kneeling beside her shook his head. 'She's dead,' he said.

Silvanus looked at Aladdin, alarmed. 'Let's put her in the back and get out of here – *now!*' he shouted, and slipped his gun into his belt. Aladdin and Silvanus lifted Nadia off the road, lay her in the back of the van and then climbed in beside her. 'Let's get out of here!' shouted Aladdin, slamming closed the back doors of the van.

Tyres screeching, Teodora crossed to the opposite side of the road, mounted the footpath to avoid traffic, which had come to a complete standstill at the intersection, and then turned into a side street and accelerated, barely missing an oncoming garbage truck.

'My God, she's dead,' whispered Silvanus, cradling Nadia's head in his lap. That's when he noticed the blood dripping from the side of the stretcher next to him. 'He's been hit as well!' he shouted, pointing to Stolzfus. 'How bad is it?'

Aladdin leant across to investigate. 'Difficult to tell. There's a wound in the right side of his chest. Lots of blood. *What are we going to do?*'

'We stay calm and proceed as planned,' replied Teodora, trying to concentrate on the traffic. 'We go to the warehouse and change vehicles. Then we can have a closer look and evaluate the situation.' Teodora knew that the next few minutes were critical, as all hell would break loose behind them as soon as the authorities realised what had happened. They had to get to the abandoned warehouse before helicopters were in the air looking for them.

Nadia's dead, thought Teodora, tears streaming down her face. *Dear God, it can't be!*

'She's gone,' said Silvanus quietly, climbing over from the rear into the front seat beside Teodora. 'Stolzfus has been hit as well ...'

This is a catastrophe, thought Teodora, her mind racing. They had been in tight spots before, but never one quite this bad. She knew it would take all of her ingenuity, determination and self-control to get out of this one. This was not the time to become emotional. There would be time to grieve later. To steel herself, Teodora thought of that other moment of great tragedy many years ago in Albania. She could see her dead mother lying on the table, her chest wide open with a man leaning over her, holding a scalpel. Then the man's face swam into focus. The face she would never forget.

Now refocussed, Teodora looked at Silvanus sitting next to her. 'We'll make it, you'll see,' she said. 'I still have things to do. Get the first-aid kit ready, we're almost there.'

14

London: 15 June, 2:30 pm

Teodora drove through a deserted scrap-metal yard on the outskirts of London, wove the van through row upon row of rusting car bodies, turned into the open entrance of a dilapidated warehouse and stopped the van. Exhausted, she closed her eyes for a moment, steeling herself for what was to come. Then she got slowly out of the van, walked to the rear and opened the back doors.

Nadia was lying in a pool of blood next to the stretcher. Her eyes were closed, her pale face serene. *She looks so peaceful*, thought Teodora, beginning to choke. Overcome with emotion and unable to hold back the tears, she reached in, took Nadia's limp hand and just stood there for a while, motionless and silent, letting the pain and grief wash over her. Silvanus walked up to her from behind, put his arms around her shoulders and held her tight. Teodora let go of her sister's hand and turned around to face Silvanus. 'How could this have happened?' she whispered, barely able to speak.

'She knew the risks; we all did.'

'Except she paid the price – for us all.'

'She did.'

Teodora wiped away the tears. 'Then let's make sure it wasn't in vain,' she said. 'Come, we have work to do and we haven't much time.'

First, they quickly wrapped Nadia's body in a blanket and put it into the back of another van they had left at the warehouse the day before in preparation for the next stage of their getaway. Then they began to examine Stolzfus. Still heavily sedated from the drug, Stolzfus hadn't moved and was breathing normally. Aladdin, who knew about first aid and had treated gunshot wounds before, albeit superficially, examined the wound.

'How serious is it?' asked Teodora.

'Impossible to tell. The bleeding has stopped, but the bullet is in there, somewhere. Must be bleeding internally. He needs surgery urgently, that's for sure.'

'He's only good to us alive,' said Teodora, 'and there isn't much time. Let me think ...'

Teodora turned around, walked away from the van, ran her fingers shakily through her short hair and just stood for a while, deep in thought. She always did some of her most creative thinking when the team had their backs to the wall.

'Silvanus, can you please get my satellite phone,' she said quietly.

Silvanus did as she asked and handed her the phone. Teodora dialled Alessandro's number and walked over to the open roller door, looking for better reception. The phone call lasted for several minutes. Teodora became animated and raised her voice several times, which Silvanus thought was unusual. Then she made a second call and seemed to calm down.

Aladdin turned to Silvanus as they anxiously watched Teodora making the phone calls.

'I wonder what she's up to?'

'Don't worry, she'll come up with something,' said Silvanus, trying to reassure his brother. 'She always does.'

'I hope you're right. But with Nadia dead ... I don't know.'

'We'll know soon enough. Here she comes.'

'I just spoke with Alessandro and Raul,' said Teodora, sounding calm and composed. 'Alessandro is in Florence with his father ...'

'And?' prompted Silvanus.

'They understand the situation and our predicament. Apparently, it's already all over the news. Put Stolzfus in the van. Leave him on the stretcher exactly as he is. The less we move him the better. He will get the medical attention he needs in a couple of hours. Let's hope he can last until then.'

'How did you manage that?' asked Aladdin.

'I'll tell you on the way, but first we have to torch the other van. You know what to do; the accelerant is over there. Use plenty of it.

That should start the warehouse fire and cover our tracks. This place is like a tinder box. Let's move, guys. We have to get out of here fast! The next few hours are critical.'

A few minutes after the team left the warehouse in the second van and turned into a quiet street, something in the warehouse exploded, igniting the dry, rotting timber beams holding up the tin roof. Moments later the roof collapsed, setting fire to hundreds of old tyres and sending a column of black, acrid smoke high up into the clear afternoon sky like an accusing finger pointing to heaven.

Following the GPS on her dashboard and staying well within the speed limit, Teodora followed the route she had carefully mapped out earlier. It would lead them through suburban back streets to the A3 motorway, the fastest route to their destination: Portsmouth.

'Are you going to tell us?' asked Silvanus as soon as they had reached the motorway and were heading south. 'Or do you want the suspense to kill us?'

'As you know, *Nike* arrived in Portsmouth yesterday and is berthed at the Port Solent Marina,' began Teodora. 'Alessandro has been there several times before and knows the harbourmaster. He does regular business with him ... Mafia stuff.'

'What does that mean?'

'The harbourmaster can be trusted. You know why? Because lots of money will change hands and as usual, money talks.'

'And this will help us?'

'Absolutely. The harbourmaster is arranging for a doctor as we speak. An expert in gunshot wounds. The doctor will be waiting at the marina.'

'He can arrange that?' said Aladdin, shaking his head. 'So quickly?'

'As I said before, money talks.'

'And Rodrigo? What did he say about all this?' asked Silvanus.

'He was very understanding. Very calm. He said keeping Stolzfus alive was all that mattered and we should do whatever it takes to achieve that. He said he would take care of Alessandro, who seemed really pissed off when I spoke to him. I think Rodrigo has Alessandro in the palm of his hand. That deal Rodrigo promised him must be really something.'

'Good for us.'

'Sure is. We could do with a break.'

Major Andersen was sitting in the back of an unmarked police van parked at the crime scene. It was a mobile incidents room used by the Metropolitan Police, mainly to deal with terrorist attacks. She had just finished giving the detectives her detailed eyewitness account of what had happened, when the senior officer in charge climbed into the van.

'I completely understand your frustration, Major,' said the officer after he had patiently listened to the major's concerns. 'But you must understand, *we* are running this investigation and I can assure you that we are doing everything we can.'

'Is that so? Here we are, more than an hour after what must surely be one of the most brazen kidnappings imaginable, with one of your officers dead and several civilians wounded, and you say you have no leads?'

The officer held out his hands and spread his fingers, but didn't reply. He had been instructed to keep the Americans out of the investigation.

'I find this difficult to believe,' continued the major, frustration in her voice. 'We both know that forensically speaking, the first hour after an attack like this is critical.'

'The best thing you can do is leave this to us, Major. MI5 will keep you and your government informed. As you can imagine, there's a lot at stake here.'

'That's an understatement,' snapped the major, but realised she was getting nowhere. To have lost Stolzfus on her watch in such a dramatic way was a disaster. And now to find that there was nothing she could do to rectify this, was rubbing salt into a festering wound. Soon, she would have to call her superiors in Washington and explain ...

'I'm sorry, Major,' said the officer and stood up. 'I have to go ...'

The trip along the A3 was quick and uneventful until they left the motorway just before Portsmouth.

'Jesus! Look over there!' Aladdin cried out, pointing ahead. 'A breathalyser!' A police officer stood in the left lane and was waving cars into a bay by the side of the road. Several cars were already in the bay being attended to by police.

'That's all we need!' said Silvanus, reaching for his gun.

'Put that away,' said Teodora calmly, and made a split-second decision. She slowed down and pulled to the left to let two of the vehicles travelling behind her pass. 'We can't afford a shootout.'

'What are you doing?' demanded Silvanus, anxiously watching the police officer come closer.

'Taking a gamble; watch.'

By now, there was only space for two cars left in the bay. The officer waved down the two cars in front of Teodora and then waved her on. 'Smile boys,' said Teodora as she waved back and then accelerated.

'That was close,' said Aladdin, taking a deep breath.

'Everything we do is like that, isn't it? We live on the edge, don't we chaps?' replied Teodora, smiling for the first time since Nadia had been shot. 'And we wouldn't have it any other way, would we?' She found that a dose of adrenaline was the best way to deal with pain.

They reached the marina ten minutes later and pulled up in front of the harbourmaster's office on the pier. *Nike*, one of the largest vessels at the marina, was berthed well out of sight at the far end of the crowded jetties full of sailing boats and pleasure craft.

Nike's captain, a man called Giacomo whom Teodora had met before, was waiting for them on the pier.

'The doctor is already on board, waiting.' Giacomo pointed over his shoulder. 'Your keys, please.'

Teodora handed him the keys to the van. 'There's a body ...' she said quietly, choking on the word.

'I know,' said the captain. 'Now please go on board quickly, all of you, and leave the rest to us. We'll dispose of the vehicle. It's all arranged.'

Silvanus looked impressed. 'Not bad,' he said as he followed Teodora and Aladdin across the gangplank. Two deckhands were already at the van, and had covered Stolzfus and the stretcher with a tarpaulin before lifting it out of the back. To a casual observer it would have looked like they were taking luggage and supplies on board. Vessels moored at the marina were being loaded all the time.

The doctor, an Indian man in his fifties, was waiting in the saloon with his medical kit. As soon as the deckhands brought in the stretcher, he went to work. First, he felt Stolzfus's pulse. Then he cut away his shirt and cleaned the wound. After that, he began to carefully explore Stolzfus's abdomen and chest with the tips of his fingers.

'He needs surgery, of course,' said the doctor. 'The bullet has to be removed.' He turned around and faced Teodora and Silvanus, who were watching him anxiously. 'Unfortunately, I can't do that here. He needs a hospital.'

'How bad is he?' asked Teodora.

'Difficult to tell. He looks stable for now.'

'Could he travel?'

The doctor shrugged. 'I could give him something.'

'How much time does he ...?' asked Silvanus.

The doctor shrugged again. 'Depends. I have seen patients with gunshot wounds like this go for days without surgery. Others died within the hour without it. It all depends on the damage inside, and the risk of infection is huge.'

Aladdin looked at Teodora and Silvanus. 'So, where to from here?'

'I have discussed this with Alessandro already,' said the doctor, who had overheard the question. 'We expected something like this. There could be a solution.'

'What kind of solution?' asked Teodora.

'A long shot.'

'Can you tell us more?' said Silvanus.

'It's better if you hear that from Alessandro. He wants you to call him. While you do that, I'll prepare the patient. Every minute counts here ...'

Teodora nodded, pulled her satellite phone out of her pocket and dialled Alessandro's number.

15

Leaving Portsmouth: 15 June, 5:00 pm

Teodora spoke with Alessandro for several minutes, then put down her phone and just sat there in silence, staring vacantly into space. *This is amazing,* she thought, trying to digest what Alessandro had just told her.

'Well?' prompted Silvanus. 'What's that long shot all about?'

'Hard to believe ...'

'Come on, tell us,' said Aladdin, frowning.

'Later.' Teodora walked over to the doctor, who was giving Stolzfus an injection. 'Can he last twenty-four hours like this?' she asked.

'Possibly. I'll rig up some drips and leave instructions. Whatever that drug was, it's incredibly powerful. We'll keep him sedated. One of the crew here has some medical experience. That should help. Apart from that, it's in the lap of the gods.' The doctor shrugged again.

Teodora nodded and was about to ask another question, when Giacomo burst into the saloon, looking alarmed. 'We have to leave – *now*!' he said. 'The harbourmaster just called. He's received instructions from the police to close the marina. Doctor, you better go ashore now, or you will have to swim.'

The doctor closed his bag. 'I need just a couple of minutes with Carlo to tell him what to do.'

'All right, but hurry!'

Teodora looked at Silvanus. 'Outside, now! Come with me, guys,' she said and headed for the door.

Ashore there was feverish activity as the crew prepared to cast off. The powerful engines had started and *Nike* was about to depart and head out to sea.

'I didn't want to be overheard,' said Teodora as soon as they were outside, alone. 'What Alessandro has come up with is truly astonishing.'

'Come on, tell us!' said Aladdin.

'There goes the doctor,' said Silvanus, waving. The crew secured the gangplank and *Nike* began to move away from the berth.

'All we need is twenty-four hours,' said Teodora, 'because by then—'

Before Teodora could complete her sentence, Giacomo came running up the stairs, looking worried. 'We must prepare,' he said, 'quickly!'

'Prepare for what?' asked Silvanus.

'A visit from the MDP.'

'What's that?' asked Aladdin.

'Come inside and I'll tell you, but there isn't much time. You have papers with you?'

'Of course,' said Teodora. 'We never go anywhere without them. But why?' The Spiridon 4 each had separate false passports and other IDs prepared for every assignment. A master forger in Turin made sure they looked authentic and passed even the most stringent scrutiny.

'Because you may need them soon.'

'All right. Tell us,' said Teodora as they followed Giacomo into the saloon. She noticed that the stretcher with Stolzfus had gone, and two crew members were hurriedly setting the dining table with glasses, small plates and serviettes.

'You are expecting visitors?' asked Silvanus, pointing to the ice bucket with a bottle of champagne in the middle of the table next to a platter full of canapes. 'Or is all this just for us?'

'Unfortunately, yes; visitors,' said Giacomo. 'But not the kind we want.'

'Please tell us,' said Teodora.

'MDP is the Ministry of Defence Police. They have a marine unit stationed right here in Portsmouth and other naval bases around the country. The instructions to close the marina came from them. They protect the naval base here and are involved in counter-terrorism policing, patrolling the waterfront and carrying out other water-policing duties. They have a fleet of fast launches and RHIBs – rigid-hulled inflatable boats – that can outrun almost anything. The officers are all heavily armed pros with broad powers. We've come across them before.'

'And we'll welcome them with canapes and champagne?' said Aladdin. 'Is that it?'

'Not quite. All of this is for you, the charter party. You have chartered this vessel in Monaco and are on a pleasure cruise. We have just taken on supplies in Portsmouth and are on our way to France. I have all the necessary papers to support this, and the harbourmaster will back us up if necessary.'

'Understood,' said Teodora, impressed.

'Please go to your staterooms. Your luggage is waiting there for you. Get out of those clothes and change into something comfortable. You are on a cruise, having fun, remember? Then come back here, have a glass of champagne and relax. Leave your papers in your cabins, but have them ready, and leave the rest to us.'

'What about the patient and my sister's body?' asked Teodora quietly.

'All taken care of. This vessel has a number of special compartments ... if you know what I mean ... and the crew knows the drill. We have been through something like this before. The MDP never stays long. If the papers are in order and all looks okay, they leave. The main thing is to look the part, but I would imagine you are used to doing that?'

'We are,' said Aladdin. 'One filthy rich, spoilt tourist coming up,' he said and headed for the door. 'A priest and a playboy all on the same day? Not bad. What do you think, guys? Back in five. Don't drink all the grog.'

Giacomo had his binoculars trained on the entrance to the harbour, and his fingers crossed. With every passing minute, the likelihood of a visit from the MDP was fading. He was about to put down his binoculars and change course when he noticed something: a plume of sea spray. *Porco Dio!* 'Here they come!' he called out. A small, rigid inflatable that looked like a rubber duckie with two powerful outboard motors at the back came racing towards them. One officer was steering, two others stood in the back, armed with machine guns.

Giacomo reached for the microphone and switched on the intercom. 'We are about to be boarded. Everyone take your positions. You know what to do.' Then he pressed another switch to pipe pleasant background music through the upper deck and slowed down the vessel.

As soon as the RHIB pulled up alongside, the officer driving the boat activated the loudspeakers. 'This is the Ministry of Defence Police. Please stop your vessel, we are coming on board.'

Giacomo waved at the boat from the bridge in reply and stopped the engines. Then he went to the lower deck to meet the officers who were climbing on board. 'I am Giacomo Cornale, the captain,' he said. 'Welcome on board. How can I help you?'

'The harbourmaster told us you left the marina just before he closed it,' said one of the officers, a young woman holding a machine gun.

'That's right,' said Giacomo. 'We are on our way to France.'

'We have a few questions,' said the other officer, a man in his forties and of senior rank. 'We would like to see your papers and we would like to see everyone on board with their passports – and that includes the crew.'

'Certainly,' said Giacomo. 'May I ask what this is about?'

'Routine inspection,' replied the young woman, sidestepping the question.

'I see. This way, please. Let's start on the bridge. All of my papers are there.'

'These are really good,' said Aladdin, putting another canape into his mouth. He reached for the bottle and filled their glasses. 'Remember, we are on holidays, enjoying ourselves; cheers.'

'They are taking their time,' said Silvanus, frowning. 'I don't like this ...'

'Wipe that look off your face and relax,' said Teodora. 'Here they come now; smile, boys.'

Giacomo stepped into the saloon, followed by the two officers. 'These are my guests I told you about,' said Giacomo, pointing to the table. 'Apart from the crew you have already met, there is no-one else on board.'

'Wow!' said Aladdin, holding up his glass and pretending to be a little tipsy. 'Uniforms and machine guns, just like in the movies. How exciting. Good afternoon. May I offer you a glass of champagne?'

The female officer smiled. Aladdin's charm had hit the mark. 'No thank you,' she said. 'This won't take long. We would like to see your passports, please.'

'They are in our cabins,' said Teodora. 'We can get them if you like.'

'Please do.'

Teodora left the saloon first. Aladdin and Silvanus stood up and Silvanus put his arm around his younger brother. 'Come on, mate, you heard the lady,' he said. 'Let's get the passports.' Playing their part to perfection, Aladdin and Silvanus grinned at the officers and left the saloon together.

'Long lunch,' said Giacomo and shrugged. 'A little too much champagne ...'

The officers did not reply. Instead they kept looking around the room. Giacomo noticed they had body cameras attached to their uniforms that were filming everything.

Teodora returned first and handed her passport to the senior officer. Silvanus and Aladdin walked in moments later and handed theirs to the young woman.

'You only stayed in port for one night. Why such a short visit?' asked the senior officer, leafing through the passports.

'That's right. We were going on to Padstow to meet some friends at Rick Stein's restaurant,' said Silvanus. 'You know it?'

The senior officer shook his head.

'They changed their minds and stayed in France. We only found out this morning. We are going over there now to meet them.'

'Where?'

'Boulogne,' said Teodora.

The idle rich, thought the senior officer and handed back the passports. 'That will be all,' he said. 'Thank you.'

'Are you sure you won't have a glass before you go?' asked Aladdin, slurring his words just a little.

'No, thank you,' said the young woman. 'Have a safe trip.'

'Well done, guys,' said Teodora after the officers had left and Giacomo had restarted the engines. 'This would never have worked had we engaged outsiders.'

'You can say that again,' said Aladdin and refilled their glasses. 'Let's drink to that. I think we deserve it. Cheers.'

'Now, tell us about that long shot, Teodora,' said Silvanus, sitting back in his comfortable leather chair and taking another sip. 'What did Alessandro tell you?'

'In less than twenty-four hours we'll have a rendezvous at sea, off the French coast. Giacomo knows exactly where.'

'What kind of rendezvous?' asked Silvanus.

Teodora smiled. Now that the tense moments had passed, she could relax a little. 'We will meet a hospital ship and Stolzfus will get all the medical attention he needs.'

For a long moment there was silence.

'You can't be serious,' said Aladdin at last.

'But I am.'

'How can that possibly be?'

'The Mafia is very resourceful and well connected. This is another good example.' Teodora paused and took another sip of champagne.

'Tell us!' said Silvanus impatiently.

Before Teodora could reply, Giacomo walked into the room with a chart under his arm. 'I just spoke to Alessandro and told him about what just happened,' he said. 'Needless to say he was very pleased and promised the crew a large bonus ... I also spoke to the captain of the *Caritas*. The ship has just passed the Strait of Gibraltar and is steaming north at full speed to meet us—'

'I don't understand,' interrupted Silvanus. 'What is the *Caritas*?'

Giacomo turned to Teodora. 'Haven't you told them?' he asked.

'Not yet. I couldn't ...'

'Ah. Well, the *Caritas* is a hospital ship run by a charity – like the Mercy Ships. You've heard of them, surely?'

Silvanus nodded.

'The ship operates mainly in Africa and was on its way from Dakar to Malta. It is registered in Valletta, and therefore spends a lot of time in Malta. That's where her owners live. Alessandro has contacted the owners and asked them to divert the ship and meet us ...' Giacomo unfolded the chart, put it on the table and ran his finger along the west coast of France, 'about here,' he said. 'We should reach this point in about twenty-four hours if there are no storms, and at the moment none are predicted.'

'Are you serious?' asked Aladdin, looking incredulous. 'Alessandro is sending us a hospital ship to treat Stolzfus?'

'Exactly,' said Teodora. 'You didn't expect that, did you?'

'It certainly pays to have the right clients,' said Silvanus.

'We have rendezvoused with the *Caritas* a few times before,' said Giacomo. 'I know the captain well. The Giordanos are major sponsors of the charity and frequently do business with the ship's owners. You could almost call them business partners. You get my drift?'

'We do,' said Silvanus, laughing.

'All we need to do now,' said Teodora, turning serious, 'is to keep Stolzfus alive until we get there, and hope the Royal Navy doesn't send a warship to intercept us.'

'Highly unlikely. We just entered international waters,' said Giacomo, laughing. 'We should be all right here, especially after Aladdin charmed that young officer and played his part so convincingly. I don't think they suspected anything.'

'Here's to you, Aladdin,' said Teodora and lifted her glass. 'As this is our last assignment, you can always take up acting and make that your next career. Cheers.'

Just before Giacomo left the saloon, Teodora walked up to him. 'A quick word?'

'Certainly.'

'About my sister ...' Teodora was struggling to find the right words and finding it difficult to hold back the tears.

'Yes?'

'Could we bury her tomorrow, at sea?'

'Of course.'

'Could you do the ...'

'Certainly. I would be honoured. We usually do this at first light ...'

'Thank you. This means a lot to me.'

16

Somewhere off the Atlantic coast of France: 16 June, before sunrise

Teodora turned off the light on the bedside table, lay her head on the pillow and listened to the mesmerising hum of the engines. Exhausted and craving much-needed sleep after a day with so much sadness, she was desperately trying to forget, hoping in vain the gentle rocking of the boat would send her to sleep. But sleep wouldn't come. Instead, the face of her dead sister – composed and serene – kept floating into her mind's eye, impossible to blot out.

And with Nadia's face came memories, conjured up with alarming clarity out of long-forgotten, hidden corners, reminding Teodora that she had lost much more than a sibling; she had lost part of herself. Coming to terms with the cruel finality of death is always a struggle, but for a twin, it is infinitely more than that. Exhaustion can distort reality, and Teodora refused to accept that her sister was no more. She couldn't accept that Nadia's dead body was lying in a small compartment a few feet away, awaiting burial in the morning. *I have to say goodbye*, she thought, *before it's too late and she descends into the deep*, *gone forever.*

Feeling better, Teodora sat up and turned on the light. The light seemed to banish the ghosts, but the reality they left behind was no less disturbing. Teodora opened the cabin door and looked down the deserted corridor, the brass fittings gleaming in the dim nightlight like eyes of demons watching. *It's just over there*, she thought, remembering the concealed compartment Giacomo had shown her just before she had gone to bed. Teodora tiptoed down the corridor, opened the door to the compartment, took a deep breath and turned on the light. Still wearing her torn leathers covered in blood, Nadia was lying on a narrow bunk.

'We can't bury you like that,' whispered Teodora, and began to unbutton Nadia's jacket. It took her more than an hour to undress her dead sister, wash her body and then dress her in fresh clothes. While she was doing this, she kept talking to her. In a strange way this seemed to calm Teodora, as a sense of peace embraced her broken heart and eased her sorrow.

Only the shoes to go, thought Teodora. She tied the shoelaces and stood up. *That's better. Now you are ready, and so am I.* Then she bent down and kissed Nadia tenderly on the forehead. 'Goodbye, my darling,' she whispered, stroking Nadia's hair, and then turned off the light, left the compartment and went back to bed. This time, sleep came almost at once, as stubborn refusal was replaced by stoic acceptance of death as an inevitable part of the journey.

As the first glow of the morning sun drove away the darkness and lit up the horizon with a strip of pink gold, Giacomo stopped the engines. The entire crew had assembled on deck and was standing to attention. The engineer had sewn Nadia's body into sailcloth as tradition demanded, and had tied a heavy iron weight around her feet, which would quickly take her to the bottom of the ocean.

Looking like a mummy, Nadia's body was lying on a narrow wooden plank. The plank was resting on the handrail and could be tilted. Teodora, Aladdin and Silvanus stood next to it and looked silently out to sea, waiting for sunrise.

Teodora had asked Giacomo not to conduct a formal service, and she didn't want any speeches either. Her sister would be farewelled with love, she had told Giacomo, and love didn't need words. While they had both been brought up as devout Muslims, Teodora and Nadia had drifted away from their faith after their parents had been killed. A merciful God would never have allowed that, they argued, and turned their backs on religion.

As the brilliant disc of the morning sun rose out of the dark waters of the Atlantic, heralding a new day, Teodora placed her shaking hands on the plank. 'Ready?' she whispered, waiting for

Giacomo's signal. Giacomo lifted the small boson's whistle to his mouth and began the familiar boatswain's call by opening and closing his hand over the hole to change the pitch.

Aladdin and Silvanus stepped forward and together they tilted the plank until Nadia's body slid over the edge and plunged into the water below.

For a while, the three friends held hands and watched the spot where Nadia had entered the sea and disappeared out of their lives, leaving only memories and a bittersweet feeling of sorrow that would stay with them for a long time to come.

During the night, Stolzfus had rapidly deteriorated. His sweat-covered body was racked by a severe fever, and he appeared to be in pain and hallucinating. Giacomo had called the *Caritas* several times to obtain some urgent medical advice. The best the doctors had been able to come up with was to keep Stolzfus cool, keep the drips going – and hurry.

Teodora joined Giacomo on the bridge after the burial to thank him and to talk about Stolzfus.

'It was very moving,' said Giacomo. 'I buried my brother the same way.'

'What happened?'

'It's a long story ...'

'Stolzfus is in a bad way,' said Teodora, changing the subject. Giacomo obviously didn't want to talk about his brother's death.

'We are doing all we can.'

'I know. So, what's the answer?'

'Speed. The sooner we meet up with the *Caritas*, the better. It's his best chance. I just spoke to the captain. He is going as fast as he can and so are we. If we keep up this speed we should meet about here.' Giacomo pointed to a spot in the Atlantic on the chart in front of him.

'When?'

'All going well, about five this afternoon. But there's a possible problem ...'

'Oh? What?'

'The meteorologists call it an extratropical storm.'

'What's that?'

'A capricious storm, some call it a "zombie cyclone". I've been watching it for a couple of days now. It's weird. The storm formed about two weeks ago in the central North Atlantic and has been meandering through the Atlantic as a cyclone, fluctuating between tropical storm strength and Category 1. It even has a name: Hurricane Patrick.'

'And why is this a problem?' asked Teodora, looking apprehensive.

'Because as of an hour ago, Patrick was headed for the coast of France, right here.' Giacomo stabbed his finger at the chart. 'And unless the storm changes direction, the place we are hoping to meet up with the *Caritas* is directly in its path, here.'

'Good God!'

'Under normal circumstance, we would change course right now to get out of its way if possible. But we can't do that, can we? See my dilemma?'

'Of course. Stolzfus.'

'Quite. And then we have the added problem of having to transfer him to the *Caritas* at sea. To do that in the middle of a storm like that? I don't know ...' Giacomo shook his head.

'So, what are we going to do?'

'Proceed as planned and hope for the best. As I said before, this storm is very unpredictable. Anything's possible.'

'And the *Caritas*?'

'Doing the same, for now. We are both keeping a close eye on the storm and our fingers crossed. Being at sea is like that.'

Teodora put her hand on Giacomo's arm. 'Thanks, Giacomo,' she said.

'No problem.'

'I meant the burial.'

'I know ...'

All went well until about two in the afternoon when dark storm clouds appeared on the horizon to the south, the wind picked up and the sea became choppy. Stolzfus had deteriorated further and his blood pressure had dropped alarmingly.

Giacomo called everyone to a meeting on the bridge. 'I just spoke to the captain of the *Caritas*. He's much closer to the storm than we are at the moment and is heading straight for it. Could be pretty rough, he said.'

'So, what's the plan?' asked Silvanus.

'I also spoke to Alessandro. He would like us to give it a go, if possible. But of course, it's my decision.'

'And, have you decided?' asked Teodora, watching Giacomo carefully. She realised the entire project was hanging in the balance. If Stolzfus didn't get medical attention soon, it would be too late.

'We go ahead as planned for the time being. If it gets too rough, we may have to pull out. I will not endanger my—'

'Of course not,' interrupted Teodora to make it easier for Giacomo. 'No-one wants that. And the *Caritas*?'

'She's of course much bigger than we are, and therefore better equipped to ride out a storm like this. The captain is prepared to take her through it. So, it's all up to us now. It's between us and Patrick.'

'We better batten down the hatches then,' said Aladdin cheerfully, 'and have a couple of Guinness?'

'Might be a good idea,' replied Giacomo, his mouth creasing into a wry smile.

As Teodora, Aladdin and Silvanus left the bridge, they could see bolts of lightning criss-crossing the storm clouds to the south and hear the rumble of thunder in the distance. To Teodora it sounded like a warning, telling them to stay away, but she realised of course that staying away wasn't an option.

17

MI5 HQ London: 16 June

Major Andersen arrived early. An urgent appointment had been arranged for her by the CIA to find out more about the disastrous events of the day before. The major had submitted her report to her superiors in Washington shortly after the rebuff from the Metropolitan Police officer in charge of the London investigation had brought her enquiries to such an abrupt and frustrating standstill. To her great relief, she was told that the director of the CIA understood her position and no blame for the fiasco could be attributed to her in the circumstances. In fact, he had gone a step further. He asked her to stay in London to represent the CIA and liaise with the authorities, but discreetly carry out her own enquiries to get to the bottom of the disaster as quickly as possible.

As far as the press was concerned, the spin doctors had already gone into overdrive in an attempt to keep the full extent of the incident out of the public domain. As Stolzfus's collapse in Westminster Abbey had been witnessed by hundreds and televised around the world, it was impossible to keep that away from the press.

However, Whitehall and the Metropolitan Police had gone to great lengths to make sure there was no connection between the Stolzfus incident and the subsequent ambulance attack. Officially, that was being treated as a separate terrorist incident with an information embargo under a national security umbrella. The last thing the UK authorities needed was a curious press sniffing around and interfering with their investigations at a time when embarrassingly little was known about what really happened. The simple question being asked by those in charge was: *what happened to Stolzfus?*

The unofficial word leaked to a curious press was that he had sufficiently recovered from a minor medical episode and had returned to the United States in the Air Force plane that had brought him across the Atlantic. To everyone's relief, the ever-hungry newshounds seemed to have accepted that, at least for the time being, and had focused on the more interesting Hawking memorial service instead.

It was therefore hardly surprising that the major's involvement was considered a nuisance by MI5, which unfortunately couldn't be ignored. The Americans had a point. Stolzfus had disappeared while in their care and his brazen kidnapping had been witnessed by one of their own: a high-ranking CIA officer and one of the few reliable eyewitnesses of the attack. To ignore the major and keep her out of the investigation was therefore not an option. Instead, she had to be treated with kid gloves and given the impression of full cooperation without allowing the Americans too much access, or say, in what was going on, especially not before the full facts of the incident were known. This delicate task had fallen on Daniel Cross, one of the MI5 officers involved in the investigation.

Cross looked at his watch and smiled. He believed letting someone wait was an art. Let them wait too long, you caused aggravation and offence. See them immediately, you gave the impression you were eager to see them and they were important. The most effective approach was somewhere in the middle and Cross, an arrogant man, fancied himself to know exactly what that entailed.

Immaculately dressed and with polished shoes so shiny they would have made a drill sergeant proud, Cross swept into the waiting room. His carefully cultivated accent was supposed to suggest Oxford, but he hadn't quite managed to erase giveaway undertones of his childhood in Hackney, one of the poorest parts of London.

'I am so sorry to keep you waiting, Major,' he said, extending his hand. 'You know how it is. We are slaves of the urgent. Please come in.'

What a pompous little man, thought Andersen as she followed Cross into his office. She hated limp handshakes and decided the best way to deal with him was to ignore his affectation and pander to his ego instead to get what she wanted.

'Thank you so much for making time to see me this morning,' she said, giving Cross her best smile. 'I'm sure you appreciate our concern. This is a most serious matter.'

'Of course, of course. Please take a seat.'

Cross pointed to a small conference table by the window. The major noticed that Cross already had a slim folder waiting for him on the table. It was obvious he had carefully prepared for the meeting.

'I understand you would like to know where we are up to with our investigation, right?'

Is he stating the obvious to feel his way, or just being patronisingly rude? thought the major. She decided it was most likely the latter.

'That would be most helpful, thank you, because so far all I've received is a cold shoulder, especially from the Metropolitan Police.'

'That is most regrettable. I will try to rectify this.' Cross reached for the file in front of him and opened it. 'Your plane landed at six-oh-five yesterday morning, and Professor Stolzfus remained at the airport until eleven am. An unmarked police car was provided by the Metropolitan Police to take you and the professor from the airport directly to Westminster Abbey, where you arrived at eleven-thirty am.'

Why is he telling me all this? thought the major. *I was there!* She decided not to comment.

'As soon as you and the professor got out of the car, you made your way to security at the Great West Gate and entered Westminster Abbey, correct?'

'Correct.'

'Now comes the interesting bit,' said Cross. He turned over a page and then paused, obviously for effect. 'Moments after you went through security, Professor Stolzfus met someone he knew. Can you remember who that was? After all, you were with him all the time.'

'Yes, a priest in traditional dress with a Greek name. He introduced himself as Christos something—'

'Alexopoulos,' interrupted Cross.

'Yes. That was the name.'

'It may have been the name, but it wasn't the real Father Alexopoulos.'

'Oh?'

'Because the real Father Alexopoulos was discovered comatose by a housekeeper in his room at a hotel in East London. Someone had broken into his room, drugged him and stolen his identity papers and invitation to the service, and then entered Westminster Abbey in disguise, *pretending* to be Father Alexopoulos.'

'How extraordinary. Do you know who that was?'

'We are working on it.'

'And why is this relevant?' asked the major.

'Because after we reviewed the appropriate security footage it became clear that the only physical contact Professor Stolzfus had with another person since leaving the airport was with that man. When they shook hands.'

'Are you suggesting that something happened when they shook hands?'

'Yes. We believe the professor was poisoned. We've come across something like this before. Quite recently in fact, with similar consequences. Very sophisticated and effective.'

It was clear to the major that Cross was trying to impress her with certain progress that had been made so far in the investigation, to cover up the fact that the culprits were still at large and the authorities had no idea what had happened to Stolzfus, or where he might be.

'What happened to the priest? Has he been apprehended?' asked the major.

'No. He left the Abbey shortly after the handshake.'

'And?'

'Disappeared.'

'What? No security footage? No leads?'

'No. Not at this stage.'

'I see. Any leads from the hotel room?'

'Forensics are still working on it.'

'Are you saying that someone who knew exactly who Father Alexopoulos was and that he had an invitation to attend the Hawking service, managed to break into his room, steal his identity papers and then by impersonating him, entered through security at the Abbey, somehow managed to poison Professor Stolzfus and then left unchallenged and disappeared into thin air?'

A little taken aback by this blunt summary of the facts, Cross took his time before replying. 'That is the situation at the moment, Major, but I can assure you, we have mobilised all available resources to work on this around the clock.'

No wonder I've been given the cold shoulder, thought the major. This was extremely embarrassing for both the Metropolitan Police and MI5. They'd been made to look like fools. *And we haven't even touched on the ambulance incident and the abduction. What a fiasco!*

Cross was clearly annoyed and now he became quite curt. The meeting wasn't going as planned and he decided to cut it short. He only gave the ambulance attack the briefest attention and glossed over the real issues raised by the major, by stating that enquiries were in progress and then quickly shutting down any questions she raised.

Sensing that the briefing was about to come to an abrupt end, the major decided to follow up one particular point that to her stood out and warranted further probing. She couldn't quite explain why, but she decided to follow her instincts.

'You did say that all major ports were immediately put on alert shortly after the ambulance attack, and authorities were notified to keep an eye on any departing vessels, right?

'That's right,' snapped Cross.

'You also said that one particular vessel came to the attention of the Ministry of Defence Police, the MDP in Portsmouth, and it was actually intercepted and boarded.'

'Yes. You can see we've been very thorough.'

'Do you know *why* it attracted the attention of the MDP?'

'You really want to know?'

It was clear that Cross had no idea and was considering the question a nuisance and waste of time.

'Yes, I would.'

'We received a tape – it's somewhere on the master file – I listened to it this morning,' Cross lied. 'The officers recorded the entire incident. Standard procedure.'

'Could I have a copy?'

'I'm afraid that isn't possible.'

'I see. Could I perhaps listen to it here?'

'You really want to do that?'

'Yes please,' said the major, standing her ground. 'If you don't mind.'

'Very well then. I'll ask my secretary to arrange it,' said Cross, irritated, and turned up his nose. He closed the file in front of him – barely touching the cover – as if he didn't want his meticulously manicured fingernails to come into contact with something that irked him, and stood up. 'That's about it for now. If you don't mind waiting outside ...'

'Thank you. You have been most helpful, Mr Cross,' said the major, unable to keep the sarcasm out of her voice. 'I will let my superiors in Washington know.'

18

In the eye of the storm: 16 June

Throughout the afternoon, *Nike* had made excellent progress and appeared to be skirting around the storm. At one time, Giacomo almost thought Patrick had changed direction and was moving away from them. The sea, however, told a different story. The waves coming towards them from the south became higher and more powerful as the afternoon progressed and the wind was picking up too. *Caritas* was reporting something similar as the two vessels were closing in on each other.

Hurricane Patrick was an enigma. The meteorologists watching the storm in various countries didn't know what to make of it and referred to it as a true 'zombie' where anything was possible, and issued a severe weather alert.

Teodora had barely left Stolzfus's side and was watching him carefully, aware that he was deteriorating fast. His breathing was erratic and he seemed to have slipped into some kind of coma. Racked by a severe fever, his body began to shake uncontrollably every few minutes and he was sweating all over.

'I thought I would find you here,' said Giacomo, walking into the small sick bay. 'How is he?'

'See for yourself.'

'Not looking good.'

'No. How much longer?'

'About two hours.'

Teodora looked at Giacomo. 'Something's worrying you,' she said. 'I can sense it.'

'It's this storm. I've been watching it for hours. I can't put my finger on it, but ...'

'What are you saying?'

'I've been at sea since I was fourteen. My father was a fisherman in Sardinia and so was my grandfather. The sea is my life. It's in my blood and you develop a sense for …'

'A sense for what?' said Teodora.

'Danger. The sea is behaving in a strange way ... I thought I should tell you.'

'What do you suggest we should do?'

'Normally, I would have changed course a long time ago and moved away from the storm, but we are doing the opposite, we are moving right towards it. I feel as if the storm is watching us, waiting. I'm sorry, I don't want to alarm you, but I thought you should know.'

'Thanks, Giacomo. If we don't pull this off, he won't make it.'

'I know, but ...'

Before Giacomo could complete the sentence, the intercom crackled into life and a loud voice boomed through the speakers: 'Giacomo to the bridge, urgent! Giacomo to the bridge!'

Giacomo ran up the stairs and burst into the bridge. 'What is it?' he demanded. Outside it was almost dark and heavy raindrops began to drum against the roof and the windows. Soon the rain turned to hail, and hailstones the size of golf balls started hammering against the roof of the cabin and the deck outside.

'There; look!' shouted the helmsman and pointed straight ahead.

'Good God! *Give me the wheel!*' Giacomo grabbed the small wheel with both hands, his knuckles turning white, and stared at the wall of water coming towards them. 'I've never seen anything like it,' he whispered, frantically turning the wheel to position *Nike* so that she could take the impact and ride the wave.

Giacomo grabbed the microphone. 'Strap yourselves in wherever you are and keep your heads down! We are in for one hell of a ride. Good luck!' he shouted. The giant wave was more than twenty metres high and *Nike* climbed up on one side and then plunged into a deep trough on the other, landing with a thud so violent that it made the entire vessel shudder and sent flying anything that wasn't tied down. By now the rain and the hail were so heavy it was impossible to see anything. Already the next giant wave was upon them and *Nike* was climbing again. Then lightning lit up the bridge with a ghostly light followed immediately by thunder so loud it hurt the eardrums.

Silvanus and Aladdin were crawling along the dark corridor towards the sick bay. It was impossible to stand up as the vessel was lurching violently from side to side. They knew Teodora was with Stolzfus and they wanted to see if she was all right or needed help.

Teodora was sitting on the floor under Stolzfus's stretcher. She was bleeding from a deep cut to her forehead and holding onto a post. Broken glass littered the floor.

'Are you all right?' shouted Silvanus, dodging the broken glass as he crawled towards her.

'I think so.'

'And Stolzfus?'

'Strapped in.'

'Can you believe this?' asked Aladdin, leaning against the wall, retching. 'This came out of nowhere,' he said, and was violently ill again.

'What's next?' said Silvanus. 'There's no way we can transfer him to the *Caritas* in this.'

'We ride it out, I suppose,' said Teodora, wiping blood out of her eyes that had trickled down her forehead.

'Will he make it?' asked Aladdin.

'Don't know.'

'Will *we*?' asked Silvanus.

'I don't know that either.'

For the next half hour, *Nike* rode the giant waves coming towards her with relentless persistence like a ghost ship sailing through a nightmare. At one stage, Giacomo thought the waves were getting bigger as the climbs took longer and appeared steeper. The troughs on the other side of each crest looked like an abyss ready to devour them, or tear them apart as *Nike* crashed into the bottom, just to rise up again with a shudder and repeat the entire gruelling process again, and again.

It took all of Giacomo's skill to prevent the vessel from rolling and being crushed by the massive force of the giant waves. He was an excellent seaman who didn't lose his cool and knew instinctively how to deal with what the unpredictable Hurricane Patrick may decide to throw at them.

Then, something totally unexpected happened. The storm clouds parted, the waves calmed down and a patch of blue sky appeared overhead. Hesitantly at first, but becoming bigger by the second until a shaft of sunlight burst through, banishing the turbulent nightmare that only minutes ago had been threatening their lives.

'Can you believe this?' said the helmsman standing next to Giacomo. 'No wonder they call it a zombie storm. Where did it go?'

'Nowhere,' replied Giacomo, looking at the radar screen. 'The storm's all around us. In fact, we are right in the middle of it, about here.' Giacomo pointed to the screen. 'This is the eye of the storm. I've only seen this once before. It's deceptive. You think you have made it and are safe, but that's not so.'

'How long does this last?'

'Hard to say. Some eyes are quite wide, but with this storm, I wouldn't want to—'

'There; look!' shouted the helmsman, pointing straight ahead.

Giacomo reached for his binoculars. 'I don't believe it! It's the *Caritas*!' He said, becoming excited. 'If we act quickly, we might just make it.'

'Make what?'

'Transfer the patient. Get everything ready!'

Giacomo called the captain of the *Caritas*.

'I can see you,' said the captain as the *Caritas* and *Nike* closed in on each other at full speed. 'You came out of that wall of water like the *Flying Dutchman* surfing out of hell. It was quite a sight.'

'Let's hope luck says with us for a little while. If the conditions stay like this and the sea calms down a little more, we could attempt a transfer; what do you think?'

'I agree. We are ready. If you manage to come alongside on my port side, we should be able to lift him on board with the deck crane and we'll cover you from the wind. We'll do it just as I told you before. Strap him into the stretcher and we'll lift him on board that way. We've done this many times before. As long as the sea is calm enough for you to come close, it should be okay.'

'Done! At this speed, it won't take us long to get to you.'

'Let's hope this eye doesn't blink before we've got him safely on board, otherwise ...'

Teodora had been watching the *Caritas* come towards them for a while – the white ship gleaming in the bright sunshine like a beacon of hope – as the crew was making preparations to transfer Stolzfus to the hospital ship. 'Is it over?' she asked, as she and Silvanus joined Giacomo on the bridge.

'No. This is merely a brief lull as we pass through the eye of the storm. Look over there,' said Giacomo and pointed to a ring of dark clouds in the distance. 'That's the eye's wall. An area of violent thunderstorms that surrounds us on all sides. We are in the middle of a severe weather event. Once we reach the other side of the eye, we'll cop it again, just as before, perhaps even worse.'

'Oh? How much time do we have?'

'Difficult to say, especially with this storm. The eye usually has a diameter of somewhere between thirty to sixty-five miles. But with this storm, anything is possible. Things can change very quickly. That's why we have to move fast. This is our only chance. It's a small, unexpected window of opportunity. The fact we both arrived here at the same time is a bit of a miracle. At least one of the weather gods has been smiling on us – so far.'

'So, what's the plan?' asked Silvanus.

'Quite simple, really, weather permitting. We pull up next to the *Caritas* and try to get as close to her as possible so that her deck crane can reach us. That's the tricky bit and it all depends on the wind and the swell. The *Caritas* will protect us from the wind, which is blowing from the south. If we can do this, we attach the stretcher to a sling and the patient is lifted safely up and across, and we pull away. That's about it. Stolzfus remains strapped to the stretcher just as he is right now. Look, we are almost there,' said Giacomo. 'Here she comes.'

Built in 1953 as a small ocean liner for an Italian cruise company, the one-hundred-and-twenty-metre-long *Angelina* had been bought as scrap metal in 1978 for one million US dollars by a charity registered in Malta. Over the next three years, the ship underwent a major refit and was transformed into a hospital ship with three operating theatres, a ward with forty-five beds, X-ray machine and laboratory, and was renamed the SS *Caritas*.

'Here we go,' said Giacomo and slowed down the *Nike*. The *Caritas* had done the same some time ago. The two vessels passed each other with only a hundred metres separating them. Giacomo turned the *Nike* around and then put on speed to catch up with the *Caritas*. By now the ocean had calmed down even further, and the wind had momentarily dropped to make getting close to the *Caritas* possible, as an eerie, tense silence descended on the bridge.

Carlo had disconnected the drips and the crew brought Stolzfus up on deck. Racked by fever and still perspiring profusely, he appeared to be convulsing and struggling against the tight straps pressing against his chest and legs.

'So far so good,' said Giacomo and skilfully manoeuvred the *Nike* even closer.

'If we can hold it like this,' said the captain of the *Caritas*, 'it should work. The deck crane is swinging across to you right now.'

Teodora looked up and could see the steel arm of the crane directly above them, with a cable and a sling at the end swinging wildly from side to side. After several failed attempts, one of the crew managed to snare the sling with a boat hook and pulled it down towards the stretcher waiting on deck.

'Okay, guys, this is it,' said Giacomo. 'You know what to do.'

As the crew was attaching the sling to the stretcher, a mighty clap of thunder shattered the silence and wild storm clouds began to race across the sky, quickly closing the narrow blue window above and obscuring the sun. The crew stepped away and one of them gave the crane operator working on the *Caritas* above a thumbs up. By now, heavy raindrops mixed with small hailstones began to fall and the wind was picking up again, pushing the *Nike* dangerously close to the *Caritas*. As soon as the stretcher was lifted up and cleared the deck, Giacomo pulled the *Nike* away, just as another giant wave was forming at the edge of the storm wall and came racing towards them out of the gloom.

'Everybody inside, *now!*' Giacomo shouted through the microphone. 'Secure all hatches and get down on the floor. Quickly!'

The impact of the huge wave was violent and swift, and only Giacomo's quick thinking saved the *Nike* from colliding with the *Caritas*. Hurricane Patrick hadn't just blinked; it was closing its eye, punishing everyone who dared get in its way.

'It's out of our hands now, guys,' said Teodora, sitting on the floor behind Giacomo who was clutching the wheel. 'We've done our bit.'

'We sure have,' said Silvanus, holding onto the doorframe to steady himself as the *Nike* crashed into another trough on her way south towards the Strait of Gibraltar and, hopefully, into the calmer waters of the Mediterranean.

'Do you think he'll make it?'

Teodora shrugged. 'Don't know. But if he's not alive in thirty days, we don't get paid. You know that. That's what was agreed.'

'The medical team on the *Caritas* is excellent,' interjected Giacomo, who had overheard the question. 'They know all about gunshot wounds. Africa is full of violence … I'm sure they are operating on him right now. There's one particular surgeon who's quite amazing. They call him *Babu* …'

'How curious,' said Teodora. 'What does it mean?'

'It's Swahili. It means grandfather, but in Tanzania where he got the name, it means healer …'

PART II
BABU

'Difficulty is a miracle in its first stage.'
Amish proverb

19

Nuba Mountains, Sudan: 17 June

'We are almost there,' said Tukamil, a tall, muscular Nuba guide, and pointed to a village in the distance. Jack wiped away the sweat running down his neck with his handkerchief and looked at the round mud huts thatched with sorghum stalks that shimmered in the morning haze. He held up a faded photograph showing the Nuba Mountains with the village in the front.

This could be it, thought Jack and traced the outline of the mountain ridge in the photo with the tips of his fingers. For the past week, he and his guide had traversed the remote valleys of the Nuba Mountains in the south of the Sudanese province of Kordofan. With rutted animal trails instead of roads leading into the bush, which were often almost impossible to traverse in the battered old Land Rover he had rented in Khartoum, progress was slow and the heat almost unbearable.

The photograph reminded Jack of Madame Petrova, a former Russian ballerina in her nineties whom he had visited in a nursing home in France a few years ago. It was during that visit he had come across that vital clue about his mother and her mysterious disappearance in the Nuba Mountains more than forty-five years ago. She had been on an assignment for *National Geographic* at the time, photographing the Mesakin Quissayr Nuba in a remote village. According to some vague government sources there had been some kind of massacre in the area, but no enquiries appeared to have been made about her disappearance.

As Jack had just finished writing another book, he decided to take a break and do something that had been in the back of his mind for a long time: picking up the trail that had ended so abruptly and find out more about his mother's disappearance. He knew it was a long shot, but Jack was used to long shots and thrived on a challenge like this. It was also a good chance to clear his mind after some intense writing at Countess Kuragin's chateau in France, before another adventure crossed his path as invariably seemed to happen.

'This is the village I was talking about,' said the guide. 'It's called Fungor. The Nuba living here are different from the Mesakin. Different language, different customs, different characteristics …'

'What do you mean?'

'You'll see; come.'

Tukamil stopped the car in front of a rectangular-shaped family compound. Surrounded by a fence of narrow wooden posts interwoven with straw, the compound consisted of two mud huts facing each other, with two long wooden benches between them and an open fire in the middle.

'The *omda* is expecting us,' said Tukamil. 'Wait here.'

'The omda?'

'The old man I told you about. I spoke with him a few days ago ...' Tukamil went into one of the huts and returned moments later leading a frail-looking old man by the hand.

'This is the omda, the chief of the village,' said Tukamil. 'Come over here and let him touch you. He's almost blind.'

Jack walked over to the old man and stood in front of him. The old man looked at Jack with unseeing eyes – white, milky cataracts had reduced his vision to merely a blur – and began to run his hands over Jack's head and face.

'He sees with his hands,' continued Tukamil.

After a while, the omda stopped and said something to Tukamil in a strange-sounding language and then sat down on the bench.

'I have asked him to repeat what he told me the other day. That way you can judge for yourself ...'

Tukamil had made enquiries on Jack's behalf about a certain event that had taken place in the area forty-six years ago.

Jack sat down on the other bench and looked expectantly at the old man.

Like most old men, the omda lived in the past. There wasn't much life left for him in the present and he therefore took refuge in a time he could remember with great clarity and pride. Unlike the turbulent, uncertain present, the past had stability and meaning. As a respected elder and great storyteller, the omda often sat around the fire in front of his hut, which he shared with his granddaughter, and told stories to mesmerised children who listened in wonder and hung on his every word.

The stories were mainly about the spectacular ceremonies and the bloody, ritual knife-fights that had taken place in the village only a few decades ago, but these events had been gradually lost as brutal wars, famine and social upheavals had taken their toll, decimating the population and eroding the little that was left of age-old traditions and customs that used to hold village life together and gave meaning to being a proud Nuba.

'The omda can clearly remember the day the young white woman with golden hair came to the village again,' translated Tukamil. 'This caused great excitement, especially among the girls, preparing themselves for the *nyertun*.'

'What's the nyertun?' asked Jack.

'The love dance. It follows the *zuar*, the ferocious knife-fighting practised around here.'

'Fascinating.'

'The golden-haired woman had visited the village before and had taken many photographs. The reason the girls were so excited was because of the pictures she had brought with her this time. The girls had never seen photographs before and there was lots of laughter and finger-pointing as they recognised themselves and their friends in the pictures.'

This all fits, thought Jack as he remembered the last batch of photographs sent to *National Geographic* by Natasha Rostova from Khartoum in 1972, which he had recently discovered in the publication's archives. The photos portrayed village life and the intriguing customs of the South-East Nuba she had visited before. After a lot of painstaking research and calling in favours, Jack had managed to piece together Natasha Rostova's last trip into the Nuba Mountains before she disappeared. He had even discovered a letter to her editor explaining that she had to go back one more time to photograph something extraordinary, never before captured on film. Unfortunately she didn't say what it was, but Jack had a date and now, it would appear, he also had a place – Fungor – and an old man who said he was there and could remember what happened.

Transported by his memories, the omda travelled back in time to that fateful day in April that had changed everything ...

Fungor: 14 April 1972

Rumours had circulated for days that a zuar, a knife fight, was about to take place. No-one knew exactly when or where, but as there were only three villages that practised knife-fighting, it had to be in one of them. This caused great excitement in Fungor, especially among the girls, because a knife fight was always followed by a nyertun, a dance of love.

This time, the fighters from Kau, a neighbouring village, were coming to Fungor to fight. These fights were inter-village contests; fighters from the same village never competed against one another. The exact time and place of these contests and the identity of the combatants who would be fighting each other was decided by the witch doctors, who wielded great power in the villages.

Preparations for the fight started early that day. The art of face and body painting had been perfected by the South-East Nuba over centuries and had the sole purpose of enhancing the wearer's appearance. Great care was taken, especially when painting the face, which was a reflection of the wearer's artistic skill, imagination and personality, as the fighters tried to outdo and impress one another with intricate designs and originality. This in turn had an impact on their reputation as fighters, which would enhance their prowess and performance.

Their performance in the arena was of huge importance, not only for reasons of prestige; it also had a direct bearing on their love life, as the girls would choose partners during the dance of love. Successful fighters would also be courted by married women, who would sleep with them after the fight. Such was the prestige of those fighters that instead of resenting this, the husbands were proud if such a fighter chose to sleep with one of their wives and left them with child.

Because Natasha was very popular in the village and her white skin and golden hair a much-envied curiosity, especially among the women, she had been granted permission by the elders to photograph not only the preparations for the fight, but the fights themselves. Normally, no women or girls were allowed; their presence during the fights was strictly forbidden. While the men were fighting, the women and girls were busy adorning themselves for the dance of love that would follow later.

Natasha was carefully watching one particular warrior, a tall, muscular young man of about twenty, with a body so perfect it would have made Michelangelo reach for his sketchbook. He had already oiled his naked body all over and was gleaming in the sunlight like a god. Holding a small broken mirror in one hand, he was beginning to paint his face, applying white paint with a small stick to accentuate his eyes by making them appear larger, like the eyes of an owl. He saw Natasha look at him and gave her a big smile as if to say *Do you like it?*

Natasha took countless photos that morning and was about to change her film, when shrill cries from men who were posted on rocks above the village as lookouts announced the arrival of the fighters from Kau. The much-awaited contest was about to begin.

Natasha decided to follow the 'owl man' and make a photographic study of his fight. Evenly matched against a young fighter from Kau, who had painted his body and face with striking leopard spots, the first bout was about to begin. The excited spectators surrounding the arena were watching the referees who officiated and whose word was law, and were waiting with great anticipation for the raised-hand signal.

For a while, the two fighters circled each other with graceful, ballet-like moves, simulating attack and defence with staves. Soon, the staves were discarded, and the fight began in earnest involving the main weapon: sharp wrist blades strapped to the hands. Owl man lunged first and caught his opponent off guard, inflicting a deep cut to the back of his head that began to bleed profusely.

Carefully watched by the referees, the two opponents circled each other again. This time, the leopard man lunged, but was skilfully parried by the owl man who inflicted another blow to his opponent's head. As he turned away, the owl man received a terrible blow to the back of his head, which was the main target in the ferocious bout. After that, the blows continued, inflicting deep cuts and causing a lot of bleeding. However, the injuries were rarely fatal and usually didn't cause permanent damage. The combatants were evenly matched and neither would give up.

In pain, drunk on violence and yearning for glory, the perilous ballet continued until the leopard man, covered in blood, could no longer go on and the owl man was declared the winner, much to the delight of his supporters who were howling with joy. Caught up in the excitement of the fight, Natasha cheered as well, as her jubilant champion had sand sprinkled on his wounds and palm fronds wrapped around his head to stop the bleeding. Looking like a Roman emperor enjoying a victory procession, the owl man left the arena cheered on by excited spectators who had a new hero.

Rather than resting and nursing their injuries, the bloodied fighters would reappear a short time later – freshly bathed, oiled and with their faces repainted – to attend the dance of love they had all been waiting for.

It all began with the drums. Ancient rhythms buried deep in the blood came alive on that hot afternoon and soon the girls appeared, many of them escorted by their mothers. Preparations for this event had started early that day and had taken hours. First, their naked bodies were covered in oil to make them shine and accentuate long, supple limbs and firm breasts. Then their hair was given particular attention and adorned with ostrich plumes, shell buttons and brass clasps.

As the drumbeats grew louder the naked girls began to dance. Swaying their hips in time to the rhythm of the drums and holding long leather whips, they moved around in groups of two or three, but soon separated as the dancing became more expressive and wilder. That was the moment the young fighters appeared and joined in, their painted, naked bodies also covered in oil. In contrast to the wild gyrations of the girls around them, their movements were measured and slow.

Standing under a tree nearby, Natasha was furiously taking photos. The swaying bodies of the girls and the stunning painted faces of the fighters were a photographer's dream. Excitement rippled through the spectators and the drums began to beat faster – when owl man made his entrance.

Covered entirely in black paint, an honour reserved for exceptional champions, he towered over the other fighters dancing around him, his white owl-face mask providing a striking contrast to his gleaming black frame. Holding a staff in his right hand, he began to dance, his muscular, athletic body gleaming in the hot afternoon sun. Natasha moved closer to better capture the spectacle with her Leica, well aware that she was witnessing something extraordinary that would send the editor at *National Geographic* into raptures.

From time to time, a dancing fighter would stop, bend backwards and let out a blood-curdling cry that seemed to whip up great excitement among the spectators and send the girls into an erotic dancing frenzy. Known among the Nuba as *shakla*, the cry mimicked the call of a bird of prey.

After a while, owl man stopped dancing and walked away from the gyrating girls to an area known as the *rakoba*. This marked the beginning of the next stage of the dance of love. Sitting on large stones, the fighters kept their heads bowed without looking at the girls dancing nearby.

Owl man sat down next to them and did the same. All the fighters had strings of small bells tied around their right ankles and kept moving their legs ever so slightly to make the bells jingle. This was part of the age-old ritual and was meant to show their excitement about what was to come: the girls were about to choose their mates.

Owl man didn't have to wait too long. One of the dancing girls, a striking beauty with long, athletic legs, separated from the others and came dancing towards owl man until her swaying, sweat-covered body almost touched his. Then suddenly, she swung one leg over his bowed head and rested it on his shoulder. Owl man didn't move and kept staring at the ground, but his heart was beating faster than the drum.

Holding her breath and crouching down low, Natasha took a photo and captured that perfect moment on camera, before the girl stepped away from her chosen mate and, still dancing, slowly left the rakoba.

The drums continued to beat and the dancing continued late into the night. After dark, owl man and the other fighters met up with their new mates and made love with a consuming passion that would leave them trembling for hours. It also made them oblivious to the mortal danger closing in on the village.

The Arab slavers had carefully chosen the time for their raid. Paid informers had told them about the zuar at Fungor and the dance of love that would involve the entire village and last well into the night.

Just before midnight, the slavers struck. Armed men closed in from all sides, making escape almost impossible. Even the bravest fighters had no chance against automatic weapons. Resistance was futile, but owl man put up a valiant fight. As one of the slavers burst into the hut where he lay with his young lover and began to pull the screaming girl away from him, owl man managed to put his arm around the slaver's neck from behind and snap it. Moments later, another slaver set the hut on fire with a torch. As owl man staggered outside, coughing and barely able to see because of the smoke, the slaver lifted his gun and shot him in the chest, killing him instantly. Three days later, the girl was sold on the secret slave market in Khartoum.

The omda paused and stared into the distance, the painful memories almost too much to bear. 'The village never recovered from that,' translated the guide. 'Most of the girls and young women were taken, and so were many of the men and boys. Most of the fighters were killed. It was a massacre ...'

'What happened to the golden-haired woman?' asked Jack.

'She too was taken by the slavers. So were my wife and two daughters. I was badly wounded, but survived. Our village was burned to the ground.'

'How dreadful,' said Jack sadly, shaking his head.

The omda turned his head towards Jack and stared. 'What is your interest in the golden-haired woman, after all these years?'

Jack touched the little cross hanging around his neck with his fingertips and took his time before replying. 'You are not the only one who lost so much that day,' he began, choosing his words carefully. 'The golden-haired woman was my mother.'

The omda nodded, as if he had been expecting it. Then he stood up slowly and said a few words to the guide.

'He wants to give you something,' said the guide and helped the old man walk into the hut.

The omda and the guide returned a few minutes later. 'Please come closer,' said the guide. 'He wants to see you.'

Jack walked over to the omda and stood in front of him. The old man ran his shaking hands over Jack's head and face just as he had done before. Then he stopped, reached into his robe and put something into Jack's hands. Jack looked down. As soon as he realised what it was, tears began to well up until he could barely see. Then he embraced the old man and held him tight. 'Thank you,' he whispered and then let go.

He wiped away the tears and held up the camera against the light. The lens was broken and the case badly scratched, but the name – Leica – was still clearly visible. His trip hadn't been in vain. He now had two things that had once belonged to his mother.

As they approached Khartoum two days later, Jack received a call on his satellite phone. It was Rebecca Armstrong, his publicist, calling from New York.

'Where are you? I can hardly hear you,' she said.

'In the Sudan.'

'What are you doing there for Christ's sake?'

'It's a long story ...'

'Isn't it always?'

'You got the manuscript; I needed some time out.'

'Jack, I need your help.'

'Oh? What about?'

'It's about my brother.'

'The reclusive genius reaching for the stars?'

'Yes. I suppose you haven't heard, bearing in mind where you are, but Zachariah has disappeared ...'

'What are you talking about?'

'It's a long story ...'

'Touché! You are breaking up ...'

'I'll text you the details, but could you go to London?'

'What? *Right now*?'

'Yes. It's really important. You have to meet someone.'

'I can hardly hear you. Who?'

'A CIA agent.'

After that, the connection cut out and all that remained was frustrating static.

Jack put away his phone and smiled as a familiar feeling raced through him. A feeling of excitement and anticipation he knew well. New stories and challenges always seemed to find him when he least expected it. The cryptic phone call from Rebecca had all the hallmarks of a new adventure, and Jack was ready for one.

Instead of going to his lodgings, Jack went to the airport in Khartoum and booked the first available flight to London.

20

Port de Fontvielle, Monaco: 19 June

Alessandro watched *Nike* being slowly manoeuvred into her usual berth. He had hoped for an earlier arrival, but the journey through the Mediterranean had been slower than expected due to heavy winds caused by the tail end of Hurricane Patrick, which had finally run out of puff after wreaking havoc along the French Atlantic coast.

Alessandro walked on board as soon as the crew had secured the vessel and went straight to the bridge to talk to Giacomo. 'How was it?' he asked.

'Tough. About as tough as it gets, but we managed the transfer. No problem.'

'Any damage?'

'No. Just some broken glass and a few scratches on the furniture. Nothing major.'

Alessandro slapped Giacomo on the back. 'Well done! Don't worry, I'll look after you and the crew. But first, there's something urgent we have to attend to. Right away.'

'What?'

'I want the entire vessel thoroughly cleaned top to bottom. No trace of the professor or the body must remain, clear? I'm talking fingerprints, clothing, medical things; forensic stuff. Nothing!'

'Why?' asked Giacomo, frowning.

'I just had a call from the harbourmaster in Portsmouth. He had a visit from MI5 asking questions about *Nike* ...'

How come?'

'Don't know. But we have to be careful. We could get a surprise visit. It may take some time, but they are bound to find us here if they are looking for *Nike*.'

'Understood.'

'Do it now and then send the crew home; extended shore leave. And tell them to keep their mouths shut. They know what happens if they don't. You stay here. I know you can handle the situation and you have all the papers to back up everything.'

'Done.'

'Where are the others?'

'In the saloon. We had a rough journey ...'

The mood in the saloon was subdued. Everyone was exhausted after the terrifying storm and five days at sea. But worst of all was the uncertainty. There had been no news from the *Caritas* about Stolzfus. Alessandro had made it clear: no contact between the vessels after the dramatic patient transfer.

'Before you say anything,' began Alessandro as soon as he stepped into the saloon and sat down, 'let me say this: I am so sorry about Nadia; a terrible loss. You have handled this assignment in an exemplary way. I don't know of anyone else who could have done better.'

'Thanks, Alessandro,' said Teodora. 'Not everything goes to plan all of the time. Ours is a risky business. The unexpected happens.'

'I appreciate that, but most of the time it's not the problem that's the problem, but what you do about it.'

'Absolutely,' agreed Silvanus, relieved by Alessandro's approach to a tricky situation. After all, he was the client and held the purse strings.

'And that brings me to where we're at right now ...' continued Alessandro.

Stolzfus. The elephant in the room, thought Teodora. 'And where is that, exactly?' she asked.

'Damage control.'

'In what way?' asked Silvanus.

'I just instructed Giacomo to scrub the vessel top to bottom. MI5 has shown an interest in us. I have no idea exactly why, but they obviously suspect something. We may be searched. We have to be careful and thorough.'

'We always are,' said Aladdin quietly.

Teodora made eye contact with Silvanus and nodded. It was time to ask the obvious question. 'How is Stolzfus?' she said, cutting to the chase. 'And where is he?'

Alessandro sat back and looked pensively at Teodora. 'He's still on the *Caritas*. I have good news, and bad news,' he said. 'It's complicated.'

'Good news first,' said Teodora.

'The bullet has been removed and he's alive.'

'And the bad news?' asked Silvanus apprehensively.

'He's on life support in a coma. There has been considerable internal damage. The surgeon called it severe, and a miracle he was able to hold on for that long and survive that transfer at sea.'

'The prognosis?' asked Teodora.

'According to the surgeon who carried out the operation, not good. Stolzfus is unlikely to come out of the coma and will have to remain on life support indefinitely. Otherwise ...'

'No good news, then,' said Silvanus, 'when you look at this objectively.'

'Not entirely,' replied Alessandro, smiling for the first time.

'What are you getting at?' asked Teodora.

'There is this surgeon in Malta. He's one of the owners of the *Caritas* and the driving force behind the entire charity operation. He has an exclusive private clinic on the island and is well known for organ transplants and other controversial, some would say experimental, procedures. His methods are unconventional and he has many critics, but he's considered by some to be a genius when it comes to innovation and state-of-the-art surgery. He has successfully performed certain high-risk operations that no-one else has attempted before.'

'*Babu*,' Teodora cut in.

Alessandro looked at her, surprised. 'How do you know about him?'

'Giacomo told us.'

'Babu is just a nickname. His real name is Professor Ambert Fabry. He worked for years on the *Caritas*. Surgery for the destitute and the desperate he called it, mainly in Africa before he opened his clinic in Malta. He's quite famous and very sought-after in certain circles. We've used him on several occasions ... He doesn't ask too many questions and produces some outstanding results. For a fee, of course. A big one.'

'And you've told us all this because …?' said Teodora.

'At my request, the surgeon on the *Caritas* approached him about Stolzfus ...'

'And?' prompted Silvanus.

'Fabry has already examined Stolzfus and has an idea ... apparently quite a radical one.'

'What kind of idea?'

'Don't know yet. Rodrigo and I are meeting him the day after tomorrow in Malta to discuss the case.'

Teodora held up her hand. 'Where do you think this is heading?'

'We'll know more after the meeting.'

'You realise of course this isn't just a matter of keeping Stolzfus somehow alive,' added Teodora. 'This is not just about the body. It's all about the mind. You heard what Rodrigo said. Keeping Stolzfus alive is all that matters, and we should do whatever it takes to achieve that. That's what this is all about.'

'Fabry is well aware of this.'

'Interesting ...' said Silvanus. 'And where does that leave us?'

Alessandro smiled. The conversation was reaching the predictable, pointy end, and in the end it was always about money. 'Rodrigo and I have already discussed this. Here's the deal: If Fabry comes up with something that will bring Stolzfus out of his coma with his mind functioning and he manages to keep him alive, indefinitely, we pay you the full fee on the proviso that you pay for Fabry's services. Whatever the cost.'

'And how much would that be?' said Teodora.

'About a million, US.'

'Quite a surgeon,' said Aladdin, shaking his head.

'There's a lot at stake here,' said Alessandro. 'The risks are high.'

'We understand that,' said Aladdin.

'What do you say, guys?' asked Teodora.

Teodora looked first at Silvanus and then at Aladdin. Both nodded.

'It's a deal,' she said. 'We'll make this work; for Nadia.'

'Excellent,' said Alessandro, looking pleased.

'Do you want one of us at least to come with you to Malta?' asked Teodora.

'No. You've done your bit. Extremely well, if I may say so. I want you all to go home, cover your tracks, lie low and leave the rest to us.'

21

Time Machine Studios, London: 20 June

The afternoon flight from Khartoum arrived late. Every time Jack visited London, he stayed at the Time Machine Studios. To do otherwise was unthinkable, as it would have insulted his close friend Isis, who insisted on providing a permanent suite for Jack in her spectacular apartment overlooking the Thames. Apart from Countess Kuragin's chateau in France where Jack did most of his writing, the Time Machine Studios was Jack's second home. He rarely visited Australia these days and spent most of his time in Europe or travelling.

Boris, Isis's bodyguard-cum-chauffeur, was waiting for Jack at Heathrow. Clearly pleased to see Jack, the huge man – a former champion wrestler – gave him a rib-crushing bear hug and opened the door of the black Bentley.

'Welcome back,' he said and skilfully manoeuvred the big car along the motorway headed into the London afternoon traffic choking the streets. 'Your phone call from Khartoum caused quite a stir.'

'It did?' said Jack, letting himself sink deeper into the comfortable leather seat in the back. 'Lola's been busy then?' he continued. Boris saw his mischievous grin in the rear-view mirror.

'You can say that again. She's arranged everything you asked for. Everyone's here.'

'Excellent!'

'Ms Armstrong flew in last night, and Miss Crawford arrived this morning from New York. I picked her up from the airport myself. They are both at the apartment with Isis, waiting.'

'Like the good old days.'

'Something like that,' said Boris, laughing.

Isis's spectacular apartment – a cube-like architectural steel-and-glass marvel oozing industrial chic constructed on top of a converted warehouse – was more like an art gallery than the home of a retired billionaire rock star turned philanthropist. Lola Rodriguez was waiting for Jack at the glass lift on the top floor. She was Isis's loyal PA and personal pilot, and had shared many an exciting adventure with Jack in the past.

'A little thinner than last time, but otherwise in reasonably good shape,' pronounced Lola. She gave Jack a big hug and kissed him on both cheeks. Jack patted the smiling stone Buddha next to the lift on its forehead for good luck, and followed Lola into the spacious lounge full of exotic artefacts from Africa and Oceania.

Rebecca Armstrong, Jack's publicist who was now also running Jack's publishing company in New York, and Celia Crawford, a journalist working for the *New York Times*, were sitting next to a Maori war canoe beside the panoramic window.

'I came as soon as I could,' said Jack and dropped his well-worn duffel bag on the floor.

Rebecca stood up and embraced Jack, tears in her eyes. 'Thanks, Jack. I knew you would.'

'And you dropped everything and came as well?' said Jack, turning to Celia. Celia put down her champagne glass and looked at Jack, a coquettish twinkle in her eyes.

'How could I refuse?' she said. 'Jack Rogan's siren call is irresistible. Just think of the stories we did together. The Blackburn affair in Somalia, the fall of the British Government, Emil Fuchs and the forged Monet ...'

'Thanks, Celia,' said Jack. 'I can't promise anything, but something tells me this could be big.'

As soon as Rebecca had texted Jack some of the sketchy background information about her brother's sudden disappearance she had found out so far, Jack had immediately contacted Celia in New York and asked her to join them. He knew from past experience that a journalist of her calibre and with her connections would be invaluable in any investigation and add considerable clout from the very beginning. When a man of Stolzfus's international standing was involved in something so intriguing, a sensational story was in the making, and there was no-one more qualified to break such a story than Celia Crawford.

'Where's Isis?' asked Jack, looking around.

'Right here,' said a voice from the top of the stairs.

As usual, Isis, the consummate performer, couldn't resist making an imposing entry, even when close friends were involved. Her full name was George Edward Elms – Lord Elms, since her father's tragic death in 2011 – but millions of fans around the world knew her as Isis, the legendary, transgender rock star and lead singer of Time Machine. Dressed in an impossibly tight black bodysuit by one of her favourite Paris designers that showed off her hourglass figure and wearing impeccable, if a little too theatrical make-up, Isis came slowly down the stairs. 'What a wonderful surprise,' she said, blowing kisses to her friends seated in the lounge below. 'All of us together again. How wonderful!'

Jack walked over to the stairs and held out his hand. Isis took his arm and, walking side by side, they swept into the room. 'Do you like my short hair?' asked Isis, frowning.

'You look ten years younger,' said Jack, smiling.

'Not too radical?'

'Not at all; just stylish.'

'That's what Lola said. Growing old is such a bitch, don't you think; and staying slim such a bore?'

'Can't say I've thought too much about it. Champagne?'

'Absolutely! I'm parched, darling.'

'So, what's all this about?' asked Jack after his second glass of champagne. 'I got this phone call from Rebecca three days ago asking for help, while I was in the middle of the jungle.' Jack lifted his glass. 'Well, guys, here I am; cheers!'

'We thought it best to wait for you before discussing any of this,' said Rebecca, looking serious. 'This is all I've been able to find out so far; very frustrating. It isn't much, and I am really worried ...'

'Tell us,' said Jack.

'The last time I spoke to my brother was just before he was due to fly to London to attend the Stephen Hawking memorial service here in Westminster Abbey. That was six days ago. He rang me to tell me all about it. He was so excited. He rarely travels, you see.'

Rebecca put down her empty glass and looked at Jack. 'Just before the service began, Zachariah had some kind of fit and collapsed in Westminster Abbey. It was all on TV—'

'I saw it,' interrupted Celia. 'It was very dramatic. I was in the newsroom and all of us were glued to the screen. We even saw him being taken to an ambulance on a stretcher.'

'I heard it on the news and tried to call him on his mobile. Not surprisingly, there was no answer. Then I rang the Marshall Space Flight Center. I've visited him there often and have met his boss, Chuck Weinberger.' Rebecca paused, collecting her thoughts.

'And?' prompted Jack.

'I was put through to Weinberger and he appeared vague, evasive. That wasn't like him, but I don't think he knew very much himself. Then I rang the big London hospitals: nothing. I called Weinberger again the next day, and that's when he gave me Major Andersen's number.'

'Who's Major Andersen?' asked Jack.

'A CIA agent, a woman who accompanied Zachariah on his trip to London.'

'Did you speak to her?' asked Celia.

'Yes, but it wasn't easy. I called her several times but she didn't answer her phone. I did get through to her eventually. It was a strange conversation.'

'In what way?' asked Jack.

'It was obvious she was expecting my call. Nothing surprising about that, I suppose, but she seemed to know a hell of a lot about me. It was a bit creepy ...'

'How come?' asked Celia.

'She said I was listed as the next of kin in Zachariah's employment contract. She spoke about him as if he was ... dead.'

Rebecca paused, close to tears. Jack put a comforting arm around her and they sat in silence for a moment.

'Did you ask her about ...?' prompted Jack quietly.

'Of course, but like Weinberger she seemed evasive and reluctant to tell me anything. It wasn't until I told her that I would come to London straight away to make my own enquiries that she opened up a little.'

'How?' asked Jack.

'She said it was all in the hands of MI5 and the Metropolitan Police, and that she herself didn't know too much about what happened or where Zachariah was. As you can imagine, I became very upset and told her that just wasn't good enough. To my surprise, she agreed and asked me to call her as soon as I arrived in London.'

'Did you?' asked Celia.

'Yes, this morning.'

'And?' prompted Celia.

'She told me she had arranged a meeting with MI5 for tomorrow morning at ten, and then I would find out more from one of the officers in charge of the investigation, a Daniel Cross ...'

Isis shot Jack a meaningful look and burst out laughing.

'What's so funny?' asked Rebecca, frowning.

'You won't believe this,' said Isis, 'but Jack and I have met agent Cross before.'

'You're joking, surely,' said Celia.

'Oh no. Daniel Cross is a difficult man to forget. I met him on the morning my parents were attacked in their home here in London and my father was killed. Daniel Cross was the investigating officer.'

'Incredible,' said Celia, shaking her head. 'What a coincidence.'

'A most annoying little man,' continued Isis. 'I called him an arrogant little prick. Sir Charles Huntley, my lawyer, was with me at the time. I can still remember exactly what he said about Cross.'

'What did he say?' asked Rebecca.

'That – and I quote – "the world is full of arrogant little pricks. The secret is to know when and how to cut off their little balls",' replied Isis, grinning.

'I've also met Cross,' Jack cut in. 'I remember him well. A dreadful little man. But little men like that can be useful. You just have to know when and how to cut off—'

'That's just great,' interrupted Rebecca.

'Don't worry,' said Jack. 'I'll come with you and we'll ask Sir Charles to come with us as well. He's very well connected. That should unsettle the pompous Mr Cross and get us some more information. It did last time.' Jack turned to Isis. 'What do you think?'

'Excellent idea. I'll call Charles straight away.'

'All right, guys, that's enough for now,' said Lola and stood up. 'Dinner is about to be served. Follow me.'

The vast open living and entertaining space in the multi-storey apartment was cleverly divided by exposed steel stairs and glass partitions. The dining area, located on a gallery level above the lounge, had uninterrupted views across the Thames right up to Tower Bridge, which was a spectacular backdrop when lit up at night.

Isis was in her element. She loved entertaining friends in her home and showing off her spectacular, eclectic art collection. Used to being the centre of attention, she told outrageous stories about her concerts, many of them performed outdoors in front of tens of thousands of adoring fans. These stories transported her, at least for a few moments, to some of the most exciting times of her life. Sadly, her dramatic collapse on stage in Mexico City in 2011 caused by a life-threatening brain tumour, had marked the beginning of the end of her days as a performer.

After dinner, Isis showed her guests some of her iconic costumes, which were on display throughout the apartment. 'Jack will remember this one,' she said, and pointed to a striking Aztec-inspired bodysuit in a glass cabinet.

'How could I forget?' said Jack. 'The "Thank You" concert in Mexico City in 2012. It was the beginning of your Crystal Skull Tour after your operation.'

'We arrived in a fleet of convertible vintage cars, remember?' said Lola.

'I was lying on a stone altar on top of a pyramid erected in the middle of the arena, bathed in green light,' reminisced Isis. 'Listening to a lonely drumbeat echoing through a stadium packed with a hundred thousand fans holding their breath.'

'And then suddenly, the drumbeat stopped,' Jack cut in. 'I still get goosebumps just remembering that tension, that incredible silence before Time Machine's guitars screamed into life and began to play your signature song ...'

'*Resurrection*,' whispered Lola.

'Ah, yes; what a great number that was. First, I lifted my right hand and pointed to heaven, like so.' Isis pointed towards the ceiling, her gesture theatrical. 'Then I sat up and turned towards the crowd who were chanting "Isis, Isis" below me as laser lights came on, casting lifelike jungle images across the pyramid.'

'And then you did something your doctor had strictly forbidden,' said Jack, pointing an accusing finger at Isis.

'How could I disappoint my fans? They were all expecting it ...'

'What?' asked Rebecca.

'I'll show you ...'

'No! Don't!' said Lola, looking concerned.

'Lola's right; please don't!' said Jack and put a restraining arm around his friend's waist. 'What Isis did that night was a somersault off the altar,' he continued. 'It was one of her iconic moves. Boy, did the crowd cheer. And then she began to sing. It was a triumph we'll never forget.'

'Thanks, Jack,' said Isis, her cheeks aglow with excitement. For an entertainer like Isis who lived in the past, rare moments that brought the past to life were precious.

'Is it here?' asked Celia, turning to Isis.

'What exactly?'

'*Little Sparrow in the Garden*?'

'Ah, the painting. It's here.'

'Could we see it?' said Celia.

'Of course. It's upstairs in my study. Follow me.'

They all got into the glass lift and went up to the top floor. Surrounded on three sides by a terrace, Isis's study occupied the entire floor. Gold and platinum records rubbed shoulders with various awards and trophies, and rows of photographs and custom-made guitars covered one entire wall.

'Welcome to my memory lane,' said Isis and switched on a spotlight. 'There it is.'

Monet's *Little Sparrow in the Garden*, which had caused such a sensation during an auction in 2014, stood on an easel facing the window, next to a large antique oak desk. Isis had bought the painting for thirty-five-million pounds, which was then donated to charity by its rightful owner, Benjamin Krakowski, in memory of his parents who had been killed by the Nazis.

Celia walked over to the painting and smiled as she remembered meeting Emil Fuchs in his Swiss mansion. After the auction, Fuchs, a reclusive art collector in his nineties, had claimed that he owned the original painting, and that the Monet sold at auction was a fake and the buyer had been duped.

Jack, who after a long search had discovered Krakowski's lost painting hidden in a sarcophagus in the Imperial Crypt in Vienna, had provided credible provenance for the painting, which had suddenly been challenged by Fuchs. To avoid a huge scandal and embarrassment, Jack and Celia had approached Fuchs to try to resolve the matter and an expert, Jacques Moreau, was called in to examine Fuchs's painting.

Celia turned to Jack standing next to her. 'I can still see Fuchs looking at the painting with his magnifying glass after Moreau had pointed to that amazing "signature".'

'Proof that Fuchs's painting was a forgery, albeit a very good one?' said Jack, laughing.

'Well, if you want to see that signature, you have to come over here,' said Isis and turned on another spotlight. On the other side of the desk stood another easel with a painting. It was Fuchs's forgery, which he had left to Isis in his will.

'There it is, right here,' said Jack and pointed to a certain spot in thc lily pond.

'What is it?' asked Rebecca, bending down to see better.

'A tiny Star of David and a small heart under the rock, here. See?'

'I can see it. And this is a *signature*?'

'It sure is, and a famous one at that. It was the way David Herzl, a notorious Jewish master forger who lived in the Warsaw Ghetto, signed his paintings. With the Star of David, obviously for David, and a small heart for Herzl, which in German means heart. In its own way, this is a masterpiece.'

'Ingenious!'

'Oh yes.'

Rebecca reached for Jack's hand and squeezed it. 'Thanks, Jack,' she said, lowering her voice.

'What for?'

'For coming, and for this amazing evening ...'

'Isis arranged that.'

'But only because of you. For the first time since Zac collapsed, I feel ...'

'Don't worry,' said Jack. 'We'll get to the bottom of this, I promise.'

'What I meant to say was, I no longer feel so alone.'

'Good. And tomorrow, you will meet an interesting little man and if he doesn't play ball, we'll cut off—'

'*Stop it!*' said Rebecca, laughing for the first time since hearing that her brother had disappeared.

22

MI5 HQ London: 21 June

Daniel Cross hated pressure from above. He walked impatiently up and down in his office, fuming, with his hands folded behind his back. He had deeply resented the phone call from his superior officer earlier that morning instructing him to provide full cooperation and transparency in the Stolzfus investigation.

The meeting with Major Andersen and Stolzfus's sister couldn't have come at a worse time. Just when the frustrating and highly embarrassing investigation was beginning to show some promising green shoots, he would have to share everything with the CIA. And if that wasn't enough, he had just been informed that Rebecca Armstrong had retained Sir Charles Huntley as her legal representative, who would also be attending the meeting. He and Sir Charles had crossed swords before in the murders of Lord and Lady Elms a few years ago. Cross was still smarting from the encounter, which had ended in a disaster that had almost cost him his career.

Cross looked at his watch and decided to let his visitors wait a little longer. He would provide cooperation, not capitulation.

Jack, Sir Charles, Rebecca and Major Andersen were sitting in Cross's waiting room. Rebecca was chatting with the major and the two of them appeared to be getting along very well. Sir Charles had rung his contacts in MI5 the night before and prepared the way. He knew that Jack's unexpected presence would unsettle Cross and remind him of the humiliating Elms case. However, it was decided not to bring Celia along as well, as the presence of a high-profile journalist could jeopardise the meeting, perhaps even abort it. MI5 was very sensitive when it came to publicity.

'Remember what I told you,' said Sir Charles, turning to Jack who sat next to him. 'Let the major and I do the talking. To have you sitting in as an observer will be enough to unsettle the pompous little man. Silence can often have a greater impact than words shouted from the rooftops.'

'All right by me,' said Jack. 'I'm really looking forward to this. And thanks again for stepping in at such short notice. You know, in a way this is deja vu. Isis certainly seems to think so.'

'It is a bit like that. Look, here he comes now.'

Cross swept into the waiting room and walked over to the major without looking in Sir Charles' direction. To Jack, this appeared quite pointed and deliberate. He was sure it was intended to put Sir Charles in his place and send a message that his presence wasn't considered important or relevant. Sir Charles had noticed this as well and smiled. Such clumsy tactics didn't faze him in the least. As a prominent lawyer with a fearsome reputation who had access to the highest echelons of London society and power, he moved in circles that Cross could never hope to even get close to.

Portly but distinguished-looking, in his late sixties with thinning grey hair, Sir Charles was at the height of his profession. Dressed in an impeccable pinstripe suit that whispered Savile Row, he adjusted his silk bow tie and looked forward to the encounter that was about to unfold.

After the major had introduced Cross to Rebecca, Cross turned casually to Sir Charles. That's when he noticed Jack standing next to him. For an instant, Cross's face registered shock and disbelief, but he recovered quickly.

'Good to see you, again, Sir Charles,' said Cross affably, extending a limp hand. 'You seem to be involved in all the important cases in town these days,' he added in a patronising tone.

'That's what I do, Mr Cross. And, of course, you remember Mr Rogan,' continued Sir Charles, pointing to Jack. 'Isis and the Time Machine?'

'How could I forget?' said Cross frostily, turning to Jack. 'And what, may I ask, is your interest in this matter?'

'Ms Armstrong is a close friend. She's also my publicist and runs my publishing company in New York, and she's asked me to come along as a friend for moral support. As you can imagine, this is a very distressing matter for her. I hope you don't mind.'

'Not at all,' replied Cross, gritting his teeth. 'Please do come in.'

Sir Charles had decided to let the major take the lead. He liked to stay in the background and then pounce at the right moment.

'Thank you once again for seeing us this morning, Mr Cross,' began the major. 'As you can imagine, Ms Armstrong is most concerned about her brother and has come all the way from New York to find out what has happened to him. As an alarming amount of time has now passed since his disappearance, there is now an urgency about this ...'

'Completely understandable,' said Cross and opened the little file in front of him. He had decided to focus on the major and Stolzfus's sister and ignore Sir Charles and Jack. He would treat them as if they weren't present at all.

'I'm pleased to tell you, Major, that we have made considerable progress since our last meeting.' Cross slowly opened his file to keep them in suspense.

The major looked at him expectantly but didn't say anything.

Cross took a large black-and-white photograph out of the folder and pushed it across the desk towards the major. It showed the wreck of a van being lifted out of the sea by a mobile crane perched on top of a cliff.

'We have reason to believe that this is one of the getaway vehicles used in Professor Stolzfus's abduction.'

'*One* of the getaway vehicles?' said Sir Charles, raising an eyebrow. 'How many were there?'

'Two. The first one was torched at an abandoned warehouse just outside London. The only thing left was a burnt-out shell.'

'And this one, where was this discovered?' asked the major.

'On a lonely stretch of the coast a few miles south of Portsmouth. A fisherman saw the vehicle plunge into the sea and alerted the local police.'

'No doubt the vehicle was forensically examined?'

'Of course.'

'Any leads?'

'Unfortunately, no. The badly damaged vehicle was submerged for several hours in the sea. However, this made us revisit that vessel we talked about last time.'

'The *Nike*? The one the MDP boarded just after it left Portsmouth? The body camera video?' said the major.

'Yes. She was supposed to go to Boulogne but she didn't. Instead, *Nike* sailed all the way to Monaco. The vessel is registered there. Home port.'

'Do we know who owns it?' asked Sir Charles.

Cross turned slowly towards Sir Charles. 'Yes, we do,' he said, looking at a page in his folder. 'The vessel is owned by a corporation linked to the Giordano family ...'

'Florence Mafia,' whispered Jack.

Cross looked stunned. 'You seem very well informed about high-profile criminal elements, Mr Rogan,' he said. 'How do you ...?'

'It's a long story,' said Jack. 'There was a very public assassination in Florence two years ago during the funeral of Mario Giordano, the son of one of the prominent Mafia families operating in Florence. You must have heard of it, surely? I was there ...'

Cross shook his head. 'I must say, Mr Rogan, you certainly have the knack of turning up in the most interesting places and at times when extraordinary events seem to happen. One could almost be tempted to say you must have somehow been involved in them all. I wonder, is that the case here?'

'Involved, no. Interested, yes. I like to help friends.'

'Ah. Is that what it is?' said Cross, unable to keep the sarcasm out of his voice.

'Surely this is important new information,' interjected the major. 'Are you treating this as a significant lead?'

'Of course. *Nike* is being searched in Port de Fontvielle as we speak.'

'Are you suggesting that after Professor Stolzfus was abducted from the ambulance, he was taken to Portsmouth in that van you located and then smuggled out of the UK on *Nike*?'

'Possibly.'

'That means he must have been on board the vessel when it was intercepted by the MDP,' said the major, shaking her head.

'Perhaps.'

'What about the charter party on board *Nike*?' asked the major. 'I saw close-ups of their passports in the MDP video.'

'All fake. We are tracing the crew right now.'

'This is more than just a lead, surely,' said Sir Charles. 'This is compelling evidence clearly pointing in a certain direction, don't you think?'

'Yes, but unfortunately there is more ...' Cross looked at Rebecca. 'I am afraid I have some troubling news about your brother.'

'In what way?' Rebecca almost shrieked.

'Our investigators obtained some photos and video footage taken on iPhones by bystanders who witnessed the incident. We know the injured motorcycle police officer fired two shots before he was killed. The first bullet hit one of the kidnappers, a woman, who was killed instantly. Her body was taken away in the getaway vehicle.'

Cross paused, collecting his thoughts. 'We now have reason to believe,' he continued, 'that the second shot accidentally hit Professor Stolzfus in the side of his chest as he was being lifted into the back of the van.'

For a while there was silence.

'This puts an entirely new complexion on the matter, doesn't it?' said Sir Charles. 'To abduct a man who has been incapacitated by drugs is one thing; to abduct someone who has just been shot at close range and seriously injured is something else, right?'

'Correct.'

'Are you saying my brother could be dead?' whispered Rebecca.

'That is possible. Such an injury would require urgent medical attention. Needless to say, we've checked all the hospitals and contacted all the medical practitioners in the area; nothing.'

The major put an arm around Rebecca, who reached for her handkerchief and began sobbing. 'Would you like to wait outside?' she asked. Rebecca shook her head.

'The few facts your investigation has uncovered so far,' said Sir Charles, 'seem to suggest that the Mafia is behind the Stolzfus abduction. One of the abductors was killed at the scene and Stolzfus seriously injured, perhaps even fatally. The abductors reached Portsmouth in a getaway vehicle that was dumped into the sea, before they managed to leave the UK on a vessel owned by a notorious Mafia family, despite being intercepted by the MDP. Would that be a fair summary?'

'Yes,' said Cross, sounding annoyed.

'Is that all you have?' asked Sir Charles.

To hell with instructions, thought Cross and closed his file. 'For the moment, yes,' he lied. He had decided to hold back one crucial piece of evidence that had just come to hand that morning. There was no way he would allow Sir Charles and Rogan to make a fool of him again. If anyone was to solve this matter, it would be MI5 and no-one else.

'I can see my client is quite distressed,' said Sir Charles and stood up. 'And no wonder,' he continued, preparing his parting shot. 'It seems to me that the horse has well and truly bolted here, and all you are doing is playing catch-up.'

Cross stood up as well. 'You are of course entitled to your views, Sir Charles, but I can assure you that isn't so,' he said haughtily.

'Well, in that case, we'll let the public decide.'

'What do you mean?' demanded Cross.

'We think it's time the public learned about this fiasco. I am sure that Ms Armstrong will want to go to the press with this. After all, you didn't insist on confidentiality regarding anything you told us here today.'

'I thought that was understood,' said Cross, running a hand through his carefully parted hair.

'Not by us, it wasn't,' retorted Sir Charles, sensing that Cross was definitely on the back foot.

'This could seriously jeopardise our investigation,' snapped Cross, moving into damage control. He knew he was being cleverly outmanoeuvred by Sir Charles.

'I doubt it,' said Sir Charles, heading for the door. 'I don't think things could get any worse. Good day to you, Mr Cross. May I suggest you keep an eye on the papers? Who knows, you might even get a new lead.'

23

Valletta, Malta: 21 June

Malta International Airport was busy as usual. Tourists from every corner of Europe arrived in droves every day to enjoy the attractions of this popular destination. Inhabited since around 5900 BC, the strategic location of these islands in the Mediterranean – Sicily being only one hundred kilometres away, and the African coast three hundred to the south – had greatly contributed to its long and colourful history.

Since joining the EU in 2004 and replacing the Maltese lira with the euro, Malta had become a haven for shady financial institutions setting up elaborate money-laundering schemes and it therefore wasn't long before the Mafia had moved in. And it did so in a big way, buying up properties and businesses and infiltrating all arms of government with bucketloads of money, triggering corruption and compromising the rule of law.

Alessandro's plane was arriving from Florence, and Rodrigo was flying in from London half an hour later. Alessandro was approaching this meeting with Professor Fabry with some trepidation. With so much riding on it, and with the entire Stolzfus matter hanging in the balance, he knew the meeting could have a significant bearing not only on Alessandro's future, but on the future of the entire Giordano family business for decades to come. While his father had met Fabry several times before and had done business with him for years, Alessandro had never met the controversial doctor and only knew him by reputation.

Located in an imposing stone building next to Fort Saint Elmo in the historic centre of Valletta, dating from the days of the Knights of St John in the sixteenth century, Fabry's exclusive private clinic was only a short taxi ride from the airport.

The receptionist, an immaculately dressed young woman who spoke several languages, ushered Alessandro and Rodrigo into a spacious, vaulted waiting room on the ground floor. Filled with paintings and antiques, it looked more like the foyer of an exclusive boutique hotel than the waiting room of a private hospital. Moments after Alessandro and Rodrigo had sat down on a couch facing a large stone fireplace, one of the wooden side doors opened. Professor Fabry entered and quickly walked over to the fireplace to greet his guests.

Tall and slim, in his mid-forties with a tanned face and a muscular physique, he looked more like a movie star on holiday than one of the leading, albeit controversial, surgeons in Europe, if not the world.

'You remind me of your father,' said Fabry, shaking Alessandro's hand. 'You look just like him, only a little younger of course.'

Fabry had presence and knew how to put people at ease. His manner was easygoing and relaxed, inspiring confidence and trust. Women especially were drawn to him by his charm and magnetic personality. Yet this affable, urbane facade was hiding a ruthless, calculating man consumed by ambition and blind self-belief without moral compass, who would stop at nothing to get what he wanted.

'How was your flight from Colombia?' asked Fabry, turning to Rodrigo. 'I was there last year. It's a long way. Is this your first visit to Malta?'

'It is,' said Rodrigo, feeling instantly at ease in the fascinating man's presence.

'Would you like some tea?'

'Yes please.'

'Forgive me if I appear somewhat in a hurry, but I have a busy operating schedule this afternoon. So if you don't mind, we should get straight down to business,' said Fabry after the receptionist had served tea.

'Perfectly fine by me,' said Rodrigo, who appreciated the no-nonsense, businesslike approach of the man who quite literally, held the future of the critical project they had come to discuss in his hands.

'Then let's go to my office,' said Fabry and stood up. 'I can explain everything much better there.'

Fabry's office was on the first floor, with tall windows overlooking the bustling harbour. He motioned to two chairs facing a large chrome-and-glass desk next to the floor-to-ceiling windows.

'I never tire of this view,' said Fabry and pointed to the windows. 'The history in this place is amazing. Fort Saint Elmo is just over there – the Great Siege of Malta, 1565?'

Alessandro looked bemused and Rodrigo shook his head, so Fabry continued. 'A watershed moment in European history. The Phoenicians arrived in the eighth century BC and were conquered by the Persians in 539 BC. In the fifth century BC the islands became an important Carthaginian naval base and played a crucial part during the Punic Wars in the third century BC. Then in 218 BC, Malta was incorporated into the Roman province of Sicily; it became part of the Roman Republic and stayed under Roman rule until the fifth century when the Vandals and the Goths invaded the island. The Arabs arrived in the ninth century ...'

A pedantic man like Fabry couldn't help but recite his practised spiel to impress guests. The looks on Rodrigo and Alessandro's faces told him that as always, he had succeeded.

'I could go on and on, but enough of ancient history. One of my passions, I'm afraid.' Fabry paused and turned on the light of a glass display board behind his desk used for examining X-rays.

'You may not be aware of this,' he continued, 'but Malta has been known for centuries as the hospital of Europe. And for very good reasons, right up to today. Medical tourism is booming here and we have incredible, state-of-the-art facilities, excellent medical staff and very high standards. The reason I'm telling you all this is because of what I am about to suggest. There is, in my view, no better place to carry out what I have in mind than right here. Not only for medical reasons, but for other critically important matters that will become apparent shortly.'

'May I assume that you are fully aware of who we are talking about here and how – let's call him the American patient – has come to be here, and why?' said Rodrigo, who wanted to make absolutely sure there was no room for misunderstandings before the discussion went any further.

'I am,' said Fabry. 'I appreciate your concern, but Alessandro and his father have explained everything.'

'Then you are aware of the risks?'

'Absolutely. They will be reflected in my fee, should you decide to go ahead,' said Fabry, flashing his professional smile.

Rodrigo nodded, feeling more comfortable after this assurance. This was the kind of language he understood and expected from a man like Fabry.

'I have closely examined the patient,' began Fabry. 'He has life-threatening internal injuries caused by a gunshot wound and the delay involved in having the bullet removed. He is presently on life support on the *Caritas* and cannot, in my view, survive without it. Not for much longer in any event. I don't believe recovery is possible.'

Fabry paused to let this sink in.

'Then why are we here?' asked Rodrigo.

'A fair question in the circumstances. Because I believe there is a way, albeit a risky one, to address the problem.'

'*There is*?' said Alessandro, forever hopeful.

'Yes. But I have to warn you. What I am about to propose has never been done before. It is very radical and many of my colleagues would say it isn't possible. But I think otherwise.'

Rodrigo looked at Fabry. He hadn't expected this. 'What exactly *is* this radical way?' he asked.

'Here, let me show you.' Fabry pinned a large X-ray to the illuminated glass board and stepped back. 'This is an X-ray of the patient's head, neck and shoulders that we took yesterday, seen from the front. The patient's problem, in essence, is multiple organ failure. In short, his body is shutting down, dying, but I believe he has a healthy, working brain. I tested its functions. And it is that brain we want to preserve, right?'

'Yes, but—' began Rodrigo.

Fabry held up his hand. 'I believe we can do just that.'

'How?'

'By preserving the healthy, working brain, and discarding the dying body.'

Rodrigo was the first to speak. 'You can't be serious.'

'But I am. Allow me to speak frankly. I believe it can be done, and our patient and the unique circumstances of this case provide all the necessary elements to make this a reality. I have waited for years for an opportunity like this,' said Fabry, becoming excited. 'Apart from anything else, that's what's in it for me. I get a chance to perform something that has never been done before and if I succeed – and I believe there's an excellent chance that I will – then your professor will live with his extraordinary mind intact for many years to come.' Fabry paused, folded his arms and leant against his desk. 'That's what's in it for you,' he added quietly.

'Incredible,' said Alessandro. 'Almost too hard to believe.'

'It is. Just like anything new and revolutionary at first appears incredible and too hard to believe until we get used to it, accept it and realise it actually works. This is no different.'

'Can you give us some more detail about how this would work, without being too scientific?' asked Rodrigo. 'I would like to get my mind around this before we go any further.'

'Certainly.'

Fabry pointed to the X-ray and then briefly explained the complex procedure he had in mind.

Both Alessandro and Rodrigo listened in silence, totally fascinated by Fabry's riveting account of a procedure that seemed fantastical and Frankensteinian.

What Fabry didn't tell his guests was that he had already experimented for several years on humans, perfecting the procedure while he had been working on the *Caritas* in Africa.

'We have all the necessary medical staff right here,' continued Fabry. 'With all the expertise and experience required to do all that. As you know, we mainly do transplants in our clinic. I myself have been doing transplants for over twenty years ...'

Rodrigo held up his hand. 'My head is spinning, Professor,' he said. 'I think this is more than enough for now, especially for a layman like me.'

'Hardly surprising,' said Fabry, smiling. 'It's a lot to take in.'

'My client is a businessman. He understands risks and percentages. If I understand you correctly, if we do nothing, the patient will die very soon.'

'Correct. That's a certainty.'

'So, the question I would like to put to you is this: if we go along with what you suggest, are you able to provide us with a likely success ratio?'

Fabry turned to face the X-ray behind him and looked at it in silence. 'Seventy–thirty in favour of survival,' he said quietly.

'For how long?' asked Rodrigo.

'Several years.'

'With the brain intact and able to communicate?'

'Absolutely.'

'Extraordinary. What do you think, Alessandro?'

'It's your call, but we are certainly prepared to go along with it.'

'And Spiridon?' said Rodrigo.

'Already taken care of,' said Alessandro, looking smug.

'I have to make a phone call.'

Fabry nodded. 'Alessandro and I will go down to reception. You can join us after you've made the call.'

'Perfect,' said Rodrigo and waited until Fabry and Alessandro had left the room. Then he took his encrypted satellite phone out of his briefcase and dialled Cordoba's number in Colombia.

Rodrigo joined the others in reception a few minutes later. 'My client has one question,' he said.

'What is it?' asked Fabry.

'What about a donor body? Obviously without that, this cannot work.'

Fabry smiled. It was the question he had expected. 'You can safely leave that to me, Mr Rodrigo. It's included in my fee. As I said before, all we do here is transplants and sourcing organs. That's what we are known for. We have our sources. That is another reason why Malta is the perfect place for this kind of business ...'

'In that case, gentlemen, we have a deal,' said Rodrigo and held out his hand. Fabry walked over to him and shook it.

24

Chief Prosecutor's office, Florence: 22 June

Jack looked down at the familiar terracotta rooftops of Florence and the silver band of the river Arno snaking lazily through the city below. Peaceful and serene in the first light of the early morning sun, it was difficult to imagine that this splendid city full of priceless art and architectural masterpieces should harbour so much violence and bloodshed. *Feels good to be back*, thought Jack as he remembered the astonishing events that had brought him to Florence two years earlier, culminating in the dramatic and very public assassination of Salvatore Gambio, a notorious Mafioso, at a funeral service. Jack just managed to catch a glimpse of the iconic cupola of Santa Maria del Fiore – the Duomo – before the plane made a turn and lined up for landing.

After the frustrating MI5 meeting with Cross the day before, Jack had decided to fly straight to Florence and meet with Chief Prosecutor Antonio Grimaldi to pursue the Mafia connection that now appeared to be at the centre of the Stolzfus case.

Major Andersen had remained in London to keep in touch with MI5, as she had been instructed to do by her superiors in Washington, and Sir Charles promised to make further enquiries through his extensive network of contacts.

Jack had persuaded Rebecca to return to New York with Celia, as there seemed little point in her staying in London just to be waiting for news. He believed keeping busy would be the best way for Rebecca to cope with the stressful situation.

Everyone agreed to stay in touch and share information. Celia was standing by to break the story of Stolzfus's bizarre disappearance when the time was right and more information was to hand. However, it was understood that timing the release correctly would be critical because once this story got out, it would take on a life of its own and there would be no way of stopping it. If things went wrong, the damage could be considerable.

Grimaldi, renowned Mafia hunter with a fearsome reputation and survivor of several assassination attempts, stood up as his secretary opened the door and admitted Jack. Genuinely pleased to see his friend, he embraced Jack and then pointed to a plateful of crostini on the coffee table. 'Your favourites,' he said, smiling. In Italy, food and friendship were never very far apart.

'From across the road?' asked Jack, taking one.

'Where else? They have the best.'

'My God, these are good,' said Jack, munching happily. He had called Grimaldi the day before and briefly told him about Stolzfus and the likely Florence Mafia connection. To his surprise, Grimaldi seemed to know a lot about the matter already.

'So, not all is well in Florence I hear,' began Jack, reaching for his second crostini.

'No, it isn't. It just goes on and on. After Gambio was shot, there was a brief period of calm. Turns out it was the calm before the storm and it wasn't long before the Giordanos and the Lombardos were at each other's throats and began to fight over Gambio's territory. Bodies were floating in the river again.'

'Who won?'

'For the moment they seem evenly matched, but things are changing.'

'In what way?'

'We've made significant progress, not only here in Florence but in the whole of Italy, closing down the drug supply routes and moving against the Mafia generally. An entirely new generation is now fighting these guys and they are not prepared to put up with the old ways.'

'But that's good news, surely?'

'Up to a point. But you can't catch a shadow. The faster you move, the faster it moves. Every time we close in, they somehow manage to evade us and move out of reach. Because Italy was becoming too hot, the Mafia decided to move its operations elsewhere. Out of our reach.'

'Where to?'

'Malta. They seem to control the entire country. As you know, it's a republic now with its own international airport and the euro as its currency, which has made Malta incredibly attractive to the Mafia. Add to this its strategic position in the Mediterranean and the fact that the Mafia controls virtually all arms of the government, it makes pursuing them there very difficult for us. In fact, they are laughing at us, you know?'

'In what way?'

'The Mafia, too, has a new generation at the helm. Smarter, better educated, very savvy. They use Italy to park their money and buy up legitimate, respectable businesses, and do their shady business elsewhere, like Malta. Their children go to the best schools here, they live like princes in palaces and are slowly "buying" respectability.'

'I didn't know it was that bad.'

'It is, but we do what we can. We've been closely watching the Giordanos lately, especially Alessandro, who seems to be taking over from his father. He is charming, ruthless, but not very smart, which makes him unpredictable and dangerous. Something is definitely going on. A power shift of sorts between the families. That's why I was quite surprised when you rang yesterday about him in connection with this Professor Stolzfus matter. But yours wasn't the first call.'

'What do you mean?'

'MI5 contacted the *Squadra Mobile* – our elite police force in Florence – the day before asking for information about the Giordano family, and our help.'

'In what way?'

'To search the *Nike* in Port de Fontvielle. We have excellent contacts in Monaco and collaborate all the time.'

'And did you; search the vessel, I mean?'

'Yes.'

'And?'

'I've asked Cesaria to join us. She should be here any moment. She can tell you much more about it than I. She was there.'

'How is Cesaria?' asked Jack, remembering the bright, courageous young police officer from two years ago who had played such a vital part in the rescue of Lorenza da Baggio and Tristan Te Papatahi, who had both been kidnapped by the Mafia.

'She's now the acting chief superintendent of the Squadra Mobile,' said Grimaldi, smiling. 'After Conti's horrible death in Istanbul, she was the most suitable officer we had who could take over.'

'But she's so young ...'

'Yes, and that's exactly why we appointed her. She has the fire within that's needed in this deadly game. She hasn't been disillusioned or corrupted. She still knows what's right and what's not. She still believes in the fight ...'

'Just like you, my friend?'

'Yes, but our ranks are thinning. You know her background ... her father...'

'I do.'

Just then the door opened and Cesaria burst into the room. 'You are here already,' she said, and hurried over to Jack.

'No wonder I love Florence,' said Jack, enjoying her embrace. 'I don't know another place where a chief superintendent of police gives you a hug like this so early in the morning.'

'And I don't know another man who has been through so much with me as you have,' replied Cesaria. 'You were there when Conti died,' she continued, tears in her eyes. 'I still find it difficult to talk about.'

'I understand. Here, have one of these before they all disappear,' said Jack, pointing to the few crostini left on the plate. 'Knowing you, you've probably worked through half the night without eating a thing.'

'You know me too well.'

'So, what exactly is your interest in the Giordano family and *Nike*?' asked Grimaldi.

Cesaria and Grimaldi listened attentively without interrupting as Jack took them step by step through the Stolzfus matter and the MI5 briefing with Cross the day before.

'And you think the Giordanos are behind this Stolzfus abduction?'

'It would seem so.'

'A Jack Rogan hunch,' teased Cesaria, 'just like last time?'

'A little more than that, I hope.' said Jack. 'There's quite a—'

'I think you are right,' interrupted Cesaria.

'You've searched the *Nike*?'

'We have.'

'And?' prompted Jack.

'Nothing. Absolutely nothing. But even nothing can be a clue.'

'In what way?'

'The forensics team concluded that the vessel had been meticulously cleaned top to bottom with chemicals just hours before they came on board. Now, that by itself tells you something. A vessel isn't cleaned like that without good reason, shortly after arriving in the harbour at the end of a long journey.'

'True. But we need more, don't you think?'

'We do. And we have more.'

'You have?' said Jack. 'I knew I came to the right place.'

'It would seem that your Mr Cross at MI5 hasn't told you everything,' said Cesaria and reached for her briefcase.

'What do you mean?'

'He sent us this yesterday.' Cesaria handed Jack a large black-and-white photograph. It was an aerial shot of a circular, rotating storm cloud taken from high above. There was a large hole in the centre of the cloud and in the middle of that hole, one could just make out two small shapes, one quite larger than the other.

'What am I looking at?' asked Jack.

'This is an aerial photograph taken by a weather satellite on sixteen June off the west coast of France. The meteorologists were tracking a hurricane, Hurricane Patrick, a rogue storm that was behaving in a strange way.'

'And this is relevant because ...?'

Cesaria pointed to the large hole in the middle of the storm cloud. 'Because of this here. These are two vessels quite close to each other, as you can see, in the middle of the storm, quite literally.'

'Right.'

'We have followed this up with the meteorologists in France and asked for clarification, and this is what they came up with. This is why I was working so late last night ...' Cesaria handed Jack another photograph. It was an enlargement of the first photo and showed a large ship and a smaller vessel next to it, taken from above. Cesaria paused to give Jack some time to have a close look at the photograph and digest the implications.

'And the best news is, we have been able to identify the two vessels,' continued Cesaria. 'The large ship is the *Caritas*, a hospital ship operating mainly in African waters, and the smaller vessel is, wait for it, *Nike*.'

Jack looked stunned. 'This is extraordinary,' he said. 'And Cross didn't say a word about this.'

'To be fair, he didn't know the whole story at the time.'

'I suppose not, but still ...'

'You know what spooks are like,' said Grimaldi, smiling. 'All cloak-and-dagger and reluctant to share information because they want the glory all to themselves. Not like the Squadra Mobile we have here in Florence.'

'So, what does all this mean?' asked Jack.

'We believe the injured professor was transferred to the hospital ship during the storm on the afternoon of sixteen June. The *Nike* returned to Monaco and was scrubbed – "forensically cleaned" would be a more accurate way to put it – to erase all traces of Stolzfus having been on board. At the moment we have nothing on *Nike* or the crew. We spoke to the captain, Giacomo Cornale, a loyal Mafia soldier who knows how to keep his mouth shut. We've come across him before. The crew was already on leave and therefore difficult to trace quickly.'

'And the charter party with the false passports?' asked Jack.

'Left as soon as they arrived and disappeared without a trace.'

'And the *Caritas*,' said Jack. 'Do we know where she is now?'

'We do. In Malta.'

'Amazing,' said Jack, shaking his head. 'What do you know about this hospital ship?'

'It's owned by a syndicate and run by a charity. And guess who has a big stake in that?'

'Who?'

'The Giordano family.'

'It's all coming together.'

'That's also the end of the good news,' said Cesaria.

'Why?'

'Because we have little chance of getting any cooperation from the authorities in Malta. The Mafia dominates everything there, even the police; especially the police.'

'We've been watching the *Caritas* for quite some time now,' said Grimaldi. 'Suspected refugee smuggling from Africa, drugs, and something more sinister: trafficking in body parts.'

'Charming. What a lovely hospital ship,' said Jack, shaking his head. 'And run by a charity. Donations from all over the world to support the vulnerable and the poor in need, I suppose?'

'Something like that,' said Grimaldi. 'Registered in a Mafia stronghold we can't get near.'

'So, are we saying that the injured, kidnapped Stolzfus could be on board the *Caritas* in Malta?'

'It's the most plausible explanation,' replied Cesaria. 'Classic Mafia. They like to have all the angles covered. They like to be in control. The only thing we don't understand at the moment is why they have kidnapped such a high-profile scientist during such a public occasion, with so much risk attached. This isn't really like the Mafia at all. Normally they do such things quite differently, and the target and the motive are usually obvious and clear from the beginning, but not here. This is quite different, and that's what puzzles us. And on top of it all, there hasn't been any contact. No demands; nothing. That certainly doesn't fit either.'

'Perhaps Stolzfus is dead,' suggested Jack.

'Could be,' said Cesaria.

'So, is this the end of your involvement?' asked Jack.

'It is for the moment. We've provided everything MI5 has asked for. It's their case, not ours.'

Jack nodded, looking vacantly into space for a moment.

'What will you do now?' asked Grimaldi.

'I'm catching the afternoon train to Venice to visit Tristan and Lorenza. A long-overdue visit. If they were to find out I was here without dropping in, well ...'

'Give them our regards,' said Grimaldi and stood up to farewell his friend, signalling that the meeting was over.

'It doesn't stop here, does it?' said Cesaria after they left Grimaldi's office together. 'For you, I mean.'

'Of course not,' said Jack, giving Cesaria a cheeky smile. 'This is just the beginning.'

'I thought as much. But please be careful, Jack. You know better than most just how dangerous these people are.'

'That's why I'm going to Venice to ask for Tristan's help. You know he has a sixth sense ...'

'Just as I suspected,' said Cesaria, shaking her head. 'You and Tristan ...' She gave Jack a peck on the cheek. 'What did Countess Kuragin call you? An incorrig ... something-or-other—'

'Incorrigible rascal,' Jack completed her sentence. 'It's a term of endearment, you see.'

'Oh. Is that what it is?'

'Maybe not all the time; it depends ...'

'Take care, Jack; I mean it. And you know where to find us. My door is always open. Should you need something, anything, all you have to do is call me.'

'I know that. Thank you.'

'Even incorrigible rascals need help from time to time; admit it.'

'We sure do.'

25

Palazzo da Baggio, Venice: 22 June

Jack had decided to surprise Tristan and Lorenza. Instead of calling them from the railway station to let them know he was coming, he caught a water taxi. Jack had visited Venice only once since their wedding, and the trip along the Canal Grande brought back memories of the dramatic events two years earlier that had almost cost Tristan his life. Lorenza's abduction after she had won the *Top Chef Europe* crown, followed by Tristan's disappearance and the strange Mafia ransom demands, which ended in tragedy in Istanbul, had stretched the da Baggio family to its limit. However, their wedding in the Sistine Chapel in Rome, presided over by the pope, had healed everything and had marked the beginning of a wonderful future for two special people who were very dear to Jack.

It was already getting dark as the water taxi passed under the Rialto Bridge, and Jack knew he was almost there. Lorenza and Tristan had turned the old da Baggio family palazzo into an exclusive boutique hotel complete with a Michelin Star restaurant – Osman's Kitchen – run by masterchef Lorenza, which was booked out weeks in advance.

In the elegant foyer full of paintings and antiques that had graced the da Baggio family home for centuries, the receptionist looked at Jack in surprise. She hadn't expected any guest arrivals because the hotel and the restaurant were already completely booked out. And besides, the man standing in front of her certainly didn't look like someone who could afford the astronomical hotel tariffs and lofty prices charged in the high-class restaurant, where two hundred euros was the starting point for a reasonable bottle of wine. Dressed in a pair of khaki slacks, open-neck shirt and a somewhat crumpled linen jacket that had seen better days, Jack looked like a lost tourist who'd found himself in the wrong place.

'May I help you, sir?' asked the frosty receptionist.

Sensing her displeasure, Jack put down his duffel bag and pointed to the gorgeous floral arrangement on the marble reception desk. 'Magnificent,' he said. 'I love flowers. Do you?'

'Have you come to discuss flowers, sir, or is there anything else I can help you with?' asked the receptionist sarcastically.

'Oh, I hope so. I would like a room, please, preferably one with a view over the canal. Old memories, you see.'

The receptionist was bemused. Was this guy for real? 'This hotel is fully booked, sir. Has been for weeks.'

'Oh well. Dinner then,' said Jack, enjoying himself. 'Would you have a table—'

'The restaurant is fully booked as well, I'm afraid,' interrupted the receptionist, exasperated.

'That's very disappointing. I've come such a long way, you see, just to be with my—'

'Is there a problem?' said a voice coming from behind Jack.

Jack slowly turned around.

'*Jack?*' said Tristan, his eyes wide with astonishment. 'I don't believe it!' Tristan hurried over to the reception desk and hugged Jack tight. 'What are you doing here? I thought you were in Africa.'

'It's a long story.'

'Wait till Lorenza sees you,' said Tristan, taking Jack by the hand. 'She's in the kitchen, come.'

'Good. I'm starving.'

Jack looked at the receptionist and winked as he went past. 'I don't think I'll be needing that table now; thanks anyway,' he said and followed Tristan into the kitchen.

Over the years, Jack and Tristan had developed a close bond and had shared many adventures. When Jack first met him, Tristan was fourteen and in a coma after a serious accident. In fact, he had been in a coma for several years, watched over by his mother, Cassandra, a Maori princess and psychic. When Tristan unexpectedly came out of his coma, Cassandra told Jack that her son could 'hear the whisper of angels and glimpse eternity' and that his psychic powers were much stronger than hers. Jack had never forgotten her words.

Tristan pointed to a small table at the back of the elegant dining room, a discreet distance away from the other diners. Lorenza, who was busy in the kitchen, said she would join them as soon as she could.

'Dinner and a chat?' said Tristan, smiling. 'You obviously haven't eaten all day, right?'

'You know me too well.'

'Let's remedy that, shall we?' Tristan called one of the waiters over and ordered some pasta, followed by veal 'Osman', a signature dish of the restaurant that he knew Jack would enjoy.

'This is really strange,' said Tristan. 'Just this morning I had this feeling ...'

'What feeling?' asked Jack, enjoying his second bowl of veal and pasta with truffles, washed down with a fine Chianti from Tuscany.

'That you would turn up.'

'Well, here I am. See? We can always rely on that sixth sense of yours, and that is exactly why I'm here.'

Nodding to some of the diners who appeared to know her well, Lorenza, who was the star of the restaurant, came over to the table. 'How is it?' she asked and sat down next to Jack.

Jack gave her a peck on the cheek. 'Superb. What else?'

'Are you going to tell us why you've turned up like this? Out of the blue without letting us know you're coming? Is it just to surprise us, or is there more to it?' asked Lorenza, looking excited.

'Sure, but first I would like to finish this,' said Jack, tucking into the last bits of the veal with gusto. 'This is amazing!'

'Thanks, Jack,' said Lorenza. 'One of my grandmother's recipes.'

Jack looked around the crowded, exclusive restaurant and pointed to the Ottoman recipes displayed in heavy, ornate frames on the walls next to numerous awards the restaurant had won.

'Remember those, Tristan?' he said. 'What we had to go through to get them back?'

'How can I forget? It's what brought Lorenza and I together.'

'You two have transformed this place. It's absolutely stunning. I'm very proud of you.'

'Thanks, Jack. So, what has brought you here?' asked Lorenza again and put a hand on Jack's arm. 'It's not just to see us, is it?'

'No ...' Jack took a sip of wine and put down his serviette. 'It all started with a phone call I received in Africa a week ago,' he said, lowering his voice. 'A friend asked for my help.'

'Sounds familiar. What about?' asked Tristan, his curiosity aroused.

'It's all about a famous astrophysicist, Professor Zachariah Stolzfus. He disappeared mysteriously in London twelve days ago.'

'And your connection to ...?'

'He's the brother of Rebecca Armstrong, my publicist.'

'Ah. Can you tell us more?'

'It's all very hush-hush at the moment. The authorities are tight-lipped about it all ... very political.'

'Until you stepped in and made a fuss?' said Tristan, who had heard it all before.

'Something like that, but what we do know is that he's been abducted – most likely by the Florence Mafia. We also know that he was seriously injured during the abduction. Shot. I just spoke to Chief Prosecutor Grimaldi and Cesaria in Florence, and it would appear that the professor is being held on a hospital ship in Malta.'

'By the Mafia?'

'In a roundabout way, yes.'

'How interesting,' said Tristan.

'And, of course, you promised to investigate,' said Lorenza. 'Right?'

Jack looked a little sheepish but didn't reply.

'I thought so.' Lorenza looked at Jack. 'I have a bad feeling about this,' she said. 'You and Tristan ...'

'What's on your mind, Jack?' asked Tristan, smiling. He knew his friend well and therefore realised at once where this was heading.

'There's something I would like to do. Right now. It's urgent.'

'What?'

'Somehow get on this hospital ship in Malta and have a nose around.'

'To see if the good professor is being held there? Is that it?' said Tristan.

'Yes.'

'And how are you planning to do that?' asked Lorenza.

'I have an idea, but I need Tristan's help.' Jack turned to Lorenza, sitting next to him. 'Do you think I could borrow your husband for a couple of days?'

'Do I have a choice?'

Jack shrugged. 'Why don't you ask him?' With that, Jack stood up and went to the bathroom.

As Jack walked past a table for two near one of the tall windows overlooking the canal, he noticed something out of the corner of his eye. Two women were holding hands and looking intently at each other. One of the women began to laugh, and it was that laugh that triggered something in Jack. He stopped, turned and looked at the woman.

It can't be, he thought and took a closer look. The woman must have noticed him staring at her, because she turned her head and looked at him.

'Izabel?' said Jack and slowly came closer.

At first the woman didn't say anything and just stared at Jack. Then her face lit up. '*Jack?*' she said and stood up. 'What are *you* doing here?'

'Looking for you, of course,' said Jack, covering his surprise with charm.

'Sure,' said Izabel and embraced Jack. 'Come, let me introduce you. This is my friend Teodora. Teodora, this is Jack Rogan.'

Teodora pointed to Jack's neck. 'Ah, the man with the cross. Pull up a chair and join us.'

Jack looked nonplussed. 'How did you know ...?'

'I told Teodora all about you and how you saved Soul,' said Izabel, a shadow of pain flashing across her beautiful face.

'Ah.'

'But what brings you here?' continued Izabel.

'The couple who run this place, Lorenza da Baggio and her husband, Tristan, are good friends of mine. They are just over there. Would you like to meet them?'

'Is that Lorenza da Baggio, the *Top Chef Europe* winner?' asked Izabel.

Jack nodded.

'Yes please! I would love to meet her.'

'I'll arrange it.'

Tristan had prepared a table on the terrace with a splendid view across to the Rialto Bridge, and everyone moved outside. Introductions were made and Tristan ordered champagne.

'When did you arrive?' asked Izabel.

'A couple of hours ago ... you?'

'Teodora and I have been here for two days. A little break ... we are leaving tomorrow.'

'Jack's on a mission, as usual,' Tristan cut in and poured some more champagne.

'What kind of mission?' asked Teodora.

Jack waved dismissively. 'Long story.'

'He's trying to find someone who went missing in London. A famous astrophysicist,' said Tristan.

Teodora sat up as if prodded with a hot poker and stared at Jack.

'What a fascinating life you lead, Jack,' said Izabel. 'Don't you think so, Teodora?'

'Absolutely,' said Teodora, recovering quickly. 'Would that have something to do with that scientist who collapsed in Westminster Abbey during the Hawking memorial service?'

'Ah, you know about that?' said Jack.

'It was all over the news.'

'Yes, that's him.'

'What's your interest in this?' Teodora asked casually. She watched Jack carefully and took another sip of champagne.

'He's the brother of my publicist.'

'Ah,' said Teodora.

By now, the restaurant was almost empty and it was time to call it a night.

'Well, this is it for me,' said Izabel, turning to Jack. 'We've had a long day, and I'm sure you did too.'

'Five am start in London. Then a meeting in Florence and a train trip to get here.'

'You must be exhausted.'

'I am, but delighted to see you. Pity you are leaving tomorrow ...'

'We have to, quite early. We are driving back to Teodora's home on Lake Como. Why don't you join us for breakfast and we can have another chat before we go?'

'Good plan. Let's do that.'

Jack stood next to Tristan on the terrace and was watching the vaporetti and water taxis going up and down the canal, lit up by the colourful lights of the restaurants dotted along the banks.

'What a magical place,' he said after Izabel and Teodora had gone to their room, and Lorenza had gone back to the kitchen to close up.

'Another drink?' said Tristan.

'No, thank you.'

'I don't know if you noticed, but there's something odd about Teodora,' said Tristan.

'What do you mean?'

'When you mentioned the professor, she looked quite shocked.'

'Can't say I noticed.'

'And there was something else ...'

'What?'

'Danger. The woman radiates danger.'

'In what way?'

'Difficult to explain. It's an aura. I've felt it many times in the past, and I felt it tonight. Strongly. She's like a coiled-up, venomous snake, ready to strike.'

Jack knew better than to dismiss Tristan's observation. He had been around Tristan too long and had witnessed his incredible intuition and insights often.

'I think she knows something about the professor she isn't telling us,' continued Tristan.

'How interesting. I wonder why ... There is something else you should know, Tristan.'

'Oh?'

'I'm about to call Lola and Isis.'

'Why?'

'To ask for their help. I don't think we can get on board this hospital ship without them.'

'How come?'

'I'll tell you in the morning. Now, let me go to my room and call them before I fall asleep right here. I also want to call Celia in New York and ask her to do some urgent digging for me. I want to know more about this surgeon in Malta who seems to be running the charity. He's most likely working for the Mafia. And I want to know more about this hospital ship, the *Caritas*. Celia has all the resources available at the paper to do this quickly. And she knows she's getting the story. So, that should be enough fuel for a little midnight oil.'

For a while Jack looked pensively at the silent facades of the palazzos lining the canal like sentinels of the past, frozen in time. 'And I can tell you, I can see a big story in all this, and it's coming towards us like a tsunami out of the dark,' he continued. 'The question is, are you ready for it, my young friend? Could be dangerous.'

Tristan took his time before replying. 'I said yes the moment you asked me,' he began quietly. 'I have a great life here, but I do miss our ...'

Jack put his arm around Tristan. 'I know,' he said. 'Everything has its price.'

'Don't tell Lorenza this, but I could do with a little time away from here. I need some of the old excitement; a new challenge of sorts, if you know what I mean.'

'I do, but be careful what you wish for,' said Jack and slapped Tristan good-naturedly on the back.

26

Venice: 23 June

Jack was an early riser. He was the first guest to make it down to breakfast on the terrace, its manicured hedges still covered in glistening morning dew. Venice early in the morning had a special magic. Because the mist hadn't quite lifted yet, only the tops of the buildings were visible, giving them a surreal, stage-like appearance, and the muffled traffic noise drifting up from the busy canal below sounded eerie, distant and distorted. Even the familiar bells sounded different, but Jack was oblivious to all this because he was busily working on his laptop.

The information he had requested about Professor Fabry and the *Caritas* had just come through. *Celia has been a busy girl*, thought Jack, impressed by the detail and the speed with which the material had been assembled. The more he read about Fabry, the more astonishing his story became. Shaking his head, Jack pushed the laptop aside, sat back and took another sip of coffee. *If only part of this is correct, this guy must be one of the most skilled surgeons on the planet*, he thought. *Genius, or monster?*

Because he was so focused on what he had just read, Jack didn't notice Izabel walking over to his table until she put her hand on his shoulder and bent down to give him a kiss on the cheek.

'Don't tell me you've been here all night,' she said and sat down next to him. 'A penny for your thoughts?'

'Feels like it. I've just read something amazing.'

'What about?'

'A surgeon who lives in Malta; Professor Fabry.'

'What's so special about him?'

'Have you heard of *Our Bodies,* the exhibition?'

'Isn't that about real human bodies that have been preserved in some unique way and used as anatomical exhibits?'

'Yes. The exhibition has been hugely successful; it's toured the world, attracting millions of visitors.'

'So, what's so interesting about it?'

'Well, the preservation process is called vivification. Fabry uses the proceeds from the exhibition, which is run by a charity registered in Malta, to operate a hospital ship, the *Caritas.* It's very much like the Mercy Ships organisation, which provides medical services in poor third-world countries.'

'But that's wonderful, isn't it?'

'Not entirely. There's a dark side to this. Fabry and the exhibition have been plagued by scandal and controversy from the beginning.'

'In what way?'

'It's all about the bodies – where they come from and how they've been obtained. Has there been donor consent, or have the bodies been obtained in some other, more sinister way?'

'What do you mean?'

'The *Caritas* operates mainly in Africa, often in war-torn countries with many casualties, and it has been rumoured that bodies have been sourced without consent for vivification and use in the exhibition. This has raised major ethical and legal considerations.'

'How ghoulish.' Izabel looked shocked.

'Fabry has strongly denied this, maintaining that all bodies have been sourced from willing donors, but he has never been able to prove it. And it gets worse.'

'In what way?'

'Fabry is a very gifted surgeon, albeit a controversial one. He has many critics. Some call him a genius because he has perfected certain surgical procedures and techniques that mainstream surgeons argued would never work. Others call him a charlatan. He has a clinic in Malta and specialises in organ transplants.'

'So?'

'There's been a lot of controversy about the origin of some of the organs. Their legitimacy has been questioned and he has been accused of trafficking in body parts. Some say the Mafia is involved.'

'Wow!'

'There's more ...'

'*There is*?'

'His background is murky and there is even a cloud hanging over his medical qualifications. Apparently, he changed his name for some reason. A few years ago, there was a rumour that he was a Kosovar doctor who was involved in an organ-harvesting racket during the Kosovo war. This was all part of a UN war crimes investigation, but it was closed down and didn't go anywhere.'

'This is all very fascinating,' said Izabel, 'but why are you so interested in this man?'

'Because I am going to meet him tomorrow.'

Izabel shook her head. 'You are an amazing guy, Jack. No wonder your books are so interesting and popular.'

'Enough of this,' said Jack and closed his laptop. 'Let's have some breakfast. Where is Teodora?'

'She's usually a morning person, but she looked so exhausted last night I've left her sleeping ...'

'Ah. I don't want to pry, but you two looked very happy last night ...'

'We are.'

'Have you known her long?'

'No. Just a couple of weeks. We just clicked. For the first time since Soul died, I feel so ...'

Jack put his hand on Izabel's arm. 'No need to explain. I'm very happy for you.'

'Thanks, Jack. Soul's death almost destroyed me.'

'Life goes on. Is Teodora also in the fashion business?'

'No. She lives in a fabulous house on Lake Como. We are going back there today. As you know, I live in Milan, so it's quite close.'

'What does she do?'

'I don't really know, but she's very rich. Serbian.'

'Hmm. Interesting ...'

'Her sister died quite recently. Totally unexpected. They were close. That's why we came here for a little break. I know all about grieving ...'

'Ah, here comes our breakfast,' said Jack, changing the subject. 'Fresh pastries and coffee. I'm in heaven.'

Teodora joined them for breakfast shortly after, and Tristan offered to take them in his beloved boat to the Piazzale Roma, which was close to the AVM Venezia car park.

'You are in for a treat,' said Jack. 'Wait till you see this boat. It's a classic. An original Riva Aquarama. It's been in several movies.'

'No way!' said Teodora. 'Does it still have the original Cadillac engines?'

Tristan looked impressed. Few people knew about that. 'Absolutely. Two hundred and fifty horsepower per engine. Top speed forty-five knots. We can outrun just about anything on the water here in Venice. The hull is sheathed in mahogany and varnished to show off the woodgrain,' boasted Tristan.

'Teodora has a Lamborghini Centenario roadster,' interjected Izabel. 'You should see her drive it. Like a pro, I tell you.'

'*You have one of those*?' said Tristan, turning to Teodora. 'Six-point-five litre, V12 engine, zero to one hundred in two-point-eight seconds?'

'That's the one,' said Teodora, smiling. 'Only forty Centenarios were built: twenty coupes, and twenty roadsters.'

'And you have one of them. Amazing.'

'We should just leave them to it, Izabel, what do you think?' said Jack and reached for another pastry.

'We should. She looks so happy,' said Izabel quietly. 'Coming here was a good idea. We must do it again.'

Half an hour later, they were on their way. Tristan manoeuvred the boat out of the mooring under the palazzo and through an iron-studded wooden gate, opening straight onto the canal. Teodora held Izabel's hand and was enjoying the deep throb of the powerful engines bouncing off the wet, moss-covered stone walls, promising speed and excitement.

'This little beauty was my wedding present,' shouted Tristan, accelerating through the busy morning traffic outside. 'It used to belong to Lorenza's late brother. Hold on; here we go.'

Tristan pulled out into the middle of the canal as Lorenza had taught him, found a gap in the traffic and put on speed. The powerful boat roared past barges, gondolas and vaporetti packed with waving tourists.

'What do you think?' said Jack, enjoying the spray hitting his face.

'Exhilarating,' replied Teodora, her wet cheeks glowing with excitement. With only centimetres to spare, Tristan steered the boat expertly past lumbering barges and massive bridge pylons.

'Are there no rules or speed limits here?' shouted Izabel.

'There are,' replied Tristan, 'but no-one cares. This is Italy, remember?'

Tristan made a sharp right-hand turn in front of a water taxi and slowed down. 'Almost there,' he said. 'Piazzale Roma is just over there.'

'Thank God,' said Izabel. 'I thought sitting next to Teodora in the Centenario was tough enough, but this is something else.'

'You've become an excellent driver, Tristan,' said Jack.

'Lorenza is a good teacher. She wouldn't let me take her baby out alone until she was sure I could manage. It took almost a year,' said Tristan, grinning.

Tristan pulled up at the vaporetto stop, which was totally illegal. Jack helped Izabel and Teodora with their luggage and they said goodbye.

'You must visit me sometime at Como,' said Teodora as they shook hands. 'And good luck with the professor.'

Tristan saw a vaporetto approach, horn blaring, and took off.

'Can we go somewhere quiet?' said Jack, 'I've something to tell you.'

'Sure. Let me show you my favourite caffetteria; it's on the way.'

Tristan turned into a quiet side canal and tied up the boat at a small pontoon. 'This is it,' he said and pointed to a few stools in front of a narrow opening in a wall. 'Best coffee in Venice; locals only.' Tristan seemed to know everyone at the caffetteria and ordered two lattes.

'I know you've been busy all night,' said Tristan, and pointed to two empty stools. 'So, what's the plan?'

'Lola says hello,' began Jack. 'Fancy a ride in the *Pegasus*?' *Pegasus* was Isis's private jet.

'Are you serious?'

'Absolutely.'

'When?'

'Tomorrow. Lola and Isis are flying in from London and picking us up at Marco Polo airport in the morning, and then we are flying to Malta to meet someone … intriguing.'

'Care to tell me about it?'

'Sure. I think I've found a way to get us on board the *Caritas* without having to break any laws.'

'How have you managed that?'

'Simple, really. With the promise of money. Always a sure thing. That's why I told you yesterday that we needed Isis to make this work.'

'How exactly?'

'The *Caritas* is operated by a charity. It has an interesting website and is always looking for donations. Isis is a well-known, high-profile philanthropist. She supports numerous charities worldwide. So, I asked Lola to get in touch with the man who runs the charity – Professor Fabry in Malta. She emailed him a letter last night – on Time Machine letterhead – and told him that Isis was interested in making a substantial donation. The letter also stated that Isis would be in Malta tomorrow and would like to visit the *Caritas* if possible, and meet the doctors running the operation before making a decision about a donation.'

'Clever plan,' said Tristan, nodding appreciatively. 'There was a reply already, I take it?'

'Professor Fabry will meet us personally at the airport in Malta and take us on board the *Caritas* to show us the ship. I suppose arriving by private jet helps. How's that?'

'Exactly what I expected from you, Jack. Another coffee?'

Teodora joined the A4 autostrada at Mestre and accelerated, giving the Centenario an opportunity to show what it could do.

'What an interesting man; Jack,' said Teodora, enjoying the extraordinary power of the V12 engine as the car flew past a convoy of trucks.

'He is. Very charming.'

'And you two now share a special bond.' Teodora pointed to Izabel's neck. 'The little cross. I could see it's very special to him.'

'It is. As I told you, it used to belong to his mother. He was in Africa just recently, trying to find out what happened to her all those years ago.'

'Fascinating.'

'He's always involved in unusual stuff.'

'Like trying to find that missing professor?'

'I suppose so. And there was something else that was really interesting he told me this morning. It's about a famous doctor in Malta, a surgeon.'

'Oh? What about him?'

'Apparently, he runs a charity supporting some hospital ship and has a travelling exhibition with real human bodies, would you believe. I think it's called *Our Bodies.*'

'I've seen it in the States. It's incredible. So, this doctor is behind that?'

'Yes, but apparently it's all very controversial.'

'How come?'

'Because of the bodies. Some say the bodies have been obtained without consent in Africa. He's got a clinic in Malta specialising in transplants and has been accused of trafficking in body parts.'

'How awful,' said Teodora, her interest aroused.

'It is. Apparently, he was investigated some years ago by a UN war crimes tribunal.'

'What about?'

'Somc organ-harvesting racket.'

'Where?' asked Teodora, barely able to speak.

'I think Jack said Kosovo, during the war. *Watch out!*'

Babu! thought Teodora, her head spinning. She almost lost control of the car and nearly hit a truck travelling next to her.

'What are you doing?' shouted Izabel.

'Sorry,' said Teodora, taking deep breaths to calm herself. 'I think we need a break.' She slowed down, changed lanes and took the next exit.

'Do you believe in destiny?' said Teodora.

Izabel looked at Teodora, surprised. 'Why do you ask?'

'Because I've just seen it at work.'

27

Professor Fabry's surgery, Malta: 23 June

Fabry slipped the phone into his pocket, sat back and looked pensively down to the harbour below. He could just see the *Caritas* tied up at the wharf. *This is it*, he thought. *We'll do it today. The first in vivo cephalosomatic anastomosis ever carried out.* The day he had been dreaming about for years had arrived. Everything was lining up perfectly. The last missing piece had just fallen into place. The phone call from the hospital he had just received had seen to that. A fisherman had been rescued from a sinking boat during the night. According to the doctor in emergency, the man was in a coma and on life support with severe, irreparable brain damage, and unlikely to see out the day. His family was by his side and discussions were in progress to turn off the life support. The man, in his early thirties and with a young family, was an organ donor.

Fabry had an arrangement in place with the doctors at the hospital regarding organ donors. He would offer generous payments to relatives and give assurances that the donated organs of the loved one would make a huge difference to someone in great need. Charming and persuasive, Fabry was always believable and usually got what he wanted.

A useless brain and an otherwise strong and healthy body, thought Fabry as he watched the *Caritas*. And down there was a useless, dying body with an extraordinary, healthy brain and a million-dollar price tag. *Perfect; exactly what we need.* All he had to do was bring the two together. And Fabry believed he knew exactly how that could be done. He rang his assistant and told her to meet him at the hospital to examine the dying patient. He wanted to make absolutely sure the body was suitable and compatible before making arrangements for the historic operation later that day.

Two hours later, Fabry met his team in his office. The dying patient at the hospital had turned out to be a perfect match, and fifty-thousand euros had eased the family's pain of losing the breadwinner. The wife had agreed to have the life support turned off and her husband's body donated. Fabry made arrangements to have the patient immediately transferred to his clinic. The life support would be turned off there when the time was just right. As a generous patron of the hospital, Fabry had no difficulty in making sure the hospital cooperated with this somewhat unusual arrangement, and they didn't ask any questions.

Fabry had two experienced operating teams at the clinic that specialised in transplants. He decided to use both teams for this operation because he knew it could last up to eighteen hours, involve several specialists, and most likely stray into uncharted territory. Fabry had often discussed the possibility of an in vivo head transplantation with his teams. In fact, some members of the team had already experimented with him on live humans, trying to perfect various aspects of the revolutionary procedure while they were working with him on the *Caritas* in Africa. On two occasions, some limited motor function had been achieved after an in vivo head transplantation. What had eventually killed the patients was rejection and other associated complications. But recent advances in immunology and especially stem-cell research had come a long way since then to overcome this problem.

One month earlier, Fabry had conducted a full-scale cephalosomatic anastomosis (CSA) rehearsal on two recently deceased cadavers, including neck-surgery, orthopaedic surgery, vascular surgery, gastronomical surgery and, of course, neurosurgery, in preparation for a live human CSA.

'My friends, I believe we will make history today,' said Fabry and paused to look at each of his team member's expectant faces. 'We have a patient on the *Caritas* right now with a perfectly healthy brain, but a severely injured body that is about to shut down. And then as you've heard, we have just received a dying patient in a coma who has a fatally damaged brain after almost drowning, but an otherwise strong, healthy body. The body has been donated with full family consent and the life support is about to be turned off, by us. This is exactly what we've been talking about and waiting for. This is the perfect scenario and I believe we must take advantage of it, right now. We are ready to do what has never been done before, but time is of the essence. You all know why. We will carry out the first in vivo CSA – today!'

Fabry turned around and pointed to the X-ray on the illuminated glass board behind his desk. It was the same X-ray of Stolzfus's head, neck and shoulders he had shown to Alessandro and Rodrigo two days before.

'The CSA will be conducted in the standard neurosurgical sitting position. We will sever the patient's head at the base here,' Fabry drew a line with his finger across the base of the neck, 'and then attach it to the new, healthy donor body we've just received. In short, we will carry out an in vivo head transplantation.'

At first there was silence in the room as Fabry's surprise announcement was beginning to sink in. While the team members were all familiar with the various steps involved in the revolutionary procedure, it had never been carried out on a live patient before.

'Don't look so surprised. I know we can do it. We have all the necessary consents in place, so you don't have to be concerned about that. If something does go wrong, there will be no repercussions.'

Fabry had a strict privacy policy in force at his clinic that ensured patient–donor anonymity and confidentiality at all times. The identity of the parties involved was never disclosed. 'We will split into two teams,' continued Fabry. 'One team will work on the donor body and keep it functioning after the head has been removed, the other will work with me to sever the head from the damaged body, which we will discard. As you know, this is the most critical part of the entire procedure. The cut has to be as precise as possible to ensure that the spinal cord can be reattached. I will use the latest diamond blade for this. Fusing the spinal cord of the head to that of the new body is the real challenge here; uncharted waters, I'm afraid, but definitely possible. Of course, we have to reconnect the head to blood vessels, the oesophagus and airways. With me so far?'

'Sure, but what happens after we've severed the head?' asked Fabry's assistant, a young doctor from Ghana.

'We know we can keep the unconscious, severed head alive by keeping it below fifty degrees Fahrenheit to avoid brain damage,' continued Fabry, warming to his favourite subject. 'Of course, the head will have to be hooked up to two pumps to provide continuous blood flow and oxygen while we get the donor body ready, and the head can be attached. However, we do know the brain can survive intact under deep hypothermia for up to an hour without blood supply. That should be sufficient time for us to complete all the vascular anastomoses and thus restore blood supply.'

Fabry paused. 'One other critically important issue I would like to mention right now,' he continued, 'is this: we have to make absolutely sure that we transfer the head with the larynx and the recurrent laryngeal nerves intact to preserve phonation. We must be able to communicate with the patient once he's been reawakened.'

'And then?' asked one of the other doctors.

'We then use an adhesive – polyethylene glycol – to connect the head with the spinal cord of the donor body, supported by an eleven-hole titanium plate held in place by vertebral screws. After that, the patient will be fitted with a cervicothoracic orthosis brace before we induce a coma for a month or so to allow blood vessels and nerve networks to regenerate. This is a complex, multi-specialty procedure. I firmly believe that present in this very room right now, we have all the necessary interdisciplinary expertise and experience required to succeed. And one more thing ... we will film the entire procedure to ensure we have a detailed record of everything. Time is obviously of the essence here. We better get started. This is a team effort. Any questions?'

It took several hours to prepare the operating theatre for the groundbreaking procedure. Surgery commenced at three pm and lasted just under eighteen hours.

Fabry was on a high. The patient was alive and had come through the complex surgery with his brain intact. In the end, everything had worked out better than expected. Professor Stolzfus had kept his old head and his memory, and had received a new, healthy body that had saved his life.

An old head on young shoulders, thought Fabry, smiling. He took off his surgical gown and went from team member to team member, congratulating each one personally. They had encountered several tense, nail-biting moments during the epic CSA, with the threat of failure and the shadow of instant death never too far away, but somehow ingenious solutions had been found, often in unexpected ways, to overcome each of the problems.

Exhausted but elated, Fabry went up to the roof terrace on top of the building. He wanted to be alone to savour the moment of personal triumph he had longed for so desperately, and for so long. *I knew it could be done*, he thought, drinking in the cool, refreshing air, which felt particularly invigorating after eighteen stressful hours in the operating theatre.

Now, everything he had done in the past, all the questionable practices, those early, dark horror years in Albania, the trafficking in body parts in league with the Mafia and the many reckless, experimental surgical procedures carried out on the *Caritas* without consent or regard for the patients' rights or wellbeing, seemed perfectly justified. Pioneers had to take risks, Fabry told himself. Guilt had been washed away by success, and conscience devoured by blind ambition and ego in the name of science and glory.

Never one to dwell in the past or be troubled by moral considerations, Fabry looked across to Fort Saint Elmo that divided Marsamxett Harbour from the Grand Harbour, and contemplated the future. *There could be a Nobel Prize in this*, he thought, letting the morning sun caress his face. A couple of hours' sleep in the office and then off to the airport to meet a legendary rock star with buckets of money. Life was good.

Little did Fabry know that at the very pinnacle of success, dark forces were gathering all around him, and the terrible day of reckoning was coming closer with relentless certainty.

28

Visit to the *Caritas*, Grand Harbour, Malta: 24 June

Pegasus landed at three-thirty pm sharp at Malta International Airport as scheduled, and taxied to the designated bay reserved for private jets. Lola, who was flying the plane, had arranged a brief stop at Venice Marco Polo Airport to pick up Jack and Tristan on the way.

Fabry watched the sleek aircraft make a sharp turn and come to a sudden stop. Moments later, the door opened and Isis appeared at the top of the stairs. Looking like a glamorous movie star in a striking Valentino creation, she adjusted her dark glasses and Chanel headscarf and looked around. Aware that she was being watched by the officials waiting at the bottom of the stairs to check passports, she began to walk slowly down the stairs, one step at a time, careful not to get her insanely high heels caught in the steel grooves.

'Welcome to Malta,' said Fabry, extending his hand. 'Is this your first visit?'

'No. I've been here before,' said Isis, giving Fabry her best smile. 'We shot a promotion video here at Fort Saint Elmo a few years ago for my album, *Siege*. We used the Siege of Malta as our theme. I love history, you see, and I incorporate historical themes into my music and my performances. The video was very popular.'

'If you are interested in history, you've certainly come to the right place,' Fabry continued breezily. 'There's probably more history on these islands than any other place in the Mediterranean I can think of. You must allow me to show you around, if you have time,' he prattled on.

'I would like that very much, thank you, but first we should visit the *Caritas*. After all, that's the reason we are here ...'

'Of course. Everything is ready. We'll go there straight away. The whole of the *Caritas* is at your disposal. I'm sure you'll be impressed.'

'I have heard a lot about the *Caritas* and the wonderful work you do. That's why I wanted to see it for myself. But first, allow me to introduce you to my friends ...' Isis pointed to Jack and Tristan standing behind her.

'What did I tell you?' whispered Jack, squeezing Tristan's arm. 'She's got him wrapped around her little finger already. All we have to do is tag along and watch.'

Tristan nodded and stepped forward to shake Fabry's hand. As he looked briefly into Fabry's eyes, a strange feeling came over him, like he was looking into a murky, bottomless pool full of dark promises, drawing him in. *A well of accusing souls*, thought Tristan, recognising the unsettling feeling he had experienced before, usually in situations of acute danger. The feeling became stronger as he touched Fabry's cold hand. *This man has killed, many times. We have to be careful!* On this occasion, Tristan, who could hear the whisper of angels and glimpse eternity, glimpsed only misery and horrible death.

Fabry took his visitors straight to the *Caritas* to meet the captain and the medical team. Everyone had been fully briefed, knew the drill and was ready to impress the famous visitor. It was all about loosening the purse strings. Used to such occasions, the medical team knew exactly what to do and say. After all, the *Caritas* was run by a charity and depended on donations to keep it afloat, literally, and Fabry was an experienced fundraiser who knew exactly which levers to pull.

As soon as they stepped on board, Tristan was momentarily overwhelmed by signals and impressions assaulting his finely honed senses from all sides, like a tide of pain screaming for attention.

Jack noticed that Tristan appeared to be uncomfortable and in a daze. 'What's wrong?' he asked, reaching for Tristan's arm to steady him.

'This place. I've never felt anything quite like this before,' replied Tristan, shaking his head.

'What do you mean?'

'Difficult to put into words.'

'Try.'

'Pain. And evil.'

'Sounds promising.'

'You don't seem to understand. Horrible things have happened here. And there's something else ...'

'What?'

'Danger.'

'Great. Just what we need.'

'We have three fully equipped operating theatres on board,' said one of the doctors showing them around, 'and a ward of fifty beds—'

'We have heard a lot about your famous travelling exhibition – *Our Bodies*,' interrupted Jack, changing the subject. 'Can you tell us something about that?'

'We use that exhibition to raise money for our charity, which as you know runs this ship,' said Fabry, stepping in. He clearly didn't like the question and appeared keen to move on.

'I'm absolutely fascinated by the concept,' said Isis, picking up the thread. 'As I understand it, you are using *real* human bodies ...'

'Yes, we are.'

'And you prepare them right here, on this ship,' said Jack, watching Fabry carefully, 'using a unique, revolutionary procedure? I think it's called vivification?'

Fabry looked at Jack, instantly on guard. *How does he know all this?* he wondered. 'Where did you hear that, if I may ask?' he said casually.

'We have our sources,' said Isis, answering the question for Jack. 'Before I make a substantial donation, I like to find out as much as possible about the recipient. With so many imposters and so much corruption around, it is often difficult to find the genuine article. And then of course, there's my own reputation to think of, if you know what I mean ...'

'I certainly do,' said Fabry, smiling. 'And what would you consider a substantial donation?' he added casually.

'A million pounds, say, over three years?' said Isis, baiting the hook.

Fabry looked impressed. Donations like this didn't come along too often, and the cash-strapped charity could certainly do with the money. He realised that to secure the donation, he had to somehow impress his visitors and give them confidence in the charity's work.

'May I speak frankly?' said Jack, realising the right moment had arrived to introduce the subject of real interest.

'Of course,' replied Fabry.

'The exceptional work the *Caritas* is doing in third-world countries is well known and needs no further explanation. We have no problem with that. What does cause us some concern, are the rumours ...'

'What kind of rumours?' interjected Fabry, frowning.

'Rumours about the bodies that are being used in the exhibition and for anatomical teaching purposes. As you no doubt know, allegations are circulating that many of the bodies have been obtained without consent, or worse. Before Isis can put her name to a donation, we have to be satisfied, you know ...'

'I completely understand,' Fabry cut in again. 'I can assure you, all of the bodies we use have been donated with full, informed consent.' Fabry paused, collecting his thoughts. He realised that more was needed to put this controversial matter to rest and get Isis over the line, and the best way do to that would be by providing a convincing, current example, or better still, a demonstration.

Fabry, a quick lateral thinker, was already coming up with a possible solution to this thorny problem.

'Normally, we do not take visitors behind the scenes, so to speak, and show them how we prepare the bodies, or how we obtain them,' he said. 'This is a delicate subject. As you can imagine, there are ethical and legal issues involved here.'

'Exactly our point,' Jack said.

'However, in this case, I am prepared to make an exception,' continued Fabry. 'But please keep all this confidential,' he added, lowering his voice in a conspiratorial tone.

'Of course,' said Isis.

'Only yesterday, we received the body of a fisherman who was badly injured at sea and drowned,' said Fabry. 'His body has been donated to us by his widow. We are preparing it right now for vivification. Parts of the body will be used in our exhibition and for anatomical teaching purposes in universities. I will show you the consent documents and the body, and explain the procedure. I will also show you our extensive donor registry. Would that help?'

'It certainly would,' said Isis.

'I hope you are not squeamish.'

'No, we are not,' said Jack, making eye contact with Tristan.

'In that case, please follow me.'

Fabry led the way down into the bowels of the ship. A large space next to the engine room had been converted into what looked like a laboratory with large vats, freezers and all kinds of strange-looking pipes and equipment. It reminded Jack of an exotic boutique brewery he had visited recently in France. Several technicians in white coats were bent over a steel table lit up by strong floodlights from above.

'This is where we prepare the body,' said Fabry and pointed to the table. 'Come, have a look.'

'What happened to the head?' asked Jack, looking at the naked, headless cadaver.

'The head was badly damaged and had to be removed,' said Fabry. 'We will use the rest of the body, in this case the heart and the lungs, in situ. We have a specific request from a university in the US for this. They will use the specimen in their anatomy classes. Much more effective than dissecting recently deceased cadavers. And, of course, reusable.'

Tristan stared at the headless body. Certain images were floating into his mind's eye with alarming clarity, but none of them had anything to do with drowning. He could see a shaved head being removed from the body and carried away. It wasn't damaged, but seemed strangely alive. He also saw something else: a bullet entering the body. Tristan took a step closer and looked at the side of the chest. He could just make out a bruised area that looked like a small wound. Tristan closed his eyes, trying to focus to see more, but the image drifted away, leaving behind a strange feeling of sadness and loss.

'So, what's the first step,' asked Isis, 'in preserving the cadaver?'

'There are four steps in this process,' said Fabry, sensing that his visitors were impressed and interested. 'Fixation, dehydration, forced impregnation in a vacuum, and hardening. But before we do any of that, one of our surgeons will be dissecting this body to expose the chest cavity as requested by the university. After that, the specimen will be placed in a bath of acetone in that vat over there.' Fabry pointed to a large, cylinder-shaped container. 'This will draw out the water.'

Tristan turned to Jack. 'It's him,' he whispered. 'I can feel it.'

'What do you mean?'

'This is Stolzfus.'

'You can't be serious!'

'I am. Have a close look at the right side of the chest. Bullet wound.'

'Jesus!'

Fabry continued to explain the complex vivification procedure in detail, addressing each of the four steps. It was obvious that he was passionate about the subject. 'I will now show you the consent documentation and our donor register if you like. It's upstairs.'

Fabry turned to the technicians standing around the table. 'All right chaps, we'll do the rest in the morning. You can finish now, but leave the body where it is.'

One of the technicians pulled a plastic sheet over the headless body and took off his gloves.

'Thank you,' said Jack. 'Absolutely fascinating. I think we have seen enough here.'

Used to reacting quickly under pressure – a skill acquired from his days as a frontline war correspondent – Jack made a snap decision. He waited until no-one was looking, stooped down a little, quietly dropped his phone on the floor and then kicked it under the vat as he went past.

Fabry smiled as he looked at the table in front of him. He could just see the outline of the truncated body under it. *Thank you, Professor.* A million dollars US for the transplantation, and a million pounds in donations from a gullible rock star with more money than sense. *Not bad for a day's work,* he thought. And the rest of his body would be immortalised for teaching purposes tomorrow. No waste here! Fabry then turned around and followed his visitors up the stairs.

29

Port of Valletta, Malta: 24 June, evening

Fabry was in his element. After leaving the *Caritas*, he insisted on showing his guests some of the main historic attractions of Valletta before they were due to return to the airport and fly back to London. He first took them to the Upper Barrakka Gardens to show them some of the city's old fortifications, with splendid views of the Grand Harbour and across to the towns of Vittoriosa, Cospicua and Kalkara. Then he took them to the spectacular St John's Co-Cathedral, ending up at the Grand Master's Palace in the centre of town.

'This spectacular palace was commissioned by Master Fra Pietro del Monte in the sixteenth century as a residence for the Knights of Malta and contains one of my favourite battle scenes,' enthused Fabry. 'Come, let me show you.' Fabry led the way to the staterooms on the upper floor.

'I know you will like this,' he said to Isis. 'Especially with your interest in the Great Siege of fifteen sixty-five.' Fabry pointed to a series of murals depicting dramatic battle scenes of the knights fighting the Ottoman Turks.

'And then I must show you a portrait of the Grand Master Jean de Valette, the founder of our city. It's right here ...'

Jack turned to Tristan standing next to him. 'Let's do it now,' he whispered. Tristan nodded.

Jack had briefly discussed his improvised plan with Tristan when they had found themselves momentarily alone in the cathedral.

'*Oh no*!' said Jack,' holding up his little notebook with the rubber band around it he used for taking notes. 'I don't believe it!'

Fabry looked at him, surprised. 'What's wrong?'

'My phone; I must have dropped it. I usually carry it in my back pocket with my notebook. Damn!'

'Where could you have lost it, do you think?' asked Tristan, right on cue.

'I had it on the ship, I'm sure of it. When I pulled out my notebook to jot down something about that fascinating vivification process ... I'm sure it was still in my pocket.'

'Could you have lost it then?' asked Fabry, trying to help. The last thing he wanted was for the visit to end on some sour note, like losing a silly phone.

'Yes, that's quite possible, come to think of it. So much was going on ... the phone sometimes gets caught in this rubber band here. Stupid, I know.'

'Let's go back to the *Caritas* and have a look,' said Fabry. 'It's on the way.'

'Could we?' said Jack. 'I feel naked without my phone. And losing it would be such a nuisance ...'

'No problem. I know what it's like. I'll call the captain right now.'

Jack winked at Tristan and smiled.

The captain and one of his officers were waiting for them on top of the gangway. Isis had decided to stay in the car and Fabry stayed with her to keep her company.

Perfect, thought Jack. So far everything had gone exactly to plan.

'We already had a quick look around in the lab,' said the captain. 'Unfortunately, nothing.'

'Could we please go back there? I'm sure I had it with me then. What if we call my number? That could help. If we don't find it there, perhaps we can quickly retrace our steps?'

'Good idea,' said the captain. 'Follow me.'

Illuminated by dim, flickering ceiling lights at the end of a dank corridor, the deserted laboratory looked eerie, the strange shapes of the vats and the many pipes casting crazy shadows across the slippery steel floor.

It's just as we left it, thought Jack as he looked at the polished steel table with the covered body. He walked over to the table and stood directly next to it. 'I stood right here when I took out my notebook,' he said. 'Tristan, could you please call my number?'

'Sure.' Tristan pulled out his phone and dialled Jack's number. Within moments, a dial tone – a cheerful rendition of *Waltzing Matilda* – could be heard coming from somewhere in the lab.

'It's here!' cried Jack, pretending to be surprised. The captain and the officer turned instinctively towards the sound, listening to see where it was coming from. Tristan quickly stepped forward and stood between them and Jack, who by now was bending over the table. As the phone kept ringing and it became apparent that the sound was coming from somewhere under one of the large vats, the officer went down on his hands and knees to have a closer look.

Now! thought Jack, and quickly reached his left hand under the plastic sheet covering the body on the steel table. He could clearly see the outline of the body under the sheet and dug his fingernails deep into the soft flesh of the neck stump, tearing away as much tissue as possible. It was all over in a second and Jack quickly withdrew his hand.

'Here it is,' said the officer, and handed the phone to Jack.

'Thank you so much, gentlemen,' said Jack and turned off the phone. 'I feel such a fool.'

As he walked towards the waiting car, Jack held up his phone. 'Found it,' he said.

'Excellent,' replied Fabry, pleased. 'That didn't take too long.'

'No, it didn't. But it sure made a difference. I don't know how to thank you.'

One hour later, *Pegasus* was in the air. Isis opened a bottle of champagne and Tristan carefully wrapped a clean bandage around Jack's left hand, making sure the tips of his fingers were completely covered to avoid contamination. This was a precaution suggested by Cesaria to preserve the integrity of the tissue sample.

'I don't know how you keep coming up with these ideas, Jack, but I must say, this was absolutely ingenious,' said Isis, letting the cork pop. 'This deserves a toast.'

'I knew we needed proof. Tristan's intuition may be enough for us, but I don't think it would be enough to convince the Squadra Mobile, or MI5 for that matter.'

'I suppose not.'

'But they do understand DNA. And that's what we've got. Right here under my fingernails.'

'Classic defence wounds stuff,' Tristan cut in. 'Very effective.'

'Do you know how many murderers have been convicted because their victims had some of their attacker's DNA under their fingernails?' said Jack.

'Very clever,' said Isis and filled the glasses.

Jack had called Cesaria in Florence as soon as they were in the air and explained the situation. Lola had changed *Pegasus*'s flight plan and they were due to land in Florence in just over two hours. Cesaria would meet them at the airport and take Jack straight to forensics to extract the tissue from under his fingernails for DNA testing.

Jack had also called Rebecca in New York and told her the sad news. In all probability, her brother was dead, and his mutilated body on the *Caritas* in Malta. However, to make absolutely sure that was the case, her DNA was needed for comparison. Rebecca said she would catch the first available flight and meet them in Florence.

'I can't tell you how long it's been since I've had so much fun,' said Isis, lifting her glass. 'Thanks for making me part of the team.'

'Never a dull moment with Jack,' said Tristan. 'How I've missed this!'

'So, you don't mind bumming around with an incorrigible rascal then, guys?' said Jack, grinning.

Isis lifted her glass. 'Let's drink to that. To our very own incorrigible rascal. Cheers!'

30

Chief Prosecutor's office, Florence: 26 June

As one of the most tenacious and successful Mafia hunters still alive in Italy, Chief Prosecutor Grimaldi thought he had seen just about everything and that nothing could surprise him. Yet, when he looked at the whiteboard behind his desk he used for making notes and working out connections in ongoing cases, he had to admit that the latest intelligence regarding certain activities involving the Giordano family in the alleged abduction of Professor Stolzfus, seemed almost too far-fetched to be believed.

Grimaldi had read the report prepared by Cesaria Borroni, acting chief superintendent of the Squadra Mobile, several times overnight. Borroni was one of his finest officers and certainly not one known for speculation or hasty conclusions. And Jack Rogan had proved himself many times over as a reliable and trustworthy, albeit unconventional, source. Grimaldi had worked with Jack on the notorious Gambio case two years ago and would trust him with his life.

When Grimaldi didn't understand something, he always followed a golden rule: he asked the officers involved to explain it to him in person.

Grimaldi listened to the familiar bells of Santa Maria del Fiore announcing the hour, and smiled. *There will be a knock on the door just about now*, he thought and stood up.

Cesaria looked at Jack and Tristan standing next to her. 'Ready?' she said. 'This is it, boys.'

Jack nodded. Cesaria knocked and opened the door.

'How is it when you two come to see me, remarkable things seem to happen?' said Grimaldi. He walked over to Jack and embraced him.

'It's his charm,' said Cesaria. 'Villains find it irresistible.'

'Ah. That must be it. And this must be Tristan,' said Grimaldi, letting go of Jack. 'I've heard a lot about you, but we've never actually met. *Ars Moriendi* and Lorenza da Baggio?'

'And I've heard a lot about you, sir. In fact, for the last day or so, Jack hasn't stopped talking about you,' said Tristan. He stepped forward and shook Grimaldi's hand.

'Take a seat and let's start from the beginning,' said Grimaldi. 'You can take it I've carefully read your report, but I want to hear it all from you.'

Cesaria had expected this and was ready.

'As we know, Professor Stolzfus was abducted in London on fifteen June. All indications so far seem to suggest that the Mafia was behind it; the Giordanos, to be precise.'

'Why?' asked Grimaldi.

'Frankly, we don't know.'

'That worries me. The Giordanos do nothing without a good reason. Certainly not something so high profile and risky.'

'That worries me too, but there it is.'

'Please continue.'

'You will remember what first alerted us to a possible Mafia connection was that satellite photo showing the *Caritas* and *Nike* meeting in the middle of a storm off the coast of France?'

'It's right there,' said Grimaldi and pointed to the photo stuck on the whiteboard. 'But we searched the *Nike* in Monaco and found nothing.'

'Wiped clean.'

'Perhaps.' Grimaldi sounded sceptical.

'That's where the matter rested until now,' continued Cesaria.

'Ah, yes. Jack and Tristan's adventures in Malta,' said Grimaldi, shaking his head. 'Unbelievable stuff, I must say. Private jet, famous rock star and all.'

'You better hear the rest from Jack,' said Cesaria, ignoring the remark, and sat back in her chair.

Jack described the recent trip to Malta with Isis and Tristan, and how and why the meeting with Fabry had been arranged to gain access to the *Caritas*. He described the discovery of the grisly headless body in that strange laboratory, and told Grimaldi how Tristan's intuition and the discovery of a possible gunshot wound had led them to believe it could be Stolzfus.

'Let me get this right, Jack,' said Grimaldi. He lit a small cigar and let the smoke curl towards the open window. 'Tristan here sensed something when he looked at the headless corpse, and that was the reason you pursued the matter further?'

'Yes. Tristan has certain psychic powers. I have seen them at work many times. It would be a mistake to dismiss them as fanciful nonsense. I certainly don't.'

'And neither do I,' Cesaria cut in. 'As you will see in a moment, Tristan's intuition led to certain *incontrovertible* evidence about that body's identity.'

'All right. Let's hear it.'

'You would have read in the report how I obtained that DNA sample,' continued Jack.

'I certainly have. It read like something out of a movie: Bruce Willis meets science fiction.'

'But true nevertheless,' said Cesaria. 'It is a reliable chain of evidence.'

'We could do with a little imagination like that in the Squadra Mobile from time to time. What you think, Cesaria?' said Grimaldi. 'When we get really desperate.'

'Unfortunately, I have no officers of Jack's calibre on the force who could pull off something like that.'

'I suppose not. Go on.'

'Professor Stolzfus's sister arrived yesterday and gave us a DNA sample. A forensic comparison has been made with the DNA extracted from the cadaver tissue under Jack's fingernails.'

'And?'

'Here's the report,' said Cesaria. 'I just received it.' Cesaria opened her briefcase, took out an envelope and placed it on the desk in front of Grimaldi.

'What does it say?'

'Perfect match: brother and sister. The body belongs to Professor Stolzfus. There can be no doubt about it.'

For a long moment there was utter silence, only broken by the sounds of the familiar church bells chiming in the distance and the tourist hum drifting up from the busy street below. Grimaldi stubbed out his cigar in the ashtray and looked at Jack. 'Extraordinary,' he said, shaking his head. 'I just don't understand it. Something is missing here. Something big, and that worries me. This isn't like the Mafia at all.'

'There's a lot more behind all this,' said Tristan, speaking for the first time. 'I could feel it on the *Caritas*.'

'Can you be more specific?' asked Grimaldi.

Tristan shook his head. He realised this was not the time or the place to disclose what else he had felt in the presence of Stolzfus's body. That would have to wait for another more suitable occasion because if he were to disclose it now, he knew for certain he wouldn't be believed.

'So, where to from here?' demanded Grimaldi. 'What do you suggest, Cesaria?'

'So far, we haven't told MI5 or the CIA anything about this. Before we do, we should try to secure the body. Once we do that, we have all the evidence we need to go public with this story and blow it sky high. As you can imagine, this would be an international sensation and put huge pressure on the Giordanos and on Malta generally. Something we've been waiting for ...'

'And how do you suggest we do that?'

'You would have read in the report that the body was being prepared for vivification,' said Jack, stepping in.

'Ah yes, that too sounded quite bizarre,' said Grimaldi. 'More science fiction?'

'The process is complicated, takes a long time – several months in fact – and will be carried out on the *Caritas*. It is therefore unlikely the body will be moved as long as we don't rock the boat and spook those involved. That's why keeping a lid on this for the moment is so important. Fabry told us the *Caritas* is about to return to Africa on another mercy mission. The ship's departure appears imminent ...'

'What's on your mind?' asked Grimaldi.

'I think we should ask the coastguard to intercept the vessel and search it,' said Cesaria.

'On what grounds?'

'Illegal trafficking in body parts would be a good start. Possible immigration breaches, people-smuggling – the whole crew appears to be African – perhaps even slavery. In any event, if we can identify and secure the body and link it to our investigation, we would have sufficient grounds, surely.'

'And how would we identify the body?'

'Jack and Tristan could help us there and guide us to the body on board the *Caritas*. With the body secured, we have everything we need to expose a monstrous crime. And with Jack identifying the body, we have the chain of evidence that would stand up in court. The international pressure would be enormous, and we stay a step ahead of MI5 and the CIA. If we can implicate the Mafia in this and put the spotlight on Malta, it would be a big coup, don't you think?'

Grimaldi nodded. He liked that angle. As usual, Cesaria was pressing all the right buttons. Pursuing the Mafia had become far more complicated recently, and a huge international case like this could be just what was needed to close in on the Giordanos and smash their hold on Florence. 'Let me think about it.'

'Is that a yes or a no?' asked Jack.

'It's a maybe.'

'We haven't much time.'

'I realise that. But enough time for an early lunch perhaps? Usual place across the road?'

'I thought you'd never ask,' said Jack, and stood up.

31

Somewhere off the coast of Sicily: 28 June

Jack had always found waiting the most difficult thing to do. Restless by nature, enforced inactivity was incompatible with his personality and grated on every fibre of his usually sunny and optimistic disposition, making him irritable and cranky. Yet, enforced inactivity was precisely what had been thrust upon them by Grimaldi's decision to give them only forty-eight hours before he would have to disclose the location of Stolzfus's body to MI5 and the CIA. He said beyond that, he couldn't justify sitting on this vital piece of information any longer without causing an international incident.

What that meant was that unless the *Caritas* left Malta within that timeframe, intercepting the ship to secure Stolzfus's body would not be possible. Jack had spent most of his time at the Squadra Mobile HQ, hounding Cesaria and her colleagues as they waited for news from the port authorities in Valletta about the supposedly imminent *Caritas* departure.

'You know we are running out of time,' said Jack, sipping his fifth cup of coffee that morning.

'I am just as anxious as you,' replied Cesaria, running her fingers nervously through her hair. 'But there's nothing further we can do. The coastguard vessel is standing by in Palermo. From there, it's only a short distance to the intercept point off the coast of Tunisia. Everything is ready.'

The only one who appeared calm was Tristan. He had assured them several times that morning that all would be fine. Rebecca had decided to stay in Florence and wait for the outcome. If her brother's body was in fact recovered, she would take it home for burial. She had gone to a museum to take her mind off the disturbing subject and the tense waiting. With their participation successfully completed, Isis and Lola had returned to London.

Moments later, one of Cesaria's colleagues, a young woman, burst into the room. 'Just had a call from the harbourmaster. The *Caritas* will sail at three pm this afternoon and head for Gibraltar.'

'Okay, guys, this is it,' said Cesaria. 'We're on! We have five hours before the *Caritas* is due to leave Valletta. Let's get to the airport.'

'See? I told you so,' said Tristan, reaching calmly for his jacket.

'He can be very infuriating at times,' said Jack, following Cesaria to the door.

'Yes, being right can be infuriating, but also helpful, don't you think? You have no idea what Grimaldi had to go through to get this approved. I know he made all kinds of promises about the Mafia. Thank God it's coming off.'

'Look at it this way: if we pull this off, Florence and its law enforcement agencies will be in the spotlight – worldwide. A very favourable one.'

'And this will put the wind up the Mafia here, for sure,' added Cesaria. 'And that is precisely what Grimaldi is counting on. The Mafia hates the spotlight just like a frightened rabbit hates headlights.'

Jack had kept Celia informed as promised, and she was standing by in New York to break the story. She hadn't left her desk in two days, which had kept her editor on edge, as he could sense a big story in the making. As a high-profile, multi-award-winning journalist at the *New York Times*, Celia was well known for her tenacity and legendary contacts around the world. When asked how she was able to get access to people and stories others could only dream about, and open doors that remained firmly shut to her competitors, she answered with only one word: *trust*. And it was because Jack could trust her implicitly that he had kept her in the loop.

This was an excellent arrangement that had worked well for them both in the past. Both understood the power of the media and how to keep a step ahead of the establishment, in this case the CIA and MI5. This added further excitement and danger to the unfolding story.

The flight from Florence to Palermo on a plane provided by the Italian navy took less than two hours, and they were on board the powerful coastguard vessel, the *Alberto Condotti*, by two pm. The captain had been fully briefed and had received his orders. They would intercept the *Caritas* off the Tunisian coast on its way to Gibraltar and search the vessel. This would happen sometime during the night, which would further add to the drama.

The *Alberto Condotti* had taken up position just off the western tip of Sicily and was waiting for the *Caritas*. At that point, the distance between Sicily and the Tunisian coast was less than three hundred kilometres. It was a clear night with good visibility and the sea was calm.

'There she is,' said the captain and pointed to a cluster of lights on the horizon. He put down his binoculars and gave some orders. It was just after one am.

'What happens now?' asked Cesaria.

'We sail towards the *Caritas* and should intercept her right here.' The captain pointed to a spot on the map in front of him. 'We will make radio contact shortly and ask her to slow down because we are coming on board. We will then ask her to stop altogether, which will take a little time. Then we launch one of our inflatable boats and board the vessel. That's the protocol.'

'And if they don't comply?' said Jack.

'We have a protocol for that too,' said the captain, smiling. 'But I'm sure it won't come to that. Ships are searched in these waters all the time. The asylum-seeker and people-smuggling problems here are very serious, some would say out of control. The *Caritas* will assume we are coming on board for that reason.'

'And you would like us to come with you?' asked Jack.

'Of course. Apparently you will show us where to find the body. We carry body bags and have a morgue on board, so transporting the body won't be a problem. You will be supplied with suitable clothing and, of course, life jackets. These are my orders.'

'Understood. I suppose we better get ready then?'

'Yes, you should do that. One of my officers will explain everything.'

'Thank you, Captain,' said Cesaria. 'You have been most helpful.'

'My job.'

Everything unfolded exactly as the captain had described. The *Caritas* slowed down and then stopped completely to allow the coastguard to come on board.

Caritas's captain waited on deck with two of his officers and watched the boarding party come up the temporary gangway that had been lowered. He didn't look particularly concerned, as the *Caritas* had been searched before in these volatile waters. In fact, on one occasion a year ago, the *Caritas* had been involved in the rescue of African asylum seekers whose boat had capsized during a storm just off the Libyan coast.

Everything changed when the coastguard officer in charge advised the captain that he had information to suggest that the body of Professor Zachariah Stolzfus, who had recently been abducted in London, was on board the *Caritas* illegally.

The captain became quite agitated. He protested and strongly denied the accusation and assured the officer that he had all the required paperwork to explain everything that was carried on board, and that included bodies and body parts that were regularly treated on board as part of the charity's *Our Bodies* exhibition program conducted by Professor Fabry of Valletta. That's when he noticed Jack standing behind the officer, and paled. At first he hadn't recognised him in the dark-blue waterproof jacket and life vest, the coastguard baseball cap making Jack look like one of the boarding party.

'Good morning, Captain,' said Jack and stepped forward to lead the way. 'We meet again, and so soon. Thank you for your help the other night. It made such a difference! Please follow me, gentlemen.'

Not surprisingly, the laboratory next to the engine room was deserted. The polished steel table in the middle was empty, and the truncated body was nowhere to be seen. The entire lab looked tidy and appeared to have been scrubbed clean recently, as parts of the floor were still wet.

Cesaria walked up to Jack. 'What now?' she asked.

As Jack looked around the dimly lit chamber, he remembered Fabry's explanation of the complex vivification process. *The acetone bath. He must be in the acetone bath*, he thought, searching for the large, cylinder-shaped container Fabry had shown them. That's when Jack noticed Tristan walk across to one of the large vats in the corner. Tristan pointed to a blue light flashing on a panel. 'He's in here,' he said calmly.

'Are you sure?' asked Cesaria.

'Let's find out.'

The captain, who had overheard the exchange, walked over to the coastguard officer in charge and began to protest. 'Yes, there are body parts in there being treated right now, but we have a register that can clearly account for them all. Everything we do here is strictly legitimate.'

The officer held up his hand. 'Please open the vat.'

'This is preposterous! I can't do that! It would ruin the process.'

'Please open the vat,' repeated the officer.

'All the technicians are asleep.'

'Wake them.'

'I will lodge an official complaint about this. I can assure you, everything we do here is strictly legitimate,' the captain said again, looking indignant.

'Just like the rendezvous with the *Nike* in the middle of a storm off the coast of France the other day?' said Jack.

The captain's jaw dropped, a look of utter disbelief on his face. 'I ... I have to make a phone call,' he stammered.

'The phone call will have to wait,' said the officer. 'You have to wake one of the technicians and open the vat – right now! One of my men will go with you.'

The captain and the officer returned a few minutes later with a sleepy looking man in white overalls. The man walked across to the vat and punched some numbers into the blinking panel. As soon as the blinking stopped, the lid opened all by itself. Jack climbed up a ladder attached to the vat and looked inside. 'He's in here,' he said, covering his nose. The potent fumes drifting out of the vat were overpowering.

'What I want you to do right now,' said the officer, addressing the technician, 'is to get that body out of there and place it on that table.'

'That isn't easy. This is an acetone bath ... I will need help and it will take some time.'

'Get help. We are not leaving without it.'

'This body was donated to us in Valletta a few days ago,' said the captain. 'It belongs to a fisherman who drowned. I have all the necessary documentation to prove it.'

'Show it to us by all means, but my decision stands. You can take this up with the relevant authorities in due course,' said the officer, remaining firm.

Cesaria walked over to Jack. 'Are you absolutely sure this is Stolzfus?' she whispered, looking concerned.

'I am. I saw the bullet wound, but the body has been changed somewhat since I saw it last.'

'What do you mean?'

'The chest has been opened, exposing the heart and—'

'How bizarre,' interrupted Cesaria. 'But you're sure it's him?'

'I am.

'I hope you're right because if you're not, this case will collapse and we are finished.'

'Don't worry. Didn't you hear what Tristan said? That should put your mind at rest. He's never wrong about matters like this,' said Jack, a smile creasing the corners of his mouth.

'A psychic assurance by someone who can hear the whisper of angels and glimpse eternity? Great! That should really go down well when I have to explain what happened here,' said Cesaria.

'Relax. Can't you see? You have the spirit world on your side. It doesn't come any better.'

'And I thought Tristan was infuriating ... Ha!' mumbled Cesaria, pretending to be cross, and turned away.

32

Villa Rosa, Lake Como: 29 June

Teodora looked at Izabel lying next to her and gently stroked the hair of her sleeping lover, careful not to wake her. *Why is it,* thought Teodora, *that the darkest hour of my past is trying to rob me of the happiest moments of the present?*

After Izabel had unwittingly provided that fatal clue about Fabry on their way home from Venice – causing Teodora to almost crash the car – Teodora had immediately instructed her Ukrainian hacker to investigate Fabry. What he had come up with in such a short time was astonishing and filled Teodora's heavy heart with a mix of incredulity – and elation.

It was a saga of ingenious deception and meticulous reinvention of a man who had gone to extraordinary lengths to hide all traces of his criminal past in Kosovo during the war, only to re-emerge as a celebrated surgeon living the high life in Malta. Apparently, he had been able to achieve this with the help of the Mafia, who had used his services for many years to conceal criminal activity. This involved the disposal of bodies without leaving a trace, treating gunshot wounds without the victim having to go to hospital, and even providing face transplants to give certain people a new appearance and identity.

But despite all this, and despite forged identity papers, degrees and qualifications, and even a hushed-up name change – from Dritan Shehu to Ambert Fabry – rumours of a shady past had haunted Fabry ever since he had been investigated by a UN war crimes tribunal after the Kosovo war.

At one stage, investigators had come close to exposing him as the notorious 'Dr Death' who had been responsible for the killing of countless Serbs for body-parts trafficking after the Kosovo war. Two witnesses had come forward who were prepared to testify, but they were both killed in a village on the Albanian border just as they were guiding investigators to gravesites that would have provided vital evidence in the case against Fabry. After that, the investigation collapsed and the case was closed. It was rumoured the Mafia had been behind the killings.

Fabry went to ground and disappeared for a few years to work on the *Caritas* and let the accusing dust settle. It was during that time that he had established the controversial, but highly successful, *Our Bodies* venture, backed and financed by the Mafia.

The information provided by the hacker was convincing. Teodora was left in no doubt that she had finally found her elusive Dr Death who had so brutally murdered her parents during that fateful night in Kosovo and harvested their organs to sell on the black market. Even the change of name from Dritan Shehu to Ambert Fabry was ingenious: *Ambert* meant 'light' in German, and the Albanian name *Dritan* meant the same – light. The choice of Fabry as a name was also significant, because Wilhelm Fabry, who had lived in the sixteenth century, was often referred to as the 'Father of German surgery' and was one of Fabry's heroes and role models.

Since that moment, Teodora couldn't get the spectre of Fabry out of her mind. Even in her sleep, dark thoughts haunted her, robbing her of much-needed rest and preventing her from exploring feelings of long-lost love that had so unexpectedly been rekindled by meeting Izabel. Every waking hour was now dominated by violent visions of retribution. Nadia's recent death only added more fuel to this all-consuming obsession that taunted Teodora's mind and raced through her body like a fever.

Teodora was convinced that fate had finally dealt her a winning card to face her past and set things right, and nothing and no-one would stand in her way to follow what she believed was her destiny. She looked at her sister's dramatic death as part of the price that had to be paid for that card she now held in her hand, shaking with rage.

Exhausted, Teodora closed her eyes. She was desperately trying to get a few hours of much-needed sleep before daybreak, when her mobile on the bedside table began to ring. Instantly awake, Teodora sat up and answered the phone. It was Alessandro.

'Sorry about the hour,' he said, 'but we have a crisis.'

Teodora got out of bed and walked out onto the terrace overlooking the silent lake bathed in moonlight. 'What kind of crisis?' she asked.

'Once again, I have good news and bad—'

'Good news first,' interrupted Teodora impatiently. She was getting tired of Alessandro's annoying way of approaching important subjects. Rather than dancing around them, she preferred a more direct, businesslike approach.

'Stolzfus has survived the critical operation and is in recovery.'

'Prognosis?'

'Apparently quite good. He should live—'

'But that's great news, surely?'

'It is, but what happened yesterday isn't.'

'What happened?'

'It's all still a little vague, but the *Caritas* was raided yesterday at sea and searched by the Italian coastguard.'

'And why is that a problem?'

'Because what was left of Stolzfus's body was on board and has been taken away by the coastguard for analysis ...'

'*What?*' Teodora almost shouted. 'Are you serious? How could that have possibly happened?'

'I still don't know much about this, but Professor Fabry is behind it all ...' Alessandro sounded vague and defensive, and Teodora realised at once that things hadn't gone quite as planned in Malta.

'Needless to say, Rodrigo is furious.'

'Understandable. I'm a little confused here. Where is Stolzfus now?'

'Still in Malta. In a coma under Fabry's care. Apparently, it will take quite some time for Stolzfus to come out of the coma. Only then will the full effect of the surgery be known.'

'Where does that leave us now?'

'That's the reason I called. There's a bigger problem.'

'*There is?* Tell me.'

'A senior police officer of the Squadra Mobile here in Florence was present during the raid and seemed to know a lot about Stolzfus and the abduction in London. And there was another person present as well, a man who seemed to know even more ... The Squadra Mobile has been investigating us for years. They obviously believe we are somehow involved and that is, as you can imagine, a problem for us.'

'I can imagine.'

'I have just spoken to Rodrigo. He blames Fabry and wants to cut across this mess and take over ...'

'In what way?'

'He has a proposal. A plan, and it involves you ...'

'How?'

'He wants to meet us here in Florence as soon as possible. He will tell us then. This is really urgent. Can you get here?'

'Sure. What about Aladdin and Silvanus?'

'At this stage, Rodrigo asked only for you.'

'I'll drive down first thing this morning. It shouldn't take me more than four hours. I'll be there around nine, depending on the traffic.'

'Great; thanks,' said Alessandro, sounding relieved. 'See you when you get here.'

Teodora looked pensively across the still lake she loved so much. The first light of the new day was beginning to creep hesitantly across the sky, banishing the pale moon. A strong believer in destiny and fate, Teodora felt calm and composed. She was certain that destiny had shown her the way to Fabry, and realised this would culminate in the ultimate showdown she had been dreaming about for such a long time. Her parents' murder would be avenged, of that she was now sure, and her promise fulfilled. And only then would she finally have peace and be able to turn away from what was left of Spiridon and begin a new life. Hopefully, she thought, with Izabel.

Teodora walked back into the bedroom and for a long moment watched Izabel sleeping peacefully in her bed. Careful not to wake her, she bent down, kissed her tenderly on the forehead and then tiptoed out of the room to get ready for her trip to Florence.

33

Giordano villa, Florence: 29 June

It took Teodora just under four hours to drive from Lake Como to Florence. Traffic was light that early in the morning – she had left just after five am – and that had allowed her to put the Centenario through its paces without getting booked for speeding. Feeling exhilarated and relaxed after the drive, Teodora got out of the car, walked past the security guards and the snarling dogs, and as she headed towards the imposing entrance of the Giordano villa, the door opened and Alessandro came out to meet her.

'That was fast,' he said, kissing Teodora on the cheek. 'Raul is here already, having breakfast with my father. I wanted to catch you before we go inside.'

'Oh? Why?'

'Dad is very uneasy about all this.'

'How come?'

'I suppose you haven't heard. It's about the article ...'

Teodora looked puzzled. 'What article?' she asked.

'The article in the *New York Times* about Stolzfus ...'

'Is there a problem?'

'Come in and see for yourself. It's a bit of a bombshell!'

'Sounds intriguing. How about some breakfast first?' said Teodora. 'I'm starving.'

'You've come to the right place. Follow me.'

Rodrigo and his host were sitting at a large wooden refectory table in the kitchen, which was Giordano's favourite place in the villa. Giordano's mother was slicing bread and Giordano was serving coffee.

'Smells good,' said Teodora. 'I could kill for a cup.'

'Coming from you, that sounds dangerous,' said Giordano, smiling, and handed Teodora a cup. 'Great to see you; sit down.'

'Thanks for coming so quickly,' said Rodrigo, but I believe we have to act fast if we want to stay in this game,' he added, looking serious.

'What kind of game?' asked Teodora, putting some thinly sliced prosciutto and provolone on a thick slice of bread that was still warm.

Without saying a word, Rodrigo pushed a copy of the latest *New York Times* across the table towards Teodora. Teodora looked at the headline on the front page, and paled:

> ***Missing scientist turns up as headless corpse***
> *The headless corpse of world-renowned scientist Professor Zachariah Stolzfus was recovered by the Italian coastguard from the* Caritas, *a hospital ship operating out of Malta. The grisly discovery ...*

Aware that everyone was watching her, Teodora put down her half-eaten sandwich and read the rest of the sensational article, the ticking of the large clock on the kitchen wall the only sound cutting through the tension in the room. The article by Celia Crawford read like the script for a James Bond movie. It began with the alleged poisoning of Stolzfus in Westminster Abbey during the Hawking memorial service, followed by the dramatic ambulance attack resulting in the professor's abduction and disappearance. It even referred to the *Nike* and *Caritas* meeting in the middle of a hurricane, and provided an aerial photo, which added to the drama.

It then went into considerable detail describing the night raid on the *Caritas* and the recovery of the headless body by the Italian coastguard, culminating in the formal identification of the body in Florence by Stolzfus's sister. Acting chief superintendent Cesaria Borroni of the Squadra Mobile in Florence was specifically mentioned as a reliable source, linking the abduction to the Mafia. Jack – referred to as an international celebrity author-cum-private investigator working for the rich and famous – was also mentioned as someone who had provided valuable information and leads to the Italian authorities about a possible Mafia involvement in the matter.

The article then touched on a broader picture, with veiled allegations of MI5 and CIA incompetence, possible conspiracies and cover-ups by the Metropolitan Police in London, culminating in the woeful failure to protect one of the world's leading scientists while he attended the memorial service of a famous colleague in Westminster Abbey.

The article concluded with this question:

How is it possible that the police in Florence and a private investigator appear to know more about this shocking matter than MI5, the CIA and the Metropolitan Police combined? Who is responsible for this heinous crime, and what steps are being taken to bring the perpetrators to justice? Justice and decency deserve an answer!

'Wow!' said Teodora and put down the paper. 'This will certainly put a chilly wind up law enforcement agencies around the world.'

'It will do much more than that,' said Rodrigo. 'It will put enormous pressure on MI5 and especially the CIA, to mobilise and solve this case quickly. This article is a great embarrassment, and Americans in particular cannot tolerate loss of face or criticism. Take it from me, all stops will now be pulled out and huge resources invested in this.'

'I agree,' said Giordano. 'And the Squadra Mobile here in Florence, and Chief Prosecutor Grimaldi in particular, will use this case to make life very difficult for us. And that is a major concern.'

'How did all this blow up so quickly, and why right here in Florence?' asked Teodora. 'How did the Squadra Mobile get its hands on all this information?'

'Good question,' interjected Alessandro. 'We believe it's all because of one man.'

'*One man?* Which man?' asked Teodora.

'Jack Rogan, the celebrity author.'

'Are you serious?'

'Absolutely,' Giordano weighed in. 'We have come across him before. He was involved in the Gambio matter a couple of years ago right here in Florence. In fact, he was present in the church, standing right next to Chief Prosecutor Grimaldi and myself when Gambio was shot. He was in the thick of it all right, helping the police.'

'What's his interest in all this?' asked Teodora.

'He's a bit of an enigma,' said Rodrigo. 'Incredibly well connected. He's a former journalist turned writer who follows up big stories and then writes books about them. He's done this very successfully for quite some time and has been involved in some high-profile cases over the years. Notoriety seems to follow him everywhere. He loves controversy and the limelight. He has even collaborated with the *New York Times* on several occasions, and was instrumental in breaking a number of sensational stories. Just like this one.'

Teodora didn't mention that she had met Jack by chance just a few days ago in Venice. She thought it was better to keep this to herself for the moment. 'So you think he's supplying information to the police here in Florence?'

'We know he is,' said Giordano.

'How do you know?' asked Teodora.

'I make it my business to know. We have our sources. Reliable ones. In the Squadra Mobile and in the prosecutor's office. That's how we stay a step ahead of those who want to harm us and destroy our business. That's how we survive.'

'And that is precisely what we have to do right now,' said Rodrigo. 'We must stay a step ahead of the game if we want to conclude this delicate project successfully. And I believe we can do just that, but we have to act quickly.'

'And how do you propose to do that?' asked Teodora.

'Through information. It always comes down to information,' said Rodrigo. 'And most important of all, we have to buy time.'

'Why? I don't follow,' said Teodora.

'You will in a moment,' said Giordano, turning to Rodrigo. 'Tell her!'

Rodrigo picked up the paper and held it up. 'I believe everything in here has come from one man: Jack Rogan. He appears to be in the middle of this and the source of intelligence flowing to the police here in Florence, and to the *New York Times* in the US. He even turned up in Malta with a rock star who claimed to be interested in making a large donation to the Caritas Charity a few days ago, and met with Fabry. We now know that was all a pretence. What Rogan was really doing was gathering information. We need to know what he knows, where it's all coming from, and why he's so interested in all this. But most important of all, we must stop the flow of information.'

'How?' asked Teodora.

'That's where you come in,' replied Rodrigo. 'As you can imagine, Fabry is very embarrassed about the Stolzfus body fiasco. He wasn't supposed to keep what was left of it, but to destroy it and make it disappear – not preserve it for an exhibit. For whatever reason he didn't do that, and we have just seen the consequences of his mistake.'

Rodrigo took a sip of coffee and looked directly at Teodora. 'Fabry is desperately trying to make up for the disaster. He has done a remarkable job with the head transplant. No question about it. I believe there isn't another surgeon alive who could have done that. We have come such a long way in this, and it would be a great tragedy to see it all fall apart at this late stage.'

'So, what's on your mind?' asked Teodora.

'We have to take Rogan out of the game.'

'How? You want us to *kill* him?'

'No, it's more complicated than that. He's worth much more to us alive than dead.'

'Please explain,' said Teodora.

'Fabry is prepared to waive his fee for the transplant – about one million US – which you agreed to pay. In return, we want you to abduct Rogan and deliver him to Fabry in Malta for interrogation. I understand he's an expert in interrogating people.'

'He sure is that,' said Alessandro. 'He's helped us out several times before. His methods are a little, let's say unusual, but his results are outstanding, and as you can imagine, he's very keen to get his hands on Rogan.'

'Where's Rogan now?'

'That's the best part: right here in Florence.'

'I'll have to talk to the others.'

'Understood.'

'When do you want it done?'

'As soon as possible, but no later than tomorrow. Rogan could leave here any time ...'

'And how are we supposed to get him to Malta?'

'All taken care of,' said Alessandro, glad to be able to contribute. 'The *Nike* is on her way to Livorno as we speak. We'll take Rogan to Malta on the *Nike*. It's about six-hundred and sixty nautical miles. Should take us no more than a day and a half at most. Giacomo is standing by.'

Teodora nodded, trying to stay calm. She was finding it difficult to control her excitement. Not only had destiny shown her the way to Fabry, it was now delivering him to her as well. All she had to do was convince Aladdin and Silvanus to take on the assignment, and the rest would fall into place all by itself. Once in Malta, she would be able to deal with Fabry on her terms.

'And what about Stolzfus and the rest of our agreement?' she asked. 'We have to hand him over to you in Morocco, alive and with his mind intact. That's the deal as I understand it.'

'It is, but that's why we need time,' replied Rodrigo. 'According to Fabry, Stolzfus isn't ready to be moved just yet. He cannot even be moved out of his surgery at this stage without risking, well, death. Once he's well enough to travel, you deliver him to us in Morocco as agreed, and my client will then take it from there. But to be able do that safely, we obviously need time and the authorities off our backs. We can't afford a raid on Fabry's surgery. Not right now. But no-one suspects that Stolzfus could possibly be alive after his body has been found. Not even the resourceful, intrepid Mr Rogan. That's our best protection for the time being.'

'Isn't Fabry going to be investigated, especially now after the *Caritas* raid?' asked Teodora.

'That's very likely, but he has a lot of powerful friends in Malta who can protect him and cause delays, at least until we can move Stolzfus.'

'I understand,' said Teodora. 'And if we do all this and deliver Stolzfus to you in Morocco, our contract is at an end and we get paid in full?'

Rodrigo looked at Giordano sitting at the other end of the table.

Giordano nodded.

'Half now, the other half when Stolzfus comes out of his coma and begins to talk to us,' said Rodrigo.

'In that case, I have to make a couple of calls,' said Teodora and stood up, the thought of Fabry finally being within her grasp making her tremble with excitement. The moment she had been dreaming about for such a long time was coming closer.

34

Florence: 30 June

Normally Teodora would have walked away from an assignment that allowed so little time for planning and preparation, but the situation she found herself in wouldn't allow that. Caution had become a victim of necessity. At least Alessandro had been able to provide some of the much-needed information and logistical support on the ground required to put a rough outline of a workable plan together, but Teodora knew that most of the essential steps would have to be improvised and crucial decisions made on the run, which was always fraught with danger.

At the same time, she also knew that she had three vital elements working in her favour: she had met Jack before and knew what he looked like; she had obtained his phone number from Izabel the night before; and, most important of all, she had the element of surprise on her side, with a team of highly trained professionals to back it up.

After the meeting at the Giordano villa the day before, Teodora had immediately contacted Aladdin and Silvanus and explained the situation. As expected, they agreed to do the job and arrived in Florence by train during the night. They checked into a small hotel near the railway station and waited for the morning before linking up with Teodora.

Jack, Tristan and Rebecca were all staying in a hotel close to Squadra Mobile HQ. Cesaria had arranged this for convenience, as most of their time had been spent on police business and, sadly, in the morgue. With Alessandro's help, Teodora had been able to secure a room for herself in the same busy hotel, popular with tourists. This was a key component of her daring plan, and the only way she could see the ambitious assignment had a chance of success before Jack caught the train to Venice later that morning, as she knew he had planned.

Teodora had arranged for Aladdin and Silvanus to meet her at her hotel at five am. This would be their one and only opportunity to discuss the plan in person before it had to be implemented. They all knew this wasn't ideal, but it was the only way forward in the circumstances. They also realised that since that sensational article in the *New York Times* that had trained the international spotlight firmly on the good professor and his disappearance, the entire Stolzfus assignment was now under a cloud of uncertainty and hung in the balance by a thread. But they had carried out delicate assignments on the run before and knew the risks.

Just before five, Teodora went down to the hotel foyer to meet Aladdin and Silvanus and took them back to her room on the first floor.

'We came as soon as we could,' said Silvanus.

'I can see you didn't sleep much,' said Aladdin and pointed to the bed, which hadn't been used.

'No, I didn't. I spent the little time I had to put together something I believe will work.'

'All right; let's hear it,' said Silvanus and put his Glock on the small table by the window.

'As I've told you, Jack Rogan, the target, is staying right here in this hotel on the third floor. He is due to check out this morning and catch a train to Venice with a friend, Tristan, who is also staying here. The good news is, I've met them both before – socially. Entirely by chance, a few days ago. They have no inkling about my involvement in the Stolzfus matter and therefore will not suspect anything.'

Silvanus looked at Teodora, impressed. 'You are full of surprises as usual. And this is going to help us?'

'It sure will.'

'How?'

'Sit down, boys, and I'll tell you.'

Silvanus and Aladdin listened in silence as Teodora took them step by step through every detail of her daring plan, right down to phone signals and seating arrangements in the breakfast room she had checked out the night before. It all came down to split-second timing and, of course, a little luck. But Teodora was convinced that luck favoured the brave.

'So, what do you think, guys?'

'We are flying by the seat of our pants and taking considerable risks, but I like it,' said Aladdin. 'I think it can be done.'

'So do I,' said Silvanus, who particularly liked the million-dollar windfall that came with the unexpected assignment. As seasoned professionals, they all thrived on a challenge and liked to consider themselves some of the best in the business. And as this was most likely to be their last assignment, the huge publicity surrounding the Stolzfus matter had a particular cat-and-mouse appeal; egos always played a big part in high-profile cases like this.

'All right. Check phones and watches,' said Teodora, 'and then it's almost time for me to go down to breakfast and start the show. You two will, of course, stay right here and wait for my signal.'

Aladdin and Silvanus looked at each other and nodded, the intoxicating adrenaline rush had already begun.

A few minutes after seven, Teodora sat down at a small table in the back of the breakfast room with a clear view of the entrance and ordered coffee. She knew Jack was an early riser and expected him to be one of the first to come down to breakfast. She was right. Ten minutes later, Jack and Tristan appeared and the hostess who was waiting at the door showed them to a table.

'Before Rebecca comes down, there's something I have to tell you,' said Tristan and ordered some tea.

'Oh? What?'

'Something that has troubled me for some time now. I could hardly sleep last night. I couldn't get this music out of my head. And then there was something else ...'

'What kind of music?'

'I've worked out what it is.'

'Tell me.'

'Tchaikovsky's *Lost Symphony.*'

'Okay, and this caused you to lose sleep?'

'It did, because the first time we saw that disfigured body on the *Caritas*, I heard the same music. And then there was this strange feeling ...'

'What kind of feeling?'

'I wasn't going to mention this before because it's quite absurd. But when we went with Rebecca yesterday to view the body at the morgue, there it was again, only stronger and more compelling.'

Jack reached for his cup and looked at Tristan. He had seen that troubled expression before. It told him that Tristan was wrestling with something he couldn't quite explain, but realised it was important and therefore had to be shared. It had to do with his intuition and his psychic powers, which from time to time seemed to overwhelm him. The blessing struggling with the curse.

'Care to tell me about it?'

'Only if you promise not to laugh.'

'Promise.'

'I firmly believe Stolzfus isn't dead ...'

'Do you realise what you are saying? Based on what? We got the wrong body, is that it?'

'And there is something else ...' said Tristan, sidestepping the question.

'What?'

'Danger.'

'What kind of danger?'

'It's about you, and it's imminent!'

'*About me?* Tell me later. Here comes Rebecca now.'

Teodora was carefully watching Jack's table and biding her time. When the three of them got up and went to the buffet, she made her move.

Teodora walked calmly across to the buffet table, took a plate and positioned herself next to Jack. 'Ham looks nice, don't you think?' she observed casually, and put some ham on her plate.

'Teodora!' said Jack, surprised, 'What are you doing here?'

'I could ask the same question, but of course I know the answer. You've been in the news and all over the papers.'

'Is Izabel with you?'

'No, she stayed in Como. I drove down yesterday; urgent business.'

'You're by yourself then?'

'Yes.'

'Come and join us.'

'I will; thank you.'

'You remember Tristan,' said Jack and pointed to Tristan standing next to him.

'Of course. Our charming host from Venice.'

'And this is Rebecca Armstrong, Professor Stolzfus's sister,' continued Jack, lowering his voice. 'She's here to—'

'I know,' interrupted Teodora and walked back to the table with Jack. 'It's in all the papers ...'

Tristan was carefully watching Teodora sitting opposite. She was making small talk that to him appeared somewhat contrived. Her mind and attention were somewhere else, and she seemed distracted and tense. Tristan was trying in vain to interpret the signals radiating from her. All were vague and confusing except for one: *danger*.

Jack was oblivious to all this and appeared to be enjoying himself. *Now*, thought Teodora and reached into her pocket to press the send button on her mobile, sending a message to Silvanus to make the phone call. Moments later, Jack's phone began to vibrate in his breast pocket.

Teodora held her breath. She knew this was the tricky moment. Would Jack answer the phone or ignore it?

'Excuse me,' said Jack, 'I must take this. Travel arrangements ...' Jack pulled out his phone and the ringing stopped, but he saw that he had a message: 'I have information about Stolzfus. Come to your room now,' it said, 'alone.'

Teodora watched Jack out of the corner of her eye. *This is it*, she thought, realising that the next few seconds would define the entire project. Success or failure on a knife's edge. It all depended on whether she had read Jack's character correctly.

Jack slipped his phone back into his pocket and put down his serviette, his mind racing. *What the heck*? he thought and stood up. 'Please excuse me, I'll be back in a moment,' he said and hurried to the door. Teodora smiled. Curiosity had won the day. Tristan watched Jack walk away from the table, a feeling of dread making him choke.

Jack stepped out of the lift on the third floor and looked around. The corridor seemed deserted. *It's a bloody hoax*, he thought and was about to turn around and get back into the lift, when he felt something hard pressing against his back.

'This isn't my finger, but a silencer on a Glock,' said a voice speaking softly. 'Get back into the lift.'

Jack did as he was told. He glanced at the tall man standing next to him. Another man was standing behind him, pressing the gun against his back. 'We are three friends going down to the car park,' said the man standing next to him. 'Behave accordingly if you don't want the gun to go off; clear?'

Jack nodded.

'Good,' said the man and pressed the button.

The lift went straight down to the basement without stopping. The car park was deserted. 'The BMW over there,' said the man next to Jack. 'Get into the back seat.'

Teodora could feel her mobile vibrating in her pocket. It was the prearranged signal telling her that everything had gone according to plan. 'A little more of that delicious fruit, I think,' she said, smiling at Tristan, and stood up. An icy shiver of fear raced down Tristan's spine as he watched Teodora walk towards the buffet table. Instead of stopping to get another plate, she kept walking towards the exit.

The black BMW headed east along the Viale Filippo Strozzi to join the SGC Firenze-Pisa-Livorno towards Livorno. Jack was sitting in the back seat next to Silvanus. Aladdin was sitting in the front next to

Teodora, who was driving. The three of them were speaking Albanian, which Jack couldn't understand. They covered the ninety kilometres to Livorno in just over an hour and boarded the *Nike* a short time later. Alessandro's men were waiting for them at the harbour to dispose of the BMW they had sourced earlier and couldn't be traced. A short time later, the *Nike* was on her way south, sailing towards Malta.

35

On the *Caritas*, Main Harbour, Malta: 1 July

'We meet again, Mr Rogan,' said Fabry cheerfully as he swept into the brightly lit laboratory deep in the dark bowels of the *Caritas*. 'And so soon. An unexpected pleasure, I must say.' Wearing a white coat and surgical gloves smelling of chloroform, he walked over to the steel table in the middle of the chamber and looked at Jack. It was the same table on which only a few days ago Stolzfus's truncated body was being prepared for vivification.

Barely able to move because of the tight leather straps tying him to the table and cutting into his bare chest and legs, Jack was lying on top of the table, naked, and blinded by the bright lights trained on him from above.

'I wish I could say the same,' said Jack, squinting at Fabry.

'As you have shown such a keen interest in our vivification process, we thought it would be only fair to allow you to experience it firsthand, so to speak.'

'What do you mean?'

'We have just recently lost a precious specimen, which was in an acetone bath over there. It was confiscated by the Italian coastguard. But you know about all that don't you, Mr Rogan? You were right here when it happened,' continued Fabry, looking serious. 'We need an urgent replacement – and you look like a perfect specimen to me.'

'You can't be serious!' croaked Jack, who had barely slept a wink since his abduction in Florence and the twenty-hour sea voyage on the *Nike* from Livorno to Malta, locked in a tiny cabin without windows.

'But I am; deadly serious. Before we begin, let me explain the main steps of the process to you again ...'

'This is insane,' protested Jack, squirming on the table.

'You are right. It may be a little too much information because after the first step, you will be in no condition to follow the others.

Once you are placed into that acetone bath over there, well ... do I make myself clear?'

Over the years, Fabry had perfected the dark art of interrogation by using fear and suggestion as his main tools, and had elevated this technique to such an effective level that even the most stubborn and determined subjects capitulated in the end, answering all questions willingly and truthfully. An experienced medical practitioner, Fabry realised that using psychoactive drugs like scopolamine, ethanol, midazolam, or sodium thiopental as a 'truth serum' was notoriously unreliable and therefore ineffective, and what the Mafia needed was accurate information – quickly.

Fabry had come up with a much better way. As all the information to be extracted was locked in the mind of the 'subject', it was only logical that one should focus on the mind when trying to obtain that information. Fabry's approach varied from subject to subject and was tailored to suit the personality and character involved, but his approach and technique were the same.

First, the subject was deprived of sleep for at least twenty-four hours before the interrogation began, to weaken any resistance and thus make the mind more pliable. In essence, this had already happened to Jack during his uncomfortable sea journey.

In Jack's case, Fabry had decided to use the vivification process and the very location of the interrogation, namely the intimidating laboratory on the *Caritas* where the actual bodies were being prepared, as his main 'suggestion tools'. The fear of fear was far more effective than fear itself.

'You may not have noticed, but there are several people present who are looking at you right now,' said Fabry. 'They are standing over there, watching.' Fabry pointed over his shoulder. 'Shortly, some of them will ask you questions. You have a choice. You can decide to answer the questions, truthfully of course, or decide to stay silent. If you choose the latter I will begin the vivification process, which I can assure you will not only be excruciatingly painful, but irreversible. The same applies if you lie or try to deceive by giving wrong answers. I'm sure you understand. So in the end, you see, it's all up to you.'

Standing in the shadows, Teodora was watching Fabry going through his chilling descriptions, preparing Jack for the horror to come. As soon as she had set eyes on Fabry earlier that evening, she realised at once that she was looking at the man who had butchered her parents all those years ago. The face, the voice, the bearing of the man all aligned with the memory of the terrified girl who had witnessed it all. Fabry's face was etched into Teodora's memory, never to be erased.

Alessandro had arrived earlier that evening by plane with Rodrigo, and both had questions of their own. They wanted to hear what Jack had to say about the Stolzfus matter in general, and about MI5, the CIA, and especially the Squadra Mobile and the perceived involvement of the Mafia. But what caused Teodora to tremble with excitement was the phone call she had received earlier from Giordano in Florence, who of course had the ultimate say in the Stolzfus assignment as he was the client who had engaged them and paid the bills. Even his son didn't know precisely what Spiridon had been instructed to do and why, although Teodora suspected that Rodrigo was in on all this.

But what even Giordano couldn't possibly have known was that Teodora had an agenda of her own as far as Fabry was concerned. Ironically, what Giordano had instructed her to do played perfectly into her hands. Not only would she be able to wipe out the monster who had haunted her all these years, but she would get paid for doing so.

Just before they had entered the laboratory, Teodora had spoken briefly to Aladdin and Silvanus about their latest instructions. Being thorough professionals, they accepted the instructions without question and were standing by to carry them out. As usual, Teodora was in charge and would direct the matter.

'Before we begin,' said Fabry, 'let me show you the implements I will use in preparing you for vivification in case you do not answer the questions. First, this is the scalpel I will use to make an incision here, and here.' Fabry held up the scalpel and pointed to an area on Jack's chest, the touch of the cold steel making Jack's skin creep.

'And then, I will have to remove your eyes. To do that, I will use this here ...'

Fabry continued for a few more minutes, explaining the process with clinical efficiency, which only added to the horror. This was of course quite deliberate and intended to intimidate and terrify the subject into submission, and prepare the way for the questioning to come.

Jack listened in silence and evaluated the situation, his mind racing. He had been in tight spots before and knew that keeping calm and focused was essential if he wanted to get through this alive. He had no doubt that the best way forward was to cooperate fully from the beginning and answer all the questions. After all, he wouldn't place anyone in danger, and as Stolzfus was dead, anything he was about to say or disclose couldn't harm him either.

'So, Mr Rogan, are we ready?'

Jack just stared at Fabry without saying anything.

'Very well, let us begin.' Fabry lifted his hand, which was obviously a signal. Moments later, music drifted through the cold chamber, softly at first, but becoming louder by the second, adding drama and a level of excitement to what was about to happen.

Good heavens, thought Jack. *Tchaikovsky's* Lost Symphony! *It's what Tristan kept hearing ... What does it all mean, I wonder?*

Then the questions began. First, Alessandro wanted to know what Jack's involvement and interest was in the Stolzfus matter. Jack explained that Rebecca Armstrong – Professor Stolzfus's sister who was running his publishing company in New York – had asked for his help after she had found out that her brother had disappeared.

The rest of the questions were all about MI5, the CIA and the Squadra Mobile, and what they knew or suspected about a possible Mafia involvement in the Stolzfus abduction. Jack answered all the questions willingly and accurately, and explained how the Mafia had first come to the attention of MI5 because of the *Nike* leaving Portsmouth on the very day Stolzfus had been abducted. He then mentioned the *Nike–Caritas* aerial photo during the hurricane, which had become the catalyst in the Mafia connection as both vessels had strong Mafia ownership links.

'And were you the one who supplied information to the *New York Times*?' asked Rodrigo.

'Yes, I was,' answered Jack. 'Celia Crawford, the journalist who wrote the article, and I have collaborated on several high-profile cases before.'

'And have you also been supplying information to the Squadra Mobile in Florence?' asked Alessandro.

'Yes, I have. I have worked with the Squadra Mobile before, especially acting chief superintendent Borroni and Chief Prosecutor Grimaldi.'

'The Gambio matter?'

'Yes.'

'And are they aware that there may be a possible link between the Stolzfus abduction and the Giordano family?'

'Yes, they are. The *Caritas* and Professor Fabry here have come to their particular attention for obvious reasons, and the recent discovery of Professor Stolzfus's body provided all the proof needed to make the necessary connection. It put the matter beyond doubt.'

'And MI5 and the CIA are aware of this?'

'They are. In fact, Major Andersen, who is in charge of the CIA investigation, arrived in Florence yesterday.'

'Do you know what the next steps are in the investigation?' asked Alessandro.

'Yes. I believe a raid on Professor's Fabry's surgery here in Valletta is imminent, and Professor Fabry and the captain will be investigated about the Stolzfus body found on the *Caritas* and certain other matters involving the Giordano family and the Mafia in general. The Squadra Mobile is particularly interested in the drug supply chain from South America and the role the *Caritas* and her crew have played in smuggling drugs into Malta.'

After that, there were no more questions.

'Well, that seems to be it,' said Fabry, and reached for his scalpel. 'I think it's time we begin the vivification process.'

'What do you mean?' croaked Jack, staring at the blade only a few centimetres from his face.

'You are about to find out—'

'I have a question, *Dr Shehu*,' interjected Teodora.

Fabry froze and slowly put down the scalpel. Then he turned around and looked at Teodora, who was pointing a gun at him.

'I-I don't understand,' he said.

'Oh, I think you do. I would like to take you back to the twenty-fifth of October 1999. A family arrived in the middle of the night at a farmhouse near Burrel in Albania. A man and a woman with two young daughters; twins. I'm sure you remember. Do you know what happened to them?'

'I don't know what you are talking about,' said Fabry hoarsely.

'The girls were given to the owner of the farmhouse, and he raped them. And, of course, you know what happened to their parents, don't you?'

'This is crazy! Alessandro, do something!' shouted Fabry.

'There is nothing I can do,' said Alessandro, and pointed to Aladdin standing next to him with a gun in his hand.

'Both parents were shot in the back of the head,' continued Teodora. 'On your orders. Their bodies were then opened up by you, and some of their organs were removed. For sale on the lucrative black market in the Middle East—'

'You are mistaken,' interrupted Fabry, his voice sounding shrill. 'That wasn't *me*!'

'Yes it was!' shouted Teodora and took a step forward. 'I saw you do it myself, through a crack in the stable wall. I was one of the twins. The day of reckoning has arrived, Dr Death! Justice at last!'

'What are you talking about?'

'You did say you needed a replacement for that specimen you lost the other day. Well, I think we've just found it, don't you, guys?'

'I think you are right,' said Silvanus. 'And a much better one than Mr Rogan here.'

Teodora walked over to Fabry and lifted her gun. 'My parents were both shot in the back of the head,' said Teodora. 'Get down on your knees. *Now*!'

'Alessandro!' shrieked Fabry. There was no reply.

Slowly, Fabry got down on his knees. Teodora walked up to him from behind and pointed her gun at the back of his head. For a long moment she just held it there, remembering her parents as Tchaikovsky's *Lost Symphony* reached its climax. Then she whispered, *'Go to hell!'* and pulled the trigger.

'That's some justice,' said Jack and looked at Teodora standing next to him.

'It's not over yet,' said Teodora and untied the leather straps restraining Jack on the table. 'Silvanus and Aladdin will need some help; give them a hand.'

'What do you mean?' Jack sat up, wiped some of Fabry's blood off his face and rubbed his chafed wrists.

'To drop this despicable piece of filth into the acetone bath over there and begin the vivification process, what else?'

Alessandro turned to Rodrigo standing next to him. 'Did you know about this?'

'I did. Did you?'

'I had no idea.'

'But your father ordered it.'

'When?'

'After breakfast at the villa.'

Alessandro shook his head, feeling suddenly quite small.

36

On the way to Tangier: 1 July, morning

After Fabry's dramatic execution on the *Caritas*, Teodora knew they had to move fast and leave Malta. A visit from the authorities was imminent; it was only a matter of time before Fabry's body was discovered because it was almost certain that the *Caritas* and Fabry's clinic would be searched. Jack had said as much, and Teodora and Rodrigo had no doubt he was telling the truth.

Giordano had explained to Rodrigo the necessity of eliminating Fabry. Fabry had become a dangerous liability, putting the entire project in jeopardy. And, of course, there was a lot more Mafia business at stake that only Giordano would have known about ... It had also become clear that Stolzfus could no longer remain at the clinic and had to be removed from Malta as a matter of urgency, regardless of the risks involved. No-one suspected Stolzfus could possibly be alive and it was imperative to both Giordano and Rodrigo to keep it that way. Ignorance was always the best cover.

Fortunately, Fabry had left Stolzfus in the care of a gifted young surgeon from Ghana, who jumped at the opportunity to accompany Stolzfus on his journey to Colombia. As an illegal asylum-seeker working on the *Caritas*, he knew all too well how precarious his position was, and the promise of a new life in Colombia proved irresistible. It was the way Fabry had kept his staff in check, made sure they did his bidding and kept their mouths shut, irrespective of legal or ethical considerations. Fabry believed in the power of fear and money, and manipulated his staff and the crew on the *Caritas* accordingly.

Stolzfus was still in a coma but seemed to be making good progress. Fitted with a cervicothoracic orthosis brace and in a sitting position in a wheelchair, the blood vessels and nerve networks were regenerating faster than expected. The prognosis looked good, provided there were no unexpected mishaps or complications. A long sea journey had its risks, but with an experienced surgeon watching over him round the clock, the Ghanaian surgeon was optimistic it would work.

The moment of reckoning would come later, when Stolzfus was brought out of his coma and reawakened. It would only be then that the full impact of the revolutionary surgery could be assessed. Phonation was of course a critical issue here. It was imperative to be able to communicate with Stolzfus once he had been woken. That was the reason great care had been taken to transfer his head with the larynx and the recurrent laryngeal nerves intact. But it would only be possible to find out if that had in fact worked once Stolzfus was conscious. The same applied to his motor functions.

With Stolzfus safely on board and in the care of the surgeon, *Nike* was ready to continue her journey to Tangier, the agreed handover port in Morocco. Teodora, Aladdin and Silvanus would all stay on board and accompany Stolzfus on the final leg of his long journey to Morocco. At the last minute, Rodrigo had added another condition to the agreed arrangements: Jack too, was to be taken to Tangier and then sent on with Stolzfus to Colombia.

Just before the *Nike* was due to leave Valletta, Teodora found herself momentarily alone with Rodrigo after Giacomo had been briefed and left the saloon to prepare the departure. Rodrigo would not travel with them, but return to Florence with Alessandro and meet them in Tangier two days' later.

'We've been through a lot together in a short time,' began Teodora, speaking softly. 'It's been quite a journey since our first meeting in your office in New York.'

'It sure has,' said Rodrigo, wondering where this was going.

'As our contract is shortly coming to an end, I would like to ask you a question if I may.'

'Go ahead,' said Rodrigo and lit a cigarette.

'I'm intrigued. Why would a billionaire Colombian drug baron go to such astonishing lengths and spend millions to abduct a famous physicist, keep him alive in such an extraordinary way, and then take him to the other side of the world? For what?'

Rodrigo smiled. 'It's a good question, but I am not at liberty to give you an answer. Instead, I will ask *you* a question: What would you have been prepared to do had there been a way to save your sister?'

Teodora was taken aback. 'I would have done anything to save her,' replied Teodora without hesitation. 'Absolutely anything at all.'

'You see, you have your answer. My client's position is no different. Most important things in life come down to a few basic issues that really count. This is such a case. We try to protect what is close to our hearts at all cost, and are prepared to sacrifice almost anything to achieve this, often in crazy, totally illogical ways and against our own interests. Does this make sense?'

Teodora nodded. 'It does,' she said, remembering how she had felt about her late parents and Fabry just a short while ago. 'But where does Jack Rogan fit into all this? You are taking him back to Colombia with Stolzfus? Why?'

'It's complicated, and my client is a complicated man, but a very shrewd and far-sighted one with incredible instincts and a brain wired for strategic thinking – like that of a general on a battlefield.'

'That doesn't answer my question.'

'Jack Rogan is a unique, extremely well-connected individual with access to people in high places, including the world media, and my client needs just such a person to carry out an important part of his plan. This makes Rogan very useful and valuable. Stolzfus and now Rogan are both part of that plan. Just like Fabry had to be silenced, Stolzfus and Rogan have to be kept alive. It's all about the big picture. Simple as that.'

'I see ...'

'The *Coatilcue* has already docked in the Port of Tangier and is waiting for us. As soon as you arrive, she will sail for Colombia with Stolzfus and Rogan on board.'

'Funny name for a ship.'

'Coatilcue was an Aztec goddess who gave birth to the moon, the stars and Huitzilopochtli, the god of the sun and war. The cartel is named after him. My client is a strong believer in tradition. Tangier is part of the Slave Route bringing drugs from Colombia into Europe. Just like the Aztec Highway brings drugs into the US via Mexico. My client owns several ships. The *Coatilcue* is one of them.'

'And what will you do?'

'I will meet you in Tangier.'

'You realise of course that with the discovery of Stolzfus's body on the *Caritas* – and very soon Fabry's as well – add to this Rogan's abduction and the article in the *New York Times,* all hell will break loose.'

Rodrigo nodded.

'We'll have some of the most powerful law enforcement agencies in the world trying to hunt us down.'

'I'm aware of that.'

'Does that bother you?'

'No, not really. We are used to it. My client lives in the shadow of war all the time. What about you?' asked Rodrigo.

Teodora smiled. 'We are used to it as well. We live in the shadow of exposure, which would of course destroy us. It's part of what we do.'

'I think you and my client have a lot in common.'

'What do you mean?'

'You are both very good at what you do, and are both addicted to danger and don't seem to know fear. At least not like others do.'

'And you?'

'I make money out of it. I'm a lawyer.'

'That's honest.'

Rodrigo shrugged. 'I have to go. My plane is leaving in an hour. Alessandro and I are returning to Florence. Good luck, Teodora,' he said and stubbed out his cigarette. 'And don't forget, the last step is always the hardest.'

Stolzfus sat in his wheelchair, supported by a sophisticated brace. His eyes were firmly shut and he could hear and process everything that was happening around him, but couldn't feel anything. Nor could he move any part of his body. In fact, he wasn't even aware he had one. His mind, however, was as sharp and alert as ever. His self-awareness, too, had changed. It was as if he were looking from the outside in at somebody else, not himself. Certainly not his old self, and strangely, there were no emotions. No feelings of joy, or pain, no feelings of longing or regrets, only a detached awareness of his mind, and memories that linked him to his past and who he was, or more accurately, who he had been.

Stolzfus had turned into a purely cerebral being with his remarkable brain intact and functioning perfectly, where existence was now defined by thought only, and in order to occupy itself, that brain turned to its favourite subjects: physics and the universe.

In his mind, which was now free of all human distractions and limitations, Stolzfus travelled to the outer reaches of the universe and back in time to the very beginning, the Big Bang, and imagined how the universe looked at that crucial moment when time itself began, and pondered how it could have created itself. He visited black holes and looked inside, and imagined a place where gravity was so powerful that not even light could escape. And all the time he was making complex calculations, using mathematics as his language instead of speech, and storing up those calculations for future reference in the hidden recesses of his extraordinary mind.

Step by step, that mind was putting together a theory that explained everything that had gone on before, and was going on right now in the universe, and would go on in the future until the very end of time. A theory of everything that had eluded him during his previous existence was now slowly taking shape through pure imagination driven entirely by logic, and explained through irrefutable laws that were pure and eternal, and expressed through mathematics as the universal language.

Locked in a tiny cabin next to the one occupied by Stolzfus, Jack went through the turbulent events of the past twenty-four hours and tried to work out why he was still alive. As he reached for the little cross around his neck, he could hear that music again – Tchaikovsky – echoing eerily through the chamber of horrors on the *Caritas*, certain now more than ever that somehow the little cross had protected him when all had seemed lost, and death had appeared to be only seconds away.

37

Chief Prosecutor's office, Florence: 1 July, afternoon

Grimaldi walked over to the whiteboard behind his desk, and for a while just looked at it with his hands folded behind his back. 'Are you telling me that after more than twenty-four hours have passed since Jack Rogan disappeared from his hotel, we have no leads whatsoever?'

'That's not entirely correct,' said Cesaria. 'We do have something ...'

'Enlighten me.'

'This is what we know so far; in fact, it would be better if you could hear this from Tristan. After all, he was right there, and he has some additional information that could be helpful.'

Grimaldi walked back to his desk and sat down. 'All right, Tristan, let's hear it. It seems to me that once again, amateurs like you appear to know more about this case than our police,' said Grimaldi, unable to keep the sarcasm out of his voice. Tired and irritable – he had barely slept since Jack's disappearance the day before – he had mobilised every available resource to find out what had happened to the Australian writer.

Grimaldi had no doubt the Mafia was behind all this, especially as the sensational article in the *New York Times* had mentioned Jack Rogan as a source, which had triggered a raft of headlines in papers around Italy, training the spotlight once again on the Mafia in Florence and the under-resourced law enforcement agencies trying to bring the festering problem to heel. There were also the usual accusations of incompetence and thinly veiled suggestions of corruption in high places. In fact, Grimaldi had already received a call from the General Commander of the Guardia di Finanza wanting to know what progress had been made in the embarrassing Rogan abduction matter. The pressure was on, especially now that Major

Andersen of the CIA had arrived and joined Cesaria in the investigation. This had elevated the case to an entirely new level.

'As I explained to Cesaria,' began Tristan, 'this woman – she called herself Teodora – is definitely involved. It all started with a phone call and message Jack received during breakfast at the hotel. He excused himself, stood up and walked out of the room. That was the last time we saw him. Moments later, this woman got up as well and pretended to go to the buffet table, but she kept walking and left the room. That was the last time we saw her. Both Jack and the woman disappeared without a trace.

'But what could be helpful here,' continued Tristan, 'is this: I have met this woman before, just a few days ago in Venice. She and a friend were staying at our hotel, the Palazzo da Baggio. I have contacted our reception and obtained some details about the booking. It was made by a woman called Izabel Santos, who gave an address in Milan. We also have a phone number and an email address. Jack knows this woman very well. They have a connection going back many years and it was because of her that we were introduced to Teodora. It was obvious that Izabel and Teodora are very close. They were holding hands during dinner ...'

'And this Teodora just turned up here at the hotel that morning?' asked Grimaldi.

'Yes, we met her in the breakfast room. Entirely by chance, or so it seemed at the time.'

Grimaldi shook his head. 'That's too much of a coincidence for me.'

'I agree,' said Cesaria. 'She only stayed one night at the hotel. We checked her room; nothing. The bed hadn't been slept in. The reservation was made through some booking agency. She paid in cash, and the personal details provided to the hotel are obviously fake.'

'What else do we know about this Teodora?' asked Grimaldi.

'She has a villa on Lake Como, appears to be very wealthy and drives a rare car, a Lamborghini Centenario,' said Tristan.

'*What?*' said Cesaria. 'Why didn't you mention this before?'

'It didn't come up ...'

'Why is this relevant?' asked Grimaldi.

'Since we located Stolzfus's body on the *Caritas*, suggesting a strong link to the Giordanos, I arranged round-the-clock surveillance of the Giordano villa.'

'And?'

'A black Lamborghini Centenario was driven into the Giordano compound two days ago. The driver was a woman.'

'That's interesting,' said Grimaldi.

'What's even more interesting,' continued Cesaria, 'is that the car is still there.'

'Unless it was a present, someone is bound to come and collect it. No-one leaves such a car behind.'

'Exactly. And we will be watching.'

'And Izabel Santos?'

'It's a lead we are following up, but in light of what we've just heard, I don't think this is the right time. We don't want to alert Teodora that we are onto her, do we?'

Grimaldi shook his head.

'I have something that may help here,' said Andersen, who until now had only been listening. 'As you can imagine, the CIA has a huge database and an army of analysts and profilers. We ran the key elements of the Stolzfus abduction, including the very latest developments involving Rogan and, of course, the likely Giordano Mafia connection through the system.' Andersen paused, collecting her thoughts.

'Go on,' prompted Cesaria.

'We know that at least one woman was involved in the London ambulance attack,' continued Andersen. 'She was killed and her body taken away. It now seems that a second woman is involved: Teodora ...'

'What are you suggesting, Major?' said Grimaldi.

'There are only a handful of operatives active in the world today who can carry out such a complex, high-risk operation like this, and one of them is a group of two men and two women. The possibility of a second woman being involved was the key here. I just received the report from Washington ...'

'What do we know about them?' asked Cesaria, becoming excited.

'Very little, I'm afraid. They operate in the shadows and seem to be involved in only very high-profile, high-risk matters involving assassinations, kidnappings, mutilations ... their modus operandi is always original and highly imaginative. They are wanted in several countries and have been on the CIA's top priority wanted list for several years, ever since an American ambassador was assassinated in Turkey a few years ago. He was the target, but his wife and daughter were collateral damage. After every assignment they go to ground and just disappear. But there are quite specific similarities in their approach, almost like a signature, and there is a common thread.'

'What kind of similarities?' asked Grimaldi.

'All the cases attributed to this group – and there are only a handful, often years apart – appear to have a strong commercial connection. In short, it's always about money and business; big business.'

'What kind of business?'

'Drugs mainly, and money laundering.'

'And the common thread?' asked Cesaria.

Andersen smiled. She had saved the best for last. 'All the cases seem to be linked to the Mafia here in Europe.'

'Excellent work, Major. Great to have you on board,' said Grimaldi. 'So, what's our next step? I'm sure the commander is about to call me again.'

'Fabry and the *Caritas.* We are about to go to Malta, hopefully this afternoon, to have a closer look at both. As soon as the paperwork allows it, that is,' added Cesaria, rolling her eyes. 'You won't believe what I have to go through to make this possible. The Maltese authorities are dragging their feet, and I think I know why ...'

'Good luck,' said Grimaldi and stood up. 'Let's find Jack Rogan, and please keep me informed.'

As soon as they left Grimaldi's office, Tristan took Cesaria aside while they waited for Andersen, who had gone to the bathroom. 'I didn't want to say this in front of Grimaldi or the major, but Fabry is dead,' he said, looking worried. 'And I'm only telling you this because I know you will take this seriously and not just laugh and shrug it off ...'

'Come on, Tristan, how can you possibly know this?'

'I heard the music again ...'

'What kind of music?'

'It's difficult to explain.'

'Try.'

'I had a similar conversation with Jack just before he disappeared,' said Tristan, ignoring the question. 'Unfortunately, I couldn't quite finish what I had to say. You know I sense things; I have visions, I *feel* ...'

Cesaria put her hand on Tristan's arm. 'I know, and I am taking this seriously, but ...'

'There is more, a lot more, but I cannot tell you now because it would be too big an ask for you to believe it,' said Tristan. 'I'm having trouble believing it myself because it goes against every piece of logic and against everything we know, especially now that we have found Stolzfus's body.'

'Can't you tell me anyway?'

'No. But I tell you what. We are about to go to Malta to investigate Fabry. If we find him dead, as I believe we will, then I will tell you the rest because by then you will be ready to listen. And you never know, I may find out a little more about all this in the meantime ...'

'All right. Let's do that.'

'Fabry died a horrible death and Jack is in great danger,' said Tristan, looking anxious. 'We must hurry!'

The final approvals came through from Malta just after noon. With all the necessary warrants in place, Cesaria, Andersen and Tristan, together with two senior forensics officers, headed for the airport to catch the two o'clock flight to Valletta. By four-thirty, they were on the *Caritas*. Accompanied by two detectives from the Malta Police

Force Criminal Investigations Department, they began to inspect the vessel. Cesaria expected to be met by the captain, only to be told that the captain and most of the senior officers and crew had gone on leave. Apparently, the captain had left the island earlier that day for an unknown destination. When they tried to contact Fabry at his clinic, they were told that no one had seen him that day or knew where he was.

'This is odd, don't you think?' said Cesaria as she followed Tristan down to the laboratory where they had found Stolzfus's body during the coastguard raid four days earlier.

'I agree,' said Andersen. 'The captain and all the officers on leave. Sounds a bit like rats leaving the sinking ship.'

'Exactly. Or trying to be out of reach. Someone doesn't want us to talk to them. At least not now.'

As soon as Tristan entered the dimly lit laboratory that smelled of chloroform, he was once again assaulted by frightening images suggesting mutilated bodies and unspeakable pain. For a while, he just stood in the shadows and watched the forensics officers go through their paces. They began by examining the steel table in the middle of the room.

Suddenly, Tristan could hear that music again. Softly at first but becoming louder by the second. *That symphony again*, he thought, *Tchaikovsky*, and closed his eyes. Moments later, he covered his ears with his hands and opened his eyes.

'It happened right there!' he cried out and pointed to a spot next to the steel table. Cesaria walked over to Tristan and put her hand on his arm to calm him. Shaking all over and with his eyes wide open and staring into space, Tristan was looking at something only he could see.

'What happened right there?' asked Cesaria quietly.

'Death. At first I thought it was Jack, but it's not him, thank God. *It's Fabry*! He died right there.'

'Calm down. What are you talking about?'

Slowly, Tristan walked across the chamber like a necromancer and stopped in front of a large vat. It was the same vat in which the remains of Stolzfus's truncated body had been discovered. Then he lifted his right arm and pointed to the vat. 'He's in there,' he whispered.

'Who?'

'Fabry.'

At first, the forensics officers were unable to open the lid of the vat, which appeared to be firmly sealed, with blue lights flashing on a control panel. It was only after a technician could be located on the ship and came to enter the security code on the panel that they were able to open it. The forensics officers took turns to climb the ladder and look inside. Both recoiled in horror. 'Good God,' said one of them, covering his nose, and looked away.

'Is it Fabry?' asked Cesaria. The technician climbed the ladder, looked inside the vat and nodded, looking shaken. 'It's him,' he said and climbed down, 'but most of his face is gone.'

'What did I tell you?' said Tristan quietly to Cesaria.

'I don't know what to think right now,' she said, shaking her head. 'This changes everything.'

'What do you think happened here?' asked Andersen, looking quite pale.

'I think the Mafia is mopping up. Fabry had become a liability. I am certain Jack's disappearance and this here are connected. In fact, it's all classic Mafia. You stuff up, you pay for it. That's what happened to Fabry. You keep poking into hidden corners and disclosing confidential information, you have to be silenced. That's what's happening to Jack.'

Tristan was staring at a corner of the empty steel table and was tracing something with his fingertips. 'Jack was here,' he said quietly. 'Not that long ago.'

'What makes you say that?'

'He sent us a message.'

'What are you talking about?'

'This here; look.' Tristan pointed to the table.

Cesaria walked over to the table and had a look. She could just make out a cross with a tick just under the cross bar on the right-hand side.

'The Southern Cross and a tick.'

'Meaning?'

'Jack uses the Southern Cross with the slightly askew cross bar as a logo on all of his books. You would have seen it.'

'Come on ... and the tick? What about the tick?'

'Isn't it obvious?' said Tristan, a hint of a smile creeping hesitantly across his troubled face.

'The tick represents the logo of the Nike brand, of course, right here where the fifth star of the constellation would be. Jack was here, most likely on this table, and scratched this into the surface with some sharp object, most probably a knife,' said Tristan. 'It could be done very quickly with only three short strokes. You could even do it blindfolded. Jack is on the *Nike*.'

'Come over here and have a look at this,' said Cesaria, turning to Andersen.

Andersen came over and had a look. 'What are we looking at?'

'Tristan, please tell her,' said Cesaria and stood back.

38

On the *Coatilcue*, on the way to Colombia: 3 July, afternoon

The *Coatilcue*, a rusty old workhorse owned by the H Cartel, had done countless trips between Colombia and Morocco, primarily to transport coffee, but also to smuggle large quantities of cocaine into Europe, cleverly concealed in hessian coffee bags. Over the years, the cartel had acquired several large coffee plantations and was gradually moving its drug money into the lucrative – and legitimate – coffee business. The captain and his six 'security guards' were the only Colombians on board. The rest of the crew were African, mainly from poor, war-torn countries, who worked under appalling conditions and were kept in check by the armed guards, who terrorised them mercilessly.

The captain had received specific instructions from Cordoba himself about the Stolzfus transfer arrangements and had allocated a sealed-off area at the stern of the ship for Stolzfus and his doctor. It was only an hour before leaving port that he was informed by Rodrigo that one more detainee would be coming along: Jack.

The segregated area consisted of three cabins, a shared bathroom with a shower desperately in need of a thorough clean, and a small outdoor deck space. Jack was allocated a cabin next to the doctor. The rest of the ship was strictly off limits. Jack was a prisoner on the ship, with no passport, no access to a telephone or the internet, and no freedom of movement apart from the designated area.

During the trip from Malta to Tangier on the *Nike*, Jack had also been segregated and locked in a tiny cabin without access to the rest of the vessel or contact with the crew. He therefore had no idea where he was or where he was being taken. And, of course, he had no inkling that Stolzfus could be alive. But all of that changed when Teodora paid him a surprise visit in his cabin just before the *Coatilcue* was due to leave port.

'Jack, please listen to me. There isn't much time,' said Teodora as soon as the guard closed the door behind her, and she was alone with Jack in his cabin. Exhausted and disorientated after his horrifying ordeal on the *Caritas* and an uncomfortable two-day sea journey locked in a dark cabin the size of a cupboard, Jack just looked at her and shook his head.

'I certainly didn't see this coming,' he said, referring to his abduction in Florence. 'And I certainly didn't suspect you. I saw you as Izabel's friend. Someone she trusted and was very fond of. How could I have been so mistaken? I must be losing my edge. What do you want?'

'Jack, believe me when I tell you that none of this is personal.'

'So, being abducted at gunpoint during breakfast, then locked in a tiny cabin for days just to find myself lying naked on some operating table on a hospital ship, being prepared for vivification by a madman standing over me with a scalpel, wasn't *personal*?'

'No, it wasn't.'

'What was it then?'

'A job. I'm sure you must have worked that out by now.'

'One hell of a job.'

'But killing Fabry and saving your life wasn't a job. *That* was personal. A moment of destiny.'

'I don't understand.'

'You heard some of it, but there isn't time to explain it all now. Perhaps one day … Now listen. There are a few things you need to know.'

'What kind of things?'

'Stolzfus is alive—'

'What! What are you talking about?'

'Hard to believe, I know, but true nevertheless. In fact, he's right here on the ship in the next cabin with his doctor.'

'You can't be serious!'

'I am. You'll meet him soon enough.'

Jack looked at Teodora in disbelief and shook his head. That's when he began to hear that music again – Tchaikovsky – and could hear Tristan's words: *I firmly believe Stolzfus isn't dead* ... and the word *danger* ringing in his ears.

'Why?' was all Jack could utter.

'I don't know exactly why either, but what I do know is this, and you better listen because it may help you.'

'Help me?' said Jack? 'Help me in what way?'

'Survive.'

'Why are you doing this? After all that's happened?'

'It's complicated. I'm doing this for Izabel and for you, her friend she thinks so highly of.'

Teodora sighed heavily and looked pensively at Jack. 'And for myself,' she added quietly.

'All right; I'm paying attention,' said Jack and sat up.

'Good. We are in Tangier right now. You and Stolzfus are on a ship bound for Colombia. It's about to leave.'

Jack looked astonished. '*Colombia?* Why?'

'Ever heard of the H Cartel?'

'Sure, run by Hernando Cordoba, the Colombian drug baron with a son on death row in the US. Who hasn't heard of him?'

'Exactly. He's behind all this. I don't know why, but he and the Giordanos in Florence arranged everything. The entire Stolzfus saga, including your abduction. It's all related.'

'This is crazy! I still don't understand. What's the connection?'

'Money, big business, drugs; what else?'

'And Stolzfus and I somehow fit into all this?' Jack shook his head. 'I cannot see it.'

'You will soon, trust me. You are obviously important enough to them to keep you alive, and you must use your knowledge and ingenuity to stay that way. I had specific instructions to make sure Fabry didn't harm you. I also had specific instructions to kill him after you were interrogated in such a colourful manner on that table. To cooperate and not resist was smart. It made things a lot easier, not only for you, but for me as well. I believe it's all about information. What you know and certain contacts you have, especially in the media. I'm certain they want to use that in some way.'

'And Stolzfus? What about him?'

'Not entirely sure, but that too will become clear soon enough, I suspect.'

Teodora stood up and walked to the door. 'I must go,' she said. 'Take care of yourself, Jack.' Teodora opened the cabin door and was about to step outside when she stopped and turned around. 'I really like you …'

'A favour?' said Jack.

'Sure.'

'Could you contact Tristan and tell him I'm alive?'

'I will. If I manage to stay alive that long myself,' she added softly.

'Thanks for telling me all this,' said Jack.

Teodora shrugged. 'Good luck, Jack,' she said and hurried out of the room.

After the *Coatilcue* had left Tangier and it was getting dark, Jack knocked on the door of the cabin next to his. No-one came, so he tried the third cabin.

'Come in,' said a deep voice inside. Jack opened the door – and gasped.

A man was sitting motionless in a wheelchair facing the door. His eyes were closed and his shaved head seemed to be held up and supported by a strange-looking brace resting on his shoulders. A number of coloured tubes were protruding from his bare chest, and from his mouth and arms were more tubes, all connected to a machine positioned behind the wheelchair, its blinking lights like strange eyes, watching.

A tall African man stood next to the wheelchair. He walked over to Jack and extended his hand. 'I'm Doctor Agabe. I've been expecting you.' The man pointed to the wheelchair. 'This is Professor Stolzfus. He's in better shape than he looks.'

Over the next hour, Agabe, a well-spoken, highly intelligent man in his late thirties, gave Jack a step-by-step account of the groundbreaking operation performed by Fabry and his team that had made history, and had saved Stolzfus's life and given him a new body.

'Fabry's dead, you know,' said Jack.

Agabe nodded. 'I know.'

'You know how he died?'

'Yes, I do.'

'Does that bother you?'

'Fabry was a difficult, complex man. An evil genius totally devoid of morality or feeling for others, who used and disposed of people, like you or I would dispose of a paper towel. Does that answer your question?'

'I suppose it does.'

'As we are about to spend quite some time in here together before we reach Bogota, I think we should get to know each other a little. Do you play chess?' asked Agabe.

'I do,' said Jack, taking an immediate liking to the doctor. He pointed to Stolzfus. 'How long before he comes out of the coma, do you think?'

The doctor shrugged. 'We don't really know. Could be any time. He's in remarkably good shape, considering what has happened to him and what he's been through.'

'Fancy a game?' said Jack.

'Why not? It's going to be a long eight days.'

39

4 July, early morning

After the discovery of Fabry's mutilated body and the absence of the captain of the *Caritas* and most of the officers and crew on leave, which made questioning them impossible, enquiries in Malta had hit a dead end. Cesaria and Andersen returned to Florence with Tristan to continue their investigation, as Fabry's murder was now a matter for the Maltese authorities. Although clearly connected to the Stolzfus case, the situation didn't allow further involvement by Cesaria and the Squadra Mobile at that stage.

With the recovery of Stolzfus's headless corpse, and now Jack's abduction as an added complication, the case was quickly spinning out of control and turning into an international embarrassment, especially for the CIA and MI5. Another explosive article in the *New York Times* hadn't helped either and had put Andersen under considerable pressure. Washington was demanding answers.

Andersen realised it was time to think outside the square. Cesaria and the major decided to split the enquiry into two parts. Cesaria would remain in Florence with Tristan, work on the Mafia connection and keep the Giordano villa under surveillance in the hope that the Centenario would lead them to Teodora. Andersen wanted to follow up the *Nike* lead provided by the cryptic inscription discovered by Tristan on the *Caritas*. When Cesaria asked Andersen how she intended to do that, Andersen replied, 'It's time to ask a friend for help.'

The US Sixth Fleet was under the command of Vice Admiral Laura Fratelli. Andersen and Fratelli had served together for several years on aircraft carriers before going their separate ways to advance their careers. Both were crack pilots with extensive combat experience and had remained close friends. The Sixth Fleet was based in Naples at the

Naval Support Activity Naples (NSA Naples), a US military complex near the airport, and Andersen went there to see her friend. But before doing so, she had asked her superiors in Washington to contact the vice admiral and prepare the way.

'So, what can I do for you?' asked Fratelli, who was both surprised and delighted to see Andersen.

'You have read the articles in the *New York Times* about Stolzfus and Rogan, I suppose?'

'Of course. Who hasn't? Everyone's talking about it here. I've also had a long conversation with the secretary of state, and the director of the CIA. Your case is certainly going right to the top and making considerable waves in Washington.'

'For all the wrong reasons, I'm afraid. National interests are at stake here and more importantly perhaps, the reputation of the United States,' said Andersen. 'I was again reminded of this by my boss just the other day.'

Fratelli nodded, well aware of the pressure her friend was under. 'So, tell me what you've got in mind and how I can help. According to my instructions, the entire fleet is at your disposal,' joked Fratelli.

'As you know, we've just recently recovered Stolzfus's body. The head was missing. Quite bizarre really, and distressing for his sister who had to identify the body and is about to take it back to the States for burial. Without question, there's a strong Mafia link here, but a lot of information is still missing, especially a motive, which is of serious concern. And it all began with the *Nike,* a luxury motor cruiser belonging to the Giordanos, a Mafia family in Florence. There are still many gaps in this enquiry and we have a long way to go, but it is in connection with that vessel that I need your help. It's our strongest lead at the moment.'

The next day, Andersen was helicoptered on board the USS *Intrepid,* a frigate operating in the busy Strait of Gibraltar. Naval Intelligence mobilised by Fratelli in Malta and all the major ports in the Mediterranean had established that the *Nike* had left the Port of

Tangier and had passed through the Strait, travelling east. It was assumed she was on her way back to Monaco. Unfortunately, the information was sketchy as the agents had picked up the trail just after the *Nike* had left Tangier the night before. It was therefore impossible to tell who was on board or what they had been doing in Tangier during the few short hours *Nike* had spent in the harbour.

Captain Tom Roberts, Commander, Task Force 65 welcomed Andersen on the bridge of the USS *Intrepid*, and gave her a briefing.

'The *Nike* left the Port of Tangier during the night and is travelling towards us,' he said and pointed to a blip on the radar screen. 'Right here. I have received orders to intercept and search the *Nike*. This will happen in about two hours – right here. The reason for this is straightforward: based on recent intelligence, we have reason to believe that three terrorists are on board.'

'Terrorists?' said Andersen.

'Yes. Two men and a woman who were very likely responsible for the murder of the American Ambassador and his family in Turkey a few years ago. And I understand they may also be wanted in connection with the abduction and murder of Professor Stolzfus, and the more recent abduction of Mr Rogan. And that's where you come in. I understand you have means to identify the suspects?'

'I do.' Andersen reached into her briefcase and pulled out three photographs. 'These photos are enlargements extracted from body camera footage obtained by the Ministry of Defence Police during a search of the *Nike* just outside Portsmouth on June fifteen. These are the suspects we are looking for,' she said and showed the photos to the captain. They were close-ups of three faces: those of Teodora, Silvanus and Aladdin. 'If they are on board, it would be a major coup, because we have DNA evidence available from the Turkish murder scene that should allow us to make a positive identification and link them to that crime.'

'And the Stolzfus matter?'

'Circumstantial at this stage. But if Rogan's on board, that would certainly help because I can of course identify him easily and he would tie the suspects to Stolzfus as well. I was with Rogan only a few days ago.'

'But building a case would take some time?'

'Yes, it would. It's all very complicated at the moment, with several countries and law enforcement agencies involved, all baying for blood. You could call it a legal minefield wrapped in a diplomatic nightmare.'

The captain smiled. 'I've been tiptoeing around those for years.'

'So, what will happen to them if they are in fact on board the *Nike* and apprehended?'

'They will be detained and taken back to Naples for interrogation and the *Nike* will be escorted back to our base and the crew questioned. Those are my orders. We have the necessary authority to do that as part of our operations here in the Mediterranean.'

'Excellent, Captain. We need a breakthrough – desperately.'

'Let's hope I can provide you with one.'

Silvanus and Aladdin sat in the saloon of the *Nike,* drinking Scotch. It was four in the morning, but neither could sleep. The turbulent events of the past forty-eight hours saw to that.

Silvanus looked at his brother and lifted his glass. 'We've done it! Cheers.'

'Have we? At what cost? And it's not over yet.'

'Come on … don't look so gloomy.'

'Nadia's dead, and we've taken risks lately we have never taken before. We've done things on the run. Foolish and reckless things …'

'No choice, and you know it.'

'Perhaps … I don't think Teodora should have gone by plane.'

'I agree, but would you have been able to stop her?'

Aladdin shook his head.

Just before the *Nike* left Tangier, Teodora received a phone call from her housekeeper in Como. Izabel had had a nasty fall on the slippery rocks just below Villa Rosa. She had broken a leg and almost drowned. She was in hospital in Como in a stable condition. Distressed and in a panic, which was totally out of character, Teodora had rushed to the airport to arrange a flight back to Italy instead of remaining on the *Nike* and taking the much safer but slower route back to Monaco. Airports were dangerous places for people like Teodora, especially at a time like this, and she knew it. All of Silvanus's pleading and reminding her of this had fallen on deaf ears. Teodora had made up her mind and nothing he could say would change it. But she assured him she would be careful.

As usual, there was a lot of traffic in the Strait that morning and Giacomo kept a close eye on the vessels passing by. One in particular caught his attention, a US Navy frigate that appeared to have been trailing him for some time. *Why is he coming so close?* thought Giacomo. He changed course slightly and accelerated. That's when the frigate closed in.

'What's that?' asked Aladdin, pointing to the bright light illuminating the deck. He put down his glass and went outside. Silvanus did the same. Blinded by the powerful searchlights trained on them from above like the accusing fingers of some giant, Silvanus and Aladdin shielded their eyes.

'Stay where you are and put up your hands!' boomed a voice through loudspeakers from above. Squinting through his fingers, Silvanus could see the grey bulk of the frigate towering above him only a few metres away. Moments later, heavily armed marines swarmed on deck.

'Down on the floor with your hands behind your head where I can see them!' shouted one of them.

Silvanus and Aladdin did as they were told.

Accompanied by two armed officers, Andersen went up to the bridge first to talk to the captain. Giacomo went through his usual routine of being on a charter trip and produced his logs and papers. After that, Andersen went down into the saloon to talk to Silvanus and Aladdin, who were waiting for her there under guard.

'Can you tell me where you both were on June fifteen?' asked Andersen, carefully watching Silvanus and Aladdin.

Silvanus shot Aladdin a meaningful look and took his time before replying. 'Let me see …' he began. 'My brother and I were at home at my place in Milan, planning this trip.'

'Milan, you say …' said Andersen. She opened her briefcase, took out the three photos she had shown the captain earlier, and put them on the table in front of Silvanus. Silvanus looked at the photos and his heart skipped a beat.

'These were taken by the Ministry of Defence Police on June fifteen on this very vessel just outside Portsmouth,' continued Andersen. 'Unless you have found a way to be in two places a thousand miles apart at the same time, you have some explaining to do, don't you think? Would you like to start now?'

'We have nothing to say!' barked Silvanus, realising they were in deep trouble. 'Not without our lawyer!'

'That may have to wait a while because you are being detained under special terrorism legislation where the rules are quite different.' Andersen paused to let this sink in. 'With that in mind,' she continued, speaking more softly, 'I would like to talk to you about the abduction and murder of Professor Stolzfus, and the more recent murder of Professor Fabry and the abduction of Jack Rogan. Where is Jack Rogan?'

'I don't know what you are talking about!' said Silvanus.

'And then there are others who are anxious to talk to you about the murder of the American ambassador and his family in Istanbul, and assassinations in Cairo and Tel Aviv,' continued Andersen, undeterred. 'In fact, there's quite a list of interested parties who want to talk to you. But there will be plenty of time for all of this because from now on, gentlemen, yours is a world behind bars. The only question will be in whose prison you will be spending the rest of your lives. Now then, how about we start again? A little cooperation could go a long way. I'm sure you know what I mean ...'

40

On the way back to Como: 4 July

After watching the *Coatilcue* leave Tangier, Teodora went straight to Tangier Ibn Battuta Airport to arrange her flight. She decided against flying directly into Florence to collect her car and opted instead to fly to Rome and catch the train to Florence from there. While this would take longer, it was safer by far. Teodora realised it was high time to go to ground as soon as she got back to Villa Rosa. Elaborate plans to do that were in place at all times, and she knew Silvanus and Aladdin would do the same as soon as they arrived in Monaco. They had their own safe house in Corsica. It was what they had done after every assignment, especially one this risky.

All of Teodora's finely honed instincts told her that collecting her car and going back to Como could be a costly mistake, but Izabel's accident and her feelings for her had discarded caution and Teodora decided to take the risk. But in order to be able to do that, she needed Alessandro's help. There were no direct flights from Tangier to Rome. The only connection was via Madrid, with several hours between flights.

Teodora had called Alessandro to prepare the way.

'Where are you?' asked Alessandro.

'Madrid. Waiting for my flight to Rome.'

'How come?'

'I want to collect my car and go back to Como, just for a brief visit.'

'Isn't that risky? With all that's been going on?'

'It is, but I have to do this.'

'Malta's blown up big time,' said Alessandro.

'What do you mean?'

'Fabry's body has been found, of course, and his clinic taken apart. Whole filing cabinets have been taken away. This is a big operation involving security services from various countries. We know the Americans are part of it. As you can imagine, they are throwing everything at this.'

'We expected that,' said Teodora calmly.

'Sure, but not on this scale, and not so soon. Our contacts in Malta are running scared and the Squadra Mobile here in Florence is on the move and turning up the heat. You must be careful.'

'Hardly surprising, but this will settle down as long as we don't lose our cool. I need your help.'

'In what way?'

'The car.'

'What have you in mind?'

'I'll tell you; listen.'

As soon as she arrived in Rome, Teodora began to work on her disguise. First she bought a wig, a small backpack, and a large pair of sunglasses. Then she changed her clothing to jeans, tee-shirt and sneakers. Looking like one of the myriad tourists flocking into Rome during the summer, Teodora caught the train to Florence.

Feeling relaxed and quite safe for the first time since leaving Tangier – airports were notoriously dangerous places for someone like her – Teodora left the train station and walked across to the large public car park nearby. With thousands of tourists arriving it was bedlam as usual, but Teodora blended in perfectly and there was safety in numbers. She had called Alessandro earlier and told him the arrival time of the train she was on. He assured her that everything had been arranged exactly as she had requested.

Cesaria was in Grimaldi's office, briefing the chief prosecutor on the latest developments, when her phone rang. It was the surveillance team watching the Giordano villa. After a short conversation Cesaria slipped the phone back into her pocket, and smiled.

'You look like the proverbial cat who has just discovered the cream bowl,' said Grimaldi.

'Teodora's car has just left the Giordano compound.'

'Do we know who's driving?'

'One of the bodyguards.'

'Interesting. You'd better go.'

'Where's he going?' asked Cesaria, as she hurried back to her office with her phone pressed against her ear.

'He just entered a car park near the train station,' said the officer in the surveillance car.

'You are not to approach. Is that clear? I will get there as soon as I can.'

'Understood.'

Cesaria arrived at the station a short time later and linked up with the surveillance team. 'What's happening?'

'The car is over there,' said the officer and pointed to the black Centenario parked between a BMW and a Fiat some distance away. 'To get out of here they have to drive past us, right here.'

'Good work, guys!'

'Where's the driver?'

'He left the car and caught a taxi.'

'What does this tell you?'

'He dropped off the car for someone to collect.'

'Exactly.'

'There's more.'

'Tell me.'

'After he got out of the car, the guy went down on one knee next to the driver's door and did something. We couldn't see what it was from here, but it didn't take long.'

'What do you think he was doing?'

The officer smiled. 'Placing the car keys somewhere they could be easily retrieved. We have done this many times ourselves.'

Cesaria nodded. 'Let's sit back and see if you're right,' she said and pulled out the body camera photographs taken by the Ministry of Defence Police in Portsmouth. She looked at the close-ups of Teodora's face, which Tristan had already identified at the Squadra Mobile.

'Here comes someone,' said the officer sitting next to Cesaria. A young woman with long blonde hair and a backpack slung casually over her shoulder walked slowly along the row of parked cars towards the Centenario. When she reached the black sports car she stopped and, without looking around, dropped her backpack on the ground and then bent down, pretending to tie one of her shoelaces.

'You were right; look,' said Cesaria.

'Do you think it's her?'

'Hair's different and with the sunglasses it's difficult to tell from here. I'd say she changed her appearance.'

Moments later, the woman stood up, unlocked the car door, threw her backpack on the passenger seat and got in.

'This is it, boys! It's her. I put my reputation on it.'

'What do you want us to do?'

'We follow her, of course. Let's see where she's heading.'

'How do you want to handle this?'

'Carefully. I want a second team on this, and one of the best motorcycle guys from traffic. No uniform, of course. This is a very fast car and we can't afford to lose it. It's okay in this crazy traffic here, but if she takes the autostrada, it's a different matter.'

'Understood. Leave this to me.'

As soon as Teodora got into her car and turned on the engine, she relaxed. The familiar sound and throb of the powerful motor calmed her, like the hand of an old friend stroking her hair. This allowed her to focus and clear her troubled mind. For the first time in days, she felt in control and was looking forward to the long drive north back to Lake Como with the promise of an embrace from Izabel she had been longing for since leaving her early that morning five days ago.

Just what I need, thought Teodora, and skilfully manoeuvred the car through the heavy traffic towards the on-ramp that led to Strada Statale 36 del Lago di Como e dello Spluga, the autostrada to Como. She had called Izabel several times during her trip back to Florence, promising she would be home soon, but she didn't explain where she had been or what she had been doing for the past five days. This was despite Izabel demanding answers and threatening to return to Milan. Teodora realised the moment she had dreaded since meeting Izabel had arrived. If there was to be a future for them, she had to tell her lover who she really was. She knew this would test their relationship, but the time for games and deception was over; there was nowhere left to hide.

Teodora knew Izabel was expecting her and waiting for her at Villa Rosa after being discharged from Como hospital, but as time was quickly running out, she decided to tell Izabel everything with brutal honesty during the drive back to Como. As soon as she reached the autostrada, Teodora put her foot down on the accelerator and dialled Izabel's number.

Izabel was lying in a deckchair on the terrace overlooking the lake. Her right leg was in plaster and she was not allowed to put any weight on it. There was no pain, only immobility and a little frustration. But with Teodora's housekeeper fussing over her, she was coping and looking forward to seeing Teodora. Suddenly her mobile rang, and she picked it up.

During the three-hour drive, Teodora told Izabel about her life, her secret hopes and darkest fears, holding nothing back. She spoke of her childhood and what it had been like to grow up with twin sister, Nadia, on a remote farm in Albania before the Kosovo war. She told Izabel how she remembered her parents as simple, pious, God-fearing Muslims who believed in the Prophet, the Koran, and in hard work. She burst into tears as she described that night of unimaginable horror in that farmhouse in Kosovo that had changed everything, how she had witnessed her parents being killed, their chests opened and their organs harvested by a man known as Dr Death.

She told Izabel how she and Nadia had been taken in by gypsies in their hour of great need, and how they had met Aladdin and Silvanus and how Spiridon 4 had grown out of that friendship as a means of survival after another monstrous tragedy.

She spoke of loneliness, heartache and despair, of pain, guilt and sorrow. She explained how she had become a skilled assassin and one of Europe's most dangerous women, wanted in several countries, and described the heinous crimes the group had committed for money and personal gain. Teodora pointed out that if caught, she would spend the rest of her life in prison, or worse.

She then explained where she had been during the past five days. She explained how destiny and fate had brought her face to face with the monster who had haunted and tormented her all these years and how she felt liberated and free after she had avenged her parents' murder by executing the man who had so callously butchered them and destroyed her life. Sobbing, she spoke of redemption and the power of forgiveness, and how she desperately hoped that love would heal and cleanse her wounded soul.

After Teodora had finished, there was complete silence and for a long, painful moment, she thought that Izabel had hung up on her. 'Are you still there?' she whispered, fearing the worst.

'I am.'

'Shocked?'

'A little.'

'Am I going to lose you?'

'No, but only on one condition ...'

'Name it.'

'That you hurry back to me so that I can hold you in my arms.'

'I'm on my way!' said Teodora, barely able to speak. 'I love you,' she said and hung up.

Teodora took a deep breath, wiped away the tears and looked around, surprised by how far she had travelled since leaving Florence. Time seemed to have been strangely suspended by painful memories and pent-up emotions she had locked away for so long in the secret recesses of her heart.

Not long now, thought Teodora, glad that she had taken the risk to go home, albeit for just a few hours, to talk to Izabel before going to ground in her secret bolthole in Bavaria, and disappear. It was because of this distraction that she hadn't noticed she was being followed. Two unmarked police cars and a powerful motorbike had been on her tail since Florence.

Feeling both relieved and elated, Teodora remembered what she had promised Jack just before she left him on the ship in Tangiers. She called the Palazzo da Baggio and asked for Tristan. A female voice answered the phone and told her Tristan wasn't in Venice.

'I would like to leave a message for him, please. It's urgent and very important.'

'It's Lorenza, his wife, speaking. Please go ahead.'

'Lorenza, would you please tell Tristan this: Jack Rogan is alive and he is being taken to Colombia.'

'Who is this?' asked Lorenza, sounding anxious.

'A friend,' replied Teodora and quickly hung up.

'Looks like she's going all the way to Como,' said Cesaria, pleasantly surprised by the smooth, uneventful way the pursuit had been going so far. She realised it would become far more difficult for it to remain that way once they got closer to the lake, as the lack of traffic would make it almost impossible to remain unnoticed on the narrow road leading into Como. For that reason, she had contacted Como police and asked them to intercept the Centenario, should that become necessary. The police there were standing by and would use roadblocks to stop the car if required.

Cesaria's instructions were clear: under no circumstances was the car to be allowed to pass once that order had been given. Too much was riding on apprehending the subject. Allowing Teodora to get away wasn't an option.

As she approached the lake and the familiar road became narrow with numerous bends, something in the rear-view mirror caught Teodora's eye. It was a motorcycle, followed by a car she had noticed before. At first she dismissed this as a coincidence, but as she accelerated, the bike did the same, and when she then slowed down, it didn't overtake her, but slowed down as well, making sure it remained close but behind her at all times.

Someone's tailing me, thought Teodora, an icy wave of fear washing over her. *Stay calm and think. This is no time for mistakes*! If she was right, returning to her villa would be the worst decision as she would be trapped there. The only logical option was to outrun her pursuers and head north to Switzerland. Teodora knew that with her car, her local knowledge and her driving skills, she could do that. She waited until she got out of a bend and then, she accelerated.

'I think she's onto us,' said Cesaria as the Centenario put on speed and began to take corners like a racing car. Realising that their own police car was no match for the powerful Lamborghini, she contacted the motorcycle policeman in front of her and told him to try to overtake the car if possible and signal for it to stop. She also contacted Como police and asked them to put up a roadblock.

Teodora was rapidly approaching the turn-off to Villa Rosa on her left, when she heard the shrill sound of a police siren. It was coming from the motorcycle closing in fast from behind, its flashing lights a signal for her to stop.

Police! thought Teodora. *Shit!* Biting her lip, she changed gears and put her foot down.

Sitting on the terrace facing the lake, Izabel heard the sound of a police siren in the distance. As it became louder, she turned her head – and gasped. She saw Teodora's car racing along the winding road opposite the villa at an insane speed, followed by a motorcycle with flashing lights. She could also see a tractor with a trailer full of hay coming the other way. 'Oh my God!' shouted Izabel, watching as the two vehicles, whose drivers obviously couldn't see each other around the bend, came closer.

Teodora was madly cutting corners to keep her car on the road and get away from the bike. Moments later, the left-side front bumper of the Centenario clipped the large wheel of the tractor as it came around the bend. Doing one hundred and forty, Teodora lost control of the car, veered to the right and crashed through a steel barrier on top of a steep cliff, plummeting towards the lake below.

'*Nooo!*' screamed Izabel, holding her breath, as the Centenario became airborne, its engine whining like a wounded animal in agony.

Teodora saw it all happen in slow motion. First, the collision with the tractor, then crashing through the low barrier on her right, sending pieces of metal flying, followed by a strange feeling of weightlessness as the Centenario left the road and went over a cliff thirty metres above the still waters of the lake.

The last thing Teodora saw was a shaft of blinding sunlight just before her dream of coming home to Izabel was shattered as the car burst into flames, and then rapidly sank into the deep, dark waters of the lake.

PART III

THE THEORY OF EVERYTHING

'In the name of Hippocrates, doctors have invented the most exquisite form of torture known to man: survival.'
Edward Everett Hale

41

Somewhere in the Atlantic: 6 July

Jack hated confined spaces, but what he loathed more was the monotonous, mindless routine of the long sea journey across the Atlantic. The food was basic – some of it almost inedible – contact with the crew was non-existent and the young Colombian boy who delivered the food tray didn't speak a word of English. And to make things worse, it was incredibly hot and there was no air-conditioning in the cabin.

To make his situation bearable, Jack spent most of his time with Dr Agabe in Stolzfus's cabin helping the doctor to look after his patient, which took up quite a bit of time, and playing chess. During the many hours they spent together watched over by a silent, motionless Stolzfus sitting strapped in his wheelchair next to them, Jack got to know Agabe very well and fortunately for him, Agabe was a fascinating man with many interests.

'You know, every time you think about your next move, you hum the same tune,' said Agabe.

'I'm sorry,' replied Jack. 'I wasn't aware of this. Does it bother you?'

'No, not at all, but what I find curious is that the tune you are humming reminds me of Fabry.'

'In what way?'

Agabe shook his head. 'Fabry and his music. There was music everywhere. When we worked on the *Caritas* together, there was piped music in his cabin, in the dining area, even on deck. He couldn't work without music.'

'How odd.'

'It got worse in Valletta,' continued Agabe. 'He had a sophisticated sound system installed in the operating theatre in his clinic and there was music playing during every operation.'

'What kind of music?'

'Classical mainly, but he had his favourites.'

'What were they?'

'Bach. He loved Bach. We got to know Bach cantatas very well and were even humming along during operations just like you were doing a moment ago. *The Passions* of Christ and the scalpel. It was an odd combination.'

'A complex man, as you said.'

'He was complex all right, but when it came to music, he was obsessed. Every week or so, he had a new favourite composer and a new favourite piece and we had to listen to it over and over, day after day. It was quite crazy.'

'And what I was humming just now reminded you of him?'

'It did, because I recognised the tune.'

'You did?'

'Yes. It's Tchaikovsky.'

Jack looked at Agabe, surprised. '*The Lost Symphony*,' he said. 'For some reason, I cannot get it out of my head. I keep hearing it over and over.'

'You know it?'

'I sure do.'

'Strange. During the past couple of weeks or so, Fabry kept playing this symphony all the time. He played it during every operation and told us the story of its extraordinary discovery. It was only discovered recently, you know, somewhere in Russia.'

'Yes, I know.'

It was Agabe's turn to look surprised. 'You seem to know a lot about this. How come?'

'Because I discovered it,' said Jack, a knowing smile spreading across his face.

'Are you *serious*?'

'I am.'

'Can you tell me about it?'

'Sure. Do you believe in destiny?'

'Why do you ask?'

'Because what I'm about to tell you is a remarkable story about destiny, which began a few years ago and appears to be continuing here, right now. And it all began with an old lady in a retirement home in France, a beautiful music box and a letter from a desperate Tsarina, asking for help.'

'How intriguing. I cannot wait to hear it.'

'I will tell you, but you may find it hard to believe. But before I do, I would like to ask you something.'

'Please, go ahead.'

'You said Fabry played music during all of his operations.'

'Yes, he did.'

'Would that include that marathon operation involving Professor Stolzfus here?'

'Yes, of course.'

'And do you remember what music Fabry played during that operation?'

'Yes, I do. It was this piece. Tchaikovsky's *Lost Symphony*. In fact, he played it several times.'

Extraordinary. That's what Tristan could hear, thought Jack, smiling. 'Now let me tell you a story about destiny and fate, and a young man who can hear the whisper of angels and glimpse eternity.'

'Fascinating.'

Over the next two hours and during several chess games, Jack told Agabe how a letter accidentally discovered in a music box left to him by his great aunt, took him on an extraordinary journey of discovery that ultimately led him to a remote church in Russia and Tchaikovsky's lost masterpiece.

After Jack had finished, there was a palpable stillness in the cabin as the chess game continued, the occasional scraping of the pieces on the chessboard the only sound. For a while, Jack stared at the board, lost in thought, but then without realising it he was again humming the Tchaikovsky tune, just as he had done before. It was his move; a difficult one. Then a soft, strange voice interrupted the silence.

'Bishop to d3.'

Jack looked up, bemused, assuming Agabe was making a suggestion because he was taking so long. But Agabe hadn't said anything.

'Bishop to d3,' said the voice again, this time sounding a little stronger. Slowly, Jack turned around and looked at Stolzfus, who was sitting by the open window. Stolzfus's eyes were open just a little and his lips were moving, this time repeating the words without making a sound.

'Incredible! He's *awake*!' whispered Agabe and stood up without taking his eyes off Stolzfus. 'And he can speak. We've done it! It worked! Fabry was a genius.'

This is surreal, thought Jack. Slowly, he moved his bishop as suggested by Stolzfus. 'Good move, Professor,' he said, carefully watching Stolzfus. 'You must have been following the entire game.'

'I have. Not only this game, but everything. Just like your young friend who can hear the whisper of angels and glimpse eternity,' said Stolzfus, speaking very slowly and slurring his words. 'I can remember everything that happened to me since I was shot.'

'You are obviously referring to Tristan's story we've just discussed. Tristan spent several years in a coma after an accident. Somehow he was able to follow everything that was happening around him, but without being able to participate because he was locked in the coma.'

'It was the same with me ...'

'How is that possible?' said Agabe. 'For a while you were only a frozen head without a body, kept alive by a complex process ...'

'I know. I can't explain it. Admittedly, there are gaps in my recollection, but I could comprehend everything that was happening around me with great clarity and without feeling any pain or emotion. Just like now.'

'Extraordinary,' said Agabe and began to examine his patient. 'Everything looks good,' he said. 'Blood pressure and heartbeat, perfect. Astonishing.' Then he reached for his video camera and began to film Stolzfus.

'What are you doing?' asked Jack.

'Instructions. I have to record everything, just as we've recorded the entire operation. Proof ...'

'It's all about the brain, Dr Agabe,' said Stolzfus. 'We know so little about it, yet we owe it everything. Do you ever wonder how we ended up with a brain consisting of one hundred billion neurons and one hundred trillion connections? That's more than all the stars in the universe.'

How strange, thought Jack, remembering a similar conversation in a refugee camp in Somalia a few years ago. *This is exactly what Dr Rosen and I discussed after Tristan had that bad dream.* 'That's staggering,' said Jack. 'Life has come a long way since it first crawled out of the primordial soup millions of years ago.'

'I know you are interested in this subject, Mr Rogan,' said Stolzfus. 'I've read all of your books ...'

'*You have*? How come?'

'My sister, Rebecca, introduced me to them. She's very proud of what you do and gave me copies of your books to read.'

Of course. Jack shook his head. *Another moment of destiny*. 'Yes, in the beginning, progress was slow and nothing much appeared to happen,' continued Jack. 'Then, two hundred and fifty thousand years ago something occurred in the Rift Valley in Ethiopia that changed everything.'

'That's not that far from where I was born,' interjected Agabe. 'What happened?'

'An apeman did something quite extraordinary.'

'What was that?'

'He picked up a lump of obsidian – volcanic glass – and split it. He now had a razor-sharp flint, which he attached to a long piece of wood. He now had a weapon, a spear for hunting. It all went from there. Two hundred and fifty thousand years later – a relatively short period of time – apeman has become spaceman, contemplating the universe, how it began, and where it is heading. Right, Professor?'

'Yes,' said Stolzfus. 'And he's getting very close to a theory that explains everything. If he's capable of doing that, it will be his crowning achievement because then, he will know the mind of God.'

'And all thanks to a grey blob of matter we still don't fully understand, weighing about a kilo and a half. Amazing, don't you think?' said Jack.

'I totally agree with you. And to show you just how right you are, I would like to ask you a favour,' said Stolzfus, suddenly sounding very tired. The strain of talking was beginning to show.

'Of course. What favour?'

'Could you please write something down for me?'

'Sure. What exactly? I have pen and paper right here. The good doctor and I kept score …'

'A couple of equations I've been working on during the past few days.'

'That's incredible,' said Agabe. 'You did that while you were in a coma?'

'Yes. And what's perhaps even more surprising, my mind has never felt sharper or stronger. Without the distractions of life, I have been able to focus completely on solving problems that had seemed insurmountable to me for a number of years now. Suddenly, there is this clarity. I am able to travel through time and space in my imagination and look at the problems in completely different ways. The calculations are complex and it would help me if you could write them down. As you can imagine, I don't want to lose them …'

Suddenly, Stolzfus's voice became fainter until it was almost inaudible and trailed off. He closed his eyes and his breathing became shallow.

'Is he drifting back into a coma?' asked Jack, sounding concerned.

'No, I don't think so. He's falling asleep,' said Agabe, feeling Stolzfus's pulse. 'This must have been a huge effort for him and, I expect, extremely exhausting and confronting, even for a man like him.'

'I can imagine,' said Jack. 'He obviously needs rest. We should leave him to it.'

'Yes, we should. I still can't believe this.' Agabe shook his head. 'We've just spoken to a man who is being kept alive by a body that not so long ago belonged to someone else, who says he can feel no pain and no emotions, and whose astounding mind is functioning better than before, perhaps in a totally new, unique way we can't even imagine. I believe we are witnessing history here, Jack.'

'I look at it in a different way.'

'You do?'

'Yes. I believe that Stolzfus, like Tristan, can hear the whisper of angels and glimpse eternity. The only difference is he can work out what those whispers mean and interpret them. Next time he wakes up, I have to be ready to write it all down.'

'You are right. Every moment he's conscious is precious. In a case like this, we never know what's around the corner …'

'What do you think brought him out of the coma?' asked Jack. 'So suddenly and without apparent reason?'

'Don't laugh. I think it was the music.'

'What? My humming?'

'Yes.'

'Seriously?'

'I've seen this before in Africa. Music can have a profound effect on the mind we don't quite understand. I've seen witchdoctors go into a trance triggered by the sound of drums or flutes, and come out of it when it stopped.'

'Are you suggesting that somehow hearing *The Lost Symphony* that was played during the operation, brought him out of the coma?'

'It's possible.'

'Amazing. Another game?'

'Sure, but only if you promise not to hum. We don't want to wake the professor, do we?'

'Certainly not! Even a genius needs sleep. Your move.'

42

Chief Prosecutor's office, Florence: 7 July

Cesaria knew Grimaldi hated to be kept waiting. Breathless and late, she burst open the door to his office for the briefing she had arranged the day before. Andersen and Tristan were already there, chatting to Grimaldi. 'Apologies,' said Cesaria as she hurried into the room and sat down. 'I got tied up on the phone with forensics.'

'You are here now; that's all that matters,' said Grimaldi, putting his star officer at ease. He knew she was under a lot of pressure from various quarters, but the situation was serious and the Squadra Mobile was under the spotlight, which meant that he too was in the glare of scrutiny and attention from above. A breakthrough of sorts was badly needed, and Grimaldi was hoping Cesaria would deliver one. The chief prosecutor sat back in his chair and looked expectantly at Cesaria.

'The police divers have recovered Teodora's body from the lake. Unfortunately, it's very deep there and it took longer than expected. We have searched Teodora's villa and obtained her phone records, and secured computer equipment and several laptops. Forensics are examining the material right now and retrieving information.'

'That will take some time, I expect,' said Grimaldi.

'It will. But I can confirm that the cryptic telephone message left for Tristan at Palazzo da Baggio at three thirty-four pm on four July came from Teodora. It was the last call she made before she plunged to her death.'

'"Tell Tristan Jack Rogan is alive and he is being taken to Colombia",' interjected Tristan. 'Are we any closer to finding out what that could mean?'

'We are,' said Cesaria. 'I interviewed Izabel Gonzales at the villa. She had a broken leg and was waiting for Teodora. She was quite distraught. In fact, she and Teodora had a lengthy telephone conversation lasting over two hours just before Teodora spoke to Lorenza at the Palazzo.'

'Do we know what that was about?' asked Grimaldi.

'We do. Izabel cooperated fully and I am satisfied that she has nothing to do with this matter. She's unaware of what has been going on. She and Teodora had only met recently and were lovers.'

'A dead end then?' said Grimaldi, frowning.

'Not entirely,' said Cesaria, a hesitant smile spreading across her tired face. 'Somehow it's always the little unexpected things that seem to make all the difference.'

'Can you please elaborate?' asked Andersen, who until then hadn't said a word.

'I can. And it's about when and where Izabel met Teodora.'

'Intriguing,' said Grimaldi.

'It is. Izabel and her friend Claudia – both former Victoria's Secret Angels – were invited by Alessandro Giordano to spend a couple of days on the *Nike* in Port de Fontvieille. Claudia is Alessandro's present girlfriend. One of them.' Cesaria paused to let this sink in.

'When was that?' asked Tristan.

'On fifteen April. That's the day Izabel met Teodora. A chance meeting. But what's even more interesting is who else was there at the time.'

'Who?' asked Grimaldi, leaning forward in his chair.

'A man called Raul Rodrigo.'

'And he is important because ...?' said Grimaldi.

'He's the New York lawyer representing Hernando Cordoba, the head of the notorious H Cartel in Colombia,' said Andersen. 'He also acts for Cordoba's son, who is presently on death row in Arizona awaiting execution.'

'Charming family,' said Tristan.

Grimaldi smiled. Cesaria and Andersen had just provided the breakthrough he so desperately needed: a direct link between the Giordanos and the H Cartel, one of the biggest drug suppliers in

South America, and one of the most ambitious and ruthless. Hoping for just such a breakthrough, Grimaldi had arranged a meeting with Alessandro and his father for the next day. He now had exactly what he needed to apply the necessary pressure he had been looking for. Grimaldi had crossed swords with Riccardo Giordano before. He knew how his mind worked and therefore how to handle him. But most important of all, he knew his weakness and how to use this to his advantage. It had worked before and Grimaldi was hoping it would do so again.

'But that's not all,' continued Cesaria. 'Izabel overheard a conversation between Alessandro and Rodrigo on the *Nike* that could shed some light on what is going on here.'

'Oh? What conversation?' asked Grimaldi.

'About handing something over in Morocco and using the *Nike* to deliver it there.'

'Are you serious?'

'I have no reason to doubt Izabel's recollection or truthfulness.'

'Excellent work,' said Grimaldi.

Andersen nodded and turned to Grimaldi. She had just returned from the American Naval base in Naples after a marathon interrogation session involving Aladdin, Silvanus and the crew of the *Nike*. 'The pieces of the puzzle are slowly falling into place,' she said. 'But one key element is still missing here, and nothing I've heard so far is helping us with that.'

'What's that?' asked Grimaldi.

'Why a Mafia family here in Florence engaged one of the most notorious and expensive hit-squads in the world to abduct a prominent scientist, and then arranged to hand him over to a South American drug cartel in Morocco,' said Tristan.

Andersen nodded. 'Precisely. Nothing we've been able to glean from the interrogations in Naples has thrown any light on this baffling question. The two male members of the squad in custody haven't said a word and are demanding to see their lawyer, and the crew are too afraid to say anything. They are more frightened of the Mafia than they are of the CIA; no-one's talking.'

'That's been troubling me too,' said Grimaldi. 'But the Mafia does nothing without a reason, and the reason is usually calculated and clear. It's always about money and power.'

'But with Stolzfus dead, whatever arrangement or deal might have been in place between the Giordanos and the H Cartel has gone terribly wrong,' said Cesaria. 'It's all over, right?'

Tristan realised the right moment had arrived for him to step in and drop the bombshell he had been carrying around for some time now. 'Not necessarily,' he said.

'What do you mean?' said Cesaria.

Tristan cleared his throat. 'Assume for the moment that Stolzfus *isn't* dead, but has in fact just been taken on the *Nike* from Malta to Morocco—'

'But that's absurd,' interrupted Grimaldi. 'We have his body. Identified by his sister and confirmed by DNA tests.'

'Yes, you have his body, but not his *head*,' said Tristan. 'I know this is difficult to take in and appears to fly in the face of logic, but I strongly believe Stolzfus is alive.'

'Based on what, for heaven's sake?' Grimaldi said, becoming annoyed.

'Have any of you heard of a cephalosomatic anastomosis, or CSA?'

Grimaldi shook his head. 'What on earth is that?'

'A head transplant.'

'A *what?*' said Grimaldi impatiently.

'I've done some research on this fascinating subject. It would appear that Professor Fabry was somewhat of an authority on this, albeit a very controversial one. In essence, the head is removed from a damaged, dying body and surgically attached to a healthy, brain-dead body, thereby keeping the healthy brain, and therefore *the person*, alive.'

'This is fantasy, surely,' said Grimaldi.

'As far as I'm aware this has never been done successfully involving a live human, but Fabry claimed it could be done, and it was only a matter of time before a successful in vivo CSA was carried out.'

'Are you seriously suggesting that this could have happened to Stolzfus?' interjected Andersen.

'I am,' said Tristan.

Grimaldi shook his head. 'This is absurd! We are going nowhere with this and wasting time.'

Cesaria held up her hand. 'Let's not dismiss this just yet,' she said, trying to smooth the ruffled feathers. 'Let's hear what else Tristan has to say. We mustn't forget that he is capable of certain unique insights that have helped us before. Quite spectacularly, if I remember correctly, with Lorenza da Baggio's abduction, Conti and the Gambio matter.'

'It's all about intuition,' said Tristan, stepping in. 'I keep hearing this music and then I see things ... I cannot add much more at this stage, but I did tell Jack about it just before he disappeared.'

'What was his reaction when you told him?' Grimaldi wanted to know.

'A bit like yours, but Jack knows how to keep an open mind and not to dismiss what I sense, however far-fetched it might appear at the time.'

'Perhaps so, but I cannot run an investigation based on intuition, insights and "visions". I need facts and proof.'

'But you can run on gut feeling,' said Cesaria. 'I've seen you do it many times before, sir, and then find the facts and proof later to back it all up. Is this so different?' came her polite rebuke.

'Why don't we keep this possibility in the back of our minds for the time being?' suggested Andersen, trying to find some common ground. 'Just for now. But I must admit the possibility raised by Tristan has a certain seductive appeal.'

'In what way?' asked Grimaldi.

'Because it does answer many of the questions that are troubling us right now.'

Cesaria shot Tristan a meaningful look and winked. 'Good suggestion,' she said, realising that Tristan's extraordinary hypothesis couldn't go much further at that stage.

Andersen stood up and walked over to Grimaldi's whiteboard. 'Let's not worry about this and what's still missing for the moment. Let's have a closer look at what we *do* have instead and take it from there.'

'Good idea,' said Grimaldi, feeling better. 'Please go ahead, Major.'

43

On the *Coatilcue*, approaching the coast of South America: 8 July

'Queen to f3,' said Stolzfus. 'Checkmate. Sorry.'

'Damn!' said Jack. 'I didn't see this coming, Zac. Will I ever win a game?'

'Don't despair, my friend, you are doing exceptionally well. Huge improvement over the last two days. It's all about strategy and anticipation, and sizing up your opponent.'

'You only keep saying this to encourage me to continue playing so that you can beat me. Easy for you. You can see the entire game in your head. Several moves down the track. Not like me. I struggle with each move, one at a time.'

'Patience. You will master this in due course. If you want to. You are a man of action, Jack, not of contemplation. I'm a mathematician and a theoretical physicist. That's all about *thinking*. Very different. That reminds me. It's time for our little lecture. Are you ready?'

'Sure. Beats losing.'

Jack reached for his notepad and biro. Since Stolzfus had come out of his coma two days ago, he had made remarkable progress and a special bond had developed between Stolzfus, Agabe and Jack. They spent most of the day together in Stolzfus's small cabin, whiling away the long, monotonous hours by talking about physics, the mysteries of the universe and playing chess.

But Stolzfus also appeared to be working. His mind never stopped and he looked at chess as a welcome distraction from his never-ending calculations and equations, all of which Jack had to write down. It was the way he seemed to cope with his extraordinary predicament and come to terms with his new, confronting reality. He also enjoyed teaching Jack and Agabe about general relativity and quantum field theory, which underpinned all of modern physics and most closely seemed to resemble the elusive theory of everything Stolzfus appeared to be so obsessed with.

'All right, Jack, tell me about general relativity,' said Stolzfus.

'Is this an exam?'

'Not at all. I just want to see if you've been paying attention.'

Jack put down his pen and looked at Stolzfus. 'Yes, Professor. Here we go. General relativity is a theoretical framework of physics. It uses gravity to explain how the universe works in areas of high mass and large scale, like galaxies, stars and so on.'

'Very good. Now what about quantum field theory? What can you tell me about that?'

'Quantum field theory on the other hand,' continued Jack, encouraged by the compliment, 'is a theoretical framework that uses something quite different to explain how the universe works.'

'And how does it do that?'

'It uses three non-gravitational forces and concentrates on areas of small scale and low mass, like atoms, molecules and subatomic particles.'

'Excellent! You have been paying attention. I will now ask my doctor here a question. Is there a problem with these two frameworks?'

'Yes. They are mutually incompatible. In short, they can't both be right, but this problem only becomes an issue in areas of extremely small scale.'

'Correct; the Planck scale,' said Stolzfus. 'Regions that only exist in black holes and where else?'

'At the very beginning of the universe. Shortly after the Big Bang,' said Jack.

'I am impressed. I wish all of my students were so switched on.'

'We've heard nothing else over the last two days,' said Jack, rolling his eyes. 'How could we possibly have missed any of this and not be on top of it all?'

'I firmly believe there is a way to integrate these two seemingly incompatible principles into a single theoretical framework,' continued

Stolzfus, becoming excited. 'And it's all about what you wrote down yesterday.'

'If you say so.'

'But something vital is still missing,' continued Stolzfus, undeterred. 'I've seen what it is. In my sleep; just like Einstein conceived his famous E=mc2 during sleep, and it goes back to ancient Greece: Democritus. Do you want to know why?'

'Do we have a choice?' said Jack.

'And then there was Archimedes. Now, he was a real thinker. Well ahead of his time,' Stolzfus prattled on, enjoying himself. 'And then came a real giant – Newton with his gravity – and it all went from there. Kepler and one of my personal favourites, Laplace, did the heavy lifting after that. And now we have an eleven-dimensional string/M-theory as a possible contender for the theory of everything ...'

'I think I prefer chess,' said Jack. 'At least I know where I'm going, even if it's into defeat.'

'Don't look too glum, Jack. Please write this down. You never know, we may be making history today and you, my friend, could be part of it.'

'Yeah. The dumb scribe who wrote it all down.'

'Don't be so tough on yourself. I'll explain it all to you later. Now, please pay attention. Here we go ...'

Over the next hour, Stolzfus dictated calculations and complex equations at a feverish pace and made sure Jack got it all down on paper correctly. To anyone but Stolzfus and an initiated few, the numbers and complex diagrams and symbols would have appeared meaningless and strange, but they were in fact rare insights into the workings of the universe and the eternal laws that govern them, based on flashes of genius Stolzfus had experienced during the coma after his operation.

Then, in the middle of one particularly long, complicated equation, Stolzfus suddenly stopped speaking.

Jack looked up.

Stolzfus had his eyes closed and appeared to be asleep.

'He's done it again,' said Jack, putting down his pen. 'Hardly surprising. This stuff is diabolically boring.'

'He's obviously exhausted,' said Agabe, feeling Stolzfus's pulse. 'This huge intellectual effort must be taking a lot out of him is all I can say. In any event, what he's doing here is absolutely remarkable. Let's let him sleep for a while. It will do him good.'

'Fine by me. I was about to fall asleep myself. Let's go outside and get some air.'

Standing on the small deck reserved for them at the stern of the ship, Jack watched the sun sink slowly into the calm sea. It was a particularly beautiful moment, watching the mesmerising colours turn within seconds from blazing red to warm shades of mauve as the dying sun disappeared from the horizon and the stars took over and began to appear in the sky like tiny, sparkling windows into infinity.

'You know, what Stolzfus is doing here is amazing,' said Jack. 'In fact, this whole situation is quite surreal when you look at it objectively. Here we have a man who's just gone through a world-first operation that until now was considered impossible. His head's been grafted onto another man's body to keep him alive. He's strapped into a wheelchair – effectively paralysed with only his exceptional brain working – but he's able to communicate because somehow his power of speech has been preserved. And what is he doing? He's trying to solve one of the greatest remaining challenges of theoretical physics that has so far eluded the most gifted minds. He's trying to come up with a theory of everything. How? By merely thinking about it and using his imagination. Why? Because inspired by a piece of music he heard as his head was being removed, he saw a possible solution to the conundrum and has been working on it ever since, even while in a coma. Does this sound like fantasy to you?'

Agabe looked up at the stars. 'The human brain has awesome powers we don't yet fully understand. If used correctly, it can achieve astonishing things. What we are witnessing here is just that,' he said. 'Man reaching for the stars and trying to understand his place in the universe. It's an age-old quest.'

'And if this isn't enough,' continued Jack, 'we are effectively prisoners on a ship approaching South America, floating towards an uncertain future I cannot make sense of, however hard I try. Why was Stolzfus abducted in the first place and brought here? Why have I been abducted and brought here with him? Who is behind all this and what is the purpose of it all? I can't work it out. At least your position is clear. You are here to look after him.'

'Correct. But beyond that I'm just as much in the dark as you and my future is just as uncertain as yours. Does all this make you afraid?'

Jack gave Agabe a mischievous smile. 'Not really. If they wanted to kill me, they could have done that easily a long time ago. No, they *want* something from me; I just don't know what. How does that make me feel? Glad to be alive. I've been in situations like this before and they have turned out to be some of the most exciting and stimulating times of my life. I think the same is happening here, right now.'

'I hope you're right, for both our sakes.'

'In any event, we'll find out soon enough. We must be very close to South America. Perhaps another day or so and we should be there. And just as well. I don't think I can take Zac's dictations for much longer.'

'Don't say that, Jack. You could be holding the theory of everything in your hands.'

'Perhaps, but I doubt it will do us much good. I suspect astrophysics has limited appeal where we are heading and we may need a little more than a few obscure equations scribbled on a piece of paper to keep us out of trouble.'

Agabe slapped Jack on the back. 'I think you're right. In any event, I'll never forget this journey, surreal or not.'

'Nor will I.'

44

Florence: 8 July

Riccardo Giordano had only been summoned to the chief prosecutor's office once before. That had been two years ago. He remembered the occasion well. It was about the shooting of his eldest son, Mario. Grimaldi had given him certain information about whom he believed was behind the killing, and had left it up to Giordano to do something about it. What followed had been the very public assassination right in front of Grimaldi and Jack during Mario's funeral, resulting in a certain understanding between Giordano and the chief prosecutor about Mafia affairs in Florence, and an uneasy truce between the two remaining Mafia families ruling the city. Giordano had no doubt that this meeting had something to do with that, and the recent Fabry fiasco in Malta.

Giordano turned to Alessandro sitting next to him in the reception on the ground floor. He could see that his son was nervous. 'I will do the talking, is that clear?'

Alessandro nodded and lit another cigarette. 'What do you think he wants?'

'We'll find out in a moment. I know Grimaldi, remember? He's a straight shooter. With him, you always know where you stand.'

'That's what I'm afraid of.'

'Don't be. You should be more afraid of your friends than a man like him. Always remember what happened to Mario.'

At three o'clock sharp, Grimaldi's secretary took Giordano and Alessandro up to the chief prosecutor's office on the first floor.

Grimaldi smiled when he noticed the loose tie around Giordano's thick neck. It was the same tie and ill-fitting jacket he had worn at their last meeting two years ago. At seventy the man was still as a strong as an ox, and just as stubborn.

'You wanted to see us, Chief Prosecutor,' said Giordano, adjusting his uncomfortable tie. He rarely wore one because it chafed against his stubble. Giordano was no stranger to the finer things in life, but he had simple tastes and felt more comfortable in the barn or in the stables and preferred the rough kitchen table to a dining room filled with fine silver and antiques. But what he lacked in polish and finesse, he more than made up for in common sense and cunning, which had served him well in steering his family along the treacherous Mafia road from the austerity of Calabria to the trappings of Florence. A simple peasant who had once slept next to his livestock to keep himself warm during winter, now lived like a prince protected by an army of bodyguards in an opulent villa once owned by a centuries-old Florentine aristocracy.

'Thank you for coming. I know it was short notice, but what I have to talk to you about is urgent. Very urgent.'

'Oh? What's it about?'

Grimaldi lit a small cigar. He watched the smoke curl towards the open window behind him and took his time before replying. 'Two things,' he said. 'A warning … and a proposal.'

'You speak in riddles,' said Giordano dismissively.

'Let me tell you a little story and all will become clear. It's about a famous scientist, an expensive hit squad and a Colombian drug baron. With me so far?'

'I don't know what you are talking about,' said Giordano.

'You don't have to say anything. Just listen,' continued Grimaldi, choosing his words carefully. Having given Tristan's extraordinary suggestion that Stolzfus could somehow still be alive more thought overnight, he felt there was no harm in alluding to that possibility to see what reaction he would get. A skilful interrogator, Grimaldi knew how to read body language and interpret even the most subtle reactions.

'By all accounts, the scientist is dead, or so it *seems* ...' Grimaldi paused, put his cigar in the ashtray in front of him and carefully watched both Giordano and his son.

Alessandro flinched, but there was no reaction from his father.

How can he possibly know? thought Giordano, his mind racing. This could change everything.

'Two members of the hit squad – both women – are dead as well,' continued Grimaldi. 'One of them died only three days ago when her car ran off the road near her home at Lake Como during a police chase. It was the same black Lamborghini that was driven from your home and left in a car park near the train station by one of your men. The other two members of the hit squad are in custody at a US Naval base in Naples and are being interrogated. Robustly, I believe. And so are the crew of the *Nike*. In my experience, it's only a matter of time before someone talks. But I'm sure you know all this. What you may not know is that Mr Rodrigo is also being interrogated. Right now, by the CIA in New York.'

'*Rodrigo*? Never heard of him,' said Giordano gruffly. 'What has all this got to do with us?'

'Let's not insult each other,' continued Grimaldi calmly. 'You know exactly who he is. Raul Rodrigo is a high-profile lawyer working for the H Cartel. He met with your son on the *Nike* on fifteen June. We have a witness and a sworn statement. They discussed the delivery of something important. I believe Morocco was mentioned; isn't that correct, Alessandro?'

Giordano put his hand on Alessandro's knee, the gesture obvious. Alessandro didn't reply.

'I see. Then let me help you,' continued Grimaldi. He took three large photographs out of a drawer and pushed two of them across his desk towards Giordano. The photos showed Teodora, Aladdin and Silvanus sitting in front of a smiling Giacomo in the saloon of the *Nike*. 'These were taken with the body camera of one of the Ministry of Defence Police officers who boarded the *Nike* just after the vessel left Portsmouth, England on fifteen June. The two men and the woman sitting at the table are members of the hit squad, and the man standing in the background, of course you know well. He is Giacomo Cornale, the captain of the *Nike*.'

Grimaldi noticed that Alessandro had begun to fidget in his seat and looked nervous, small beads of perspiration glistening on his brow a clear sign of the turmoil boiling within. Grimaldi smiled and decided to press on.

'And then we have this here,' he said and pushed the third photograph towards Giordano. It was the aerial photograph showing the *Nike* and the *Caritas* next to each other in the middle of a storm off the French coast. Grimaldi didn't bother explaining the photo and chose to just leave it on the table to let it speak for itself. He knew from experience that saying little was often far more effective than lengthy explanations, as this gave the impression that he knew a lot more about the subject than he chose to disclose. It was a mind game he knew well and had used many times. For a while there was a tense silence in the room.

'What's on your mind, Chief Prosecutor?' asked Giordano at last.

'Very conveniently, Professor Fabry is also dead,' continued Grimaldi undeterred, ignoring the question. 'Killed in Valletta by the woman who died the other day in the car crash, and then left in a vat filled with acetone like his famous exhibits. Nice touch, but a pity. He was such a gifted surgeon. Ahead of his time, many would say. Perhaps he was silenced because he knew too much, or made some fatal mistake? Who knows? Death seems to be following this project – and you – like a bad smell. Very soon there will be no-one left. And that brings me to the first item I want to talk about: the *warning*.'

'What kind of warning?' asked Giordano.

'You have already lost one son. The warning is about the one you have left. Alessandro here.'

'What do you mean?'

'Don't take me for a fool, Mr Giordano. This is all about drugs and the drug supply from South America; the H Cartel to be precise. We've known for a long time that Malta is the entry point into Europe and that the *Caritas* and the *Nike* have played a significant part in bringing those drugs into the country. There are two families here in Florence involved and both use the H Cartel: your family, and the

Lombardos. There's been an uneasy truce since Gambio was assassinated, but tensions have been simmering lately as old rivalries have reignited. And I can guess what that's about ... the Lombardos are expanding their territory and muscling in on yours. Bodies have once again been floating in the river and as you know, I don't like that because I thought we had an understanding.'

Grimaldi paused and lit another little cigar to let Giordano stew. He was reaching the pointy end of the conversation and was deliberately taking his time. What he was about to raise was speculation, but his instincts told him that he was on the right path and therefore he decided to take the gamble. If he was right, he was certain he had Giordano exactly where he wanted him: ready to negotiate. If not, nothing much was lost and a different approach would be needed later.

'Please get to the point,' said Giordano and began to play with his tie, which was obviously annoying him. It was the first sign of unease Grimaldi had observed in his visitor.

'What do you think would happen if the Lombardos were to find out that Alessandro here has been negotiating with the H Cartel behind their backs, eh?'

'*Nonsense!*' interrupted Giordano, raising his voice.

'My guess is it was all about cutting off their supply route and giving you a free hand ...'

Grimaldi was watching Giordano carefully. The look on the old man's face told him all he needed to know. He had hit the nail on the head.

'What do you think the Lombardos would do? Take it lying down? Hardly. They would start a war and Alessandro here could well be the next body floating in the river. And after that, everything escalates and there's no way of stopping it. We've both seen this before and that is precisely what I want to prevent. What happens in London or on the high seas is a matter for MI5, the CIA and the US Navy, but what happens in my town and on my watch is very much a matter for me. And that brings me to the abduction of Jack Rogan a few days ago in his hotel not far from here. Jack Rogan is a friend – *famiglia* – and I want to know what has happened to him and why.'

Grimaldi paused and listened to the chiming of the familiar church bells drifting through the open window. It was time to play his trump card.

'I understand Rogan is being taken to Colombia right now,' continued Grimaldi, lowering his voice. 'And I want to know why, and by whom. Do you think you can help me with that?'

How on earth does he know that too? thought Giordano, sensing a serious problem in the making. And how come he suspected that Stolzfus may be alive? Someone had obviously been talking. What a stuff-up! It was time to cut a deal to get him off his back.

'And the second thing you want to talk about?' asked Giordano, trying to appear nonchalant and calm.

Grimaldi smiled. His strategy seemed to be working. 'Yes, *the proposal* ... Alessandro, would you mind waiting outside? I would like to talk to your father alone.'

Looking relieved, Alessandro stood up and without saying a word, left the room.

45

Arriving in Colombia: 10 July

Jack and Agabe stood on deck and watched the *Coatilcue* sail past El Morro Island and enter the Bay of Santa Marta. Jack wiped the sweat from his neck with a handkerchief and pointed down to the wooden pier as the ship's crew prepared for docking. The entry to the pier was blocked off by a tall barbed-wire fence patrolled by men armed with machine guns.

'If you thought of making a quick getaway, think again,' said Jack. 'Look.'

'Great! Welcome to Santa Marta,' said Agabe. 'The first Spanish settlement in Colombia … I looked it up on Google before we left Morocco,' he added, grinning at Jack.

Located on the Caribbean Sea, the busy port was used by the H Cartel as a main export point for coffee and cocaine. With its own heavily armed and fortified port facility and twenty-four hour access to its ships without interference from the authorities, Santa Marta was ideally positioned to allow the lucrative drug business to flourish. Generous payments to those controlling the harbour ensured that the cartel's operations were not interrupted.

As the *Coatilcue* was being secured and the gangway lowered, two black Land Rovers approached the barbed-wire fence. A man holding a machine gun walked up to one of the cars and looked through the driver's window. Satisfied, he raised his arm. A large gate was opened to allow the vehicles to pass.

As the cars pulled up near the ship, Rodrigo jumped out of the first Land Rover, hurried up the gangway and spoke briefly to the captain waiting for him at the top. 'How was the trip?' he asked.

'Uneventful.'

'And our precious cargo?'

'All safe and in good health. Come, see for yourself.'

'We meet again,' said Rodrigo breezily and walked up to Jack and Agabe standing in front of Stolzfus's cabin. Jack just looked at Rodrigo without saying a word as he remembered the last time they had come across each other. On that occasion, Jack had been strapped to a steel tabletop on the *Caritas*, being interrogated under the watchful eye of Fabry brandishing a scalpel in his face.

'I can't say I'm too pleased to see you,' said Jack. 'Last time we met I almost ended up as an exhibit.'

Rodrigo laughed, appreciating the humour. As a practical man only interested in results, he was hoping Jack realised that cooperation would be the best way of dealing with the predicament he found himself in. 'And the only reason you didn't,' replied Rodrigo, 'was because of the helpful and truthful answers you gave to my questions. I hope we can continue in the same spirit here. You strike me as a sensible man, Mr Rogan, a realist who understands that certain situations have a momentum of their own and demand certain actions, not all of which are pleasant. I'm sure you know exactly what I mean.'

'I understand perfectly, but I seem to have had more than my fair share of unpleasant bits lately to embrace the concept with enthusiasm as you suggest. Seven days cooped up on this rust bucket as a prisoner on a journey into the unknown, for instance.'

'Then allow me to make amends and improve things.'

Jack shrugged but didn't reply.

Rodrigo turned to Agabe. 'But first, I would very much like to meet your patient,' he said. 'Is he in here?'

'He is. Please,' said Agabe and pointed to the door to Stolzfus's cabin.

Rodrigo spoke only briefly with Stolzfus to make sure he was as lucid and alert as Agabe had indicated in his reports during the journey. Satisfied, he left the cabin and took Agabe aside. 'This is excellent. Much better than I expected. Mr Cordoba will be pleased.'

'What happens now?' asked Jack, who had overheard the exchange.

'We travel to Bogota. Mr Cordoba is anxious to meet you and, of course, Professor Stolzfus here.'

'I bet,' said Jack. 'How far is it to Bogota?'

'Less than two hours by plane. Mr Cordoba has sent his personal jet to get you there in comfort. See? I'm already working on an improvement. Gentlemen, please let's go. The plane is waiting.'

The flight from Santa Marta to Bogota was uneventful, but Stolzfus appeared to be enjoying himself. The stimulation of the flight and attention given to him seemed to have had a beneficial effect. He was not only alert, but joked with the crew fussing over him. He didn't seem to mind that they were all heavily armed young men who spoke little English, obviously had no idea who he was and looked at him as a strange curiosity.

Surrounded by armed guards, Cordoba's helicopter gunship was waiting at Bogota airport, its noisy engine running, and took Stolzfus straight to the H Cartel compound, which was only a short distance away.

Standing by the large window in his observation room overlooking the compound, Cordoba watched the helicopter land. He turned to his wife standing next to him and pointed to the man in the wheelchair being lifted out of the chopper. 'All being well, that's the man who will save our son,' he said. 'And the man standing next to him will help us do it.'

'Who's that?' asked Rahima.

'A high-profile, extremely well-connected international writer who for some reason has taken a particular interest in the Stolzfus matter. His connections – especially in America – and international reputation will come in useful in preparing the way for what we have to do to get Alonso released.'

Rahima reached for her husband's hand and squeezed it. 'Thank you,' she said. 'I know you are doing everything you can.'

'The writer was Rodrigo's idea, but I think he's right. Here they come now.'

'I better leave you to it,' said Rahima. She knew when it was time to withdraw and stay in the background. She kissed Cordoba on the cheek and hurried out of the room.

Cordoba had arranged for Stolzfus and Jack to be brought to him straight away. He wanted to see for himself how well Stolzfus had survived his ordeal. After all that had happened to Stolzfus, Cordoba took all the reports and assurances about the professor's condition and state of mind with a healthy dose of scepticism and wanted to assess the situation for himself. Cordoba always addressed critical matters personally, and insisted on meeting people who played an important part in his plans, face to face.

Being a savvy tactician, and as this matter was about people and personalities, getting to know the key players was, in his view, absolutely essential if the daring plan was to succeed. That way, he could accurately evaluate the risks involved and make an informed decision. Experience had taught him that leaving this to others could quickly turn into a costly mistake. As this was about his son's life, making a mistake was out of the question.

Cordoba stood in front of a large TV with his hands folded behind his back, watching as Agabe wheeled Stolzfus into the room. He had just watched a small segment of the video sent to him by Fabry about the Stolzfus operation. Cordoba turned off the TV and turned around. *Oh my God*, he thought. The man sitting in the wheelchair, his shaved head supported by a complicated-looking contraption, wasn't what he had expected. Recovering quickly, Cordoba stepped out of the shadows and walked towards the wheelchair. 'Welcome, Professor,' said Cordoba.

'Please stand in front of my chair so I can see you,' replied Stolzfus. 'Unfortunately, I cannot turn my head.'

Cordoba walked over to the chair and stood in front of Stolzfus. 'I'm sorry, is that better? I'm Hernando Cordoba. I'm pleased to make your acquaintance.'

'Look at me. I wish I could say the same,' replied Stolzfus. 'It's been quite a rollercoaster ride from Westminster Abbey to your fortress here in Bogota, Mr Cordoba. The mysteries I am used to are mainly about the universe, but this here is something else ... I cannot for the life of me work out why a man like you should be interested in someone like me, and go to such extraordinary lengths to bring me here.'

'Then let me enlighten you,' said Cordoba, encouraged by Stolzfus's lucid statements and the strength of his voice. 'To begin with, I would like to apologise. What happened to you was never part of our plan. Being shot was an unfortunate accident we did not expect and certainly did not intend, and what happened after that was all part of a desperate attempt to keep you alive.'

'*Why*? Why abduct me in the first place? What possible use can I be to you?'

'Because I hope that you will save my son.'

Stolzfus closed his eyes and for a few tense seconds he appeared non-responsive. Becoming concerned, Cordoba looked at Agabe. Agabe stepped forward and was about to feel his patient's pulse when Stolzfus opened his eyes again. 'I don't understand,' he said.

'As you no doubt know, my son is on death row in Arizona, awaiting execution.'

'I know, but how can I possibly assist you with that?'

'You are an important man, Professor. Perhaps more important to the US, its space program and its missile defence shield than you realise. I will let my lawyer here explain to you what we have in mind.'

Jack stood behind Agabe. *Here it comes*, he thought, mesmerised by what was happening around him.

Rodrigo walked over to Cordoba and stood next to his client so that Stolzfus could see him.

'What we have in mind here is quite simple,' said Rodrigo. 'One life in exchange for another. Your safe return to the US in exchange for the release of Mr Cordoba's son.'

Stolzfus tried to laugh, but only managed what sounded more like a throaty gurgle. 'You brought me all this way for *that?* Do you realise how insane this is?'

Rodrigo shrugged but didn't reply. It wasn't the reaction he had expected.

'That's a matter for us, Professor,' said Cordoba quietly.

'I'm not as important as you may think, Mr Cordoba, and I doubt very much if the US Government is likely to entertain such an arrangement.'

Cordoba turned towards Jack and looked at him. It was the first time he had paid him any attention. 'Perhaps not straight away,' he said. 'But that's where Mr Rogan here comes into play.'

'I do?' said Jack. 'How exactly?'

'It's nice to meet you too, Mr Rogan,' said Cordoba, ignoring the question. 'I've heard a lot about you lately ...'

Jack shook his head. 'I can't say the same about you, Mr Cordoba. In any event, I fail to see how I can possibly be of any use to you in this extraordinary endeavour.'

'Allow me to explain,' said Rodrigo, stepping in. 'I do agree with Professor Stolzfus that at first there is likely to be strong resistance by the US to our proposal. However, public opinion is a powerful tool and we both know that this president, in particular, is obsessed with social media, fake news and public opinion, and you, Mr Rogan, will help us shape and manipulate that public opinion.'

'How?'

'You seem to have excellent contacts, especially at the *New York Times*. People listen to you. We have certainly seen that in the past. You know how to shape and influence public opinion. You've done this successfully in the past ...'

A skilful advocate with extensive court experience, Rodrigo paused to let this sink in. 'You were instrumental in changing the law about abandoned Holocaust fortunes hidden in Swiss bank accounts, and you forced the banks to open their ledgers and their vaults and make restitutions. If I remember correctly, this made you *Time* Magazine's 'Person of the Year'. And then a few years later, you brought down the British Government by exposing the Lord Elms scandal. You are a man of great influence, Mr Rogan, and we would like to harness that influence—'

'I still can't see how that could possibly work here,' interrupted Jack.

'You underestimate yourself, Mr Rogan,' said Rodrigo, smiling. 'The articles you recently inspired, or shall I say *instigated*, have had a profound effect on public opinion in this very matter and have shaped how governments and law enforcement agencies have reacted to Professor Stolzfus's abduction.'

'Even if what you say is correct, how can that possibly help you here with what you propose to do? Forgive me for speaking plainly, but exchanging a convicted criminal on death row for a scientist abducted by a wanted drug baron? This is nothing more than a high-profile ransom demand involving a superpower. The Americans will never go for that!'

'We disagree, but we can discuss all this later,' said Rodrigo.

Pleased by the way the meeting had been going so far, Cordoba decided to bring it to an end because more than enough had been said – for now – and he knew that saying more at this stage could be detrimental.

'Quite so,' he interjected. 'Professor Stolzfus must be tired after his long trip. Gentlemen, please consider yourselves my guests. I will make sure you have everything you need to make your stay here comfortable. As you will see, this is a large complex. A very secure one. You are free to move around inside as you wish, but for your own safety, you may not step outside ... as you would have noticed, we have guards everywhere. Bogota is a dangerous place. Mr Rodrigo will show you to your rooms,' said Cordoba, 'and explain everything.' Cordoba nodded, turned around and walked back to his desk, an obvious gesture of dismissal.

As Jack walked to the door, he noticed a series of large photographs hanging on the wall. He stopped in front of one to have a closer look. A group of young, naked African women wearing spectacular head decorations were dancing around a fire surrounded by what looked like dense rainforest. Their painted faces reminded Jack of the love dance described by the omda he had met recently in that remote village in the Nuba Mountains. *Strange*, thought Jack as he read the inscription at the bottom of the photograph: *Xingu River, Brazil, 1971.*

Xingu, thought Jack as he turned around and followed Rodrigo to the door. *Where have I heard that name before?* And then it struck him. Of course! Madame Petrova had mentioned the Xingu Indians as one of the remote tribes visited by her niece Natasha, not long before she disappeared ...

Standing in the corridor between a security guard and Rodrigo, Jack waited for the lift to take them down to the basement. Agabe stood behind him fussing over Stolzfus, who had his eyes closed. When the lift doors opened, Jack found himself facing an elderly woman. Their eyes met and Jack could feel the fine hairs on his neck stand to attention. Something about the woman's striking eyes seemed to affect him deeply.

She too, felt something strange radiating from the man standing opposite that she couldn't quite explain. It only lasted an instant and she was about to step aside when her eyes came to rest on the little cross around Jack's neck. Rahima's heart missed a beat. She felt dizzy and had to reach for the edge of the lift door to steady herself.

'Are you all right?' asked Rodrigo and reached for Rahima's arm as she stepped out of the lift.

Rahima pointed to the little cross. 'Where did you get this?' she whispered, her lips quivering and her voice barely audible.

'It's a long story,' said Jack. Shocked by the distress and pain reflected in the woman's eyes, he decided to add something.

'This is a replica. The original belonged to my mother ...'

'Are you Australian?'

'Yes. Why do you ask?'

'Does the Coberg Mission mean anything to you?'

'*What did you say*?' asked Jack, barely able to speak.

'Coberg Mission ...'

'Yes. I was born there ...'

'*Oh my God*!' whispered Rahima, tears welling up in her eyes. She quickly turned away without saying another word and hurried down the corridor.

'Who was that?' asked Jack, following Rodrigo into the lift.

'That's Mrs Cordoba. What was all that about?'

'Don't know. She probably thought I was someone else,' said Jack casually, brushing the question aside.

46

H Cartel Compound, Bogota: 11 July

Rahima had spent most of the night in the little chapel at the far end of the garden, praying, as she tried to come to terms with what her head told her must be true, but what her heart was too afraid to believe. Red-eyed and exhausted, she stepped outside into the hot morning sun and asked one of the security guards to bring Jack to the chapel. The young guard – barely more than a boy – hurried back to the main building to fetch him. When Mrs Cordoba asked you to do something, you didn't ask questions and attended to it straight away.

A few minutes later, the guard knocked on the chapel door and opened it.

'Please ask Mr Rogan to come inside and then leave us,' said Rahima, speaking softly.

Jack stepped into the little chapel and closed the door. For some reason he couldn't explain, he felt strangely excited, his heart pounding.

Rahima was kneeling in front of the altar, facing a small Russian icon. She slowly turned around and looked at Jack standing by the door, motionless and silent like a statue. A shaft of sunlight reached through one of the small windows, illuminating his face like some kind of blessing from above and making the little cross hanging around his neck sparkle like a beacon of hope. Rahima, a devout Christian, burst into tears.

Jack didn't move and just kept staring at the little silver-haired woman kneeling in front of him. Leaning forward, she kissed the icon, slowly got to her feet and then turned around to face Jack.

'You were born at the Coberg Mission in November 1968; is that right?' asked Rahima, barely able to speak.

'Yes. When I was only a few days old, I was given to the Rogan family who lived on a cattle station close by, and became the son they couldn't have. I was taken to them by Gurrul, an Aboriginal drover who later became my mentor and friend.'

'M-my God,' stammered Rahima, feeling faint and reaching for one of the pews to steady herself. Jack stepped forward and held out his hand. Rahima took it and then embraced him. As she held him tight, her slim body began to shake uncontrollably. 'You are the son I *did* have, but left behind,' she sobbed. 'But God in his mercy has given you back to me. Here, right now. It's a sign ...'

Deeply moved, Jack was unable to stop the tears streaming down his cheeks. He too hadn't slept much during the night. A strong believer in destiny, he began to smile. 'I have been looking for you for a long time,' he whispered after a while, as a tide of mixed emotions began to well up from somewhere deep within, filling his heart with great joy. It was a feeling he had never experienced before, like seeing a welcoming light beckoning in the distance, and finally coming home after a long absence in the wilderness. As the turbulent tide of emotions that threatened to overwhelm him began to ebb, Jack looked into Rahima's eyes and recognised the same feeling: it was love. For Rahima, it was not just any love, but the love of a grieving mother aching for a lost child she hadn't dared to hope to ever see again.

For the next hour, mother and son sat next to each other holding hands in the front pew and speaking of the past. Jack told Rahima of his search for his father, and how and where he had discovered what had happened to him. He explained how murals painted on the walls of a prison cell in Fremantle Prison had pointed the way to the Kimberley in Western Australia and ultimately to the *Kimberley Queen*, the largest pearl ever found in the Antipodes.

They smiled when Jack told Rahima about Madame Petrova's memory trees and the oak tree she had planted to commemorate her lost niece, and they cried when Jack spoke of the two lonely graves at the Coberg Mission he had visited to keep a promise after Gurrul died.

'Sister Elizabeth, your mother,' said Jack, 'is buried next to Brother Francis ...'

'Your grandparents,' said Rahima.

'Yes, and Gurrul's ashes have returned to his beloved land. They all rest in peace together on the abandoned mission, but I never stopped looking for you ...'

Rahima squeezed Jack's hand. 'Why?' she asked.

'Because I needed to know ...'

'Needed to know what?'

'What happened to you. No-one just disappears without a trace. And there was something else ...'

'What?'

'Throughout all these years, I *sensed* something.'

'What did you sense?'

'That somehow, somewhere, you were still alive.'

'Really?'

'Yes. I only returned from the Nuba Mountains a couple of weeks ago. I was there, looking for you.'

'You were looking for *me*?' said Rahima, surprised.

'Yes. I visited a village called Fungor, where I met someone very interesting. An old man who remembered a young, golden-haired woman who was taking photographs of a spectacular knife-fighting ritual just before Arab slavers raided the village ...'

'What else did he tell you?'

'Many were killed, but most of the women and girls, including the golden-haired woman, were taken away by the slavers.'

'That's the day my old life ended,' said Rahima, 'and Natasha Rostova died ...'

'What happened to her?'

'She became Rahima. I was taken to the slave market in Khartoum and put up for sale.'

'And?' prompted Jack, eager to find out what happened.

'There was serious bidding and I was almost sold to an Arab trader when someone else entered the bidding. A handsome young man. His name was Hernando Cordoba, a notorious arms dealer.'

'He *bought* you?'

'Yes. From then on, my life changed for the better. We actually fell in love. Hernando was very good to me; still is, in his own way. We came to live here in Bogota, his hometown, and two years later Alonso was born. Your half-brother, who is now on death row in Arizona.'

Destiny, thought Jack, shaking his head. *This is all about destiny.*

'Can't you see? All this was meant to be,' continued Rahima, her face flushed with zeal. 'God has brought you here for a reason. It's not just about you and me. It's about Alonso as well; where he is and what he is facing. I have been on my knees here praying for hours since Alonso was sentenced to death. I was begging for his life. I believe God has heard my prayers and sent you ...'

For a while, Jack and Rahima sat in silence, lost in thought as they tried to come to terms with everything.

'The moment of unimaginable joy of finding you is marred by fear that is tearing my heart apart. Fear for Alonso,' whispered Rahima. 'This is a bittersweet moment and only you can set things right.'

'How?'

'By helping Hernando to save our son. I'm sure that's why you've been sent here, now, at this crucial time. This is no coincidence. This is fate; the hand of God.'

Rahima turned to face Jack and put the tips of her fingers on the little cross. 'Please promise me, my son.'

'What?'

'To do everything you can to save Alonso.'

'I promise,' said Jack, putting his hand on Rahima's and pressing it to his chest.

'And one more thing,' continued Rahima. 'Please keep all this to yourself for the time being ...'

'Oh?'

'Hernando is a complex man. He's changed over the years. He has a lot on his mind right now. To find out who you are would only—'

'I understand,' interrupted Jack, sensing that Rahima was struggling to find the right words.

'And will you promise?'

'I promise,' said Jack.

Rahima bent down and kissed the back of Jack's hand, the touch of her lips making him choke with emotion.

47

Naval Support Activity Naples: 13 July

'Vice Admiral Fratelli will see you now,' said the young officer, the polished buttons on her smart uniform gleaming like tiny beacons. 'Please come with me.'

Andersen, Cesaria and Tristan stood up and followed the officer along a brightly lit corridor and then up some stairs to the first floor. Despite the late hour – it was just after ten pm – it was a hive of activity at the NSA Naples, home to the US Naval Forces Europe and the US Sixth Fleet.

Andersen had received instruction from her superiors in Washington that afternoon to go immediately to Naples and report to Vice Admiral Fratelli, who had some important information in the Stolzfus matter.

'We came as soon as we could,' said Andersen and introduced her friend, the vice admiral, to Cesaria and Tristan.

'I heard a lot about you,' said Fratelli and shook Tristan's hand. 'As I understand it, you were the one who first suggested that Professor Stolzfus could be alive.'

'That's correct, but I don't think anyone believed me.'

'Hardly surprising, but someone in Washington obviously did and in a way, that changed everything.'

'I thought this was about the men in custody here ...' interjected Andersen, who had assumed that Aladdin or Silvanus, or perhaps the crew of the *Nike* must have talked.

Fratelli shook her head. 'By way of background to what happened this morning, I have been instructed to tell you this—'

'Oh? By who?' asked Andersen, annoyed that she hadn't been briefed.

'The highest level. The secretary of state. And please remember that all of this is classified.'

Andersen bit her lip in anticipation as Fratelli continued.

'After it became clear that the Mafia was involved in Professor Stolzfus's abduction and that the abduction appeared to be somehow linked to the H Cartel in Colombia, it was decided to bring the execution of Alonso Cordoba forward. As you know, Alonso Cordoba is the son of Hernando Cordoba, the wanted head of the H Cartel. Alonso is presently on death row in Arizona, awaiting execution.'

'We know that,' said Andersen, becoming impatient. 'But how is this relevant?'

'You'll see in a moment,' said Fratelli calmly. 'The execution was brought forward to put pressure on Hernando Cordoba.'

'Why?'

'Because Washington suspects that Stolzfus's abduction has something to do with Alonso's execution.'

'That's absurd!' interrupted Andersen. 'Based on what?'

'Certain intercepted telephone conversations and internet traffic.'

'What kind of conversations?'

'Conversations between Raul Rodrigo, the lawyer who has recently been interrogated in New York, and Hernando Cordoba, his notorious client. The CIA have had Rodrigo under surveillance for some time.'

'So, what happened this morning?' asked Andersen.

'Alonso Cordoba was due to be executed at nine am this morning. A last-minute appeal lodged by Rodrigo had been dismissed, clearing the way for the execution to go ahead, but it didn't.'

'Why?'

'Because of this. Watch.'

Fratelli pointed to a large TV in the corner of her office and pressed a button on the remote control on her desk. 'This recording was delivered by Rodrigo to the US ambassador in Bogota this morning, a few minutes before the execution was due to start.'

After a couple of seconds, a man lying on an operating table came into view. It was Stolzfus. Then the camera swung around and showed a man wearing a surgical gown, face mask and scrub cap standing in a brightly lit operating theatre. First, the man pointed to Stolzfus and explained his life-threatening injuries. Then he explained the complex operation he was about to perform to save the patient's life.

'That's Fabry,' said Tristan, pointing to the screen. Step by step the man in the gown described what a cephalosomatic anastomosis was, and what it involved. He pointed out that it had never been performed on a live patient before, but that he was confident it could be carried out successfully. After that, clips from the various stages of the operation were shown, including the surgical removal of Stolzfus's head and a close-up of another body without a head in a sitting position, strapped into an operating chair.

Cesaria gasped as the camera showed a team of surgeons attaching Stolzfus's head to the headless body, the music playing in the background sounding eerie and surreal.

'That's the music I kept hearing,' said Tristan, becoming excited, 'Tchaikovsky's *Lost Symphony* ...'

To Cesaria, the surgeons and theatre nurses in their green scrubs and face masks, hovering over the patient, looked like actors in some bizarre play, their deliberate, slow movements and strange-looking instruments sending shivers down her spine.

Fratelli stopped the video and looked at Andersen. 'What do you think?' she said.

Andersen shook her head. 'Incredible! Do we know if the operation was successful?'

Without saying a word, Fratelli pressed the remote again and the video continued. After a brief pause, the camera zoomed in on a man sitting in a wheelchair, his shaved head supported by an elaborate frame.

Andersen gasped. 'It's Stolzfus,' she said. 'I don't believe it!'

Then the man's eyes opened and he began to speak, his voice sounding distant and strange, like an echo from somewhere deep within. He was conscious and appeared lucid. 'Castle to b3,' said the voice as the camera swung around and showed a chessboard on a small table in front of the wheelchair, before coming to rest on another man sitting opposite.

'That's Jack!' Tristan almost shouted and pointed to the screen. Jack looked at the camera and smiled. 'Checkmate again,' he said, shaking his head. 'I can't win against this guy. That's what you get when you have a genius as your opponent!'

'We believe this was taken last week on a ship heading for Colombia,' said Fratelli. 'But wait; it gets better.'

The next scene showed the man in the wheelchair in a tropical garden full of exotic-looking plants. 'I love sitting out here and looking up at the sky,' said the man, his voice sounding strong, 'and thinking about the universe ...'

'And now comes the really interesting bit,' said Fratelli. 'Watch and listen carefully.'

The next scene showed a shortish, elderly man standing next to the wheelchair with one hand resting on Stolzfus's shoulder.

'I am Hernando Cordoba,' said the man, 'speaking to you from Bogota. My son Alonso is about to be executed in Arizona. To the US I say this: If you want to enjoy the benefits of Professor Stolzfus's extraordinary talents again, please stop the execution because if you don't ...' Cordoba paused, letting the threat find its mark, 'the professor's genius will benefit someone else. You must decide now,' he continued, 'because there isn't much time! The professor's fate is in your hands.' Then the screen went blank.

'He didn't mention Jack!' was the first thing Tristan said.

'We wondered about that too,' said Fratelli, 'and what role Mr Rogan is to play in this complicated business, but the intelligence consensus seems to be that Cordoba wanted to focus on Stolzfus without causing distractions, and that's the reason he didn't mention Rogan. But he did show him to us in the video as someone who is obviously in Bogota as well, and close to Stolzfus. They were shown playing chess.'

'So, Jack Rogan's abduction is considered a distraction? Is that it?' asked Tristan.

'Not by us,' said Fratelli. 'But it's unclear at the moment why he has been abducted and what Cordoba has in mind. However, the fact he has been taken to Colombia makes him important. A man like Cordoba does nothing without good reason.'

'There's something else that struck me as rather strange,' said Andersen.

Fratelli looked at her friend. 'I know what you are going to say.'

'"If you want to enjoy the benefits of Professor Stolzfus's talents again",' continued Andersen, '"the professor's genius will benefit *someone else*". Odd, isn't it? Cordoba's threat is focusing on Stolzfus's *talents*, not his life.'

'Correct, and we believe that's an important clue and quite deliberate.'

'In what way?' asked Cesaria.

'What is in play here is Stolzfus's *mind*; what he knows and what he is capable of,' said Fratelli. 'As one of the most gifted scientists on the planet, his value is his mind, not his life as such. Cordoba knows this and is telling us that he knows.'

'Yes, I thought that too,' Andersen agreed. 'Cordoba has gone to extraordinary lengths to keep Stolzfus alive and his brain functioning. He is clearly showing us this in the video. Playing chess and *winning*?'

'So, what does all that mean?' asked Cesaria.

'Cordoba is giving the US a chance to get Stolzfus back,' said Tristan, 'in return for his son. If they don't go along with this, then he will make arrangements with someone else. I believe that's what this is all about. That's the real threat here. Not killing Stolzfus, but keeping him alive and giving him to someone else to use.'

Fratelli looked at Tristan, surprised by his insight. 'That's what our analysts think as well. There are a number of parties standing in the shadows around the world who would not only pay a fortune, but do whatever it takes to get their hands on Stolzfus or, more accurately, his mind.'

'Cordoba is playing a clever game,' said Andersen. 'And a very dangerous one. It takes a special man to threaten a superpower.'

'Desperate people do desperate things,' said Tristan.

'Do you think Washington will go along with this?' asked Andersen.

'Don't know. I think that's why you've been ordered to return to Washington as soon as possible,' said Fratelli. 'I have a plane standing by to take you to Rome right now. You are booked on a flight to Washington first thing tomorrow morning.'

Andersen nodded. She had been expecting something like this.

'And one more thing,' continued Fratelli. 'I've been asked to persuade Tristan to go with you. Because of Jack Rogan, I suppose ...'

Andersen looked at Tristan, the question on her face obvious.

'No persuasion needed,' said Tristan, 'I'm ready.'

'I was hoping you would say that,' said Andersen. 'And I can promise you that from now on, I will look at your "intuition" in a completely different way. And as for Jack, I will do everything in my power to get him back safely.'

'And let's not forget,' interjected Cesaria, 'Tristan can hear the whisper of angels and glimpse eternity ...'

'Could come in useful,' said Andersen, smiling.

'Thanks, guys. Jack needs us,' said Tristan. 'This is serious. That's why I'm going along with all this.'

On the flight to Rome, Andersen sat next to Cesaria. 'What about your own investigation? The Mafia in Florence?' she asked, watching Cesaria carefully.

'As you know, Grimaldi met with Riccardo Giordano a few days ago and put a proposal to him,' said Cesaria.

'What kind of proposal?'

'Remember, Grimaldi knows Giordano well. As chief prosecutor in Florence, Grimaldi has one main aim: to keep the city safe and the Mafia contained, especially with the growing drug problem spiralling out of control.'

'And how is he hoping to achieve that?'

'By putting pressure on the Giordano family. Alessandro's involvement in the Stolzfus matter has given Grimaldi the perfect opportunity to do this.'

'Oh?'

'The proposal is as simple as it is ingenious. Once again, Grimaldi is using old Mafia rivalries to get his own way. In this case, the rivalry between the Lombardos and the Giordanos, the two Mafia families controlling the lucrative drug business in Florence. By going behind the Lombardos' backs and negotiating with the H Cartel direct – most likely about the drug supply – Alessandro has put the uneasy truce between the two families in jeopardy. Should this come to light and the Lombardos find out about this, Alessandro's life would be in serious danger. Should he be killed, this would trigger another bloody Mafia war in Florence, which Grimaldi wants to avoid at all cost. Effectively, the drug supply line through Malta involving the H Cartel is dead, at least for now. This affects the Lombardos and the Giordanos equally. But should the Lombardos find out that Alessandro was in some way responsible for this, and why, well ... then his days would be numbered. In Mafia circles you don't get away with something like this. Honour and reputations are at stake here.'

'So, what's the proposal?'

'Grimaldi suggested that the Giordanos get out of the drug business in Florence, and Alessandro leave Italy at once. The Giordanos have extensive business interests in Chicago. This would remove a possible trigger for another war with countless casualties on both sides. With the South American drug supply now seriously interrupted, the drug business in Florence has been dealt a serious blow, giving the authorities the upper hand to contain the problem.'

'Is that likely? I mean, the Giordanos getting out of drugs altogether?'

'Giordano gave Grimaldi his answer yesterday.'

'*He did*? And?'

'He agreed. He wants to keep his remaining son alive. Remember, he already lost a son two years ago during a turf war with Salvatore Gambio, and he is getting on in years. Moving the family into legitimate businesses has been his aim for years.'

'And Alessandro goes free? Is that it? His involvement in the Stolzfus abduction goes unpunished?' asked Andersen, becoming agitated. 'He's the one who hired—'

'Yes,' interrupted Cesaria. 'He seems to have been the facilitator, but the high-profile Stolzfus abduction and the Fabry fiasco in Malta have all been committed outside Italy in different countries, and are therefore matters for Great Britain and the US to sort out, not us. This is for MI5 and the CIA to resolve, not the Squadra Mobile in Florence. The crimes have been committed in other jurisdictions, not in Italy. We have received clear instructions from Rome to stay out of this ...'

'What about Jack Rogan?' said Andersen. 'He was abducted on your turf! On your watch. He just falls through the cracks?'

Cesaria shrugged. 'We are working on that.'

'I see,' said Andersen. 'Looking at the situation objectively – and from your point of view – I do understand.'

'I knew you would,' said Cesaria, grateful for Andersen's reassurance. 'These matters are never easy at this level.'

No, they are not, thought Andersen. But letting Alessandro off the hook and go free wasn't an option. A strong believer in justice, Andersen's mind was already working overtime as she began to explore an opportunity to use what she had just learned to her advantage. And it was all about how to get Alessandro ...

48

CIA HQ, George Bush Center for Intelligence, Virginia: 14 July

'Excited?' asked Andersen. She looked at Tristan sitting next to her in the large waiting room. Tristan nodded. She still found it difficult to believe that Tristan had been asked to accompany her.

Despite a specific appointment arranged by the director of the CIA herself, it had taken them over an hour to navigate the complex security arrangements giving them access to 'Langley', as the CIA headquarters at 1000 Colonial Farm Road in McLean, Virginia was known colloquially. Andersen had been to the director's office before and knew the drill and how long it could take. She had therefore allowed plenty of time because being late was unthinkable.

Dr Rosalind Hubert, a woman in her late fifties, stood up and walked to the door to welcome Andersen and Tristan as they were admitted to her office by a security guard. Passing her in the street, no-one would have suspected that the petite, smartly dressed woman with short, greying hair and large horn-rimmed glasses was the director of the CIA, and one of the most powerful women in the United States.

'Good flight?' asked Hubert.

'Yes, thank you,' said Andersen and introduced Tristan.

'Ah. The man who can hear the whisper of angels and glimpse eternity,' said Hubert, smiling, and pointed to a man standing in the shadows next to a large conference table by the window. 'Come, let me introduce you.'

Andersen looked at the man, surprised. She had not expected the secretary of state to be present at the meeting. To have such an important man come over from nearby Washington to attend the meeting in person could mean only one thing: the subject matter was of national importance, reaching to the very top.

'You can take it, Major, that we are familiar with all of your reports in this matter,' began the secretary of state once they were all seated. 'And so is President Gump, who is taking a personal interest in this case. You may not know this, but the president is a great admirer of Professor Stolzfus. In fact, he has met him on several occasions and considers him a national treasure. We have all seen that extraordinary video ...'

'May I ask what you thought of it?'

'Of course we had it expertly analysed,' said Hubert.

'And?'

'We believe it's genuine.'

'And such an operation is feasible?'

'Yes. Some of our surgeons in the military have been looking at something like this for a while now. It's definitely possible.'

'So, it could actually be Stolzfus in the video?'

'Yes, and we are proceeding on the basis that it is.'

Andersen nodded, but didn't say anything further.

'While you were crossing the Atlantic to get here, there have been certain developments,' said Hubert. 'Serious ones.'

'Oh?' Andersen didn't like the turn this was taking. 'Serious developments' was intelligence speak for trouble and danger.

'As you know,' continued Hubert, 'the Cordoba execution was stayed yesterday morning to give us time to consider the matter.'

'Yes, I know—'

'But what you may not know is this,' interrupted the secretary of state. He lit a cigarette and looked at Andersen. 'The president has decided that exchanging Professor Stolzfus for Alonso Cordoba is out of the question. The US does not make deals with wanted criminals. In short, releasing Alonso isn't an option.'

'Has this been communicated to his father in Bogota?' asked Andersen, looking concerned.

'It has,' said the secretary of state.

'And?'

The secretary of state pointed to Hubert. 'Would you please?' he said.

'We are communicating with Hernando Cordoba through our embassy in Bogota. The ambassador is in touch with Cordoba's lawyer,' said Hubert.

'Raul Rodrigo?' said Andersen.

'Yes. We advised him earlier today that releasing Alonso wasn't going to happen and that the only possibility may be to have his death sentence commuted to life imprisonment. We left the door open ...'

'What did he say about that?' asked Andersen.

'A reply came in just before you arrived.'

'Oh? What did it say?'

'Only this,' continued Hubert. '*New York Times*; tomorrow morning.'

'That's all? How curious.'

'And ingenious,' interjected the secretary of state. 'You'll see why in a moment.'

Hubert stood up, went to her desk and picked up a sheet of paper. 'Of course, we contacted the *New York Times* straight away and made enquiries,' she said and held up the sheet of paper. 'This will appear in the paper tomorrow morning.'

Without saying another word, Hubert handed the sheet of paper to Andersen and sat down again. For a long, tense moment there was complete silence as she read the article.

'Jesus!' she said quietly. 'Are they serious?'

'Deadly, I'm afraid,' said the secretary of state, stepping in.

'And all this information came from Jack Rogan?'

The article was a complete step-by-step account of what happened to Stolzfus, including his abduction at Westminster Abbey, the groundbreaking operation to save his life, and concluded with a specific demand and a deadline.

'It did,' said Hubert. 'According to the *New York Times*, he provided all the information. He's the source and Celia Crawford, the journalist, is vouching for him. The paper even has a copy of the video you saw. We believe this now explains why Rogan was abducted and taken to Bogota. He's a high-profile go-between with international credibility. By having him contact the paper and going directly to Crawford with this, Cordoba made sure that all his demands are being taken seriously and would be reported exactly as he had in mind.'

'A very clever and effective strategy,' said the secretary of state. 'By going public with this through one of the most widely read and trusted papers in the US, if not the world, Cordoba is making sure that as of tomorrow morning, the explosive Stolzfus case is in the public domain, putting maximum pressure on the US.'

'And as you can imagine,' added Hubert, 'all hell will break loose as soon as this comes out.'

'A South American WikiLeaks?' suggested Andersen.

'Something like that.'

'Will someone please tell me what this is all about?' said Tristan quietly. 'Or shall I just wait outside?'

Hubert looked at Tristan, surprised. She wasn't used to interruptions. 'I do apologise,' she said. 'We owe you an explanation, Mr Te Papatahi. As you can imagine, a high-level security meeting like this isn't normally attended by a civilian like yourself because everything here is classified. However, these are exceptional circumstances. You have been invited to attend because Mr Rogan has specifically asked for your personal involvement in this matter. He made this quite clear during his conversation with Celia Crawford.'

'He spoke to Celia?' said Tristan. 'And asked for me?'

'Yes, earlier today.'

'Did he say why?'

'Because of who you are and what you are capable of,' said Hubert quietly. 'Apparently, you work as a team and you have worked with Celia Crawford before.'

Tristan nodded. 'I have.'

Andersen found it difficult to suppress a smile. Here was a young man who reputedly had some kind of psychic powers, talking to two of the most powerful people in the US because he could 'hear the whisper of angels and glimpse eternity'. *This case is becoming more bizarre by the moment*, she thought, but she had to give credit to Hubert for taking Jack's request seriously and going along with it.

'So, if we don't agree to the proposed exchange – Stolzfus for Alonso Cordoba – by noon on Monday; that's in about 24 hours,' said Andersen, 'Stolzfus's services will be offered to others. What others?'

'We don't know,' said the secretary of state. 'But we are taking this threat seriously.'

Andersen shook her head. 'You are?' she said. 'How will Cordoba implement this, do you think?'

'The darknet,' said Tristan quietly. 'Giving interested parties an opportunity to acquire Stolzfus or, more accurately, give them access to his incredible mind and what it can do.' Tristan paused to let this sink in. 'Cordoba hinted at something like that during the video,' he continued. 'China, North Korea, perhaps even Russia could be buyers. So could some wealthy Russian oligarchs, smelling an opportunity to make some money. And by going public with this, Cordoba is putting maximum pressure on the US administration to take the threat seriously and do something about it.'

'Correct,' said the secretary of state, looking at Tristan with renewed interest. 'And, of course, we cannot allow that to happen and Cordoba knows this.'

'Where does that leave us?' asked Andersen.

'In a jam,' said the secretary of state. 'A jam we have to get out of!'

'How?' said Andersen.

'By being clever and not losing our nerve, and most importantly, not doing anything rash. The US cannot be held to ransom, but we will not abandon Stolzfus and let the perpetrators go unpunished.'

'There is a plan?' asked Andersen.

The secretary of state nodded.

Hubert turned to Tristan and smiled. 'As you can see, Mr Te Papatahi, things are moving very quickly here. I have to ask you to wait outside for a little while ... classified matters. I am sure you understand.'

'Perfectly,' said Tristan and stood up.

So did the secretary of state. 'Great to have you on board,' he said, extending his hand. 'Major Andersen will brief you on a need-to-know basis ...'

'I understand.' Tristan shook the secretary of state's hand and walked towards the door. Just before he reached it, he stopped and turned around. 'I can see an aircraft carrier, a deserted beach and a man in a wheelchair. I can also see a blinding flash and balls of fire, and I can hear the deafening roar of jet engines ... I better not say any more because it may be classified.'

Herbert and the secretary of state stared at Tristan with stunned looks on their faces, but Andersen just smiled as Tristan quietly left the room.

49

H Cartel Compound, Bogota: 15 July

Cordoba had just read the sensational article in the *New York Times* that had sent Washington into a spin. Like a caged lion, he was pacing nervously back and forth in front of the large window in his observation room when Rodrigo walked in.

'Not quite the reaction we had in mind, is it?' said Cordoba, turning around.

'Tactics. To be expected.'

'I think they are stalling.'

'Perhaps, but they didn't say no, and they left the door open.'

'Ajar would be a better way to put it. I don't like silence. It's always ominous, like the build-up before a storm. A life sentence is unacceptable. I want Alonso set free or there's no deal.'

'We must hurry slowly. I am sure our threat is hitting the mark. You must admit the article is excellent and specifically refers to the darknet. That was the message we wanted to put out there. Now the whole world knows … the international response to the article has been enormous. It's on all the news channels around the world. It's the hottest topic at the moment and the video has gone viral.'

'Not surprising, but I want my son back. That's what this is about,' snapped Cordoba, 'not publicity.'

'We can't have one without the other. Publicity is our tool. That's what will bring Alonso back. It's more powerful than a cruise missile.'

'I hope you're right.'

Rodrigo looked at his agitated client. He hadn't seen Cordoba in such a state for a long time and realised it was time for some hand-holding.

'Rogan was excellent on the phone, by the way. He did exactly what we asked of him and the conversation with Celia Crawford went extremely well, I thought. Without Rogan, this article would never have happened. It's only because of his relationship with the journalist that the *New York Times* went ahead with such an explosive story.'

'That's not the problem here. We set a deadline and it's rapidly approaching. Yet still no word from the Americans. That worries me.'

'They have a lot to consider and to organise logistically. And don't forget public opinion. This puts the administration under enormous pressure.'

'That's what we wanted.'

'Yes, but we asked for an exchange here on Colombian soil. That's a big ask. Think about it …'

'I still don't like it. I know we had to set a deadline, but it locked us in.'

'That's what deadlines do. It's a two-edged sword.'

Being the architect of the strategy, Rodrigo could feel the heavy weight of responsibility pressing down on him and he realised that time was rapidly running out. However, as an experienced lawyer and skilful negotiator he knew how to turn a tricky situation into an advantage, and what he had just learned about Stolzfus from Agabe a few minutes ago would give him all he needed to do just that.

'In a way, the deadline is a godsend,' he said quietly, watching Cordoba carefully out of the corner of his eye.

'What do you mean?' snapped Cordoba.

Rodrigo knew it was time to drop the bad-news-bombshell that would vindicate his decision to put pressure on the Americans by setting a deadline.

'Stolzfus is deteriorating. I just—'

'*What?*' interrupted Cordoba.

'I just spoke to Agabe,' continued Rodrigo calmly. 'Stolzfus had some kind of fit during the night and—'

'Why wasn't I told?'

Rodrigo ignored the question. 'His speech is deteriorating,' he said. 'Apparently, it's because of all the tension. He can sense something's going on, which is hardly surprising. It's the stress.'

'Great! That's all we need right now. If anything happens to him, well—'

'Even more reason to bring this matter to a head right now, while we have something to bargain with.'

Cordoba thought about this for a while and then nodded. 'You are right,' he said. 'We mustn't lose our nerve; not now.'

Rodrigo smiled. His client had reacted exactly as expected. 'I totally agree. And the best way to do that is to act.'

'How?'

'By raising the stakes.'

'What's on your mind?' asked Cordoba, looking interested. As a man of action used to being in control, he liked what he had just heard.

'We put more pressure on the Americans.'

'How exactly?'

'This is not the time to be timid. We should announce an auction.'

'An *auction?* What on earth do you mean?'

'We should arrange for Stolzfus to be auctioned on the darknet.'

Cordoba looked stunned. 'Are you serious?'

'Absolutely!'

'Right now?'

'Yes. Just think about it. Now that the story is out there and the whole world is paying attention, we have the audience we need to pull this off. This won't last forever. People lose interest quickly. We set a date and a time right now and have a ticking clock, like the count-down to midnight on New Year's Eve. With the whole world watching, this would be sensational! We know there are interested parties out there … we've already had two approaches, remember?'

Cordoba walked over to his lawyer. 'I like it! No wonder I don't mind paying you a small fortune, Raul,' he said, slapping Rodrigo on the back. 'I think this is a brilliant idea. It will send the Americans nuts and we'll play our trump card in the best way possible. We always knew we would get only one shot at this. We might as well make it a good one.'

'Exactly,' said Rodrigo, pleased to see his gamble was paying off. He knew his client well and just like in the courtroom, he carefully shaped his tactics to suit the persona and the situation.

'How would you approach this?' asked Cordoba.

'We have the IT guys we need right here to set this up. They know all about encryption and how to make sure the auction site can't be shut down. That's important. It shouldn't be difficult and it shouldn't take them too long. We create a non-traceable website on the dark web with, say, the Stolzfus video and some other sensational material to create interest, and go from there.'

Rodrigo paused, and for a little while just looked out the window. 'Then we drive traffic to the site using social media,' he continued. 'This too will go viral, I'm sure of it. These things have a momentum of their own. We've seen this with women being auctioned on the dark web. You've seen what happened. This is no different. The bids are visible and so is the clock, but the bidders and their locations remain hidden and can't be traced.'

'Right. Then what?'

'First, I speak to the ambassador here in Bogota and tell him what's coming. A little advance notice should prepare the way and apply pressure. Then we ask Rogan to call the *New York Times* again, suggesting another article to announce the auction. Sensational stuff. The paper will love it. That should do it. After that, the whole world will be watching. I promise!'

'The Americans will be furious.'

'That's what we want, isn't it? Pressure. And there's no greater pressure than the public. *The mob*. Even the Romans were afraid of it.'

Cordoba, a practical man, nodded. 'Tell Agabe to keep Stolzfus calm. We need a genius with a voice or we have nothing to sell,' he said.

'Leave that to me. We start the auction clock as soon as the current deadline expires, which is in about twenty-four hours. Unless we hear from the Americans first, that is.'

'Is that likely?'

Rodrigo shrugged. 'Anything can happen here.'

'We are making some very powerful enemies,' said Cordoba quietly.

'Does that bother you?'

'Not at all.' Cordoba lit a small cigar. 'On the contrary, I like it.'

'The stakes are very high here.'

'I understand that. That's *why* I like it.'

'I thought you would say that. I better go and start the ball rolling. Time's ticking.'

'By the way, have you noticed that Rahima seems to have a new spring in her step?' said Cordoba.

'Perhaps she can sense that Alonso is coming home?' ventured Rodrigo.

'I hope you're right. She seems to be spending quite a bit of time with Rogan …'

'I noticed that too. Do you mind?'

'No. On the contrary. He's an intelligent man. Quite charming, and we need his cooperation. The more we engage with him the better. Make him feel he's part of this, not just some prisoner we dragged over here.'

'I agree. This can't be easy for Rahima. A little distraction may do her good.'

'You're right. Rogan's an interesting man … there's a lot more to him than meets the eye. Pity we couldn't have met under different circumstances.'

Rodrigo looked at his client, surprised. For someone who lived like a recluse and shied away from people, to say something like that was unusual. And what was even more remarkable was the fact that Cordoba had only met Rogan once, briefly. Rodrigo had sensed that something must have triggered this and was wondering what it could have been. *And Rahima, too, seems drawn to him*, he thought, shaking his head. For someone who studied people and their behaviour for a living, matters like this were always of interest.

Without saying another word, Rodrigo left the room and went back to his office to call the ambassador.

50

On the USS *Endeavor*, off the coast of Colombia: 16 July, 10:00 am

The USS *Endeavor*, a giant, nuclear-powered Nimitz-class aircraft carrier, was sailing in carrier strike group (CSG) formation south towards the Colombian Pacific coast. With an overall length of three hundred and thirty-three metres and a displacement of more than one hundred thousand tonnes, it was capable of a maximum speed of thirty knots. Because it was powered by two A4W pressurised water reactors, the ship could operate for more than twenty years without refuelling.

Steam catapults and arrestor wires on its angled flight deck for launch and recovery gave the ship more efficient flight operations capabilities than smaller carriers, and with more than ninety aircraft deployed, it had awesome firepower. Its strike fighters were state-of-the-art F/A-18E and F/A-18F Super Hornets. Five hundred and fifty officers and five and a half thousand enlisted crew ensured that the carrier was battle-ready at all times and capable of launching aircraft within minutes.

The CSG consisted of six additional vessels, including two guided missile cruisers, a destroyer, a guided missile frigate and two attack submarines. The principal function of these vessels was to protect the aircraft carrier from attack.

'This is amazing,' said Tristan, pointing to the enormous flight deck. It looked like a floating island of steel from above as the helicopter approached the *Endeavor* and prepared for landing.

'It's a different world down there,' said Andersen, a hint of sadness in her voice. 'It was my world not that long ago.'

'Do you miss it?'

'Sure. But launching Super Hornets from one of these things belongs to the young.'

'But you told me you kept up your flying.'

'I did, and still do. I was an instructor for several years before I joined the CIA. I probably taught most of the pilots here at some time or other.'

'Awesome!'

Moments later, the helicopter landed and Andersen and Tristan were met by an officer, who quickly ushered them off the noisy flight deck teeming with activity and personnel preparing aircraft for take-off.

'Welcome on board, Major,' said the officer, saluting smartly. 'As you can see, we are in the middle of manoeuvres. How did the refuelling go?'

The MH-60 Seahawk helicopter had a reach of two hundred and forty-five nautical miles, which meant that refuelling at sea had been necessary to allow them to reach the *Endeavor.*

'Like a charm. We landed twice on a cruiser along the way to refuel after we left San Diego.'

Amazing what real power can do, thought Andersen as she remembered the meeting with the secretary of state and her boss at Langley two days earlier. One hour after the meeting, Rear Admiral Andrew McBride was instructed to change course and sail towards the Colombian coast, and await further orders. He was also told that Major Andersen would join him shortly and explain everything. The *Endeavor* had been en route to Hawaii at the time and was due to rendezvous with another CSG for exercises before sailing to the South China Sea.

McBride was watching one of the 18F Super Hornets take off when Andersen and Tristan were admitted to the bridge.

'Good to see you, Major,' said McBride, pleased to see one of the most outstanding fighter pilots who had served under his command. 'It's been what, four years?'

'About that,' said Andersen, standing to attention.

McBride put down his binoculars and looked at Tristan. 'Your first time on a carrier?'

'Yes, sir.'

'I'll ask one of my officers to show you around while Major Andersen and I have a chat.'

'Later, perhaps if you don't mind, sir,' said Andersen. 'Mr Te Papatahi is part of this operation and has been cleared …'

McBride looked at Andersen, surprised. 'As you wish,' he said. To have a whole CSG change course at such short notice and sail towards a new destination at top speed could mean only one thing: some kind of emergency involving national security, and McBride couldn't wait to find out what it was.

'You've been following the Stolzfus matter?' began Andersen.

'Yes, of course. In fact, we've just been talking about it in here before you landed. Quite a bizarre case. Why do you ask?'

Andersen reached into her briefcase and pulled out a copy of the *New York Times*. 'Because this operation is all about the Stolzfus case.' Andersen handed the paper to McBride. 'Just came out. Front page: "Prominent US scientist to be auctioned on darknet".'

McBride read the article. 'This is crazy,' he said.

'Perhaps, but very serious and extremely embarrassing for the US in general, and the security services in particular. The public outcry about this has been unprecedented, putting huge pressure on the administration to *do something*.'

'I can imagine. To be held to ransom by a South American drug lord is unthinkable.'

'And to be threatened in this way is even worse,' added Andersen. 'To have a prominent American scientist auctioned like cattle on the darknet is not only humiliating, but, well ... it cannot be allowed to happen.'

'So, where do we fit into all this?'

'How long will it take you to reach the Colombian coast?'

'About forty-eight hours.'

Andersen bit her lip. Somehow, time was always the problem.

'Where are we right now?'

McBride pointed to a map table in front of him. 'Just off the Mexican coast; right here …'

Andersen looked at her watch. 'In about two hours, another helicopter will land here.'

'Oh? Why?'

'A very sensitive, top-secret matter.'

McBride looked at Andersen and raised an eyebrow. *Politics more likely,* he thought, but held his tongue. As a senior officer in the navy, he knew his place. Decisions that counted were made by politicians, but were implemented by men like him. The president, an elected politician, was the commander-in-chief. He had the final say. An admiral obeyed orders, he didn't instigate them. Not at that level.

'The helicopter left the Arizona State Prison Complex some time ago. It will refuel along the way, as we have done.'

'The exchange is going ahead?' said McBride, stunned. '*Are you serious?*' He couldn't imagine the US caving in just like that to a brazen demand by a wanted drug baron in a third-world country and sending an entire CSG just to make it possible. There had to be more to it.

'Yes. Stolzfus is a matter of national security. Under no circumstances is he to be allowed to fall into the wrong hands. We will do whatever it takes to get him back. These are my orders, but we have a problem ...'

'What kind of problem?'

'Time.'

'Please explain.'

'You just told me it would take about forty-eight hours to reach the Colombian coast. This would take us past the handover deadline by twenty-four hours. If that happens, the auction on the darknet will begin, unless we can renegotiate the timeframe. That's the problem. We cannot allow that to happen.'

'But surely we could get the prisoner there quicker?'

Andersen shook her head. 'The exchange cannot go ahead until the CSG is just off the Colombian coast.'

'Why?'

'Orders. All I know is that the handover will take place on a deserted beach on the Pacific coast.'

'Do we know where?'

'Not yet.'

'This operation will cost millions.'

'Much more is at stake here than money.'

McBride knew of course that apart from analysing, collecting and processing foreign intelligence, one of the main functions of the CIA was to carry out covert operations at the behest of the president; operations that officially never happened and could be strenuously denied. To McBride, this had all the hallmarks of just such a top-secret operation, and the CSG under his command was now obviously part of it. McBride knew he had to be vigilant and careful, and the best way to do that was to obey orders and not ask too many questions.

Andersen sensed his unease. 'You will of course receive orders in the usual way. I am here merely to fill in the gaps. We are all cogs in the wheel of global politics.'

Sure, thought McBride and nodded. 'And Mr Te Papatahi?'

'He will assist with negotiations.' Andersen knew this was vague, but it would have to do for now. To tell McBride that Tristan had been brought along because he could 'sense' things others couldn't and had a special spiritual bond with Rogan that could come in useful, may have taken things a little too far.

'At the moment, we are negotiating through the US ambassador in Bogota,' she continued. 'As soon as the prisoner gets here, we will try to establish contact with his father and allow him to talk to him. We hope that this will buy us the extra time we need, because it will show that we are genuine and doing everything we can to comply with the demand.'

I don't believe it, thought McBride. There had to be more to it. You didn't position a strike force like this off the coast of a foreign country just to hand over a prisoner.

Andersen pointed to Tristan. 'We will also try to arrange for Mr Te Papatahi to talk to Jack Rogan. This is important because Rogan is part of the exchange. He is to be handed over at the same time as Stolzfus. That's the deal as it stands at the moment.'

Just then an officer walked up to McBride. 'Apologies for interrupting, sir. The secretary of the navy is on the line, asking for you.'

Here it comes, thought McBride. He excused himself and followed the officer into the communications room.

51

H Cartel Compound, Bogota: 16 July, 5:00 pm

Rodrigo burst into Cordoba's observation room. 'I just heard from the ambassador,' he said, unable to suppress his excitement.

'And?'

'They are going to do it!'

'*They have agreed*?'

'Alonso has left the prison and is on his way here,' said Rodrigo, his voice sounding shrill.

'Calm down. Where is he?'

'On an aircraft carrier.'

'Where?'

'Somewhere off the coast of Mexico.'

'I don't like this. All I—'

'They are preparing for the handover,' interrupted Rodrigo. 'And they are sending an aircraft carrier to do it. We asked for the handover to take place here in Colombia. We told them somewhere on the Pacific coast. We are calling the shots here, and we'll tell them where when we are ready. What they are doing right now is making this possible, can't you see? They'll fly him over from the aircraft carrier and take Stolzfus back there. Makes sense.'

'Hm. When?'

'There's a small problem …'

Cordoba lit a cigar and looked at Rodrigo. He didn't like the way this was going. 'What kind of problem?' he asked quietly.

'They need more time.'

'*No!*' shouted Cordoba. 'They are stalling, can't you see?'

'I don't think so. It takes the aircraft carrier that long to get here.'

'How much more time?

'Twenty-four hours, that's all.'

'This is a trick! They could fly Alonso over here much faster if they really wanted to. They don't need an aircraft carrier for that!'

'They say they do. For Stolzfus. They have sophisticated medical facilities on board and remember, we were told that Stolzfus shouldn't fly at all. Not yet. Well, not long distances anyway. Let's not forget that's why we brought him over by ship. Obviously, they received the same advice. They don't want to take the risk.'

Cordoba thought about that. 'Is that what they said?'

'Yes.' Rodrigo realised it wouldn't be easy to convince his client to agree to an extension. Fortunately, he had something left in his arsenal he believed would get him over the line. 'We should ask Rahima to join us,' he said.

'Why?'

'Because of what I'm about to tell you. I think she needs to hear it too. I promised, remember? I promised, just like you did, to do everything I can to bring Alonso home.'

'All right. Let's get her. Where is she?'

'With Rogan, I believe.'

'Again? I see ...'

Rahima joined them a few minutes later. 'You wanted to see me?' she said.

'Raul has something to tell us,' said Cordoba, putting a hand on Rahima's shoulder. 'It's about Alonso.'

Rahima paled. Shaken and expecting the worst, she prepared herself.

'It's nothing bad,' said Rodrigo, noticing her distress. 'On the contrary. What would you say if you could talk to Alonso, right now?'

'Are you serious?' stammered Rahima. 'Where is he?'

'Not that far from here, and coming closer by the moment. He's on a US aircraft carrier on its way here.'

Rahima looked at her husband for assurance.

Cordoba nodded. 'It's true.'

'They are going to hand him over?'

'Looks that way.'

'And I can talk to him *right now?*' said Rahima, feeling dizzy. She hadn't spoken to her son in years.

'But only if we agree,' said Rodrigo.

'Agree to what?' asked Rahima.

'An extension. Change the time for a handover by twenty-four hours.'

Rahima turned to her husband. 'Is that a problem?' she asked, looking troubled.

Rodrigo kept watching his client. He had cleverly manoeuvred him into a difficult position. The decision to agree or to stand firm was now between Cordoba and his wife, and Rodrigo knew who would carry the day.

'Hernando, I implore you. What's twenty-four hours? We've come such a long way. We must *agree*!' Rahima looked at Rodrigo. 'Tell him! We could speak to Alonso right now?' she asked again. 'On the aircraft carrier, not in prison?'

Rodrigo held up his satellite phone. 'Yes, I have the number. I'm told they are expecting a call.'

Rahima looked at Cordoba and burst into tears.

Despite everything he had heard, Cordoba still felt uneasy about it all. To have an aircraft carrier bearing down on them just to hand over his son just didn't make sense. Something was wrong. His instincts told him to be careful, but looking at his wife he realised he had no choice but to agree. 'All right. Let's do it,' said Cordoba. 'Make the call.'

It took Rodrigo several attempts to contact the *Endeavor* on his satellite phone. After having identified himself to various officers, he was finally put through to Andersen.

'Do we have an agreement to extend the handover time?' she asked.

'Yes, we do,' said Rodrigo. 'My client agrees. Twenty-four hours. No more.'

'And you will nominate the handover time and place?'

'Yes, we will.'

'A beach somewhere on the Pacific coast?'

'Yes.'

'We will need at least five hours' notice; logistics.'

'Understood. Is Alonso with you?'

'Yes, he is right here.'

'Can we talk to him?'

'Yes, you can.'

'Please tell him that his mother wants to talk to him and bring him to the phone.'

'Will do.'

Rodrigo turned to Rahima who was standing next to him, shaking, and handed her his phone. Rahima cleared her throat. 'Alonso?' she said, her voice barely audible.

'Is that you, Mama?' asked Alonso.

'Yes, it's me,' said Rahima and almost dropped the phone. Rodrigo had to put his arm around her to steady her. 'How are you?'

'I'm fine.'

'I want you to come home.'

'I'm trying …'

Then the line went dead.

52

Somewhere on the west coast of Colombia: 18 July

Agabe was preparing Stolzfus for the journey home. Despite his best efforts to keep his patient calm and relaxed, he was worried as Stolzfus had been gradually deteriorating, especially as far as his speech was concerned. He now had great difficulty in talking, was slurring his words and frequently fell asleep in the middle of a sentence, exhausted. He was also in considerable pain, which alarmed Agabe who was navigating uncharted medical waters with limited knowledge, lack of equipment, and urgently needed medication.

Jack had done his best to keep Stolzfus focused and in good spirits by playing countless games of chess with him, faithfully writing down his many equations and following detailed instructions to draw complex diagrams of black holes and event horizons, and numbers with so many zeros it made his eyes water.

So as not to alarm him, it had been decided to give Stolzfus only a vague outline of the impending journey and its purpose, which would take them first by helicopter from Bogota to the coast for the handover, and then by another US Navy helicopter to the aircraft carrier waiting in international waters off the west coast. This would be a stressful experience for a fit and healthy person – so Agabe could only imagine what impact such a journey would have on someone in Stolzfus's precarious position, strapped into a wheelchair, paralysed, and now almost unable to speak.

Once Stolzfus was on the *Endeavor*, expert medical help would be to hand, and they would take over. The main aim was to get him there as quickly as possible without causing serious damage to his failing health, as every hour seemed to count in that regard.

Since that extraordinary encounter in the little chapel a week ago, Jack had spent a lot of time with Rahima, who had visited him every day. Mother and son had a lot of catching up to do and spoke for several hours each day about their lives. It was an extraordinary, almost surreal and very emotional encounter neither of them would ever forget.

Rahima was sitting next to Jack in his room. It was just after sunrise. She was holding his hand and it was clear she hadn't slept much during the night. 'Well, this is it,' she said, barely able to speak. 'This is the day. I pray to God all goes well.' She wiped away a few tears and looked at Jack with red eyes radiating sadness and pain. 'The lost son I have just found is leaving,' she said, 'and the son I expected never to see again is returning. What an irony.'

Jack squeezed his mother's hand in silent reply.

'It's God's will,' continued Rahima. 'I have to accept that and be grateful.'

'As soon as this is over, I will come back. I promise,' said Jack. 'Now that I've found you, my world has changed too. I have a family. I have to get used to that.'

'A little late, I know, but better now than never, don't you think?'

'I agree. When will you tell him?'

'Hernando?'

'Yes, and Alonso too, I suppose.'

'Soon. When I am strong enough to face it ...'

'I understand.'

'I can't express what I feel right now, but you have become a remarkable man, Jack. It seems all by yourself, despite everything that happened, or perhaps because of it. I am immensely proud of you. God has brought you back to me, now, right here, and given us these precious hours to spend together. There's a reason for this. I can feel it here, in my heart.'

Jack smiled. *Destiny at work*, he thought, *I wonder what Tristan would have to say about all this?* 'I have to go and help Agabe to get Stolzfus ready,' said Jack and stood up. 'I can hear him next door. This will be a fateful day. For all of us.'

Rahima nodded, embraced Jack and kissed him tenderly on the cheek. Then she wiped away a few more tears and without saying another word or looking back, left the room.

Andersen and Tristan hurried across the busy flight deck to the waiting MH-60 Seahawk helicopter. Alonso was already on board, sitting between two armed guards. The *Endeavor* had moved into position along the coast the night before after receiving the necessary coordinates from Rodrigo. However, the exact location of the designated beach for the handover had just come through, and it would take the helicopter less than twenty minutes to reach its destination.

Also on board were the pilot, a doctor and a nurse, and only four armed marines. Instructions received from Rodrigo had been quite specific in that regard, but everyone was aware that the awesome firepower of an entire aircraft carrier was only minutes away, should anything go wrong.

'Here we go,' said Andersen as she climbed into the chopper, its noisy rotor blades creating a strong draught on the pitching deck.

Who would have thought just a few days ago that something like this could be possible? Tristan wondered, following Andersen onto the Seahawk. Going to rescue a genius scientist returning from the dead? Jack sure knew how to find the stories, or was it the other way around?

A few minutes later, they could see the rugged coastline in the distance, its deserted sandy beaches a stark contrast to the dense jungle reaching almost to the edge of the water. Dark clouds hovered above a mountain range in the distance, heralding a tropical storm.

The instructions for the handover arrangements had also been specific. They were to land at the northern end of the designated beach at ten am, and wait. The pilot circled the beach once and then put down the chopper between two large tree trunks that had washed up on the beach, and turned off the engine. The four marines got out and took up their positions.

Rodrigo looked at his watch. *They should have just landed*, he thought as Cordoba's helicopter gunship cleared a hilltop, flying just above the tree canopy. The designated beach was close to one of Cordoba's secret jungle cocaine-processing plants and the beach was frequently used for illicit drug deliveries destined for Mexico. Knowing the terrain was always an advantage, and a dozen heavily armed men had arrived during the night and were hiding in the jungle, watching the beach. They even had a rocket launcher with them that could bring down a helicopter should that become necessary. Cordoba believed in always being prepared for the worst. By cleverly choosing the time and the place for the handover, he knew he had the upper hand, but he didn't trust the Americans. A wounded lion was always dangerous, and damaged pride even more so.

Agabe sat next to Stolzfus's wheelchair in the back and carefully watched his patient, who appeared to be asleep. He had given him a strong sedative because he thought that was the best way to prepare him for a journey that could easily turn into a catastrophic ordeal for someone in his condition.

'There they are,' said Rodrigo and pointed down to the beach below. The pilot nodded and carefully put down the helicopter on the southern end of the beach as directed.

Standing next to Agabe, Jack watched as Rodrigo and Andersen walked slowly towards each other on the stretch of beach separating the two helicopters. *Just like the gunfight at O.K. Corral*, he thought. *Tombstone Arizona where Alonso was arrested meets a Colombian beach where he's to be set free. Amazing.*

Jack turned to Agabe. 'I will call you when this is all over,' he said and held out his hand. 'You have my number. It's been a pleasure to get to know you.'

'Likewise,' said Agabe. 'I hope they take good care of him. I've grown very fond of our professor, you know.'

'Me too. One day, we'll look back at this and think it must have been a dream.'

'I know what you mean.'

'What will happen to you now?' asked Jack, watching Rodrigo and Andersen talking to each other.

'Not sure, but there's nothing left for me in Malta.'

'I suppose not. Can I ask you for a favour?'

'Of course.'

'Could you keep an eye on Mrs Cordoba?'

Agabe looked at Jack, surprised. 'I know you've spent a lot of time together, but why do you ask?'

'One day, I'll tell you and it will surprise you. She's a remarkable woman, trust me. Very vulnerable at the moment, especially with what's happening here. She may need someone like you by her side,' said Jack, a sudden sense of foreboding chilling his heart like an icy wind.

'All right, I will.'

'Promise?'

'Promise.'

After talking briefly to Andersen, Rodrigo walked back to the helicopter. 'This is how we'll do it,' he said, pointing to Jack. 'As soon as I give the signal, you begin to push the wheelchair over to them, understood?'

Jack nodded.

'A doctor will have a look at Stolzfus when you reach one another, which will be somewhere in the middle over there. If he's satisfied, you continue, and so does Alonso. Clear?'

'Did you tell them the professor has been sedated?' said Agabe.

'I did, and they understand.'

Just then, two men began to walk slowly towards them from the other helicopter about a hundred metres away. One was Alonso, the other the doctor. 'Now. Go!' said Rodrigo. Jack nodded towards Agabe and began to push the heavy wheelchair forward.

A moment to remember, thought Tristan as he watched Jack coming towards him, the wheels of the wheelchair digging into the wet sand and making progress difficult and awkward.

As he approached the two men, Jack kept staring at Alonso, stony-faced and silent, coming towards him in his ill-fitting orange prison uniform he had worn since leaving Arizona just a few days ago. Jack knew he was looking at his half-brother, but to his surprise he couldn't feel anything but indifference, and a twinge of embarrassment and pity. While the doctor briefly examined Stolzfus and took his pulse, Jack stared at Alonso, who avoided his gaze and looked away.

Speak to him for Christ's sake, thought Jack, choking. He desperately wanted to reach out and say something, but couldn't find the words.

Then the moment passed. Satisfied, the doctor turned to Jack. 'Let's go,' he said and helped Jack with the wheelchair. Without looking at Jack, Alonso turned away and began to walk towards his father's helicopter, and freedom.

Suddenly, a mighty thunderclap shattered the stillness of the morning and heavy raindrops began to fall, churning up the sand like rubber bullets. Then the heavens opened and bolts of lightning lit up the dark sky. The wheelchair almost got bogged down completely as the wheels sank into the wet sand, rapidly turning it into a quagmire.

The doctor was watching Stolzfus with concern when suddenly, Stolzfus opened his eyes. His breathing became erratic and an expression of panic and fear contorted his pale face as another deafening thunderclap rolled across the beach and shook the ground like an earthquake.

'*There, look*!' shouted Jack and pointed to Stolzfus's face. Stolzfus had his mouth open and blood was running down his chin and neck. He was choking.

'Good God!' shouted the doctor. 'We must get him back to the ship – quickly!'

By now it was so dark that it was almost impossible to see the helicopter through the dense curtain of rain. '*Help! Over here!*' shouted the doctor and began to wave frantically, trying to attract the attention of the marines guarding the helicopter. One of the marines saw him waving and came running over. Another followed, and together they lifted Stolzfus's wheelchair out of the wet sand and carried it across to the waiting helicopter.

'We meet in the strangest places,' said Tristan, slapping Jack on the back as he helped him lift the wheelchair into the helicopter. 'Great to see you, mate.'

'Reminds me of the *Calypso* just before she sank in Somalia, only there the wheelchair went down with the ship,' said Jack.

'And you were rescued by a chopper,' said Tristan, grinning, 'just like now.'

Moments later, the helicopter took off. Inside, the doctor tried frantically to stem the blood flow and keep Stolzfus's airways clear to allow him to breathe.

'What's wrong with him?' asked Andersen, trying to stay calm. This was the last thing she needed.

'Don't know. We have to get him back to the *Endeavor* as fast as we can,' said the doctor. 'Every minute counts!'

'He's trapped in a useless body,' said Tristan. 'He's scared. It's like drowning in a straitjacket; I know ...' Tristan turned to Jack. 'Talk to him, mate,' he said. 'He knows you and trusts you.'

Jack nodded. 'It's all right, Zac,' he said to Stolzfus, who was staring at him with bulging eyes. 'We are out of the storm and my notes are right here, see?' Jack pulled a wad of papers covered in equations and strange-looking diagrams out of his coat pocket and held them up. 'The theory of everything is safe.'

Stolzfus kept watching him. Suddenly, his face relaxed, his breathing became calmer and the bleeding stopped.

'That's better,' continued Jack, keeping eye contact with Stolzfus and his voice calm to reassure him. 'With you like this and a bit of luck, I should win the next game,' he added. Jack thought he detected a hint of a smile on the professor's anxious face.

The doctor looked at Jack and Tristan, amazed. 'Well done, guys. This should buy us some time.'

Agabe was right, thought Jack. *It's the stress.*

Andersen was watching Jack and Tristan. 'You are quite a team,' she said. 'I can see that now. Good to have you on board, Jack.'

'Glad to be here, Major. It's been an interesting journey.'

'I bet,' said Tristan and embraced Jack. 'Good to have you back in one piece, mate.'

'Was this the kind of little adventure you had in mind when we left Venice?' asked Jack, a sparkle in his eyes.

'Not exactly, and I certainly didn't count on having to rescue you on a deserted beach in South America in the middle of a storm.'

'What took you so long?'

'The navy's fault, mate.' Tristan shook his head. 'They sent an aircraft carrier!'

'Was that necessary?'

'You are an important guy, Jack.'

'Ah. Well, that explains it. Nothing to do with the professor then? But an *aircraft carrier*?'

Listening to the banter, Andersen was unable to suppress a smile. *These two have an incredible bond*, she thought. *Australians!*

53

Bogota: 18 July, 2:00 pm

To the uninitiated, life on an aircraft carrier would appear alien and strange. Several thousand highly trained personnel going about their duties with almost robotic efficiency in ridiculously confined spaces, often with little or no privacy, can only work with strict rules and relentless discipline. Obeying orders is paramount and stepping out of line unthinkable, as it could endanger the lives of many and put critical operations at risk.

Nobody understood that better than Andersen. Civilians on board like Jack and Tristan were a rare curiosity and they were kept segregated from general operations. They had to share a tiny cabin they were assigned next to Andersen's. Most of the ship was strictly off limits and the maze of corridors and different levels made moving around difficult.

To find Stolzfus in such a bad state during the handover had caught everyone by surprise. Even Jack, who had spent a lot of time with Stolzfus since he had come out of the coma, was shaken by the professor's sudden decline. Immediately after landing on the *Endeavor*, Stolzfus was taken to the sophisticated medical facility on board, equipped with cutting-edge technology and knowhow, and access to top specialists in the United States via video link for assistance with diagnosis and treatment.

Andersen was on the bridge, reporting to McGregor. 'You did everything by the book, Major,' said McGregor. 'Professor Stolzfus's condition is regrettable, but it doesn't change anything, nor would it have altered the handover in any way had we known about it earlier. Getting the professor back alive was paramount regardless of his condition, and we have achieved that.'

'If you say so, sir.'

'I have already discussed it with the secretary of state and the CIA. The professor is now in the best of hands and there's nothing further you or I can or should do about that.'

McGregor paused, searching for the best way to broach the next, extremely sensitive subject. He had only received the top-secret instructions moments before the helicopter with Stolzfus on board had landed.

'But that is not to say this is the end of the matter ...' continued McGregor, carefully watching Andersen.

'Oh? What do you mean, sir?' said Andersen, sensing a warning on her finely honed intelligence radar.

'I have just received certain orders and they concern *you*, Major.'

Andersen felt her stomach twist as apprehension gripped her. It was an unwelcome but familiar feeling she had experienced many times before, signalling something unpleasant and dangerous.

McGregor pulled an envelope out of his tunic pocket and handed it to Andersen. 'These are your orders,' he said. 'From the very top.'

Andersen opened the envelope, read the single sheet of paper inside signed by Dr Hubert, and inhaled sharply. 'When?' she asked.

'The CIA has operatives on the ground right now. As soon as they give the signal to go ahead, your mission starts. I expect within the hour at the latest. All top secret, of course. You better get ready and stand by. And remember, officially, you are part of exercises we are conducting.'

Andersen stood to attention. 'Yes, sir,' she said and saluted.

McGregor did the same. 'Good luck, Major. For what it's worth, you are by far the best-equipped fighter pilot with combat experience I have for this kind of job. You have what it takes to pull this off and I don't have to tell you what's riding on it.'

'Thank you, sir,' replied Andersen, trying to make sense of what she had just read. Then she turned around, her head spinning, and quickly left the bridge to get ready and prepare herself for what was to come.

Jack sat next to Tristan in their tiny cabin, telling him about Rahima and what it meant to him to have found his long-lost mother in such unexpected and dramatic circumstances. If Tristan was in any way surprised, he certainly didn't show it. For someone who was a strong believer in destiny and fate, such matters were part of the workings of everyday life.

'How do you feel about all this?' asked Tristan.

'Right now, I feel worried about her. She's very vulnerable, emotionally, especially with all that's been going on.'

'Hardly surprising.'

'No, it isn't. I'm just sorry I had to leave so suddenly with so many questions left unanswered.'

'I can imagine ...'

Jack pointed to the ceiling. 'I feel very uneasy about all this, Tristan. Something's going on here we don't know about. An entire aircraft carrier strike force just to rescue a scientist?' Jack shook his head. 'Hardly. There has to be more to it than that.'

Tristan smiled. 'I've been thinking that too. We are talking about a superpower here. National interests, reputations, *prestige*!'

'Exactly, and that's what worries me. A Colombian drug baron holding the US to ransom? Do you really think he will be allowed to get away with it? I don't think so. I think there's a bigger picture here.'

'What bigger picture?' asked Tristan.

'The drug problem. It's a huge political issue in the US at the moment and it's all about the South American drug supply. Elections are coming up.'

'What are you saying? This could be the opportunity Washington's been waiting for? The strong man in the White House protecting the national interests?'

'Something like that. To show force and do something about the drug problem.'

'How?'

'By teaching the drug barons a lesson they are not likely to forget and at the same time making huge political capital out of it back home.'

'Hm. And linking it all to the Stolzfus abduction the whole country's talking about?'

'Exactly! Maximum exposure, maximum impact, opportune timing, patriotic and emotional – perfect. A re-election spin doctor's dream.'

Jack could hear some noise in the cabin next door. 'That must be the major,' he said and stood up. They hadn't seen Andersen since the helicopter had landed and Stolzfus was rushed to the intensive care unit on the ship. Jack opened the door and looked outside. Andersen was just leaving her cabin. Jack looked at her, surprised.

'Going somewhere, Major?' he said, pointing to her sage-green flight suit. 'Don't tell me some of the pilots here are a little rusty and in need of a lesson?'

She looks uncomfortable, thought Jack.

Andersen shook her head. 'No, it's a little more complicated than that.'

'Oh?'

'I can't explain, I'm sorry. Orders ... must dash!'

Tristan stepped out into the corridor and watched Andersen turn around and quickly walk away. 'I can see a blinding flash and balls of fire, and hear the deafening roar of jet engines,' he called out after her. Andersen stopped and turned around, her mouth agape. *He knows!* she thought. *He used the same words in Langley. Amazing!*

'Bogota?' said Tristan. It was more of a statement than a question.

Holding his breath, Jack watched Andersen carefully. Their eyes locked and Jack thought he could detect an almost imperceptible nod. It only lasted for an instant, then Andersen turned and hurried down the corridor without saying another word.

'Jesus!' said Jack. 'They are going to attack the compound! These jets could be there within minutes and wreak havoc.'

Tristan put his hand on Jack's shoulder. 'Ticks all the boxes. I think you were right, mate; they are not going to take this lying down. The lesson Major Andersen will deliver is not intended for pilots, but for drug barons.'

'We must warn Rahima!' said Jack.

'How?'

'She always has her phone with her. I have her number and you have a satellite phone.'

'Come inside quickly. It's worth a try.'

Cordoba's helicopter had just landed in the H Cartel compound. Standing at the window of his observation room, Cordoba watched his son climb out of the cockpit, waving. A group of security guards patrolling the grounds close by cheered and clapped. Alonso closed his eyes and took a deep breath, drinking in the familiar air. Then he knelt down and kissed the ground like he had seen the pope do during his visit to Colombia in 2017, which Alonso had watched on the TV in his prison cell.

Rahima turned to Cordoba standing next to her, tears in her eyes. She reached for his hand and kissed it. 'Thank you, Hernando,' she said. 'You kept your word. I will never forget this.'

'It will come at a price; I just can't see what it is right now and that makes me nervous,' said Cordoba, ignoring her comment. 'The American ambassador has asked to see Rodrigo. He said it was urgent. I'll send him over straight away to find out what this is all about.'

Andersen sat in the cockpit of the F/A-18E Super Hornet, waiting for take-off. Armed with two of the latest air-to-surface missiles, the jet had awesome firepower. For a fighter pilot like Andersen, this was a special moment. *How I've missed this*, she thought as the flight deck crew moved the plane into position at the rear of the catapult. They were about to attach the towbar on the nose gear to a slot in the shuttle. Andersen gripped the controls and checked the indicator panels, the palms of her hands beginning to sweat. *Next comes the holdback*, she thought. In the F/A-18E the holdback was built into the nose gear.

As the flight crew raised the jet-blast deflector aft of the plane, the catapult officer known as the 'shooter' was standing by in the catapult control pod, getting the catapults ready. Now the jet was almost ready to go. The catapult officer opened the valves to fill the catapult cylinders with steam from the reactors. Suddenly, steam began to rise from the catapult as the Super Hornet prepared to launch. Soon the steam would provide the necessary power in the pistons to sling the plane forward, providing the required lift for take-off.

Now! whispered Andersen and blasted the plane's engines. The holdback kept the plane on the shuttle until the engines generated sufficient thrust. Carefully watching the piston pressure gauge, the catapult officer released the pistons just at the right moment, causing the holdbacks to release as well, thereby thrusting the shuttle and the plane forward at enormous speed. This incredible force allowed the twenty-thousand kilogram plane to accelerate from zero to 266 km/h in just two seconds, and take off. Minutes later, four other fully armed planes took off in close succession as part of an exercise.

The CIA operatives who had been watching the H Cartel compound had seen the arrival of the Cordoba helicopter with Alonso on board. Satisfied that everyone who counted was now inside the building, they gave the go-ahead.

After briefly embracing her son, who appeared strangely cold and distant, Rahima left Cordoba's observation room. Sensing that father and son wanted to be alone, she knew it was time to withdraw. The observation room was Cordoba's private domain where he received visitors and conducted most of his business. It was understood that Rahima would only enter if invited, and never unannounced.

Rahima was on her way back to her apartment on the ground floor when her satellite phone rang. Expecting a call from a friend in New York, she answered the phone. It was Jack.

'Where are you?' he demanded, his voice sounding shrill.

'About to enter my apartment. Why?'

'Please listen carefully! There's no time to explain. You are in great danger! Leave the building at once and get as far away from it as you can. Now! Run! *Do you understand?*'

'Why?' stammered Rahima, starting to panic.

'No time! *Run*!' Then the phone went dead.

Breathless and in a panic, Rahima hurried along the corridor and burst into the observation room. Alonso was standing next to Cordoba by the window. Both men turned around, surprised.

'We must go outside *now*!' shouted Rahima. 'We are in great danger. Come; now!'

'Please calm down,' said Cordoba. 'What are you talking about?'

'Jack Rogan called. We are in great danger!' said Rahima, barely able to speak. She hurried over to Alonso and took him by the hand. 'Come with me, I implore you!'

Alonso withdrew his hand and pushed his mother aside. 'I'm not going anywhere. My place is here with my father.'

'Please, pull yourself together, Rahima,' said Cordoba. 'This is nonsense. We are safe here.'

'*Noooo*!' shouted Rahima, tears streaming down her troubled face. 'My son warned us!'

'What are you talking about?' said Cordoba. 'Your son is right here.' Cordoba shook his head, suspecting some kind of stress-related medical episode brought on by Alonso's return. 'Please go back to your rooms and calm down. I mean it. I'll send someone.'

Rahima staggered out of the observation room, finding it difficult to breathe. Confused, she ran to one of the back doors leading into the garden. She was about to open the door when she almost bumped into Agabe coming the other way.

'What's wrong?' he said, looking concerned.

'Come with me!' shouted Rahima, remembering what Jack had told her about Agabe. '*Quickly!*' She took Agabe by the hand and pulled him along the path leading to the little chapel at the far end of the garden.

'We must get inside before it's too late,' she whispered. Then she pushed open the chapel door, ran towards the altar and collapsed on the floor.

Flying at 2000 km/h, it took the Super Hornet only a few minutes to reach its target. Flying high above Bogota, Andersen released the two powerful air-to-ground missiles. Precision guided by GPS, they homed in on the H Cartel compound below. Because the target wasn't moving and had been precisely identified with exact coordinates, the missiles had no difficulty finding the compound. By the time they slammed into the main building, obliterating it, Andersen was already on her way back to the *Endeavor*, having spent less than a few minutes in Colombian airspace.

Rodrigo was talking to the ambassador at the US embassy when he heard a loud explosion that shook the building. Through the windows he saw a ball of flames and a plume of black smoke rise from the compound, visible in the distance. 'Good God!' Shaking, he turned to face the ambassador standing behind him.

'That's the reason I asked you to come here urgently, Mr Rodrigo,' said the ambassador calmly. 'A little different from viewing that video you presented not that long ago, but just as realistic if not more so, wouldn't you say? I would be surprised if anyone in the compound survived this.'

Rodrigo shook his head, desperately trying to understand what he had just witnessed. 'Who? What?' he stammered.

'Isn't it obvious? Rival cartels fight one another all the time here. We've both seen it before ...'

'On this scale? *Never!*'

The ambassador shrugged. 'Be that as it may, asking you to come here saved your life. So much is clear. A little cooperation in return would go a long way to make sure it wasn't in vain.'

'What do you mean?' said Rodrigo, the lawyer in him sensing that some kind of deal was about to be proposed.

'I suggest you return to New York at once. You will be contacted at your office, by the CIA most likely. They will explain everything. My driver will take you to the airport now. Tickets have been arranged. Have a good flight, Mr Rodrigo,' said the ambassador and pressed the call button on his desk. 'There is nothing left here for you, trust me.'

54

On the USS *Endeavour*: 18 July, 2:40 pm

Flying high above the jungle, Andersen was on her way back to the *Endeavor* when she noticed dark clouds and lightning in the distance. Gaining momentum, the violent storm she had encountered during the handover on the beach earlier, had moved out to sea. Soon visibility became poor as she approached the *Endeavor*, looking like a tiny life raft floating in the vast grey ocean below.

Fuel is low, visibility poor and getting worse, thought Andersen as she began to line up for landing. As she got closer, sea mist moved in suddenly and it began to rain heavily as the *Endeavor* disappeared from view behind a curtain of dense fog. Andersen realised it would take all of her aviator skills and experience to land the jet in these conditions. Landing a supersonic jet on a floating piece of metal runway one hundred and fifty metres long was one of the most difficult manoeuvres for even the most seasoned navy pilot, but to attempt to do this almost blind and with the deck pitching in rough seas in the middle of a tropical storm was practically a death wish.

Jack and Tristan stood in the back of the Carrier Air Traffic Control Center watching the planes that had already completed their mission, land one by one. They had returned early and were able to land before the storm closed in. That only left Andersen, returning from a secret mission over Bogota, still in the air and attempting to land.

Jack could sense the tension in the control room. He looked at Tristan and raised an eyebrow as he overheard the exchange between Andersen and the landing signals officer (LSO) guiding the plane in using radio communications, and a collection of lights on the landing deck that would be difficult if not impossible to see in these conditions.

They knew Andersen didn't have enough fuel to stay in the air and wait for the storm to pass. She only had enough fuel for one, or at best two attempts to land the plane. To do this safely, she would have to snag one of four steel arresting wires stretched across the deck with the tail hook at the back of the jet. These arresting wires are attached on both ends to hydraulic cylinders below deck to absorb the enormous energy generated by a twenty-thousand kilogram aircraft travelling at 240 km/h attempting to land and come to a sudden stop in a ninety-six metre landing area. Four parallel arresting wires were stretched across the deck, fifteen metres apart. An experienced aviator like Andersen would aim for the third wire, which was the safest and most effective. To do this almost blind would stretch the pilot and the LSO to the limit and require a high level of skill and luck to perform successfully. There were only a handful of pilots in the navy who could do this in such treacherous weather conditions, and Andersen was one of them.

Instead of abating, the tropical storm was becoming more violent. Heavy wind gusts swept across the pitching deck and bolts of lightning raced across the sky like trapped snakes trying to escape. The calm voice of the LSO sounded almost surreal as he listened to Andersen and gave her instructions over the radio:

Andersen: 'Marshal, 201 checking in state 6.4.' This was the crucial fuel level expressed in pounds and reduced to two numbers. It meant that Andersen had 6400 pounds of fuel left.

LSO: '201, expect CV-1 recovery Case III approach, altimeter 29.92, marshal on the 240 radial, 21, angles six, expected push time 22.'

Andersen: '201, marshal on the 240, 21, angles six, 29.92, state 6.3 …'

I can't see anything! thought Andersen, ignoring the fear clawing at her empty stomach.

LSO: 'Deck's moving; you're a little too high.'

Using slight stick and throttle modifications, Andersen repositioned the aircraft for a good landing start by using the information on her head-up display.

Mesmerised, Jack and Tristan stared out the window, watching the grey, windswept flight deck below. Suddenly, they could see the outline of the approaching jet coming towards them out of the mist at high speed like a giant primeval bird of prey ready to attack, and they could hear the whining roar of the engines. The jet was coming in too high and moments later, it missed the arresting wires altogether. A veteran pilot like Andersen knew that instead of slowing down the plane just before landing, she had to come in at full military power, which meant at full power without afterburners. This was of course counterintuitive, but absolutely essential should it become necessary to abort the landing and take off again because the tail hook had missed the arresting wire. If the pilot didn't come in at that speed, the jet wouldn't be able to take off again and would crash into the sea instead.

Then came the LSO's call over the radio: 'Bolter, bolter, bolter. Hook skip bolter!'

'I don't like this,' said Tristan, trying to interpret the disturbing signals assaulting his brain like a warning from the future, trying to change the present. For a moment, bright flashes of light obscured his vision. Feeling frustrated and dizzy, he had to lean against Jack's shoulder to steady himself.

Taking a deep breath, Andersen checked again that the Super Hornet was at military power, and began to climb away to attempt another landing.

Andersen looked at the fuel gauge. Almost empty. *Jesus!* she thought. *Just enough for one more pass if I'm lucky.* Andersen swung the plane around and lined up for another landing. By now it was so dark she couldn't see the flight deck at all, nor the landing lights, as heavy rain descended like a final curtain, covering the *Endeavor* like a shroud.

I'm flying completely blind, thought Andersen, staring at the controls in front of her, the calm voice of the LSO the only lifeline left to guide her in safely.

LSO: 'You are doing well, 201. Steady now and a little more power. Good. You are almost down. Watch the lights. Can you see them?'

'*No! Nothing*!'

'Steady … can you see the lights now? You are almost on top of them!'

'Yes!'

For an instant, the rain curtain parted and Andersen could see the flight deck and the arresting wires below and knew exactly what to do. *Almost down*, she thought, going calmly through the required steps. But just before the tail hook could snare the third wire, which was now within easy reach, a sudden, freak windshear hit the jet from the left, forcing it upwards and sideways. The plane, by now off course, missed the tail hook by centimetres, veered to starboard, slammed at high speed into a plane parked on deck and instantly burst into flames. The violent impact of the crash sent one of the severed wings of the parked plane flying high into the air. Missing the windows of the Carrier Air Traffic Control Center by a whisker, it spun around like a huge piece of cardboard, and then crashed into the sea below. The last thing Andersen saw as the cockpit around her disintegrated was a blinding wall of fire racing towards her as the fuel tanks exploded.

'Good God!' whispered Jack as he watched the carnage below. By now, fire crews were descending on the burning planes from all sides, attempting to put out the raging fire that had engulfed the aircraft and was threatening to spread to others parked close by.

Apart from Andersen, whose charred remains were almost unrecognisable, four deck crew had been incinerated and eight others seriously injured. The Super Hornet was completely destroyed, and three other planes severely damaged. The only fortunate outcome was that the flight deck had remained intact and operational, and damage to the *Endeavor* minimal.

55

Naval Base San Diego: 19 July

Naval Base San Diego, known to locals as 32nd Street Naval Station, was the second-largest surface ship base in the United States and home of the Pacific Fleet. As big as a small town and spread over a large area, it employed twenty-four thousand military personnel and ten thousand civilians.

After the fiery crash that had killed Andersen, Jack and Tristan were escorted back to their cabin and told to remain there until their return to San Diego could be arranged. McBride was furious when he found out that Jack and Tristan had witnessed the disaster and reprimanded the officer who had given them access to the Carrier Air Traffic Control Center to watch the return of the planes. This was a clear breach of protocol and a great embarrassment, especially in such a sensitive and difficult situation.

The officer, who was also in charge of their transfer, was tight-lipped, even frosty, thought Jack, and didn't answer any of Jack's questions. The only thing he did tell them was that they would be returned to the naval base in San Diego for debriefing as soon as possible. The mood on the ship was tense and subdued. The entire crew appeared to be grieving, and it was obvious that outsiders were not welcome. The crash had taken a huge toll on everyone.

When they were taken to the helicopter waiting for them on the flight deck during the night, Jack noticed that the wreckage had been cleared away and the only evidence of the disaster was the three damaged planes still parked on deck, looking like injured birds with their singed wings clipped.

After landing at the naval base in San Diego early in the morning, Jack and Tristan were taken under guard to a nondescript building and told to wait.

'What do you think is going on here, mate?' asked Tristan and pointed to the stony-faced, uniformed guard watching them.

'Not sure, but I think we've seen and heard things we were not supposed to …'

'The crash? I still can't get my mind around it. Andersen dead? Can you believe it?'

'Not just that. There's a lot more going on here than we realise.'

'*Bogota?*' said Tristan.

Jack looked at him sadly and shrugged. 'The worst thing is not knowing what really happened. It's the uncertainty. With Andersen dead, they pulled the shutters down. Firmly!'

Tristan put his hand on Jack's shoulder, trying to comfort his distraught friend. 'I understand,' he said.

Jack had tried to call Rahima several times before leaving the *Endeavor,* but without success. Tristan's satellite phone had been useless and without reception. Jack suspected the phone had been jammed.

'And not a word about Stolzfus either; nothing,' he said. 'After all we've been through. They obviously want to get rid of us. I don't like this at all. I think we're caught up in something big here that went terribly wrong.'

Tired and irritable, Jack ran his fingers through his hair and took a deep breath.

'That's just great!' said Tristan. 'And we are right in the middle of it.'

'Is that a complaint?'

'What do you think?'

'May I remind you that coming along was your idea? You *pleaded* with me, if I remember correctly.'

'True, but I didn't know it would turn out like this, did I?'

'You wanted a change and an adventure.'

'I sure got one.'

'Would you rather be back in Venice welcoming visitors in your posh hotel, mate?' continued Jack. 'Matrimonial bliss, Venice style?'

'That hurt and you know it. You can be very annoying at times. That's why they call you an incorrigible rascal, I suppose.'

'It's a term of endearment.'

'Exasperation more like it.'

'That's below the belt.'

'Is it? Well, I can think of several—'

'Shush!' interrupted Jack, lowering his voice. 'Here comes someone.'

A naval officer in a crisp white uniform walked up to Jack and gave him a disapproving look. Jack felt like a vagrant in his crumpled shirt and jacket, a two-day-stubble sprouting on his cheeks and bags under his eyes from lack of sleep. 'Please follow me, gentlemen,' said the officer, turning up his nose. 'Dr Hubert is waiting.'

'The director of the CIA? *Here?* Interesting. How about a shower and a shave first?' said Jack. 'We must try to look our best, don't you think?'

'Please follow me,' repeated the officer, ignoring the frivolous remark.

Jack turned to Tristan. 'Arrogant bastard. Ready for the debrief, mate?' said Jack. 'I have a feeling all of our questions are about to be answered.'

'They obviously want something from us. I'm sure the top honcho didn't travel halfway across the country just to see if we're okay.'

'What do you think they want?'

'You really want to know?' said Tristan.

'Sure.'

'Our silence.'

'That's what I thought. Let's find out. Still cross?'

'No. I can't wait!'

Dr Hubert waited until the officer had left the room and closed the door behind him, then she walked over to Jack and shook his hand. 'Good to meet you at last, Mr Rogan. I've heard so much about you.'

'From Tristan, no doubt,' said Jack. 'He's a little biased. You can't believe everything he tells you.'

'Not just from him, but from many others. You are quite an enigma, Mr Rogan, and quite a celebrity. We could use someone like you in the service. Interested?'

'I would make a terrible spy and would only disappoint you,' retorted Jack, enjoying the banter. To his surprise, he had taken an instant liking to Dr Hubert and felt totally at ease in the company of the powerful woman who had most likely ordered the air strike on Bogota.

'Please take a seat,' continued Hubert affably. 'We have much to discuss, and don't mind my assistant over there. She's taking notes of our conversation. Protocol.'

'Fine by me, as long as you don't mind my appearance.' Jack ran his hand over the stubble sprouting on his cheeks. 'As you know, we've been travelling all night, and the transport hasn't been exactly business class.'

My kind of guy, thought Hubert and burst out laughing. 'Appearances have never bothered me. It's what's behind them that counts.'

Hubert sat down in a chair facing Jack and Tristan. 'Before we begin, I must establish the ground rules,' she said, turning serious.

'What ground rules?' asked Jack.

'Everything I'm about to tell you here is classified information. It will explain everything that has happened recently. It has been decided at the highest level to share it with you, but only if you agree to be bound by the secrecy rules under the relevant US legislation. All CIA operatives are bound by those rules and I must tell you, breaches have serious consequences—'

'But we are not part of the CIA,' interrupted Jack.

'For present purposes, you are deemed to be. You will see in a moment why. All of this is a matter of national security. Highly sensitive.'

Hubert signalled to her assistant, who brought two pieces of paper over to the table and handed one to Jack and one to Tristan.

'Please read this carefully. If you are prepared to sign, we can continue. If not, I will have to ask you to leave.'

Jack read the short document and looked at Tristan. Tristan nodded, as keen as Jack was to hear what Hubert had to say. Both Jack and Tristan signed the documents.

'Excellent,' said Hubert and sat back in her chair. 'I would have been very surprised and disappointed if you had refused. We have come such a long way in this matter together, it would have been a shame to see it all fall apart at this late stage.' Hubert paused and looked at Jack. 'Especially after Major Andersen so valiantly sacrificed her life for the cause,' she added sadly.

'And what cause might that have been?' asked Jack, carefully watching Hubert. A seasoned journalist, he knew how to ask probing questions and what to look for in the body language during the answer.

'The rescue of Professor Stolzfus, of course, and the destruction of the H Cartel that was behind his abduction,' replied Hubert without hesitation. 'And both objectives have been achieved, albeit at a very high price.'

'Care to elaborate?'

'Sure. The handover of Professor Stolzfus you witnessed firsthand. You were instrumental in bringing it about and were there when it happened. In fact, you were part of the package.'

'And the destruction of the H Cartel?'

'A different matter altogether. A very sensitive one. You would have seen six fighter jets take off from the *Endeavor* shortly after your arrival, correct?'

Jack nodded. *Here it comes*, he thought, expecting the worst.

'What you may not know is this: the jets were on a top-secret mission ordered by the president himself.'

'What mission?' asked Jack, sounding hoarse.

'Five of the jets hit targets hidden deep in the jungle close to the coast. Secret drug-processing plants operated by the H Cartel. All were successfully destroyed.'

'And the sixth plane?'

'Major Andersen's mission took her deeper into Colombian airspace, to Bogota. Her mission – the most difficult of them all – was to hit the H Cartel compound where you and Professor Stolzfus had been held hostage just a few hours before the strike.'

'And?'

'Our operatives on the ground confirmed that the air strike was a great success. The compound has been obliterated. Nothing left.'

'Any survivors?' asked Jack, beginning to choke. If Hubert noticed his discomfort, she certainly didn't show it and would certainly not have been aware of the reason behind it.

'We believe not. But we do know that Major Andersen paid a very heavy price for that success.'

'And the Colombian authorities had no problem with all this foreign military activity on their soil?' asked Tristan, stepping in to give Jack some time to recover.

'No. The Colombian Government knew about the mission and okayed it. They have tried in vain for years to bring the H Cartel to heel, and welcomed the air strikes. Some trade deals and promises of aid definitely helped.'

Jack shook his head.

'To keep America safe isn't always easy, Mr Rogan, and we must often do certain things we would rather forget, but that's the real world. I'm sure you know that as well as I do.'

'And Dr Agabe, who so diligently looked after Stolzfus?'

'Collateral damage, just like Major Andersen.'

'And Rodrigo too, I suppose.'

'No. We made sure he was with the US ambassador at the time of the air strike.'

'You spared *him*?' asked Jack, frowning. 'Why?'

'Because we need him to help us unravel the H Cartel business empire. There are hundreds of millions of cocaine dollars invested in the US and around the world. Proceeds of crime. Rodrigo is the only one who knows where it all is and how it all works.'

Jack looked impressed. *Clever,* he thought, nodding his head.

'And he also knows the supply routes and arrangements with the buyers, and that is what we are really after,' continued Hubert. 'He's back in New York in his office helping us with our enquiries.'

'Lucky guy,' said Jack.

'Very predictable. Typical lawyer, doing everything he can to save his skin.'

'And the release of Alonso Cordoba? *The deal*? What about that?' asked Jack.

'I'm glad you mentioned that, because this brings me to the next subject.'

'Oh?'

'The official line.'

'I don't understand,' said Jack.

'You will in a moment. Needless to say, the press and the public at large will be told a different story.'

'What kind of story?'

Hubert looked at her watch. 'In about an hour, the White House will release a statement. A nation hungry for news about Professor Stolzfus's fate will learn how a secret operation carried out by Navy SEALs from the aircraft carrier USS *Endeavour* managed to liberate Professor Stolzfus and take him back to the carrier, where he is recovering right now.'

Jack looked stunned. 'But what about the exchange? What about the release of Alonso Cordoba?'

'Alonso Cordoba was executed in Arizona yesterday morning, just before the Navy SEALs liberated Professor Stolzfus. A statement has already been released by the prison authorities to that effect.'

'Is that the official line?' asked Jack.

'It is. Alonso Cordoba is dead. Killed during yesterday's air strike together with everyone who was in the compound at the time, and that includes his notorious father, Hernando Cordoba.'

'What about the air strikes?'

'There were no air strikes. Rival cartels armed to the teeth fight one another all the time in Colombia with sophisticated weapons, including powerful rockets and so on. The Colombian Government will release a statement later today, telling the world that a violent turf war had broken out in Bogota between rival cartels, triggered by the high-profile Stolzfus affair, resulting in the destruction of the H Cartel's headquarters and the death of its notorious leader, Hernando Cordoba. Ironically, he perished at about the same time his convicted son was executed in Arizona according to US law. Poetic justice, wouldn't you say? The press will go nuts and have a field day with all this.'

'And the public will buy all that?' asked Tristan.

Hubert smiled. 'It will do more than that, it will *love* it. And so will the press. American pride and military muscle are always popular stories, especially before an election. Everyone will feel good and most importantly, the president will *look* good. A win for all with a happy ending. That's the stuff of successful foreign policy, gentlemen, and we are grateful for your contribution. Especially yours, Mr Rogan. Without your articles and the vital information you provided, this would never have happened.'

'And the *New York Times* will go along with all this?' asked Jack.

'We already spoke to Celia Crawford—'

'And?'

'She will be given a head start about the story and be one of the first to report it. In fact, she will be the one to break the story about the rescue, just as she had done with Stolzfus and his abduction.'

Clever, thought Jack. *A little bribe obviously goes a long way*. 'How's Professor Stolzfus?' he asked, changing direction.

For a moment Hubert paused, considering how best to answer, and how much to reveal. Realising that Jack and Stolzfus had forged a close bond, she decided to reveal all. 'He's in quite a bad way, I'm afraid. He seems to have lost his speech altogether,' she said.

'But that would trap him inside a useless body, unable to communicate,' said Tristan. 'A horrible fate for a man like that.'

'I'm afraid you're right. But we are doing everything we can to address this. The best medical minds in the country are working on this right now.'

Jack shook his head. 'This is dreadful. After all that's happened—'

'I have something to give you,' said Hubert, trying to defuse the rising tension.

'Oh?'

Hubert signalled to her assistant, who came over and placed something on the table in front of Jack.

'Your passport and your wallet with all your credit cards you left behind in the room safe in Florence, and your phone,' said Hubert. 'Cesaria Borroni sends her regards.'

'You can always rely on Cesaria,' said Jack. 'Thank you. We go back a long way.'

'I know.'

'I'm very worried about Stolzfus,' said Jack, returning to the subject on everyone's mind.

'So are we.'

'For a gifted scientist like him to be unable to communicate is not only a great tragedy, but a fate worse than death.' Jack reached into his coat pocket, pulled out a wad of papers and put them on the table in front of him. 'Especially during such a critical time ...'

'What do you mean?' asked Hubert.

'You may not know this,' continued Jack, 'but during our sea journey to Colombia, Stolzfus came out of his coma and was surprisingly lucid and able to communicate. In fact, he spoke to me for hours and asked me to write down certain equations and calculations relating to the theory of everything he has been so obsessed with for years.'

'Oh?' Hubert looked at the papers on the table. She hadn't expected this.

'Stolzfus asked me a favour, and I made a promise. In fact, I made two promises.'

'What kind of promises?'

'To deliver these papers to the Genius Club where he worked, because the club would understand what it all meant.'

'I see. May I have a look?'

Jack nodded and Hubert picked up the papers covered in equations, diagrams and calculations, looking like pages of a Leonardo Da Vinci manuscript.

'I will have to take these, I'm afraid,' she said, 'and have them examined by our analysts to see if they contain any matters of national security.'

'What are you getting at?'

'I'm sure you know that Professor Stolzfus worked on highly sensitive projects involving the military. Defence systems, artificial intelligence, space weapons programs and so on.'

'I know, but I made a promise,' said Jack.

'I understand that, and you have my word that these papers will be returned to you straight away if they do not contain any sensitive material. If that turns out to be the case, I will make arrangements for you to meet with the Genius Club as soon as possible so that you can hand them over and deliver the professor's message personally. You said there were two promises.'

Jack nodded. 'Yes. I also promised to meet with his sister to arrange something that was very important to the professor. As you know, she's my publicist and runs my publishing company in New York.'

'I know. Please tell me what was so important?' Hubert wanted to know.

'It may seem trivial in the context of geopolitics and national security, but to a man like Stolzfus who found himself in such an extraordinary predicament, it was hugely important, and I promised—'

'Please get to the point, Mr Rogan,' interrupted Hubert, becoming impatient.

'To look after Gizmo,' said Jack, his voice barely audible.

'*Gizmo?* Who is Gizmo?'

Jack paused, struggling with the answer because he realised it might come out the wrong way and sound like some kind of joke.

'Yes?' prompted Hubert.

'Gizmo is Stolzfus's little dog who accompanied him everywhere, even to his lectures. He's quite famous and very popular. A real personality, much loved by all.'

Hubert looked incredulous. 'Gizmo is a *dog?*' she said, shaking her head. 'We are discussing arrangements for a dog here? Are you serious, Mr Rogan?'

Tristan could see that Jack was becoming annoyed and was about to let fly. *Here it comes*, he thought and sat back, smiling. *I'm going to enjoy this!*

'Yes, I am. It may sound astonishing, perhaps even ridiculous to you to talk about something like this here, but a promise is a promise. I made a promise to a desperate man who went to attend the memorial service of a fellow scientist he admired. A man *you* and your organisation promised to protect, but failed to. And we know what happened to him, don't we? The least we can do now is to be a little generous and considerate when we pick up the pieces!'

For a long, tense moment, Hubert didn't say anything and just looked at Jack with dismay. She wasn't used to being reprimanded. 'Touché. You are right,' she said at last. 'If we ignore the little things, the human elements in what we do, we are bound to fail. I'm glad you reminded me of that. I understand where you are coming from. Would you like to pick up the little dog and meet with Stolzfus's sister soon? To honour your promise?'

'Yes, I would,' said Jack, pleasantly surprised by Hubert's reply.

'Rebecca Armstrong is back in New York right now and has been asking many questions. Especially after those explosive articles appeared.'

'I can imagine.'

'I'll arrange a flight.'

'Thank you, I would appreciate that,' said Jack, and decided to press on. 'Where is Stolzfus now?' he asked. 'She's bound to ask me.'

'In a military hospital, receiving the best treatment possible. We are doing everything we can to—'

'Does she know he's been handed over?' interrupted Jack.

'Not yet.'

'Could she see him?'

'A little later perhaps.'

'Could I?'

'Later.'

'I see. And what about the Giordano family? They get off scot-free?'

'Not entirely. Just before Major Andersen went on her Bogota mission, she sent me a detailed report about this very topic and made an interesting suggestion.'

'What kind of suggestion?' asked Jack.

'I can't disclose that right now, but if it works, I can assure you the Giordano family, and especially Alessandro, will wish they'd never heard of Professor Stolzfus. We are working with Chief Prosecutor Grimaldi and the Squadra Mobile in Florence on this right now.'

'I hope it works,' said Jack.

'So do we. Well, that just about wraps it all up for now,' said Hubert and looked sardonically at Jack and Tristan. 'May I assume we understand one another?'

'We do,' said Jack, and Tristan nodded.

'I would appreciate it if you could both stay away from the press, at least for the moment, to give us some time …'

'I understand,' said Jack.

'And you, Mr Te Papatahi? What are your plans?'

'I have to return to Venice.'

'Yes, of course.'

'Tristan has a famous wife,' interjected Jack, giving Tristan a cheeky grin. 'Italian … He *has* to get back.'

'Major Andersen told me,' said Hubert smiling. 'The *Top Chef Europe* winner.'

'Very formidable,' continued Jack, rolling his eyes. 'And like all chefs, she's temperamental, volatile and very adept with knives ...'

Tristan held up his hands. 'All right, all right—'

'I can imagine. We are indebted to you both,' said Hubert and stood up, indicating the meeting was over. 'Major Andersen will be buried with full military honours. I hope you will be able to attend the funeral.'

'I will certainly do my best,' said Jack.

Tristan nodded. 'So will I.'

'Excellent. There was one more thing,' said Hubert, looking at Tristan. 'The last time we met, Mr Te Papatahi, you said something as you left the room.'

'Yes, I told you that I could see an aircraft carrier, a deserted beach and a man in a wheelchair. I also said that I could see a blinding flash and balls of fire, and could hear the deafening roar of jet engines.'

'Exactly. Astonishing. We now know that everything you saw then has come to pass. I was wondering …'

'Yes?' said Tristan, realising at once where this was heading.

'Is there perhaps something else you can see right now?'

Tristan closed his eyes and took his time before replying. 'I can see a blackboard full of numbers and man in a wheelchair in a hall full of people, applauding.'

'Let's hope you are right again, Mr Te Papatahi. Being able to hear the whisper of angels must be quite something. Have a good flight.'

56

Goddard Space Flight Center, Greenbelt, Maryland: 21 July

Jack followed the security guard up the stairs to the first floor where the Genius Club was due to meet. Gizmo seemed to know the way and was straining on his lead and pulling Jack along the corridor. The security guard's wife who had looked after Gizmo during Stolzfus's absence told Jack that Gizmo had fretted terribly during the past few weeks. He wasn't eating properly and apparently didn't enjoy his walks, which was very unusual.

True to her word, Hubert had arranged for Jack to get access to the Goddard Space Flight Center, which had been Stolzfus's second home, to collect Gizmo and meet the Genius Club. As it wasn't the second Thursday of the month, but a Saturday, a special meeting had been convened in a hurry. Because Jack's notes didn't contain any material touching on national security, the papers had been returned to him and he was about to hand them over to the club as Stolzfus had requested.

The security guard stopped in front of a glass door at the end of the corridor. 'In here,' he said. As soon as he opened the door, Gizmo dashed inside, tail wagging, and ran excitedly up to Barbara sitting at the front, to receive his customary pat, before turning to Jake who sat next to her, for a tickle behind the ear.

An intimidating-looking lot, thought Jack as he glanced at the five members of the Genius Club looking at him expectantly. Collecting his thoughts, he was trying to find the best way to defuse the tension in the room, when his eyes came to rest on Gizmo still wagging his tail furiously. *Of course*, thought Jack, smiling. *The cute dog always works.*

'You know what they say,' began Jack, walking up to the blackboard. 'If you are not sure what to say, bring a cute dog along to say it for you. I've been told by Professor Stolzfus that Gizmo here knows more about astrophysics than I ever will,' continued Jack, feeling more relaxed.

There was subdued laughter and all eyes were on Jack. The club had been briefed by Goldberger and the CIA about the purpose of Jack's visit and the excitement in the room was palpable. They had all googled Jack and knew a lot about him.

'I don't know how much you've been told about me or why I wanted to meet you, so allow me to start at the beginning.' Jack pulled up a chair and sat down facing the five members of the Genius Club Stolzfus had told him so much about.

Barbara sensed Jack's unease and decided to step in. 'You can take it, Mr Rogan, that all of us here have read the articles about Professor Stolzfus in the *New York Times* and, as you can imagine, we have followed the story with great interest.'

Jack looked at her gratefully; the ice was broken.

'In that case, I will cut to the chase and talk about things you may *not* know. I spent five days with Professor Stolzfus at sea after he came out of his coma. We were prisoners on a small ship owned by a drug cartel bound for Colombia and were living in cramped quarters. During that time I got to know the professor very well. We were playing chess – he hardly looked at the board and I was losing most of the time anyway – and all he talked about was, you guessed it, physics and the universe.'

More subdued laughter spurred him on. Jack the storyteller was in his element and he could sense that he had his audience in the palm of his hand. Smiling, he continued.

'He also spoke a lot about you, and the Hawking Challenge.' Jack paused to let that sink in. 'He told me that you were all playing in some kind of celestial orchestra where he was the conductor, making sure that you were all playing in harmony to create an inspired symphony that was supposed to unravel the mysteries of the universe by coming up with a theory of everything.'

Jack could see by the shocked expressions on the faces in front of him that he had chosen the right approach. 'He also told me that during that extraordinary operation, which you obviously know about, he could hear music that inspired him and showed him the way—'

'What do you mean, "showed him the way"?' interrupted a young man at the back wearing a pair of spectacles so thick they gave him an almost comical look, like a pet fish staring through a water bowl.

'Professor Stolzfus believed he had found what had eluded him for years. He believed that he had finally found that inspired symphony.'

Unable to control his excitement, Jake leant forward. 'Did he tell you what that was?' he asked.

'He did more than that,' replied Jack. 'During the five days we spent together, Professor Stolzfus spoke of nothing else. In fact, he was bursting with ideas and attempted desperately to get them all out and recorded.'

'*Recorded*?' interjected Barbara, sitting on the edge of her seat and hanging on Jack's every word.

'Yes. He had all the calculations and equations in his head. All part of that inspired symphony he kept talking about.' Jack paused, reached into his coat pocket and pulled out a wad of papers, and placed them on the desk in front of him. The five members of the Genius Club stared at the papers, the excitement in the room almost at bursting point.

'Following Professor Stolzfus's instructions,' continued Jack, 'I wrote everything down: the calculations, the equations, the diagrams. Everything. I became his scribe so to speak. I also made a promise. I promised to deliver it all to you because you, unlike me, would know what it all meant. A present from the conductor, Professor Stolzfus called it, to his beloved orchestra.' Jack pointed to the papers on the desk. 'This is it here.'

Everyone was silent for a long, tense moment, then they all rose to their feet and walked up the desk to have a look. 'May we?' asked Barbara.

'Of course, it's all yours.'

For the next hour there was excited, sometimes heated discussion in the room as the Genius Club divided up the task of deciphering

Stolzfus's complex ideas. Soon, the blackboard was covered in calculations, diagrams, arrows and equations.

'Good Lord! Did you see this, guys?' asked the young man with the thick spectacles. He was furiously scribbling something on the blackboard, his nose covered in chalk. 'Bloody brilliant!'

Standing at the back of the room, Jack watched as a gifted man's genius came to life in front of him. 'Incredible,' he whispered, and patted Gizmo who sat patiently at his feet. 'We better go, mate. I think this is beyond us; even you.'

Barbara looked at Jack. 'This will take some time,' she said, beaming. 'It's absolutely amazing!'

'I can see.'

'Thank you! Thank you so much. We can't tell you what this means to us. Not just us, but to science and the world. This could make history!'

'I'm glad. I better leave you to it then,' said Jack. 'It's time for me to attend to my second promise.'

Everybody turned around and looked at Jack. 'I'm sorry,' said Jake. 'We are ignoring you.'

'Understandable.'

'What second promise?' asked Barbara.

Jack pointed to Gizmo. 'I promised to look after this little chap here. He's going to live with Professor Stolzfus's sister in New York until the professor is well enough to come back.'

'Do you think he will?' asked Jake, sounding sad.

'I hope so. And a close friend of mine who can hear the whisper of angels and glimpse eternity certainly seems to think so,' added Jack, smiling.

Hubert had not only arranged the flight and assembled the Genius Club at the Goddard Space Flight Center, she had also arranged transport for Jack and Gizmo to New York, some three-and-a-half hours' drive away. Jack suspected this was more than just a courtesy. He was certain that he was under observation and it made sense to

Jack that the CIA would be keeping a close eye on him, especially since that dramatic statement by the White House two days earlier, which had given the 'official' version of what happened in Colombia and the Stolzfus matter to a news-hungry press.

Jack was sitting in the back of the hire car with Gizmo when his satellite phone rang. It was the first call he had received since Hubert had returned the phone to him and the battery was now fully charged.

'Jack Rogan,' said Jack.

'Thank God!' said a voice at the other end. 'I've been trying to call you for days.'

The reception was bad and Jack could hardly hear what was being said. 'Who is this?' he asked, shaking the phone.

'It's me. *Agabe*!'

57

Central Park, New York: 21 July

Jack entered Central Park near 62nd Street and walked with Gizmo towards the Gapstow Bridge. As he came closer to the familiar bridge with its splendid view of the New York skyline he had photographed so often, he remembered that fateful incident in 2002 when Soul, the famous jazz singer, had what seemed like a heart attack and collapsed almost in front of him, and how his quick thinking had saved her life.

Hard to believe that was sixteen years ago, thought Jack, as he passed the very spot Soul had been lying on the footpath with a distraught Izabel by her side. Jack touched the little cross around his neck and smiled. It had protected Soul that time; pity it couldn't have done the same later. Having struggled with drug addiction for years, Soul had sadly passed away from an overdose earlier that year. *Strange how things work out*, thought Jack and stopped on the top of the little bridge. That was the reason a lonely, grieving Izabel had hooked up with Teodora.

Jack looked at his watch. It was almost three in the afternoon, the time he had arranged to meet Rebecca Armstrong by the bridge. There were two reasons for this: first, he thought that handing Gizmo over to Rebecca in the park would be less stressful for the little dog but more importantly, Jack was certain he was being watched and felt that meeting Rebecca in a public place like Central Park to discuss what he had to tell her was safer by far.

Rocked by the telephone call from Agabe earlier that day, which had taken him by complete surprise, Jack felt unsettled and had become very cautious. He still found it difficult to come to terms with what Agabe had told him and needed some time to think about what to do next. A walk through the park seemed a good way to start.

Looking up, Jack could see Rebecca waving in the distance and he waved back.

'That's a new side of you I haven't seen before,' said Rebecca, giving Jack a big hug as she reached him. Then she bent down and gave Gizmo a pat. 'An afternoon stroll through Central Park with a new dog a couple of days after being rescued by the US Navy from the clutches of a notorious drug baron in Colombia. The papers are full of it. You are an amazing guy, Jack, but why are we meeting here? Our office is just over there.'

'There are good reasons for this,' said Jack and linked arms with Rebecca.

'With you, there always are.'

'Come, let's take a walk and I'll explain. There isn't much time.'

'You look dreadful, by the way.'

'Haven't slept much in the past three days.'

'You're not in trouble, are you?'

'Not as such.'

'And what does that mean?'

'It's complicated.'

'You look like a man on the run.'

'I could never hide anything from you,' said Jack, grinning. 'I'm not on the run, just lying low.'

'Why?'

'I'll tell you.'

During the next half hour, Jack told Rebecca everything that had happened to him since she'd returned to the United States with what was left of her brother's body. He paused when it came to the Stolzfus handover on the beach three days earlier. 'Now comes the really interesting bit,' he said, lowering his voice.

'What do you mean?' asked Rebecca, frowning.

'Before I tell you, you have to promise me something. It's hugely important and a lot is riding on it.'

'What promise?'

'Not to talk about what I'm about to tell you to anyone. I mean *anyone*; clear?'

'Sure, but why? I don't understand.'

'You will in a moment. Promise?'

'Promise.'

'Zac wasn't rescued by Navy SEALs as the White House wants us to believe and the papers are telling us. He was exchanged on a secluded beach for Alonso Cordoba, the convicted Colombian drug dealer on death row in Arizona.'

Rebecca looked thunderstruck. 'You can't be serious, surely!'

'I am. I was there—'

'But he was *executed*!' interrupted Rebecca.

'No. He died together with his father and many others during a US air strike that destroyed the Cordoba compound in Bogota.'

'But that was destroyed by rival cartels fighting one another,' said Rebecca.

Jack shook his head. 'Not so. The air strike was ordered by the president himself, and carried out by the US Navy and Major Andersen personally, who then tragically crashed her fighter jet on her return during landing on the aircraft carrier. I saw that too.'

'Jesus, Jack. *This is crazy!*'

'Perhaps, and I am risking my neck telling you all this. But I believe you of all people deserve to know the truth. You do believe me, don't you?'

'Yes, of course I do, but …'

'It's a lot to take in, I know, but we haven't much time. I have a plane to catch tonight. I'm going to London to deal with another critical matter that has just come to light.'

'Oh? There's more?'

'There sure is, and I only found out about it this morning on my way here from the Goddard Space Flight Center.'

Jack and Rebecca sat down on a bench facing a pond full of ducks. Gizmo seemed to be mesmerised by the birds and was watching them intently.

'Remember where I was when you rang me and asked for my help with Zac's disappearance?'

'Sure. You were in Africa, looking for your lost mother in the Sudan.'

'Correct.'

'How is this relevant?'

Jack took a deep breath and looked at Rebecca. 'Because I found her,' he said, choking with emotion.

Rebecca looked at Jack in total disbelief. 'You *found* her? Where?'

'I firmly believe that destiny and fate brought us together in the most unlikely way imaginable. And it would never have happened without these extraordinary events we've just talked about.'

'Please tell me.'

While Gizmo was watching the ducks with his little tail wagging madly, Jack told Rebecca about the chance encounter that had led him to his mother. 'And it only came about because of this,' he said, pulling out the little cross hanging around his neck from the top of his shirt. 'And I was only given this because I saved a young woman's life just over there by the bridge sixteen years ago.'

'Extraordinary! If that's not destiny then – *Oh my God!*' said Rebecca, as the full implications of what Jack had just told her began to sink in. 'Your mother stayed behind when you left the compound with Zac? She was there when the air strike ...?' Rebecca reached for Jack's hand and squeezed it, tears streaming down her cheeks.

'Yes, she was,' whispered Jack.

'I'm so sorry!'

'Of course, I believed she had perished in the attack with all the others, until I received a phone call from Agabe this morning that changed everything.'

'Changed what?' Rebecca sniffed and wiped her wet cheeks with her hands.

Jack reached into his pocket and handed Rebecca his crumpled handkerchief, which had seen better days.

'I managed to talk to my mother on the phone just moments before the air strike and warn her, but I thought it was too late.'

Rebecca blew her nose and looked at Jack with teary eyes.

'According to Agabe, this is what happened. When my mother ran out of the building, as I told her to do, she bumped into him – literally. She told him about my warning and they ran to a little chapel in the garden behind the main building. Apparently, they managed to get inside and lie down on the floor just before the rockets hit and obliterated the compound buildings.'

'They survived?'

'Yes. The little chapel was badly damaged and the roof collapsed. My mother was injured but alive and Agabe was somehow able to carry her out. In the mayhem and chaos that followed, Agabe managed to take her to a monastery close by. The monks there took them in and are looking after her right now. She has been supporting the monastery for years and is well known there and highly regarded by the monks.'

'How is she?'

'Agabe said she's doing fine. Don't forget he's a doctor. But that's not their biggest problem.'

'I don't understand.'

'The Colombian army has been searching the area for survivors and rounding them up. Even the injured ones. They were all taken away.'

'Why?'

'Isn't it obvious? Survivors could be very embarrassing if the truth about the attack were to somehow come out. And besides, the aim was to have the H Cartel obliterated once and for all, regardless of collateral damage. I believe the Americans and the Colombians made a deal. Hubert just about said as much. And the deal was, no survivors who could contradict the official version of events.'

'Oh my God!'

'That's South America and the CIA for you,' said Jack sadly. 'Foreign policy Yankee style.'

'So, where to from here?'

'Not sure yet, but somehow I have to get my mother out of Colombia – urgently.'

'And how are you going to do that?'

'With help,' said Jack, a hint of a smile spreading across his tired face.

'Any ideas?'

'Of sorts. That's why I'm going to London.'

'Isis?'

'Very perceptive of you. I already spoke to her and Lola.'

'You have a plan?'

'We are working on it, but we have to move fast. If my mother – Rahima Cordoba, the wife of the once-feared drug baron – and Agabe were to be found, well ... they might as well have perished in the air strike.'

'I can see why the CIA don't want you around and perhaps talking to the press.'

'No, and that's not going to happen. Certainly not now with all this going on. I believe Tristan and I are the only "civilians" who know what *really* happened down there, and we've been signed up; silenced. If I were to step out of line, well, I could never come back to the US for starters, that's for sure. And as we both know, the CIA has a long reach and a long memory – as Mr Assange is about to find out. That's why I'm lying low, and that's why I am telling you all this in confidence here and not in our office.'

'I understand now.'

'What have they told you about Zac?' asked Jack, changing the subject.

'Not much, really. All I know is that he is somewhere in a military hospital, recovering. That's all.'

'That's what they told me too.'

'We can but hope for the best,' said Rebecca sadly.

'Yes, for now. But let's see where all this takes us, and never lose hope.'

Rebecca looked at Jack and smiled. 'That's one of the many things I like about you, Jack.'

'Oh? What's that?'

'You are such a hopeless optimist!'

'Not just an incorrigible rascal then?'

'That too, of course.'

'Speaking of rascals,' said Jack, 'this one belongs to you now.' Jack stood up and handed Gizmo's lead to Rebecca. 'At least two good walks a day and I am told he likes to watch television.'

'Oh, does he now? Was there anything else?'

'Not that I can think of. I'm sure you two will get along famously.' Jack squatted down and gave Gizmo a pat on the head. 'Listen here, mate, if you are nice to her, she might let you sleep on her bed.' Jack winked at Rebecca, pointed to his watch and walked away.

58

Time Machine Studios, London: 22 July

Jack was hoping that Boris would be waiting for him at the airport. The huge man was like a rock of certainty and safety he could count on. As Jack exited Arrivals at Heathrow, he could see Boris waving. It was a most reassuring sight, especially during such turbulent and unsettling times, and after a long night flight during which he had found it impossible to sleep.

'Welcome back, Mr Jack,' said Boris and gave Jack one of his rib-crushing bear hugs that Jack loved so much. It was a sign of genuine affection by a man of few words who was very fond of Jack.

'We were very worried about you,' said Boris as he merged the Bentley onto the M4 headed towards London. 'Especially Miss Lola. But that's all behind us now. You are here.' Boris looked in the rear-view mirror and smiled. Jack was asleep in the back seat.

'Jesus, Jack, you look terrible,' said Lola, who was waiting for Jack at the lift in the underground garage of the Time Machine Studios.

'That's what Rebecca said,' replied Jack. 'It's been a rough couple of days.'

'I can see that. Come, Isis is waiting upstairs.' Lola linked arms with Jack and pressed the lift button. 'We have some good news for you that will cheer you up.'

'I could do with some cheering up,' said Jack, barely able to keep his eyes open.

Isis stood next to the stone Buddha facing the lift in her top-floor apartment, holding two glasses of champagne in her hands. Wearing a dazzling crepe de Chine dress with double-flower print by Valentino and a pair of Jimmy Choo black stilettos that would have made Lady Gaga envious, she stepped forward and handed Jack a glass of champagne as soon as the lift doors opened and he walked out.

'Just what I need,' said Jack and gave Isis a peck on the cheek, careful not to smudge her perfect make-up. 'Cheers! Did you dress up just to humiliate me?' said Jack, taking a sip of champagne. 'Look at me!'

'You do have a certain rugged charm, Jack, even in your state, but your clothes are definitely only fit for the incinerator, don't you think, Lola?'

'Definitely. I'll see to it as soon as he steps into the shower, which I must say is at least a few days overdue, don't you think?'

'All right you two, enough. I'm buggered!'

'I can see that,' said Isis. 'Hungry?'

'I could eat a horse!'

'We thought so. Cook has prepared your favourite breakfast. Almost ready.'

'Time for a shower?'

'Your room's waiting.'

'Great! See you in a jiffy, guys,' said Jack and took off his jacket.

Isis looked at Lola. 'You better go with him and see he doesn't fall asleep in the shower. He can barely stand up.'

'Leave him to me,' said Lola, laughing, and followed Jack upstairs to his room. 'I know how to keep a guy awake.'

'I bet. Just don't kill him!'

Feeling relaxed after a long, hot shower, Jack was putting on his jeans when Lola walked into the room with a fresh shirt. 'Feeling better?' she asked.

'A little.'

'You know, my dad was a pilot. He taught me how to fly. He also taught me how to stay focused and alert under stress and keep fatigue under control even without sleep.'

'How?'

'Sit down over there and I'll show you.'

Jack sat down and buttoned up his shirt. Standing behind him, Lola began to slowly massage his scalp, applying pressure with the tips of her fingers to the back of his head.

'Oh, that feels good,' said Jack, closing his eyes.

'My goodness, you are so tense.'

'I'm very worried.'

'About your mother?'

'Yes. If they find her ... I just can't see how I can get her out in time.'

'There may be a way.'

'What are you talking about?' Jack opened his eyes and tensed up again.

'You are undoing all of my good work,' scolded Lola and applied a little more pressure behind Jack's ears. 'Just relax and listen.'

'All right.'

'Remember Isis was thinking about another concert tour?'

'Sure. She's been talking about it for months. Coming out of retirement to please her adoring fans and all that. Would do her good.'

'Well, she's decided to go ahead with it. And it's all because of you.'

'I don't understand!'

'Hush. Just listen. Isis has hundreds of thousands of fans in Mexico and South America. Remember that concert in Mexico City in 2012?'

'How could I forget? It was sensational!'

'After your phone call the other day, we spoke to our agents over there and they are over the moon. They can't wait to begin making arrangements and are talking about sold-out stadiums with mega crowds. Mexico City, Rio, Buenos Aires.'

'What has my phone call to do with all that?'

'You rang Isis and told her about your mother and what happened in Bogota. You asked for our help, remember?'

'Yes, but how—'

'She will tell you over breakfast. Now, just try to relax for a couple of minutes and give me a chance to banish the ghosts,' said Lola and went to work on the back of Jack's neck.

Feeling remarkably refreshed after the hot shower and the magic touch of Lola's fingers, Jack walked into the stunning dining room overlooking the Thames. Isis was seated at the table with a glass of champagne in her hand. 'That's a lot better,' she said. 'Now eat.'

'Steak and eggs? You beauty!' said Jack and began to tuck in with gusto. 'Lola said you wanted to tell me something.'

Isis looked accusingly at Lola. 'You didn't let the cat out of the bag, did you?'

'Certainly not!'

'Good. You did a lot for me and my family, Jack, when I needed it most,' began Isis and refilled her glass. 'I have never forgotten that. So, when you rang and asked for my help, Lola and I put our heads together ...' Pursing her lips, Isis took a sip of champagne. 'We believe we've come up with a way to help your mother.'

Jack pushed his empty plate aside and looked at Isis. 'How?'

'I've decided to go ahead with the tour we've talked about.'

'Lola told me.'

'We already spoke to our agents in South America. I want to make a surprise announcement to kick it all off. Something spectacular—'

'They thought it was an excellent idea,' interjected Lola. 'Especially as Isis promised to do this in person. Great TV footage. The fans will love it!'

'And this will help my mother?'

'Yes,' said Isis and pushed a glass of champagne across the table towards Jack.

'How exactly?'

'As most of my record sales are in South America, the announcement will be made over there.'

'Where?'

'Because Colombia has featured so prominently in the news lately and I have a lot of fans there, we have decided to do it in Bogota – for maximum impact and exposure.'

For a while there was complete silence as Jack digested the implications of what Isis had just said. 'What's the plan?' he asked quietly.

'Isis will arrive in her private jet in Bogota and hold a press conference to announce the tour. Journalists from all over South America will be invited to attend,' said Lola. 'We'll make sure it's quite a spectacle. There may even be an impromptu performance of one of her signature songs. It would send the crowd wild, I can tell you. I will fly the plane, and you are coming with us. You will make contact with your mother and the doctor and we will smuggle them on board *Pegasus* while all this is happening. Boris will keep an eye on you and keep inquisitive wolves at bay.'

'This sounds like something out of a Bruce Willis movie ... are you serious?' asked Jack, shaking his head.

'Absolutely,' said Isis. 'We'll work out the details as we go. We'll improvise. Don't forget, there's chaos over there right now.'

'That's what worries me,' said Jack.

'Chaos can be an advantage,' suggested Lola. 'Opens unexpected doors with unexpected opportunities.'

'True. And you are prepared to do all this for me? With all the risks attached?'

'Without hesitation,' said Isis. 'Wouldn't miss it for quids, as you were so fond of telling us when I was in trouble.'

'And where do we take my mother after we leave Colombia? If we manage to get her out of there, that is? She will be a fugitive without papers.'

'All taken care of,' said Isis, grinning, and lifted her glass. 'Tell him, Lola.'

'To France.'

Jack looked thunderstruck. 'How?'

'You asked someone else for help as well, remember?' said Isis.

'Yes, I spoke to Katerina from New York, and told her all about my newly found mother and her predicament.'

Isis turned to Lola. 'Tell him what Countess Kuragin has been up to during the past twenty-four hours.'

'We all know how well connected she is in government circles, right to the top,' said Lola. 'She called someone who called someone else who spoke to the person close to the French president who could make it all happen.'

'Make what happen?' asked Jack.

'You told us your mother was a French citizen when she disappeared somewhere in the Sudan all those years ago. Apparently, the French Government made enquiries at the time after *National Geographic* reported her missing,' continued Lola. 'There's actually a record of it all.'

'Correct. I found it.'

'That certainly helped. And now we know what happened to her. She was captured by slavers, her name was changed, and she was sold on the black market in Khartoum.'

'That's right.'

'And bought by a South American arms dealer who took her back to Colombia where she was kept – we say against her will – right up to the present day,' said Isis.

'Yes, by Hernando Cordoba, the notorious drug baron.'

'And he was recently killed in the bloody turf wars between feuding cartels, which finally set her free. Show him, Lola,' said Isis, smiling.

Lola stood up, walked over to Jack and placed some official-looking papers with stamps and signatures on the table in front of him.

'What's that?' asked Jack and picked up the papers.

'Temporary travel documents issued by the French Government to Natasha Petrova, which allow her to enter France.'

'Incredible! That was her maiden name, although she wrote under a nom de plume for *National Geographic* – Natasha Rostova. That's what made tracing her so difficult and confusing.'

'Luckily the French kept good records,' said Isis.

'You can say that again. But what about Agabe? We can't just leave him behind. Not after what he did for my mother.'

'Of course not,' said Isis, enjoying herself. 'He'll come with us and will apply for asylum in France.'

'Good God!' said Jack, feeling dizzy. 'And you did all this for me?'

'You asked your friends for help and they responded, that's all,' said Isis. 'We all know what you did when Rebecca asked for your help to find her brother, and what you went through when Katerina asked for your help to find her lost daughter in Australia. And I know what you did for me and my family. It's your turn, Jack, and we are ready, isn't that right, Lola?'

'Sure is. *Pegasus* is fuelled and standing by.'

'When are we leaving?' asked Jack, rubbing his tingling neck. 'Every hour counts here.'

Theatrical to the core, Isis lifted her glass of champagne. Jack did the same and they touched glasses. 'Tomorrow morning,' said Isis. 'Let's drink to that, shall we?'

59

Bogota: 23 July

'All right, guys, put on your seatbelts please,' announced Lola over the loudspeakers. 'El Dorado airport is just down there. We are about to land.' The twelve-hour flight from London had been exhausting, but Lola had taken turns with the two other pilots on board to fly the jet. Lola loved to fly. *Pegasus* was her baby and she used every opportunity to get behind the controls.

'She's all yours, boys,' said Lola and climbed out of her seat. 'I'll see how our passengers are getting on.'

Jack had approached the trip with mixed emotions. On the one hand, he was overwhelmed by the generosity of his friends and grateful for their help. On the other, he was deeply concerned about the daring plan to get his mother out of Colombia. He was afraid that the project had been put together in too much haste and with not enough attention to detail. Caught between the tyranny of the urgent, and common sense that counselled caution and patience, Jack had only managed a few hours of restless sleep. As they prepared to land and enter Colombia, Jack realised that events were about to overtake him. The only thing to do in a situation like this was to go with the flow, stay alert and improvise, but most important of all, to be very careful.

Just before leaving London, Jack had spoken to Celia Crawford at the *New York Times* to give her advance notice of Isis's plan to make a surprise announcement in Bogota about a South American concert tour. Isis was very fond of Celia and trusted her completely. She had worked with her before on the forgotten Monet matter involving the enigmatic Emil Fuchs and his forgery.

Resisting Celia's pointed questions was never easy, but Jack had remained tight-lipped and hadn't said a word about the real purpose of their visit, nor had he mentioned his mother. Once again, Celia and the *New York Times* had landed a coup and were about to break the sensational story of Isis's upcoming concert tour, and Celia was already on her way to Bogota to cover the event.

After several failed attempts, Jack had finally managed to speak briefly to Agabe just before leaving London and alerted him to what was about to come. After a few moments of silence, a surprised Agabe assured Jack that Rahima was well enough to travel as her injuries weren't serious. Jack told him to get ready to leave the monastery, but to say absolutely nothing to anyone. As Agabe was used to danger and working under pressure, Jack knew he was the right man for this delicate task.

Jack looked at Isis sitting opposite. *She looks so happy*, he thought. Dressed in a stunning, insanely tight Aztec-style costume covered with feathers – the same one she had worn during one of her concerts in Mexico – Isis was putting the finishing touches to her theatrical make-up.

'Thank Christ I still fit into this. What do you think?' she asked and held up a mirror.

'Guaranteed to wow,' said Jack.

'I hope so. Announcing a tour like this is always tricky. It's a balancing act. If you say too much, you leave no room for surprises; if you say too little, you kill the anticipation and everyone goes home, bored.'

'I'm sure you'll manage.'

'I'm a little rusty. It's been a few years.'

'Don't worry, it's in your DNA.'

'You really think so?'

'I do.'

'What's in her DNA?' asked Lola as she walked into the cabin and buckled herself into the seat next to Jack.

'Performing.'

'You can say that again. Just look at her. She'll be on all the South American magazine covers by the end of the week.'

'Now that we're together, I want to say something before we land,' said Jack, looking serious. 'I can't tell you what this means to me, but are you absolutely sure about this?'

Lola put her hand on Jack's arm. 'Do you really have to ask? You know we are.'

'Don't look so worried, Jack,' said Isis. 'It'll be all right. We'll get her out, you'll see.'

'Are you absolutely sure?' Jack asked again. 'Have you considered the risks?'

'We have. Don't worry; we have a lot of friends here we can rely on,' said Lola. 'And one of them is sitting right over there.' Lola pointed to Boris, peacefully asleep in his seat.

'I hear you, but this is a dangerous place, especially after what's just happened. The authorities are very nervous, especially the military.'

Isis shot Lola a meaningful look. 'You must admit, Lola has done a marvellous job in such a short time,' said Isis, changing the subject to distract Jack and put him at ease.

'She sure has.' Jack turned to face Lola. 'I can't imagine how you managed it all, and so quickly. The press, the band, the venue.'

'To persuade the TV station to secure the Santamaria Bullring for the formal announcement tomorrow was quite a coup. It will make headlines around the world. I've performed there before, you know,' said Isis. 'It was a triumph.'

Jack smiled. 'No doubt.'

'We'll use the glass coffin for my entry,' continued Isis, becoming excited. 'The fans will love it and so will the press. We won't have all the usual props of course and we'll use a local band instead of the Time Machine, but it'll do the job.'

'I've seen your coffin entrance. It's gobsmacking!' said Jack.

'Of course, in Mexico just after we met. It was Lola's idea to bring it along for this gig,' said Isis.

Apart from a couple of spectacular costumes, Lola had also brought along Isis's signature glass coffin, securely stowed in the hold of the jet. The coffin was used for Isis's spectacular entrance at the beginning of her concerts.

'I did that for a reason,' said Lola. 'And it has nothing to do with Isis's opening entrance.'

'Oh? What else then?' asked Jack.

'I think it could be a way to bring your mother on board the plane safely and unnoticed. I already discussed this with Boris and Isis.'

'Quite so,' interjected Isis. 'We've actually used the coffin to get me safely off the stage without being mobbed, and past screaming fans back to the safety of my dressing room. It worked a treat every time.'

Jack looked at Lola, shaking his head. 'You never cease to amaze me. Obviously you have a plan?'

'I do.'

'Are you going to tell us about it?'

'Later. What I want to talk about now is how we are going to manage the press. Obviously they will meet us at the airport and so will some fans. They may also be waiting at our hotel. You can't keep any secrets around here. We are staying at the Four Seasons Casa Medina, not far from the airport. You'll love it.'

After a smooth landing, *Pegasus* taxied to a designated bay reserved for the aircraft of visiting dignitaries, next to the main building. The first thing Jack noticed as Isis and her small entourage walked along the corridor leading to immigration and customs was the rather intimidating security presence of heavily armed police and military. As they approached the exit to Arrivals, Jack could hear the hum of loud voices, reminding him of excited crowds at a soccer game cheering on their favourite team. While this should have been an indication of things to come, nothing could have prepared them for what was behind those doors.

As soon as the doors opened and Isis stepped into the hall, a deafening roar greeted them and they could see a cordon of security guards trying to hold back the excited crowd pushing towards the doors. Isis, the consummate performer, stopped and slowly lifted her hands to her lips and then blew kisses to her adoring fans, the gesture sending them wild.

'We didn't quite expect this, did we?' said Jack to Lola, who was walking next to him.

'Too much of a good thing can be a problem, but then this is Colombia and Isis is revered here like a goddess. We are supposed to have a brief chat to the press over there with a photo opportunity, and then go directly to our hotel. Let's see how we go.'

Lola pointed to a small group of journalists madly taking photographs, huddled in a corner and surrounded by security guards holding back the cheering fans. Used to crowds and the press, Isis walked confidently up to the press and began to chat with them and answer questions. After a few moments, Isis held up her hand and called out something to the crowd. Suddenly, the crowd became almost silent.

'Amazing,' said Jack. 'I don't know how she does it. She completely controls them.'

'That's Isis. Being fluent in Spanish helps,' said Lola. 'Watch.' After a few minutes, Isis stepped away from the journalists and someone brought a microphone over to her.

'See you all tomorrow at the Plaza de Toros de Santamaria. *You are all invited*!' said Isis, her voice booming through the packed hall.

An excited roar rose up from the cheering crowd, followed by spontaneous applause. 'But now I need my beauty sleep, otherwise no performance tomorrow!' More cheering followed as Isis – surrounded by security guards – blew kisses and walked towards the exit.

As Jack walked past the group of journalists still taking photographs, he could see Celia, waving. Jack stopped and waved back. Celia pushed through the crowd to get closer to Jack. 'See you at the hotel; Casa Medina. Call me!' shouted Jack.

A smiling Celia gave him a thumbs up just before he disappeared behind a cordon of security guards pushing him towards the exit.

Celia called Jack a little later, and they agreed to meet in the hotel bar at ten pm. By then, the police had dispersed the fans, who had gathered outside in the dark hoping in vain to catch a glimpse of their idol. Heavy security presence inside the hotel made sure that no unauthorised persons gained access and it was only after Lola had arranged for Celia to be admitted that she was allowed into the hotel to meet Jack.

'You do get around, Jack,' said Celia, giving Jack a hug. 'Never a boring moment with you, that's for sure.'

'It's been quite a rollercoaster; you don't know half of it. Vodka martini?'

'You remembered. I could certainly do with one.'

'I've travelled more miles in the last two weeks and experienced more excitement than most people come across in a lifetime.' Jack paused as the waiter put two martinis on the table. 'It's a bit of a miracle that I'm here at all. Cheers!'

'I can imagine.' They touched glasses.

'I don't think you can.'

A seasoned journalist, Celia knew there was a time to ask questions, and a time to listen. She sensed this was a time to listen as Jack clearly wanted to talk.

'Everything I'm about to tell you is strictly off the record, understood?' continued Jack, beginning to relax and enjoying the soft jazz playing in the background.

'Absolutely,' said Celia, feeling the excitement building in her. Conversations like this were every journalist's dream. These were the rare career gems that only came along occasionally and in the most unexpected ways, if at all.

Because Jack trusted Celia completely, he told her everything that had happened to him since their last meeting in London a month ago. Celia listened in silence as Jack spoke about his abduction in Florence, and lying naked on the operating table on the *Caritas* in Malta just before Teodora shot Fabry, and thus saved his life. He then spoke about his time with Stolzfus and Agabe on the *Coatilcue* and his arrival in Bogota.

Having finished his second martini, Jack paused. He was wrestling with what to say next. Should he tell Celia about finding his mother, and what happened on that deserted beach during the storm when Alonso was exchanged for Stolzfus, just before the US air strike that obliterated the Cordoba compound? Should he tell her what *really* happened?

Celia sensed Jack's unease and reached for his hand. 'They spoke to me too, you know,' she said quietly.

'Who?'

'The CIA ...'

'Wow. Did you sign something?'

'I did.'

Jack looked at Celia, surprised. 'So did I.'

'I thought so. Don't risk it, Jack.'

'I never cared much for bureaucracy and cloak-and-dagger stuff. I've always followed my gut feelings, my instincts. Trust and legal obligations are two separate things. For me, trust always wins. That's who I am. What makes me tick. That's why I'm having trouble with this.'

'I know, Jack. But there's a time and a place for everything, and I don't think this is the right time ...' Celia reached across to Jack and gently touched his lips with the tip of her index finger.

'You're right. So, let's leave it there for now. Let's have another drink and I'll tell you about things the CIA *doesn't* know about – yet.'

'And what might that be?'

'Isis and her upcoming South American tour. And this *is* definitely for the record.'

'What a great idea! After all, that's why I'm here,' said Celia cheerfully, relieved that Jack had decided to stay silent and so avoid compromising them both.

'Tomorrow at the bullring, Isis will make an announcement. A statement would be a better way to put it. She will talk about the plight and suffering of the Venezuelans next door and dedicate the tour to a cause.'

'What cause?'

'To rid Venezuela of a ruthless dictator who's bleeding the country dry and causing untold hardship and misery to its people. She's even given the tour a name – *VenezuelAid* – VA for short.'

'I *love* that,' said Celia, reaching for her notebook and pen.

'You know Isis supports many charities and has donated millions to various causes. Well, she will donate a million US dollars of her own money to the soup kitchens providing meals at the border to the tens of thousands of refugees pouring across from Venezuela every day. But that's not all. She will donate another million to help pregnant woman give birth here in Colombia because in Venezuela, medical services have broken down, and one in two newborn babies dies.'

'This is amazing, Jack! Can I run with this?'

'Absolutely. Isis knows I'm speaking to you tonight. For obvious reasons, she can't be seen talking to you right now, and certainly not in public, but we want you to be the one to break the story.'

'I understand. Thanks, Jack! My editor will be happy.'

'I bet. But wait, there's more.'

'There is? Tell me!'

'Apart from this announcement, Isis will perform a couple of her legendary songs. No doubt this will send the crowd wild, and it will also send an important message to the Venezuelan dictator. Isis intends to unite South America with her concert tour and create a movement to oust him. The Americans will be pleased and support this all the way. The entire concert tour will be dedicated to this cause.'

Celia was scribbling furiously, her cheeks aglow with excitement. 'This is fantastic, Jack. What a brilliant idea! This is history in the making.'

'It sure is, and it will give Isis a new lease on life, especially after all she's been through.'

Suddenly, Celia stopped writing and looked at her watch. 'How can it be this late?' she said and stood up. 'I have to get this to my editor right now or I'll miss the deadline. Sorry Jack, must dash!'

Jack stood up as well and smiled. 'I'll get you a cab. Does this remind you of something?'

'Yes it does. The Waldorf in London after the Monet auction in 2014. We had a drink just like this and you told me the story about the painting and how it was discovered.'

'And you had to leave in a hurry to call your editor in New York with the story, remember? Just like now.'

'It's a bit like deja vu,' said Celia. 'Some things never change. Looks like tomorrow will be an interesting day.'

'In more ways than you can possibly imagine,' said Jack. He escorted Celia outside, gave her a kiss on the cheek, and put her in a cab.

60

Benedictine monastery, above Bogota: 24 July

The rundown Benedictine monastery up in the hills just outside Bogota was a sanctuary and place of contemplation where time stood still. The monks tended the gardens and the orchard, celebrated mass on Sundays with Gregorian chants as tradition demanded, and educated the children of the poor. Their customs and way of life had remained virtually unchanged since Saint Benedict of Nursia had established the order in the sixth century. However, without the generous support of Rahima, who for almost fifty years had lived in the Cordoba compound close by, the monastery would have closed its doors long ago. Lack of funds, civil unrest and changing times had eroded community support and respect for the monks and their work.

Jack and Boris arrived just after sunrise in a rented black SUV. A thick mist hovered over the city below and covered Bogota like a shroud, hiding the toxic turmoil boiling within.

'This place has seen better days,' said Jack as he walked along the gravel path overgrown with weeds, leading to a small belltower. Damaged by fire, the roof had collapsed a long time ago and the tolling of bells was but a distant memory.

As he came closer, he could hear soft organ music and chanting drifting across from a building behind it. Jack realised that the next few hours would be critical, and approached the meeting with trepidation. While Agabe had assured him over the phone that Rahima was well enough to travel, he had also said that the trauma of the attack and the deaths of Hernando and Alonso had affected her deeply.

An elderly monk was waiting for them at the wooden front door riddled with woodworm holes, and ushered them inside. 'We've been expecting you,' he said. 'Come. Mass is almost finished.'

As they crossed an inner courtyard, Jack could see Agabe coming towards him. Agabe walked up to Jack and embraced him. 'I can't believe you're here,' he said.

'Where is Rahima?'

'At mass. She knows you are coming and has been in the chapel praying for most of the night, preparing herself. It's how she copes with what's happened.'

Jack introduced Boris and pointed to a bench in the courtyard. 'Let's go over there. While we wait, let me tell you how we are going to do this—'

'Before you do,' interrupted Agabe, 'you should know that soldiers have come here several times looking for survivors after the attack. I don't know what would have happened had they found us. The monks here have been marvellous. Without them …'

'I understand.'

'I hope you do. This is an extremely dangerous place, Jack. As soon as we walk out of here, we are on our own and very vulnerable.'

'Even more reason for us to discuss this without Rahima.'

'Good idea,' said Agabe and looked anxiously at Jack. 'Are you seriously suggesting you can get us out of Colombia?' he asked, sounding hesitant. 'Because if you don't …'

'Yes.'

'How?'

During the next ten minutes, Jack gave a brief outline of the ambitious plan he had worked out with Lola and Boris during the night while Isis had her beauty sleep.

'You really think this will work?' asked Agabe, shaking his head.

'It has to. We'll get only one shot at this and today's the day.'

'All right. Then let's give it our best one, Jack. Here come the monks now. Mass is finished.'

'And Rahima?'

'Most probably still inside, praying.'

Jack stood up. 'Give me a moment, guys,' he said.

'Do you want me to come with you?' asked Boris.

'No, thanks. I have to do this on my own.'

The door to the little chapel was ajar. As Jack looked inside, he could see Rahima kneeling in front of the altar, alone. The scene reminded him of a medieval fresco by Ambrogio Lorenzetti he had admired in Siena not long ago. Jack walked up behind Rahima and knelt down next to her, the pungent smell of incense and snuffed-out candles drifting across from the altar stirring up long-forgotten childhood memories of loneliness and pain, and kneeling in church on hot Sundays in dusty outback Queensland, praying for rain.

'I knew you would come,' said Rahima and placed her hand on Jack's arm. 'My prayers have been answered. You are the light in all this darkness.'

Jack reached for his mother's hand and for a while just held it tight without saying anything.

'We'll get through this, you'll see,' he said. 'By the end of today, all this will be a distant memory.'

'God willing. How will you do this, my son?'

'Let's go outside and I'll tell you.'

Lola was waiting for them in the hotel car park. Security was tight and the police had almost completely surrounded the building during the night and cordoned off the street in front to hold back the crowd. 'Come, quickly,' she said. 'We have to get Rahima inside! This is Agabe's security pass. He's Isis's doctor, clear? Everyone is aware of her health problems and will not question this.' Looking anxiously around, Lola handed Jack the pass. 'Our problem isn't Agabe, but Rahima,' continued Lola, lowering her voice. Boris nodded, put his huge arm around Rahima's shoulders and walked her to the lifts.

'How do you want to handle this?' asked Jack, following Lola into her suite on the top floor.

'We didn't count on the crowd. Apparently, it's chaos at the bull-ring already. Police everywhere. We have to get out of here fast. Police have been asking all sorts of questions of the hotel management here. I think this whole thing has taken everyone by surprise. The size of it, and Isis hasn't even made an appearance, nor has she made her announcement. You can imagine what will happen when she does.'

'The crowd will go berserk.'

'Exactly.'

'Is that a problem?'

'Depends, but I think it could be an advantage,' said Lola with a mischievous little smile.

'So do I,' said Jack, the eternal optimist. 'What we need here is a little creative thinking.'

'My thoughts exactly.'

'The coffin?'

'Precisely,' said Lola. 'We have to get Rahima safely out of here and into the bullring, and from there to the airport at the end of the concert. As you know, we are not coming back here, but going directly to *Pegasus*. The crew is already there and standing by, ready to take off.'

'We have to move fast.'

'Yes. Isis is already dressed for the occasion and ready to go, thank God. She's on fire, I tell you.'

'Then, what are we waiting for?'

Boris had a protective arm around Rahima and was walking along the corridor flanked by Lola and Jack. Isis followed with Agabe and two security guards provided by the hotel, and a porter with a luggage trolley trailing behind. As soon as the lift doors opened, a housemaid stepped out of the lift and almost collided with Rahima. Their eyes met and a flash of recognition raced across the young woman's face.

Rahima turned to Jack. 'I think I've been recognised,' she said quietly.

'What do you mean?'

'The housemaid; just now. She used to work at the compound. I remember her well.'

'Jesus! That's all we need,' said Jack.

He turned to Lola, who gave him a 'shit-happens' shrug. 'Let's just get out of here!' she said.

The police provided a motorcycle escort for the SUV and the black van Lola had hired for all their gear – especially the glass coffin, which took up quite a bit of space. Jack sat in the back next to the open coffin, talking with Rahima, who was lying inside.

'A little ahead of my time,' said Rahima, a sparkle in her eyes. 'But it pays to get used to this, I suppose.'

'I'm glad you see this in the right way,' said Jack, stroking his mother's hand. 'This is necessary to get you safely out of the country.'

'I understand,' said Rahima and winked at Jack. 'I haven't had this much fun since my twenties.'

As they approached the bullring, the crowd almost blocked the entire street and they had to slow to a crawl.

'We haven't seen anything like this since Mexico, have we, guys?' said Isis, her cheeks glowing with excitement. Because of the heavily tinted windows it was impossible for the crowd to recognise Isis sitting in the front. Had it been otherwise, the mob would have overwhelmed them.

'All right, guys, this is how it will work,' said Lola, as soon as they had been escorted to the changing rooms inside the bullring that were normally used by bullfighters. Erected in 1931, the popular stadium normally had a capacity of fourteen thousand, but it was already packed with more than thirty-thousand excited fans chanting 'Isis! Isis! Isis!' The police were unable to control access to the bullring and had been overwhelmed by the crowd that had assembled at the gates since well before midnight, hoping to catch a glimpse of their idol.

Lola pointed to the glass coffin on the floor. Workers who had hastily erected the makeshift stage in the centre of the bullring overnight, had carefully carried it into the change room as directed, unaware that someone was actually lying inside. Covered completely by the elaborate costumes Isis intended to wear during the performance, it was impossible to see Rahima – lying motionless and silent and barely daring to breathe – underneath them.

'So far so good,' said Lola. 'Rahima will stay here and hide until the performance is over. Then we'll take her back to the plane the same way she came here: inside the coffin, covered by Isis's costumes. No-one will know she's in there. Simple and effective.'

Jack looked at Lola. *I hope you're right,* he thought, and helped Rahima climb out.

Oblivious to everything going on around her, Isis could hear only one thing: the chanting of the crowd, conjuring up memories of previous performances that had been the highlights of her extraordinary career. Intoxicated by long-forgotten emotions, she looked at her reflection in the mirror in front of her and liked what she saw. Dressed in a spectacular costume she had worn on one of her South American tours, Isis travelled back twenty years and saw herself as the young, vibrant megastar she once was. Then the band outside began to play one of her bestselling numbers, which usually sent the fans wild. A lump in her throat, Isis looked at Lola with dreamy eyes.

'It's time,' said Lola and pointed to the glass coffin. 'Are you ready?'

'As ready as I'll ever be,' replied Isis. *My God, how I've missed this*, she thought and climbed into the coffin.

Instead of being lifted up by a hydraulic system as they would normally use, the coffin would be carried on stage by six Colombian 'pallbearers' wearing traditional costumes while the band played 'Resurrection'. After that, Isis would emerge from the coffin and begin her stunning performance that the excited fans had come to see.

'All right, boys, let's go,' said Lola, and closed the coffin lid. 'Let the show begin!'

61

Santamaria Bullring, Bogota: 24 July

The popular morning show presenter who worked for the Bogota TV station sponsoring the event, walked up to the microphone and held up her hand. The band on the stage behind her stopped playing and slowly the excited crowd became quiet, the atmosphere in the arena electric.

'Good morning, *Bogota*!' announced the woman, her familiar voice booming through the sound system. 'The moment you have all been waiting for has arrived.'

Cheering and thunderous applause filled the arena.

The woman paused to let the anticipation grow as the cameras zoomed in. 'I give you the legendary, the fabulous, the one and only … *Isis*!' With that, the woman turned to her left and pointed to the entry into the arena where the police had cleared a narrow path leading into the bullring. Moments later, the band's drummer began whipping up the crowd with a spine-tingling solo introduction before the throbbing bass joined in and the guitars screamed into life, heralding the arrival of the megastar.

'Here we go,' whispered Jack and blew a kiss towards Isis who was looking up at him through the glass. 'Good luck, my dear friend!'

With the famous crystal skull resting on her chest, and wearing her tight-fitting, Aztec-inspired bodysuit she had worn during her famous 'Thank You' concert in Mexico City in 2012, Isis looked like an Aztec queen beginning her journey into the afterlife.

With leopard skins draped over their bare shoulders and donning spectacular headdresses made of brightly coloured feathers, the six tall, muscular pallbearers added to the drama as they lifted up the coffin and carried it slowly outside. A mighty roar echoed through the arena as the glass coffin appeared, reflecting the morning sun like a magic beacon sent by the gods to illuminate the faithful. Step by step, the pallbearers ascended the stage in the centre of the bullring, put down the coffin on a raised platform covered in flowers in front of the band and stepped back, forming a circle. One by one, the guitars fell silent, until only the beat of the drums echoed through the packed arena like the heartbeat of a sleeping giant. Then one of the pallbearers stepped forward, opened the glass lid and knelt down next to the coffin. The other pallbearers did the same and looked up at the sun as a sudden hush descended on the spellbound crowd.

Holding the crystal skull with both hands, Isis sat up in the coffin, lifted the skull high above her head and pointed it towards the sun. This was the signal for the band to start up again. The guitars were back, playing 'Resurrection', one of Isis's all-time biggest hits. The spell was broken and the crowd erupted.

As Isis stepped slowly out of the coffin and placed the crystal skull on a pedestal next to the microphone for all to see, the crowd became hysterical and began to cheer wildly. Savouring the moment of adulation, Isis looked at the sea of adoring faces and began to sing.

Joselito Barrera, the chief of the Administrative Department of Security, the country's secret police, sat in his office in downtown Bogota. He was watching the Isis concert at the Santamaria Bullring with concern, as the concert was quickly turning into a sensitive political statement no-one had expected. Isis had just announced that her upcoming South American concert tour would begin in Bogota in three months' time and would be dedicated to the many desperate refugees fleeing Venezuela. She had also announced that she would donate a million US dollars to the soup kitchens operating at the border. Barrera was about to turn up the volume, when one of his officers burst into the room.

'I think you should see this, sir,' he said and handed his boss a piece of paper.

Barrera read the note and swore under his breath. 'When?' he asked.

'About an hour ago.'

'Where?'

'At the Four Seasons.'

'This has to be a mistake. It can't possibly be right.'

The officer shrugged.

'Where's the woman?'

'Downstairs.'

'Bring her up straight away.'

'Yes sir.'

After the frightened housemaid had repeated her account of the sighting, Barrera sat back in his chair and stared at the television screen. Isis had just finished making her surprise announcement and had left the stage to change into another costume to wow her fans in preparation for a spectacular concert finale.

Could this possibly be true? Barrera asked himself, shaking his head. 'We need more,' he said to the officer standing next to the housemaid. 'Check all the CCTV footage.'

'Happening right now, sir.'

'Excellent. Let's go to the hotel to save time. And bring her with you.'

'Yes, sir!'

'That was magnificent,' said Lola as she helped Isis take off her tight bodysuit. Covered in sweat, her face aglow with excitement and breathing heavily, Isis looked at Jack standing next to her. 'How did I go?'

'You certainly haven't lost your touch, that's for sure, but your announcement is bound to create quite a stir. Here and overseas, especially in the US. Celia will have a field day with this. We gave her a free hand.'

'Good. That's exactly what it was supposed to do,' said Isis, putting on a *taleguilla* – close-fitting pants secured with tasselled chords – and a *camisa*, an embroidered white shirt worn by matadors. 'Good choice, don't you think?' said Isis, buttoning up her shirt.

Knowing that her surprise concert would take place in a bullring, Isis had decided to perform her closing number dressed as a matador in full, traditional regalia. There would even be a mock bullfight on stage she had hastily arranged with one of the pallbearers, to add to the drama.

'One song, that's it!' said Lola, an anxious look on her face. 'We've got to get out of here.'

'Two,' said Isis and gave Lola a peck on the cheek. 'From *Dead Girl Walking*. I already spoke to the band. I've been waiting a long time for this.'

'Talk to her, Jack!' pleaded Lola, exasperated. 'This is a dangerous place. We've got to get out of here! *Think of your mother*!'

Jack shrugged and helped Isis put on the *chaquetilla*, a stunning short, gold-embroidered jacket with shoulder pads. A pair of white silk knee-high stockings called *medias* and a pair of *zapatillas*, flat black slippers that looked like ballet shoes, completed the spectacular traditional attire.

'You look magnificent,' said Jack and handed Isis the *muleta*, a long red cape used to goad the bull into charging. 'Dressed to kill.'

'Thanks, Jack. This is what I live for.'

'I know. Now get out there and show them what a dead girl walking can do!'

Sirens blaring, the chief of police's car arrived at the hotel. Barrera got out and stormed into the lobby. 'We don't want any trouble,' said the manager nervously, and ushered Barrera into his office. Two police officers were sitting at a desk reviewing CCTV footage.

'Anything?' asked the chief.

'Only this so far,' said one of the officers and pointed to the screen in front of him.

'Who's that?'

'Jack Rogan talking to Celia Crawford of the *New York Times.*'

'Rogan; the famous troubleshooting author?'

'Yes, They spent an hour here in the bar together last night.'

'Interesting. Anything else?'

'Not yet.'

'Keep at it! And put on the Isis transmission.'

One of the officers turned on the large TV next to the desk. Isis was just coming back on stage dressed as a matador. Wearing the traditional *traje de luces* – the suit of light – and waving her black *montera* hat, Isis was greeted like a hero of the bullring with deafening cheers and applause.

'She's an amazing performer,' said Barrera as the band began to play 'Dead Girls Don't Cry', the award-winning track from Isis and the Time Machine's sensational *Dead Girl Walking* album that had sold millions of copies around the world.

'Here, I think I've got something,' said one of the officers, becoming excited.

Barrera walked over to the desk to have a look. 'Who's the big guy?' he asked, pointing to the screen.

'Isis's bodyguard.'

'And the woman?'

The officer pointed to the housemaid standing next to him. 'Tell us again,' he said.

'That's Rahima Cordoba,' whispered the woman, barely able to speak.

'Are you absolutely certain?' demanded Barrera.

The woman nodded, looking terrified.

Barrera shook his head, not convinced. 'We need corroboration. We have recent photos?'

'We do, but this will take time.'

'Could this woman be somewhere here in the hotel?' *Because if not* … thought Barrera, exploring the possible implications.

'We'll search the place and talk to the staff. This too, will take time.'

Collecting his thoughts, Barrera looked at the other TV. Isis had just finished singing. The band was playing a medley of her greatest hits as a man wearing only a leopard skin loincloth and holding a mask of a bull with huge horns in front of his face jumped on stage. Pretending to be a raging bull – his sweat-covered body glistening in the morning sun – he charged at Isis, who held up her red muleta to further enrage him. The ecstatic crowd cheered, enjoying the mock fight. Isis, a skilful performer, imitated the classic moves and arrogant stances of the matador to perfection as the charging bull came at her time and time again. With each pass, Isis moved closer to the open coffin until she had her back almost pressing up against it.

'*Now!*' she shouted as the bull charged past once more. The pretend bull stopped, turned around and then came straight at her again. Instead of turning to move out of the way and miss the charge, Isis stood perfectly still as the two sharp horns came closer. The crowd gasped as the horns appeared to embed themselves into Isis's chest, pushing her backwards. Pretending to be mortally wounded, Isis pressed her hands against her chest and, staggering backwards, let herself fall into the open coffin as the triumphant bull roared and left the stage.

One by one, the guitars fell silent again until only the drummer continued with the same mesmerising beat that had accompanied Isis to the stage at the beginning of her epic, jaw-dropping performance. The crowd cheered as the pallbearers returned and slowly walked up to the coffin, closed the lid and lifted it up. Lying motionless inside the glass coffin, her heaving chest the only sign of life, Isis looked like a dying hero being carried out of the bullring.

'What's happening next?' asked Barrera.

'Isis is leaving. The performance is over. They are going straight to the airport. We are providing an escort. These are the arrangements we approved. What would you like us to do?'

'Get my car. We are going to the airport.'

'Yes, sir!'

'That was sensational!' said Lola and helped Isis climb out of the coffin. 'We should improvise more often!'

'Just listen to them,' said Jack, closing the door after the pallbearers had left the change room.

The crowd outside was chanting 'Isis! Isis! Isis!' and refused to leave the bullring.

'An encore perhaps?' asked Isis, forever hopeful.

'Don't even *think* about it!' snapped Lola. 'We have to get away from here as soon as possible. I'm very uneasy.'

'What about?' asked Jack.

'That housemaid.'

Jack nodded. 'Me too.'

'Now, get your mother out of the restroom and let's get her back into the coffin and leave.'

Escorted by two police officers on motorcycles, Barrera's car entered the airport's corporate aviation area. 'Where's the plane?' asked Barrera.

'Over there,' said his aide and pointed to *Pegasus,* its sleek, aerodynamic body glistening in the morning sun like a giant bird about to take flight. A black SUV and a van were parked next to the plane and Barrera could see Isis getting out of the car with Boris and a woman. Still wearing her stunning matador costume, she began signing autographs for a group of excited luggage handlers gathered around her.

Barrera got out of his car and walked over to Isis while his men surrounded the plane. Lola saw him coming and walked up to him, feeling a wave of apprehension. Last-minute meetings like this were rarely good news.

'May I see your papers, please?' said Barrera. 'I am the chief of police.'

'Certainly,' replied Lola. 'Is something wrong?'

'Not at all. Routine,' said Barrera, smiling.

'Good, because we've already been cleared by the Colombian authorities and are about to take off as soon as our gear gets loaded.'

'This won't take long.' Barrera turned to his aide standing next to him. 'Search the plane, *now*!' he hissed, well aware that stopping the plane from leaving and detaining someone like Isis and her entourage without good reason could have serious consequences, and he certainly wasn't going to act on a hunch, or the questionable information provided by a frightened housemaid. What he needed was proof. With the eyes of the international press firmly trained on Bogota and Isis, he wasn't prepared to take any chances.

Jack stood next to the van with Agabe and watched the glass coffin being lifted out of the back. Four luggage handlers were about to carry it over to the plane and load it into the hold when Barrera walked over to him. 'Ah, the famous coffin we've just seen on stage,' said Barrera. 'Put it down, please.'

'Why?' asked Jack, frowning.

'Because I would like to see everybody's papers.'

'And you are?'

'The chief of police.'

'But we've already ...' began Jack, feeling suddenly uneasy and on guard. Looking surprised, the luggage handlers put down the coffin and stepped back.

'Right now, if you don't mind,' continued Barrera quietly and bent down to have a closer look at the coffin. 'What a fascinating contraption,' he added, watching Jack carefully. 'Could you please open it for me?'

With decades of police experience, Barrera noticed Jack's unease and decided to probe further. *He looks just like a drug smuggler about to be busted*, he thought. *I wonder why?*

'As you can see, we keep Isis's costumes in here to protect them when we travel,' said Jack, trying to buy time. 'They are very precious.'

'I can imagine. Open the lid please, Mr Rogan.'

He knows who I am! thought Jack and shot Agabe a meaningful look. Taking a deep breath to stay calm, Jack tried to open the lid. 'It's a little difficult,' he said, pretending to have a problem with the lock. 'Stuck! Is this really necessary?'

'I'm afraid it is. Here, let me help you.' Barrera reached across and lifted the lid without difficulty. 'Is there something you would like to tell me, Mr Rogan?' said Barrera, holding the lid open.

Jack shook his head and stepped back, his heart racing.

Barrera was about to reach into the coffin and look under Isis's costumes, when the feathered dress on top began to move and Rahima's face appeared.

Feeling quite ill, Jack could hear Rahima talking softly to Barrera in Spanish, but couldn't understand what she was saying. It only lasted for a few moments. After that, Barrera reached into the coffin, covered Rahima's face with Isis's costume and closed the lid. As he stood up and turned around – his face ashen – a police officer appeared in front of the open cabin door at the top of the stairs. 'Everything in order up here, sir,' he shouted.

'And down here,' replied Barrera and turned around to face Jack.

'Have a safe flight, Mr Rogan,' said Barrera. 'Shall we see you again when Isis returns for her concert?'

'Perhaps,' said Jack, barely able to speak. *I wonder what Tristan would make of all this?* he thought, shaking his head. *Destiny in action, most likely.*

After the plane had taken off and reached cruising altitude, Jack turned to Rahima, who was now sitting next to him. *'What did you tell him?'* he asked.

'One day I'll tell you, but not now,' replied Rahima. She stared out of the window and reached for Jack's hand. 'What I want to do right now is to enjoy my first few moments of freedom, and a little time with the son I didn't think I would ever see again.'

62

Kuragin Chateau, just outside Paris: 26 July

Jack was desperately trying to go to sleep, but couldn't. Feeling drained and exhausted after the turbulent events in Bogota and the long flight to Paris, his body craved much-needed sleep, but his mind refused to comply and kept him awake. Turning restlessly in his bed, Jack's mind drifted back to the bullring in Bogota and that extraordinary encounter with the chief of police at the airport, which he still couldn't explain. He imagined what would have happened had they not been allowed to leave, and broke out in a cold sweat. Suddenly wide awake, Jack sat up and turned on the light on the bedside table. It was three in the morning. *A cup of tea will help*, he thought. He got up and put on his dressing gown.

The cavernous kitchen in the basement – its stone walls whispering secret tales of generations past – was Jack's favourite place in the chateau. He loved the gleaming copper pots and pans hanging from the vaulted ceiling, and the large wooden table in front of the fireplace, with a wax-encrusted candelabra standing next to the beautiful samovar gleaming in the middle.

Cook always left a tasty morsel on the table for those looking for a late-night snack, or something to help them go back to sleep. This time, it was one of her mouthwatering orange-and-almond cakes, covered with a large linen serviette to keep it fresh and moist. A tantalising aroma of roasted almonds still lingered, teasing the tastebuds.

Jack was about to pour himself a cup of tea when he heard a soft noise behind him.

'I thought it was you creeping along the corridor,' said Countess Kuragin. 'I couldn't sleep either.'

'Tea?'

'Please. Somehow, we always seem to end up here.'

'This brings back memories,' said Jack and pointed to the samovar. 'Remember the first time we sat here in 2010, talking about Anna?'

'We had just met and I explained what a samovar was,' said the countess, 'because you had no idea.'

'Yes. A tea urn warming generations, you called it, a precious heirloom brought here by your grandmother all the way from her dacha in Russia.'

'You remembered!'

'And you sat here often with her and listened to stories about long Russian winters and sleigh rides through magic forests frozen in time,' reminisced Jack, sipping his tea.

'You made a promise that night. You promised to find out what happened to Anna ...' The countess paused, a sad look on her face as painful memories came flooding back. 'And to see if she could perhaps somehow still be alive,' she continued, unable to hold back the tears. The countess reached across the table and placed her hand on Jack's arm. 'You gave a desperate mother hope. I will never forget that. And you kept that promise and brought Anna back to me – *alive*!'

'It was meant to be,' said Jack. 'We are but instruments of destiny's bidding.'

'Isn't that a bit fatalistic?'

'Is it? How else can I possibly explain that the mother I haven't seen since I was born is right here in the chateau at this very moment, asleep upstairs in the room next to mine? How else can I explain that the chief of police let us go after he discovered Rahima hiding in a glass coffin belonging to a rock star, about to smuggle her out of Colombia in her private jet?' Jack shook his head.

'It's late and you are tired. The mind plays tricks on you when you cannot sleep and are sitting in the kitchen at three in the morning, trying to make sense of it all. Believe me, I know. I've been here often doing just that. Things always look different in the morning.'

'You're right. I haven't been able to thank you yet for all you've done for Rahima and for Agabe,' said Jack, changing direction to clear his thoughts. 'The papers, all the formalities and all the strings you had to pull to make this happen. It all worked perfectly. And now this ... you've opened your home to us all and welcomed us with open arms.'

'I owe you a debt I can never repay, Jack. Certainly not in this life. You are family, and so is Rahima. Don't forget she's Madame Petrova's niece. And Madame Petrova was one of my mother's closest friends. She played with me when I was a child and she watched me grow up.'

'And yet you don't believe in destiny?' said Jack, smiling.

'I didn't say that.'

'What will happen to Rahima and Agabe now? They can't stay here,' said Jack, looking worried.

'Why not? At least for the moment until things settle down. Rahima's been through a lot. I had a long talk to her in the afternoon.'

'What about?'

'Many things. She would like to visit Madame Petrova's memory trees in the morning.'

Jack looked at the countess, surprised. 'You spoke about that?'

'We did.'

'You do realise there's a tree there that—'

'Was planted in her memory,' the countess said, nodding. 'She knows that.'

'And Agabe? What about him?'

'His application for asylum has been lodged and is being processed. My lawyers are handling it.'

'Thanks, Katerina, this means a lot to me.'

'I know. You are worried about Stolzfus, aren't you?'

'You could always read me like a book,' said Jack and reached across the table for the countess's hand. 'Of course I'm worried about him. He's one of the big casualties in this bizarre game. It's a bloody tragedy!'

'Do you know where he is? What's happened to him?'

'Very little, I'm afraid. The CIA has been very tight-lipped about it all. National security they say. I think it's more about a national embarrassment; a monumental stuff-up that has to be covered up and kept out of the public domain. That's what I think, and that's why Rebecca has been given the runaround. I promised to help her as soon as we've sorted things out here.'

'A lot on your plate then.'

'What's new?'

'There's a book in this, isn't there?'

Jack shrugged. 'You know me too well.'

'You better get some sleep.'

'You're right. If I don't, I'll turn into one of those memory trees before my time.' Feeling better Jack stood up, gave the countess a peck on the cheek and went back to his room.

'You're up early,' said Jack, walking over to Rahima sitting in the conservatory overlooking the garden. With the morning sun streaming through the open windows and making the palm fronds glisten, the conservatory was an idyllic place where Jack had done a lot of writing during the summer.

'Come, sit next to me,' said Rahima. 'I had the best night's sleep in months. This is so beautiful here. So peaceful and serene. So *safe*.'

Rahima pointed to an exquisite little mahogany music box on the mantelpiece. 'I believe that's yours,' she said.

'Katerina told you about it?'

'She did. But she didn't tell me the whole story. She said that would be a matter for you. Apparently, it used to belong to my aunt and she left it to you in her will a couple of years ago, I believe. Is that right?'

'That's correct. There's an amazing story attached to this little gem. It's all about a letter, a desperate Tsarina and a long-lost masterpiece created by a musical genius just before he died.'

'How intriguing. Katerina did say you were quite a storyteller,' said Rahima, a glint in her eyes. 'As we are about to visit my aunt's memory trees later today, would this be a good time for you to tell me the story?'

'I suppose it would. But I have to warn you, the story isn't altogether a happy one. There's treachery, betrayal and murder, and a family tragedy so cruel, it's almost impossible to put it into words. History written in blood.'

'My goodness!'

'Do you still want to hear it?'

'Absolutely. And I'll make a deal with you. You tell me the story of the music box, and I tell you what I said to the chief of police and why.'

'You're on!' Jack settled back into his comfortable wicker chair and looked pensively at Rahima. 'I've just finished writing a novella about this,' he began. 'The manuscript is with my editor in New York right now and will be published later this year. In fact, I wrote most of it sitting over there next to the mantelpiece. The music box was my inspiration. It spoke to me ... it was like taking dictation from the past.'

'I can't wait.'

Jack stood up, walked over to the mantelpiece and pointed to the music box. 'I had it restored by a horologist in Paris specialising in antique mechanisms just like this one made by Symphonion Musikwerke in Leipzig, Germany in 1888. It works perfectly now; listen.'

Jack pulled out a small lever on the top of the box to activate the mechanism turning the disc. Moments later, a delightful Russian folk melody drifted across from the mantelpiece, reminding Rahima of her childhood spent with Madame Petrova and her family a long time ago.

'It all began when Madame Petrova died suddenly two years ago. As you know, it turned out that she was my great aunt, a connection that I only discovered by chance because of this,' said Jack. He reached inside his shirt and pulled out the exquisite little Fabergé cross he wore around his neck. 'How this eventuated is just as fascinating as the story of the music box I'm about to tell you.'

During the next hour, Jack told his mother how the chance discovery of a letter hidden a long time ago had set in motion a chain of events that brought to light a masterpiece created by a musical giant, which but for that letter, would have been lost forever. Rahima listened in silence as Jack – a natural storyteller – brought not only the extraordinary chain of events to life, but the incredible cast of characters as well. He did it in a way that transported mother and son into an extraordinary past filled with drama and tragedy so real and moving, that Rahima had tears in her eyes by the time Jack finished.

'These are some of my breadcrumbs of destiny, as I'm fond of calling them,' said Jack, 'which inspire my writing.'

'This is without doubt one of the most amazing stories I've ever heard,' said Rahima quietly. 'Perhaps we could ask Katerina to take us to see those memory trees now? This would be the right time for such an emotional visit, don't you think?'

'It would, I agree. I'll see if I can arrange it,' said Jack and stood up. 'It isn't far.'

63

Madame Petrova's Memory Trees: 26 July

Sitting next to Rahima in the back seat of the vintage Bentley, Countess Kuragin pointed to the massive wrought-iron gates as they approached the exclusive retirement home – a converted chateau popular with well-heeled aristocrats and celebrities. 'We are almost there,' she said. 'This magnificent estate used to belong to a dear friend of my mother's, a duchess. She turned it into a retirement home for artists and friends. That's how Madame Petrova – your aunt – came to live here after she left the stage and retired.'

'What a wonderful idea,' said Rahima, admiring the beautiful avenue of trees leading to the entrance.

'My mother and Madame Petrova had adjacent apartments on the ground floor. They lived here for many years,' continued the countess, 'So did the duchess. Her name was Marguerite.'

'That's where I first met Madame Petrova, as we used to call her, in 2012,' Jack interjected. 'She liked being called Madame Petrova, you see. It reminded her of her days as a celebrated ballerina. She was an extraordinary character, even in her nineties.'

'Please tell me again about those memory trees of hers,' said Rahima, looking dreamily out of the car window.

'When your aunt and my mother were invited by Marguerite to move in here,' began the countess, 'they made a pact. In fact, there were six of them living here at the time. All women; close friends who had known each other during the war.'

'Oh? What kind of pact?' asked Rahima.

'They agreed that whenever one of them passed away, the others would plant an oak tree right here in the grounds in her memory.'

'What a wonderful idea,' said Rahima, clearly moved.

'When Madame Petrova died two years ago, Jack and I planted a tree for her as she had requested, right next to ... I'll show you.'

François, the countess's gardener and sometimes chauffeur, stopped the vintage Bentley in front of the chateau. Jack got out, opened the back door and helped the countess and Rahima out of the car.

'Before we go inside, let's take a little walk to the trees. It isn't far,' said the countess.

Jack linked arms with his mother and together they walked along the crunchy gravel path behind the chateau leading to the little grove of oak trees by a pond full of waterlilies. The countess followed a few steps behind, realising that this was a very personal moment for them all.

'I came here with Madame Petrova almost exactly four years ago,' said Jack. 'It was then that I discovered she was my great aunt and it only happened because of this.' Jack pointed to the little cross hanging around his neck. 'As you know, only two of these were ever made, right here in Paris. They were designed by your grandfather and personally crafted by Alexander Fabergé, the master jeweller. Your grandfather gave one to your mother, and one to Madame Petrova, her sister, as Easter presents in 1930.'

'Yes, I know.'

'When I told Madame Petrova that I was born at the Coberg Mission in Queensland, Australia in 1968, the penny dropped. And the rest, as they say, is history.'

'It would seem so,' said Rahima.

'But this here, right now, is history in the making,' continued Jack. He stopped and pointed to a tree by the pond. 'Do you see that tree over there?' he asked.

'Yes.'

'That's *your* tree, planted by Madame Petrova herself many years after you disappeared in Africa, presumed dead. In fact, she planted it after your mother died. That's your mother's tree right there next to yours. She was known as Sister Elizabeth at the Coberg Mission. She died there just before the mission was closed. I visited her grave. That too was many years ago now.'

Rahima walked slowly over to the two trees, put her arms around the trunk belonging to her mother's tree and stood there, hugging it in silence. Then she let go of the tree, turned around and looked at Jack.

'Come over here, please,' she said. 'I want you to promise me something.'

Jack walked over to Rahima and put an arm around her.

'When my time comes,' whispered Rahima, 'promise me that you will scatter my ashes here in this place, exactly where we stand right now. I couldn't wish for more ... after all, my tree's already here.'

'I promise,' said Jack, his eyes misting over.

'Now, let's go into the chateau and have a look at Madame Petrova's apartment I've heard so much about. I have something to tell *you* ...'

Madame Petrova had been one of the most famous and flamboyantly eccentric residents in the retirement home's colourful history. At the same time, she was also one of its most generous patrons. For years she held court in her apartment, entertaining many visitors, mainly associated with the arts. Because no-one knew what to do with her treasured belongings after her death, management had decided to leave her apartment untouched for the time being. It was therefore just as she had left it, with all her personal effects – including her beloved grand piano with the many photographs – and her eclectic furniture and paintings collection all still in place.

The countess had made arrangements for them to be admitted to the apartment for a visit and had ordered tea and petits fours just as Madame Petrova used to do when entertaining her admirers in her elegant salon. As soon as Jack entered the apartment, he could feel Madame Petrova's presence. It was everywhere. He could see her standing next to the piano, pointing to photographs while talking about life at the Ritz in Paris during the war.

'This is quite eerie,' he said as they sat down in front of the marble fireplace.

'I know what you mean,' said the countess. 'It's as if she were still here.'

'Perhaps in a way she still is,' interjected Rahima, looking remarkably energised and refreshed after that emotional visit to Madame Petrova's memory trees.

She's very resilient, thought Jack, watching his mother. *I suppose she's had to be with all that's happened to her. She's a survivor.*

'As I mentioned before,' began Rahima, sitting back in her chair, 'I've something to tell you.' She waited until the maid serving the tea had left the room, and then continued. 'I don't come without means.' Rahima paused to let this sink in. 'In fact, I come here as a very wealthy woman, albeit a controversial one, for obvious reasons.'

Jack and the countess looked at Rahima, wondering where she was going with this.

'For years I've had my own bank accounts in Switzerland. I used these funds for my charitable work in Colombia,' continued Rahima. 'Apart from supporting the Benedictine mission you already know about, I built hospitals and schools for the poor and set up orphanages throughout the country. This was the arrangement I had with Hernando. I could only go on and stay with him if I was allowed to do this. And, of course, we had a son: Alonso.' Rahima paused, and looked sadly into the distance.

'Hernando understood,' she continued. 'I know what you are thinking, and you are justified in thinking it. Nothing in life is black and white. There are only shades of grey and everything has its price. The source of those funds ...' Rahima shook her head.

'I already spoke to Raul Rodrigo in New York. He has managed my money for years and confirmed that I have access to it in the usual manner. It has nothing to do with the assets of the H Cartel currently under investigation by the Americans. As you know, the CIA is tracing and trying to confiscate Cordoba assets around the world and Rodrigo is "assisting them with their enquiries", as they say. He's being forced to do so would be a better way of putting it,' continued Rahima, steel in her voice. 'The CIA has him in their grip. You don't offend America without consequences.'

Jack was beginning to glimpse a different side to his mother he hadn't seen before. He saw a confident, determined woman familiar with hardship and tragedy, and capable of dealing with both, and with looking after herself.

'Be that as it may, I never *married* Hernando,' continued Rahima. 'I am Natasha Petrova, a French citizen who lived for many years in Colombia under unusual circumstances, and who has now returned home.'

That's a bit of a bombshell, thought Jack, as the implications of what Rahima had just told them began to sink in. 'You obviously have something in mind,' he said quietly.

'I do.' Rahima turned to the countess sitting opposite. 'As my aunt had no children or other relatives we know of, this makes me her next of kin and heir, I suppose.'

'It probably does,' said the countess.

'With that in mind, do you think it would be possible for me to move in here? I've lived in a gated community for most of my life and should therefore fit in well here.'

This was a turn the countess hadn't expected. 'I don't see why not,' she said, nodding her head. 'It's an excellent idea.'

'I would immediately make a substantial donation to this establishment in my aunt's name and memory of, say, a million euros. That should open a few doors of welcome, don't you think?'

'It certainly would. They are always short of funds here. Retired artists bring with them memories, huge egos and exaggerated vestiges of fame, but little money,' added the countess, smiling.

'Good,' said Rahima. 'I can see myself living here. And it's not far from you, Katerina, and you, Jack, but I'll have my independence. And that is of great importance to me because I want to continue my charity work.'

'Oh? In what way?' asked Jack, his curiosity aroused.

'I discussed this with Isis and Agabe in the plane on the way over while you were asleep,' replied Rahima.

Jack looked at his mother, amazed.

'The best way forward would be for me to become involved with Isis's charitable foundation and stay in the background. The fewer people who know I exist, the better. Channelling funds wouldn't be difficult; Isis's lawyers could arrange everything.'

'Sir Charles,' said Jack.

'Yes, she did mention him.'

'The first thing I would like to do in that regard,' continued Rahima, warming to the subject, 'is to do something about the *Caritas*, languishing in Malta. Agabe told me all about the hospital ship and what it could do in the right hands.'

'You have been busy,' interjected Jack, unable to hide his surprise.

'I owe Agabe my life. Without him I wouldn't be here. The little chapel where we took refuge after you rang to warn me about imminent danger, collapsed on top of us. Agabe dragged me out of the rubble and carried me to safety. It was a miracle we made it to the monastery alive. It was mayhem and chaos all around us. The monks looked after me there. Agabe's medical skills were amazing. I think he would make an excellent CEO to run the *Caritas*. What do you think?'

'He would be perfect,' said Jack.

'And this could help him with his asylum application here as well, I imagine.'

'It certainly would,' said the countess. 'This is amazing, Natasha.'

'I'm glad you think so. I haven't come all this way just to whither on the vine, so to speak, and wait for my memory tree,' joked Rahima.

'I can see that,' said Jack, shaking his head.

Rahima reached for her cup and took a sip. 'Before we go, I still have a promise to keep,' she said and put her hand on Jack's arm. 'You told me that wonderful story about that music box in the conservatory this morning.'

'And you promised to tell me what you said to the chief of police,' said Jack. 'I still can't believe he let us go.'

'And you want to know *why*, right?'

'Yes.'

'Like you, I am a strong believer in destiny, Jack.'

'Wait until you meet Tristan,' said Jack, smiling.

'He's right,' said the countess. 'That boy can hear the whisper of angels and glimpse eternity.'

'So can I,' said Rahima, looking serious. 'And what I'm about to tell you is a good example.'

'Are we still talking about the chief of police here?' asked Jack. 'Or ...'

'Yes. When I pulled back Isis's costume covering my face inside the coffin and looked the chief of police – his name is Barrera – in the eye, I told him two things. He knew who I was, which made it easier. Hernando had crossed swords with him before.'

'Easier? In what way?' asked Jack.

'Because my identity gave a certain gravitas to what I had to say. First, I told him to think of the hospitals. My charitable work over the years has become well known throughout Colombia. I have poured millions into projects helping the poor and the desperate. I have many supporters.'

'And the second thing?' asked Jack.

'I told him to remember what happened to Fernando Mancilla.'

'Could you please explain?' asked the countess, looking a little confused.

Jack began to laugh. 'Fernando Mancilla was a high-profile Colombian secret police official. He was shot sixteen times in Medellin in 2002. His assassination was ordered by a drug cartel,' he said.

It was Rahima's turn to look surprised. 'How do you know this?'

'I wrote an article about Mancilla and his feud with the cartel. It was big news at the time.'

'You see, Katerina? *Destiny* ...' said Rahima.

'Are you seriously suggesting that reminding the chief of police of the hospitals you built for the poor, and the brutal assassination of a colleague, persuaded him to let you go?' said the countess.

'Yes. You have to understand the Colombian mentality here,' replied Rahima. 'You have to understand the level of fear and violence in that country. The poverty, the desperation, the culture of corruption, the superstition. By reminding him of the hospitals, I reminded him that I really care for the Colombian people, and have done a lot for the country.'

'And Mancilla?' said Jack.

'By reminding him of the assassination, I sent him a clear message of what could happen if he didn't let me go.'

'Incredible!' said Jack. 'And what's even more incredible is it *worked*!'

'A bit of luck may have played a part as well,' conceded Rahima. 'Can you imagine what would have happened had he arrested us? Isis, the megastar thrown in jail? He would have started a war he couldn't win and he knew it. I simply gave him a way out and at the same time, a way to save face – and his skin.' Rahima shrugged. 'It was all about the power of fear and self-preservation. Hernando was a master when it came to such things. I saw him use such tactics countless times.' Rahima waved dismissively. 'But enough of this for now. We have more pleasant things to talk about, haven't we?'

'We do,' said the countess. 'I have something that definitely belongs to you, Natasha. Something very precious your aunt gave me just before she died. Even Jack doesn't know about this. I've been waiting for the right moment …'

'Intriguing,' said Jack. 'What is it?'

'I've never worn it before, but I decided to put it on today because I thought the visit to Madame Petrova's memory trees would be the right occasion to hand it over.'

With that, the countess unbuttoned the collar of her blouse to reveal a slender gold chain. Rahima and Jack leant forward in anticipation.

'Good heavens!' exclaimed Rahima as the countess exposed the little jewel-encrusted gold cross she wore around her neck. Realising the significance of the moment, Jack instinctively reached for his and held it tight.

'I was only the temporary custodian of this little treasure,' said the countess. She unfastened the chain and handed the cross to Rahima. 'Had your aunt known you were still alive, she would have given it to you instead of me, for sure.'

Jack stood up and walked over to his mother. 'May I?'

Rahima nodded, tears in her eyes, and handed the little cross to Jack.

'Definitely Fabergé, I'd say circa 1930. Beautiful workmanship. Quite unique,' said Jack, introducing a little humour into the emotional moment. Rahima looked at him gratefully as he fastened the gold chain around her neck.

Destiny, thought Rahima and stood up. She walked over to the mirror hanging above the fireplace and stood there for a moment, admiring the little cross around her neck. Then she turned around, walked over to the countess and embraced her. 'I will never forget this, Katerina,' she whispered and kissed the countess on both cheeks.

'I also have something,' said Jack, realising the right moment had arrived. He reached into his coat pocket, pulled out a small parcel wrapped in plain brown paper and put it on the coffee table. 'This is for you.'

'For me? This is definitely my day of surprises.' Rahima sat down again and looked at the parcel.

'Open it.' said Jack.

'What is it? Any clues?'

'Something that once belonged to you and you left behind a long time ago,' said Jack with a lump in his throat.

Rahima reached for the parcel and began to open it. Moments later, her eyes widened in disbelief and surprise. 'Oh no! It can't be,' she stammered, tears welling as soon as she realised what it was.

'What is it?' asked the countess, leaning forward.

'Something precious from a different, distant life.' Rahima peeled back the rest of the paper and put a battered camera on the table in front of her. Its lens was broken and the case was badly scratched, but the name – Leica – was still visible.

'Where did you get this, Jack?' whispered Rahima.

'In a remote village called Fungor in the Nuba Mountains in Sudan. An old man who remembered you well gave it to me.'

'When was that?'

'About a month ago.'

'What were you doing there?'

'Looking for you. Little did I know then, that a few weeks later ...'

'Destiny?'

'What else?'

'This definitely calls for a toast,' said the countess, trying to ease the tense, emotional moment.

'Great idea,' said Jack. 'But this is a retirement home. I doubt—'

'Oh, we can easily remedy that,' interrupted the countess. 'I have a whole cellar full of the stuff back at the chateau.'

'Then what are we waiting for?' said Jack, smiling. He stood up, walked to the door and opened it. 'After you, ladies ...'

64

Greenberg Private Clinic, Boston, Massachusetts: 30 July

Jack got out of the taxi, took a deep breath and looked around. Feeling tired after his long flight – he had been travelling for more than sixteen hours since leaving Paris – Jack was preparing himself for the critical meeting he knew would have far-reaching consequences.

Set in serene, manicured grounds in a peaceful, leafy Boston suburb, the exclusive Greenberg Private Clinic was the famous treatment centre of Professor David Greenberg, one of the most gifted and sought-after brain surgeons in the United States, if not the world. Jack had received a phone call from Rebecca the day before advising him that she had finally been contacted by the CIA about Stolzfus.

Apparently, Stolzfus had been under the care of Professor Greenberg at his clinic in Boston for the past week and was about to be discharged. Dr Hubert of the CIA had suggested that Rebecca come to the clinic and meet with Professor Greenberg before Stolzfus was released, to learn firsthand what the professor had to say about the current state of her brother's health, the prognosis for his future, and how that should be handled.

When Rebecca spoke to Jack she sounded most concerned, and once again asked for his help because she remembered that Jack knew Professor Greenberg personally through Isis. She pleaded with Jack to attend the meeting with her, as so much appeared to be riding on it. Jack, who was still at the Kuragin chateau at the time, agreed at once and made travel arrangements.

Jack smiled as he remembered his first meeting with Professor Greenberg seven years earlier. Isis had been diagnosed with an inoperable brain tumour after collapsing on stage, and was given only months to live. Sir Humphrey – Isis's personal physician – had turned to Professor Greenberg for help in a desperate attempt to save his patient. Professor Greenberg had travelled all the way to Mexico to examine Isis, and it was that particular meeting Jack remembered as he walked up the tree-lined driveway leading to the entrance of the stately nineteenth-century mansion. Cleverly transformed into a state-of-the-art clinic equipped with the latest medical facilities, including a sophisticated operating theatre that Isis had donated, the impressive building radiated confidence and class.

Jack remembered the professor as a diminutive, shortish man wearing Harry Potter-shaped tortoiseshell glasses that accentuated his prominent, slightly hooked nose, which dominated his youthful, almost boyish face. *Looks can certainly be deceptive,* thought Jack. Professor Greenberg had operated on Isis, removed the tumour, which no-one had thought possible, and saved her life. As he opened the door and walked into the foyer, Jack was wondering if the professor could perhaps do the same for Stolzfus.

Rebecca had arrived earlier from New York and was waiting for Jack in the spacious reception on the ground floor. 'I can't tell you what this means to me,' she said and gave Jack a hug. 'Thank you so much for coming. I'm very nervous about this.'

'I can imagine. Have you met Greenberg?'

'Not yet. I was waiting for you …'

'How's my little mate?'

'*What?* Oh; Gizmo?'

'Yes.' This was a typical Jack Rogan question, intended to put Rebecca at ease. 'Two walks a day, I hope?'

'Is that all you can think of?' asked Rebecca, laughing and suddenly feeling more relaxed. Jack had that effect on people.

Professor Greenberg came through the revolving doors and walked up to the receptionist, who pointed to Jack and Rebecca sitting on a lounge facing a large window overlooking the gardens.

'Ah, the intrepid Mr Rogan,' said Greenberg, walking over to them. 'The last time we met was in Mexico City during Isis's "Thank You" concert six years ago, I believe.'

'That's right,' said Jack and stood up. 'It was the beginning of Isis's Crystal Skull Tour, which would never have happened without you.'

The professor waved dismissively. 'My two daughters were hoarse for days. They screamed so much during the concert they could hardly speak afterwards. It was an amazing event.'

Rebecca looked at the fascinating little man in front of her as Jack introduced Greenberg. Dressed in a pair of faded jeans, black sneakers and a tee-shirt with Bob Dylan playing a mouth harmonica printed on the front, he looked more like a middle-aged student who had never left campus than the eminent surgeon he was.

'Thank you both for coming,' said the professor, turning serious. 'The matter I would like to discuss with you is best addressed face to face. That's why I suggested you come here if possible so that you can see for yourself … I believe it's the only way I can explain what I have in mind and what's at stake here. But first, let's go and meet the patient.'

Feeling suddenly ill, Rebecca turned to Jack as they followed Greenberg up the stairs. 'I don't like this,' she whispered, sounding apprehensive.

'Don't worry. He's the best, but remember what I told you. Zac will look very different.' Aware that Rebecca hadn't seen Stolzfus after his operation, Jack had done his best to prepare her for what to expect by trying to describe the likely state he would be in.

Greenberg walked to the end of the brightly lit corridor on the first floor and opened a door. 'After you,' he said and stepped back.

Jack reached for Rebecca's hand and held it tight as they walked into the room. To his surprise, he too felt suddenly uneasy as he remembered the last time he had seen Stolzfus. On that occasion, Stolzfus had just been lifted into a helicopter after suffering a fit on a deserted beach in Colombia, and was drowning in his own blood.

Rebecca walked into the room and gasped as she looked at the strange, motionless figure sitting strapped into a wheelchair by the window. At first, she refused to believe she was looking at her brother. The shaved head held up by a metal neck brace, the pale, emaciated-looking face and open mouth and various tubes connecting him to a machine next to the wheelchair, in no way resembled the brilliant, vibrant man she had seen only a few weeks before.

'Good God,' whispered Rebecca, unable to hold back the tears. '*That's him*?'

Jack squeezed her hand in silent reply.

'He can hear you and he can see you,' said Greenberg cheerfully. 'Go and talk to him.'

Jack let go of Rebecca's hand and they walked over to Stolzfus. 'Not quite ready for that chess game you owe me, are you, mate?' said Jack. 'Don't tell me I've come all this way for nothing. We better ask the professor here to do something about that; what do you reckon?'

Greenberg began to laugh. Jack's humour was infectious and precisely what was needed to defuse the awkward moment. 'That's exactly what I want to talk to you about,' he said, noticing Rebecca's distress. 'Let's go to my office and have a chat and you can come back later for another visit. Professor Stolzfus isn't going anywhere just yet.'

'Before we do that,' interjected Jack, 'Zac will be pleased to hear that I delivered his calculations about the theory of everything to the Genius Club, as promised. However, I think they had problems interpreting what he was getting at. The blackboard was full of fancy equations when I left them to it,' Jack prattled on. 'Lots of head scratching. The guys definitely need help, because even Gizmo – who was with me at the time – couldn't come to the rescue.'

Having composed herself, Rebecca stepped forward. 'We'll get through this, Zac, I promise!' she said, a lump in her throat.

'And in case you're wondering,' continued Jack, 'Gizmo is with Rebecca, living in her apartment in New York. Two walks a day in Central Park with all the posh pooches. Lucky little bugger! We'll come back later.'

'Who is Gizmo?' asked Greenberg on their way out.

'Stolzfus's little dog who attends all of the professor's lectures and knows more about astrophysics than most of his colleagues.'

'Ah!'

Back in his office, Jack and Rebecca sat down and Greenberg handed Rebecca a glass of water. 'I knew this would be confronting,' he said. 'But this was quite intentional. I wanted to shock you.'

'In what way?' asked Jack as he looked around Greenberg's surgery. It reminded him of a similar meeting not long ago in Malta, where Fabry had tried to impress Isis by singing the praises of the *Caritas*.

'I wanted you both to see what life would be like for Professor Stolzfus if we don't do something about it,' said the professor, sitting at his desk.

'*Do something about it?* What do you mean?' asked Rebecca.

'Before I answer that, let me give you an assessment of your brother's current situation. To begin with, Professor Fabry and his team have done an extraordinary job. I would call it medical history. To my knowledge, no-one has successfully performed a head transplant on a live human patient before. Until now. Unfortunately, being the guinea pig often comes at a price; a big one.' Greenberg paused, took off his glasses and began to polish them with his handkerchief. It was a habit Jack remembered from their last meeting. By taking off his glasses and intentionally blurring his vision, Greenberg focused on something important within.

'As you have just observed, the side effects can be severe,' he continued. 'In my view, having a successful, groundbreaking operation like this is pointless if the quality of life of the patient isn't improved at the same time. Technical brilliance alone cannot justify such a radical step. In short, to prolong life without quality may celebrate the technical skills and brilliance of the surgeon, but at the expense of the patient. To be truly successful, such an operation must do both: prolong life, and at the same time provide a certain modicum of quality to make it meaningful and bearable. Unless that can be achieved, there is – in my view – no point to all this.' Greenberg put on his glasses again and looked at Rebecca. 'It's a moral tightrope. I hope this makes sense,' he said quietly.

'It sure does,' said Rebecca, feeling relieved. Greenberg had just articulated what she had felt a moment ago.

'I have been asked by the Department of State to examine Professor Stolzfus and submit a report,' continued Greenberg. 'I have done that. Your brother is in remarkably good health considering what has happened to him. All his new organs are working well and, as you have just seen, they are keeping him alive. The main problem we have is that he has no motor functions. He is completely paralysed and cannot move anything. On top of that he has lost his speech, which I don't believe can be restored. In short, he is alive, but trapped in his new body without being able to communicate in any way. Not even by moving a muscle.'

'But that's dreadful,' said Jack. 'For a man like Stolzfus, that's worse than death.'

'My point exactly. And this is especially tragic because I believe his extraordinary brain is completely intact and functioning perfectly. I have performed tests that show this. In a way, his situation is not dissimilar to that of Steven Hawking during his latter years after he lost his speech. As you know, his disability was caused by motor neurone disease, but with one major difference. He was not as disabled as Stolzfus is, and he could communicate. He did that by activating a small sensor with a muscle in his cheek. The sensor communicated with his computer, allowing Hawking to type characters and numbers on his keyboard, one at a time. Very slow and laborious, but it worked.

'When the Department of State saw my report, they lost interest. Professor Stolzfus is no longer of value to NASA and the sensitive defence programs he had been working on. In fact, I got the impression he has become an embarrassment and a liability that has to be put to bed, quickly and permanently. Asking you to come here so that I could explain Stolzfus's hopeless situation to you was obviously part of this plan.'

'But that's not how you work, is it?' said Jack.

'No it isn't. When I agreed to examine Stolzfus, he became my patient, as indeed he is right now. He is in my care and is therefore entitled to the best I can offer him.'

'And is there something you can offer him?' asked Rebecca quietly. 'In addition to the technical brilliance that is keeping him alive?'

Greenberg smiled at Rebecca. 'I believe I can. I also believe that providence has brought your brother here and placed him into my care.'

'Can you please explain what you mean?' prompted Jack.

'A few months before Stephen Hawking died, I began to work on something I believed could help him. Something revolutionary and groundbreaking, combining the latest technology – including artificial intelligence and surgery – that could transform how we deal with severely incapacitated patients like Hawking was at the time. I had been a great admirer of Hawking for years, and had followed his extraordinary ideas and theories about the origins of the universe since I was a student. When he lost his speech I began to think, what if we could do something about this? That was the trigger …'

'A trigger for what?' said Jack, sensing the growing excitement in Greenberg.

'This. Let me show you.' Greenberg stood up, walked over to a glass screen next to his desk used for examining X-rays and turned it on. A large X-ray of a human head came into view. 'This is what the brain of a genius looks like,' said Greenberg and pointed to the X-ray. 'This one belongs to Professor Stolzfus. At the moment, this extraordinary brain cannot communicate with us because of the reasons I pointed out earlier. That is not only tragic, but an enormous loss to us all. So, is there something we can do about this? I believe there is, and it's this.' Greenberg stepped forward, picked up a small piece of wire the size of a paper clip from his desk and held it up.

'What's that?' asked Jack.

'This is a device that can be surgically implanted into a blood vessel in the brain.' Greenberg turned around and pointed to the X-ray. 'Right here in this area known as the motor cortex, which controls movement. What this small device can do is pick up signals from the brain and transmit them, say, via bluetooth to artificial intelligence software. This could help an incapacitated patient like Professor Stolzfus communicate with a computer and control it – like you and I do with a mouse.'

'Is that really possible?' asked Jack, looking incredulous.

'Absolutely. A lot more work needs to be done,' conceded Greenberg, 'but I firmly believe it's possible. And an intelligent patient like Professor Stolzfus with his extensive knowledge of computers and how they work, and a passion for artificial intelligence, is the perfect candidate for a prototype.'

'Amazing,' said Rebecca. 'So, where does this leave us now?'

'When I put this to the Department of State, they were not interested. Too risky, they said, and too costly. The patient could die and that would be a disaster after all that had happened to him. I did explain that to implant the device would be quite easy. It could be done by way of simple day surgery. It would not require complex and risky open brain surgery, which Professor Stolzfus in his condition would most likely not survive. They were still not interested.'

Greenberg turned towards Rebecca and looked at her. 'That's where you come in. I believe you hold a power of attorney for Professor Stolzfus and are officially listed as his guardian at the moment. Is that right?'

'It is.'

'You could therefore give consent for such an operation should I be able to convince you of its enormous potential and likely benefits.'

'I suppose I could.'

'How would it work? Could you explain this again? asked Jack.

'In essence, the brain signals transmitted by this device would allow the patient to communicate with a computer and control it.'

'How?'

'By simply thinking about it.'

'Are you serious?'

'Absolutely!'

'Unbelievable! I think Rebecca and I need a few minutes to digest this and have a chat,' said Jack.

'By all means. Take as long as you need. You can stay in here; I will be next door. If you have any questions, just call me.' Greenberg walked to the door, stopped and turned around. 'And one more thing,' he said quietly. 'I don't want to put more pressure on you, but you have to know this if you want to be fully informed.'

'Oh?' said Jack.

'That disturbing episode you witnessed on the beach in Colombia was brought on by stress. That is also the reason I believe Professor Stolzfus has lost his speech. Stress can be a killer, especially in a patient like this. Can you imagine a more stressful situation for a man like him than what he's going through right now? Being trapped in a body that isn't even his own, totally isolated from the world?' Greenberg shook his head. 'Unless we do something about that soon, I firmly believe he will not last long. He will have another fit and die. What we need to do is give him *hope*. Hope is the strongest drug we have. I have seen it do remarkable things, many times. If you decide to go ahead and give your permission, we could tell Professor Stolzfus about this straight away and give him that hope right now. It's up to you,' added Greenberg and left the room.

Half an hour later, Jack called Greenberg into the room. 'Rebecca has made a decision,' said Jack.

'And?' asked Greenberg, his eyes bright with anticipation.

'It was a no-brainer really,' said Jack, smiling affably. 'The answer is a resounding yes!'

'I was hoping you would say that,' replied Greenberg, looking relieved. 'Let's go and tell Professor Stolzfus all about it, shall we? He should really hear this from you.'

'By all means,' said Rebecca. She walked over to Greenberg and held out her hand. 'Thank you, Professor,' she said, with tears in her eyes. 'When will you be able to start?'

'I already have. Come, let's tell the patient.'

65

Stolzfus family farm, Ephrata, Pennsylvania: three months later

Jack hired a car at Philadelphia International Airport and drove straight to Ephrata – a borough in Lancaster County – deep in Amish territory. A very excited Rebecca had rung him a week earlier telling him that Stolzfus was about to be released from the Greenberg Private Clinic.

Professor Greenberg had made history with his revolutionary device that allowed his famous patient to communicate by thought with his computer. The life-changing operation to insert the small device into his brain had been a huge success, but getting used to the brain function had been rather slow and laborious even for a man with Stolzfus's exceptional intellect.

Special computer software programs had to be developed and a custom-made computer designed and built specially for him. This took time but while progress was slow, the results were spectacular. With each day, Stolzfus's window to the world opened a little more, allowing him to step out of his intellectual prison and enter the world around him.

Each morning since the operation, Greenberg had begun his day with a visit to Stolzfus to monitor his progress and introduce him slowly to his new reality. He even managed to persuade a leading wheelchair manufacturer to develop a new, custom-made motorised wheelchair that could be controlled through Stolzfus's computer, which not only gave him mobility, but a certain amount of independence as well, because he could operate the wheelchair by giving commands just through thought alone.

Stolzfus, a quick learner, had easily mastered the many new tasks and challenges involved in operating his new digital world made possible by artificial intelligence, and had embraced it with enthusiasm and humour. While his body remained completely paralysed, his brain flourished and his new electronic tools and gadgets allowed him to express himself with a speed and clarity not experienced before.

Eager to get back to work as soon as possible, Stolzfus was constantly asking about the Genius Club and when he would be able to meet with his students to carry on his work on the theory of everything, which seemed to be consuming his mind. At the same time, Greenberg was desperately trying to shield his patient from stress, which could easily be triggered by disappointment or shock. Somehow, stress was the big danger. It was the big unknown that could quickly intrude, destroy all the hard work and reverse progress in an instant. It was the human, emotional part of the revolutionary project that was unpredictable and wasn't governed by logic, cutting-edge technology, or the complex logarithms that had made this astounding breakthrough possible.

Greenberg knew everything had its price and vulnerability, and stress was Stolzfus's weak point. He therefore didn't tell his patient that he no longer had a job, or that his former home at the Marshall Space Flight Center was no longer available and waiting for him. In fact, Stolzfus had been discarded by his former employer and was seen as an embarrassing liability, and therefore no longer of use or interest to his country. What Stolzfus didn't know either was that only a modest pension had been provided for him with an allowance for a full-time carer to look after his needs.

The astronomical cost of his rehabilitation had been financed and made possible in a completely different way. Rahima had set up her own charitable foundation and made Jack the trustee. Joining forces with Isis and her extensive charitable network, Jack had made Stolzfus's rehabilitation and 'Operation Caritas' a priority, and the first two major projects of the foundation.

The big problem Greenberg had faced was what to do with Stolzfus once the time came for him to leave the clinic. Then unexpectedly, Rebecca, who visited her brother regularly, came up with a unique solution that ticked all the boxes. Jack had been invited to come to Pennsylvania to see for himself what that solution was and how it worked. Rebecca had given him a specific date and hinted that there would be some kind of Amish celebration with a few surprises ...

Jack knew he was getting close when he began to overtake the iconic black horse-drawn, closed-top buggies just outside Ephrata. It was the first indication that he had entered the Amish heartland with its beautiful rural landscape and picture-postcard farms. Another was the fact that there were dozens of pedestrians walking along the busy road, many of them women dressed in traditional attire on their way to market.

As Rebecca had given him only vague directions to the Stolzfus family farm just outside Ephrata, Jack could no longer rely on satellite navigation and pulled over to ask for directions. A young, fresh-faced woman wearing a plain dress, grey apron, a cape fastened with straight pins at the waist and a black prayer cap bonnet on her head, put down her basket full of eggs and pointed to a group of buildings in the distance. She told Jack how to get there and wished him a good day.

Rebecca had told Jack a little about the Amish way of life. As some of the best farmers in the world, their lives revolved around agriculture and religion. Toiling in the fields, raising livestock and growing their own food was seen not only as communing with nature, but doing God's will. Their lives were governed by strict rules that hadn't changed much since they were forced to flee from their Swiss homeland in the seventeenth century, to avoid brutal persecution by the Roman Catholic Church and Protestant Reformers.

As Jack drove through the farm gate and up a long driveway to a cluster of traditional pole buildings, he couldn't help but wonder how a man like Stolzfus, who had left the strict confines of Amish life as a young man and turned his back on religion, could return to his roots as a severely disabled invalid being kept alive by the latest technology; something that was shunned by the Amish.

Rebecca saw Jack pull up and rushed outside to greet him. 'I'm so glad you could make it,' she said, giving him a big hug. 'And just in time. Zac hasn't stopped talking about you.'

'*Talking?* What do you mean?' asked Jack, frowning.

'Wait and see. You are in for a big surprise, and you won't believe who's here as well. Apart from my brothers and their families,' added Rebecca excitedly. 'This is a big day for us all, but first let me take you to Zac; come!'

Rebecca guided Jack to a large barn set a little apart from the other buildings. 'My brothers fitted out this barn specially for Zac,' she said. 'They are carpenters and they even connected electricity. The town is quite close.'

'I thought that was strictly forbidden?' said Jack.

'The elders made an exception.'

As they approached the barn, Jack could hear voices. One in particular sounded strange and reminded him of the quirky voice of C-3PO, the golden droid in *Star Wars*. Rebecca stopped in front of the tall door and looked at Jack. 'This would not have been possible without you,' she said, tears in her eyes. 'Thanks for everything, Jack. You are in for a big surprise; ready?'

'Ready,' said Jack and helped Rebecca open the heavy wooden door.

Inside, the barn consisted of a single large room with massive posts holding up a timber-frame roof. It reminded Jack of a classroom in the country. As soon as he entered, Gizmo let out a little yelp and came running towards him, panting enthusiastically, to greet him. A group of people sitting in a semicircle facing a dais at the far end of room, turned around and looked at Jack. Jack recognised several familiar faces.

The Genius Club; *they are all here*! he thought. Then his eyes went to the strange-looking wheelchair on the dais. With its large, illuminated monitor, two antennas and other gadgets mounted on its arms and back, it looked more like moon-landing gear than a wheelchair.

'Stay where you are!' commanded the strange voice he had heard earlier. 'I am coming to you.' With that, the wheelchair turned to the left, moved slowly down a ramp and came towards Jack standing at the door. 'Good to see you could make it.'

Speechless, Jack stared at the wheelchair in front of him. Stolzfus sat strapped into the chair with his head held up by a complicated, padded brace just as before. His hair had grown back, making his head look less severe and confronting. His face had filled out a little and a thin beard softened his features. The only thing that hadn't changed were his eyes, radiating excitement and intelligence. 'I can't shake your hand,' continued the voice. 'But we are working on it. Welcome to my new world, Jack.'

Feeling emotional, Jack turned once again to humour to overcome his shock. 'Not bad,' he said, recovering quickly. 'Giving a lecture already. Looks promising. I thought I better turn up and see how that theory of yours is coming along, mate,' said Jack, stroking Gizmo's head. 'I spent hours writing this stuff down, remember? And then I handed it to these guys here to see what it all meant. I hope they could make some sense of it.'

Subdued laughter in the room eased the tension.

'You won't be disappointed,' continued the voice. 'We have quite an announcement to make. We were just waiting for you.'

'Before we do that, allow me to explain what made it all possible,' said someone in the back.

Jack turned around and smiled. 'You've been roped into this too, I see,' he said and walked up to Greenberg to shake his hand.

'Just like me,' said Celia Crawford, who came over and stood next to Greenberg.

'You too?' said Jack and kissed Celia on the cheek. 'This looks more and more like a press conference than the country picnic I was promised.'

'Surprised?' asked Greenberg.

'You bet. Your patient can talk. *Amazing!*'

'He can do more than that. Here, let me show you.' Greenberg stepped out of the shadows and walked over to Stolzfus. 'The device I showed you last time we met at the clinic was implanted into Professor Stolzfus's brain, right here.' Greenberg pointed to the top of Stolzfus's head. 'A simple procedure that allowed him to begin communicating with his computer. We had one specially designed for him. This is it right here. An amazing piece of electronic engineering; revolutionary stuff. In essence, the software that was written for this can cope with complex mathematical information that can be displayed on the monitor here, and via bluetooth on the large screen over there.' Greenberg pointed to a TV screen behind the dais.

'How?' asked Jack.

Greenberg smiled. 'By merely *thinking* about it. It took a little while for our patient to master this, but as expected he was an excellent pupil. The results were quite spectacular and surpassed expectations.'

As he shook his head, Jack noticed that Celia was furiously taking notes. 'I'm gobsmacked,' he said. 'How does it work?'

'Let me explain,' said Greenberg. 'It all began with Steven Hawking. When he lost his voice in 1986 – he was forty-four at the time – many technologies combined to develop a system that allowed him to communicate. At first there was a computer program called Equalizer, linked to a speech synthesiser made by Speech Plus. The synthesiser was mounted on the arm of his wheelchair, just like this one here.' Greenberg pointed to Stolzfus's wheelchair. 'Only this one is much more powerful and can do much more. This early system allowed Hawking to communicate at a rate of fifteen words a minute. Professor Stolzfus can do fifty, and the number is growing. But the real breakthrough is the device implanted in his brain. At first, Hawking communicated with the computer by operating a mouse with his thumb. When the nerve deteriorated, making this impossible, a new way was found: a "cheek switch", which was attached to his glasses. This ingenious device used a low-infrared beam to detect when Hawking tensed a cheek muscle and used this as a signal to operate the computer. Hawking became very adept at this and mastered this extraordinary procedure to such an extent, it allowed him not only to speak, but to send emails, surf the Net and write books!'

Greenberg paused to let all this sink in. 'And he did all this by merely tensing a cheek muscle,' he continued. 'But unfortunately,

Professor Stolzfus here cannot even do that. He is totally paralysed and couldn't possibly operate the Hawking system. So, we had to come up with something different. We did, and it is infinitely better. Why? Because it operates through *thought* and therefore does away with the need for any bodily motor function altogether.'

Spontaneous applause rippled through the room. Smiling, Greenberg held up his hand. 'The best way to show you all what this really means, is to invite Professor Stolzfus to make the announcement he's been dying to make since we arrived here today.'

'Thank you, Professor Greenberg,' said Stolzfus formally and manoeuvred his wheelchair back onto the dais, his computer 'voice' sounding distant and strange, making the whole scene appear like something out of a science-fiction movie. Stolzfus positioned his wheelchair so that he could see everyone in the room in front of him. Gizmo jumped up onto the dais and settled down next to him, just as he used to do during lectures.

'For me, to not only see so many people who are close and dear to me all gathered in one room, but being able to actually *communicate* with them, is more than a dream come true. It is a miracle that only a few short weeks ago seemed impossible.' Stolzfus paused and looked at the people gathered before him.

'On my left,' he continued, are my three brothers and their wives, whom I haven't seen for years. Standing behind them is my dear father and my sister, Rebecca. Without her dogged determination and unwavering support, I wouldn't be here. Sadly, my dear mother passed away a few years ago; may she rest in peace.

'Sitting right here in front of me is a group of very special people. Gizmo knows them well. They are without doubt some of the most gifted scientists in the world today and I feel privileged to have been allowed to collaborate with them on something extraordinary that will change the way we look at our universe, our past and our destiny forever.

'You have just heard what Professor Greenberg had to say. It all speaks for itself. Without his genius, none of this would have been possible. Thank you, Professor, you are an extraordinary human being.'

There was another ripple of applause.

'When Rebecca heard that I had collapsed in Westminster Abbey on June fifteen, after being poisoned,' continued Stolzfus, 'and she was given the runaround by the authorities, she turned to Jack Rogan for help. As the true friend he is, Jack dropped everything and answered the call. What he went through to find out what had happened to me is difficult to put into words right now, but you would have read some of it in Celia Crawford's articles, which in no small way were instrumental in facilitating my rescue.'

Stolzfus turned his wheelchair slightly to the right. 'Thank you, Celia, for putting my story out there and bringing it to the public's attention.' Stolzfus paused and took a deep breath. It was strange to hear him speak without opening his mouth, or moving his lips. 'And Celia will do it again, I'm sure,' continued Stolzfus, who hadn't lost his touch for the theatrical. 'She will tell the world about what is taking place here today. And I promise you, my friends, it will change the world forever.'

More applause came.

'But back to Jack for a moment. In hindsight, perhaps the greatest and most far-reaching contribution he has made to what I'm about to announce, was to listen patiently to my often-incoherent ramblings from my imagination while I was incapacitated, about travelling through time and space. This allowed me to look at problems that previously seemed insurmountable, in different ways. And it provided that crucial missing link that eluded Hawking. Jack faithfully wrote down my calculations and complex equations without complaint, and did so for several days while we were prisoners on a ship heading to South America.

'As it turned out, those very calculations and insights formed the basis of what was to come. Without them, I doubt the extraordinary breakthrough I'm about to announce would have been possible. And that's not all. Jack delivered those calculations to my colleagues at the

Goddard Space Flight Center – they are all right here in front of me – who immediately went to work and developed those ideas further and provided the framework for what I'm about to reveal. Thank you, Jack. You are what true friendship is all about.'

More applause reverberated around the barn, becoming ever more enthusiastic.

'But enough of that for now. It's time for me to tell you why I have invited you all to come here today. I firmly believe that we are about to witness history and I wanted to share that moment with you. I assure you, I don't say that lightly and it all began six months ago with a challenge. My young colleagues here and I called it the Hawking Challenge. It was the beginning of a search for that elusive theory of everything that had evaded Professor Hawking. We believe he was actually getting very close just before he died, but sadly he ran out of time. We decided that we would try to complete what he began and finally solve what science has been searching for ever since man first looked up at the stars and wondered how it all worked.'

Stolzfus paused to let the suspense grow. 'And we've actually done just that,' he continued. 'Here, let me show you.'

All eyes were on Stolzfus as he turned his wheelchair towards the large TV screen behind him. Suddenly, strange symbols surrounded by lots of numbers began to appear on the screen like ghostly writing on an electronic wall. They were all part of a set of complex equations placed there by thought alone, flowing from the brain of an incapacitated genius directly onto the screen for all to see.

'This, my friends,' continued Stolzfus, 'is the theory of everything that I firmly believe ties together the eternal laws of nature and explains how the universe works, how it began and where it is heading ...'

After a few moments as the audience took it all in, rapturous applause erupted, even drowning out Gizmo, who was enthusiastically barking along with it.

After Stolzfus's presentation, Amish hospitality went to work. The women had been up since daybreak preparing a feast. The Amish might be known as the plain people, but there was nothing plain about the food being served that day. Large trestle tables were groaning under the volume of delicious food being served in another barn next to the large farmhouse kitchen.

'This reminds me of barn-raising parties when I was growing up here,' said Rebecca, filling up Jack's plate with scrapple. 'My goodness, I haven't eaten this in years.'

'What is it?' asked Jack, looking a little alarmed.

'A traditional delicacy. Its Pennsylvania Dutch name is *Pannhaas.* A mush of pork scraps combined with buckwheat flour and spices. Delicious! You'll love it.'

'Can't wait.' To his surprise, the scrapple was delicious and Jack even went back for seconds. But that was just the beginning. Scrapple was followed by *gritzwurst* – a pork and oatmeal sausage – cabbage rolls and other homemade specialities. Then came the sweets. Shoofly pie topped with whipped cream was Jack's favourite.

The party lasted well into the night. Neighbours arrived during the afternoon bringing more food, and extra tables were set to accommodate the visitors.

After dark, families began to leave and a convoy of black buggies travelled down the driveway. Jack stepped outside to watch the procession.

'I thought I would find you here,' said Rebecca, walking up to Jack who was sitting on a fence post in the dark. 'What an amazing day.'

'Sure was, in more ways than one,' said Jack.

'What do you mean?'

'You realise of course that Zac's life has just changed forever. As soon as news of this gets out, he will become an overnight celebrity. I can tell you, this place will be teeming with news crews by tomorrow, hoping to get a glimpse or an interview with the man who has just joined the ranks of Galileo, Newton and Kepler.'

'You think so?'

'No doubt about it. Celia has already gone back to New York to start the ball rolling. Once again, the *New York Times* will break the story. And what a story it is! How do you think this will affect your family?'

'Don't know,' said Rebecca, frowning. 'But what I do know is, they will protect Zac and his privacy.'

'Good, because he will need protecting, that's for sure.' Jack paused and looked up at the stars blazing in the clear sky above. 'Isn't it amazing that the scientist who appears to have solved the mysteries of the universe should come from such a devout and God-fearing family whose traditions and beliefs haven't changed in centuries? How do you think the Amish community will react to this when they find out that Zachariah Stolzfus, one of their own, has found a way to know the mind of God?'

'Not sure, but I hope they will be proud, just as I am,' said Rebecca.

'It's been an amazing journey,' said Jack.

'Any regrets?'

'*Regrets?* Are you kidding? I wouldn't have missed it for the world!'

Rebecca shook her head. 'Do you know what your friends call you behind your back?'

'Tell me.'

'An adventure junkie and a story magnet.'

'Not an incorrigible rascal?'

'Don't worry, they call you that too!'

ONE YEAR LATER

Queens' College, Cambridge University

Cambridge University, 'the holy city of mathematics', was blessed with a welcoming, sunny autumn afternoon to celebrate another historic milestone: the appointment of the university's next Lucasian Professor of Mathematics. Founded in 1663, this famous chair had been held by some of the greatest minds of their time, including Isaac Newton, Charles Babbage, Paul Dirac and, of course, Steven Hawking, to mention but a few.

Stolzfus's nomination had come as no surprise. However, what did surprise many – especially in science circles – was the fact that he accepted the appointment despite his considerable disability, which required around-the-clock care. Apart from that, prestigious institutions had reached out, offering Stolzfus appointments with eye-watering remuneration in the hope of keeping him in the United States.

An outspoken and disappointed, but not bitter, Stolzfus had told Celia Crawford in an exclusive interview about the shameful treatment he had received from his former employer when it seemed unlikely that he would ever be able to speak or communicate again. And that had come on top of the security services fiasco that had failed so miserably to protect him.

He also spoke of the generosity and support of Isis and her famous foundation that had made his extraordinary recovery possible, and had given him a 'voice' that allowed him to share his groundbreaking theory with the world. Apart from all that, he conceded that becoming Cambridge University's next Lucasian Professor of Mathematics and Hawking's successor was irresistible, as it would open up further opportunities for significant contributions to science.

After the publication of his celebrated paper – *Understanding the mind of God* – which set out his revolutionary 'Theory of Everything',

Stolzfus had been catapulted into the international limelight and emerged as one of the greatest natural philosophers and mathematical physicists of his day. He had of course already obtained notoriety and fame earlier through his incredible story of survival and dramatic rescue after his very public poisoning in Westminster Abbey. News-hungry media and a curious public couldn't get enough of the enigmatic, paralysed genius who was confined to a wheelchair and communicated through a computer controlled by thought alone, via a device implanted in his brain.

After Greenberg had somewhat reluctantly given his approval, and with the generous support of Isis and her foundation, Stolzfus was relocated from the family farm in Pennsylvania to Cambridge, together with his carer and new PA. After the formal award ceremony earlier that day, which due to logistical reasons could only be attended by a privileged few, Isis – Lord Elms – as she was known in Cambridge due to a long family association with the university, had made arrangements for a celebration banquet at Queens' College.

Lola had thrown herself into this task with great enthusiasm and booked the Old Hall – the famous Queens' College dining hall dating from 1448 – where the illustrious Elms family had celebrated many an important occasion in the past. In many ways, the Old Hall was the perfect setting for a historic celebration like this, as it would provide a dining experience the fifty fortunate invited guests would remember for a long time to come.

'Very suave,' said Countess Kuragin, quickly adjusting Jack's bow tie. 'There. I don't think I've ever seen you in a dinner suit.'

'Not my scene, but Lola took me shopping. Isis is well known in Savile Row—'

'I can imagine.'

'You look stunning, by the way,' said Jack and linked arms with the countess. 'You brought the family jewels along, I see. Fit for a tsarina.'

'You really think so?' said the countess, obviously pleased about his compliment. 'Rarely get to wear them these days. So, if not today, then when?'

'Absolutely. It's great to see everyone turning up. Tristan and Lorenza took time off; Professor Greenberg came over last night with Rebecca and Celia, and even Agabe managed to leave the *Caritas* and come. Wonderful! And let's not forget, Isis sent her private jet to fly the entire Genius Club over. Not bad, eh?'

'This is a real celebration, Jack. And a lot of it has only been made possible because of you.'

'Right place, right time; that's all.'

'Nothing to do with destiny then?' teased the countess.

Jack raised an eyebrow. 'Perhaps just a little. There, look at Isis,' he said, changing the subject. 'How she thrives being the centre of attention. Wearing an old-fashioned, double-breasted dinner suit, would you believe, and her short hair parted in the middle. Charlie Chaplin meets Clark Gable. The only thing missing is the moustache. Amazing!'

'You know what they say, once a performer ...'

'Oh yes, I know all about that. I think she's Lord Elms for the night. Shall we go inside?'

'Let's.'

The beautifully restored Old Kitchens next to the Old Hall was the perfect venue for pre-dinner drinks. Most of the guests had already arrived and were chatting in groups and sipping champagne. Jack took a deep breath and looked around. Soaking up the festive atmosphere in the historic room dating back to the fifteenth century, he walked over to Tristan and Lorenza.

'You look absolutely ravishing,' said Jack and kissed Lorenza on the cheek. 'Am I still in the bad books?'

Lorenza rolled her eyes. 'No, but only if you promise not to drag my husband halfway around the world, exposing him to God knows what kind of danger and turning what should have lasted a few days into several weeks.'

'He volunteered,' retorted Jack. 'I didn't force him.'

'You didn't have to. It's your *influence* I'm worried about, not your powers of persuasion.'

'I promise to do better next time,' said Jack, trying to look serious.

'What does that mean?'

'We'll find out next time, I suppose.'

'Stop, or you will get us both into more trouble,' said Tristan and handed Jack a glass of champagne. 'Here, that should help.'

'Thanks, mate. Bearing in mind what's happening here tonight, it was all worth it, don't you think?'

'Absolutely.' Tristan lifted his glass. 'Thanks for the ride, Jack.'

'It's always a good feeling to have someone like you watch over me. Cheers!'

'You mean someone who can hear the whisper of angels and glimpse eternity?' said Celia, who had overheard Jack's remark.

'Exactly. Good flight?'

'Tight schedule.'

'What's new?'

'Will you excuse us for a moment,' said Celia. She linked arms with Jack and briefly took him aside. 'Thanks for everything, Jack. You gave me the opportunity of a lifetime with the Stolzfus matter.'

'Your articles saved my life and rescued Stolzfus. I don't think the Americans would have acted without them. You were the catalyst.'

'You are both wrong,' said Tristan, who had come over with Rebecca to join them. 'It's *destiny*, that's all.'

'He would say that, wouldn't he?' said Jack and winked at Celia.

'Jack, can I have a word please?' said Rebecca.

'Sure. Something wrong?'

'No. Quite the opposite. Isis told me she's asked you to propose a toast—'

'That's right. We won't have any speeches because Zac has to retire early. Doctor's orders. God knows what today has taken out of him, both physically and emotionally. And besides, all he wants is for everyone to have a good time. I've been told to keep it short.'

'Sure, but could you somehow include this?' Rebecca reached into her handbag and handed Jack a folded sheet of paper.

'Wow! This should make him happy,' said Jack after he had glanced at the paper. Especially on top of the surprise we have in store for him—'

'What surprise?' interrupted Rebecca, looking a little alarmed.

'If I were to tell you, it wouldn't be a surprise, would it?'

'Has anyone told you how exasperating you can be?'

'All the time. I think they want us to go inside and sit down; come.'

The Old Hall – the college's beautifully restored original dining hall – was certainly impressive. With its huge fireplace, stained glass windows, wood-panelled walls and stunning, decorated raked ceiling, the hall radiated style, history and class. Long tables seating twenty guests each had been set in traditional college dining hall manner, with one table for ten set at right angles at the front, conjuring up images of formal dinners presided over by stern professors and haughty masters as tradition demanded. The table lamps and subdued lighting reminded Jack of *Harry Potter* and the Hogwarts Great Hall, only without wizards, and more intimate and inviting. As Stolzfus wasn't going to stay long and certainly wouldn't be dining, it had been decided to begin the dinner with a toast in his honour.

As soon as all the guests were seated, Isis stood up, the accomplished performer in her enjoying the excitement and ripple of expectation around the room as everyone fell silent.

'It gives me great pleasure, my friends,' began Isis, speaking slowly, 'to welcome you here tonight to celebrate a truly historic occasion. Professor Stolzfus will join us in a moment but before he does, I must tell you that he will only be able to stay for a short while; doctor's orders. We will therefore start the evening in a slightly different way. I have asked Jack to say a few words and propose a toast. And he has a little surprise for you as well. After that, there will be no more speeches and Professor Stolzfus will retire. But not us.

We will celebrate well into the night and enjoy a wonderful dinner and many a glass of wine to honour a very special man.' Isis paused and pointed to one of the doors. 'Here he comes now!'

Everyone stood up and began to clap enthusiastically as the newly appointed Lucasian Professor of Mathematics entered the hall and manoeuvred his wheelchair across the room to the large fireplace at the far end. From there, he was able to see everyone in the room.

'Thank you for coming, my friends,' said Stolzfus, his voice sounding distant and strange, and out of place in the formal, yet intimate, atmosphere. 'I can't tell you what it means to me to see you all here tonight. As I haven't quite mastered the art of speaking eloquently through thought alone and still have a long way to go, I decided to leave that to others for the time being. I am much better with numbers, but that would stretch our friendship for sure.'

Subdued laughter echoed around the room.

Isis looked at Jack and nodded.

Jack stood up, cleared his throat and looked at Stolzfus.

'To ask a storyteller to say a few words, propose a toast and "keep it brief" is always risky, but I promise to do my best,' he began. 'I had it all worked out and knew exactly what I would say. But then, just before we came into the room, I was handed a note.' Jack paused and held up a piece of paper and turned to face Stolzfus. 'This is it here,' he said. 'It's a message from your father. When I read it, my carefully prepared speech paled into insignificance and I decided to let *this* message do the talking, because all the eloquence in the world couldn't equal it and express better what I had hoped to say.' Jack, an experienced public speaker, paused again to let the anticipation grow.

'"Words cannot describe how proud I am of you and what you've achieved, my son",' he began to read. '"My only regret is that your dear mother isn't here to see it. When I first saw you in your wheelchair, my heart sank and I thought that your life as we knew it was over. But how wrong I was. Often the path we have to follow is difficult to understand and paved with nails. Yours had more than most could bear. Yet, you never gave up and didn't despair, and never lost sight of who you are and where you were heading. You were given a precious gift: an extraordinary mind capable of extraordinary things. At first, I struggled with what you were doing and what you were hoping to achieve. When you told me as a boy that one day you would know the mind of God, I didn't understand and thought it was blasphemy. But again, how wrong I was. It wasn't blasphemy, but quite the opposite. To want to understand something like that, is to honour it. And you have done just that in a big way, and I can now see that this wouldn't have been possible without God's will and without a path paved with nails. When I was a boy, my father told me something as we were toiling in the fields one hot summer afternoon. I had slipped and fallen and badly hurt my knee. I have never forgotten what he said and would like to share it with you now on this, your big day. What he told me is in fact an old Amish saying: *Difficulty is a miracle in its first stage.* As long as you remember that, you will never lose your way and will always be able to cope with anything life throws in your path, because the miracle is still to come. Your loving father, Amos".'

At first there was complete silence, then the hall reverberated with thunderous applause, but Stolzfus kept staring into the distance – his face expressionless and silent – like a sculpture in one of Madame Tussauds' wax museums. Yet inside, his heart was jumping with joy. He had just been handed a precious gift he had longed for ever since he was a boy: the approval of the father he loved and admired, but from whom he had grown apart over the years.

Jack held up his hand. 'This brings me to the little surprise Isis mentioned earlier,' he said. 'It has taken a great deal of planning, ingenuity and cunning, and most important of all, a careful circumnavigation of baffling bureaucracy, rules and regulations to make this possible. And, I forgot to mention, a private jet and a trip across the Atlantic. Curious? I hope so!' Jack turned to Lola sitting next to him. 'Would you, please?'

'With pleasure.' Lola stood up and quickly left the room. Moments later, one of the doors opened and she returned with

Gizmo by her side, straining at his lead and pulling her towards the wheelchair. Lola stopped and let him off the lead. Gizmo ran up to Stolzfus and began jumping up and down, his tail wagging madly.

'Ladies and gentlemen,' said Jack, holding up his glass, 'now that the guest of honour has arrived, please charge your glasses and be upstanding. To Professor Zachariah Stolzfus, the newly appointed Lucasian Professor of Mathematics! May his extraordinary mind keep travelling through time and space to the far reaches of the universe, dazzle us with new insights and discoveries, and so bring us a little closer to knowing the mind of God.'

Afterword

Dr Hubert, director of the CIA, had a long memory. Acting on the report submitted by Major Andersen just before she perished in that fiery crash on the *Endeavor*, and supported by recent intelligence received about Alessandro Giordano, she knew it was time to act.

After the destruction of the H Cartel in Colombia, Chief Prosecutor Grimaldi had all but wiped out the drug culture in Florence with the help of Cesaria Borroni and the Squadra Mobile. This had hit the Lombardo family particularly hard because they had depended on the Colombian drug supply to sustain their business. A growing resentment and open animosity had developed between the Lombardos and Giordanos, but the latter had also found it easier – and more lucrative – to adapt to the new situation by moving into legitimate businesses, both in Italy and overseas.

After his father retired to a small farm in the country, Alessandro remained in Florence and was now running the thriving family business empire and was rapidly expanding his influence and Mafia domination there.

When CIA operatives, through their Italian agents, provided the Lombardos with proof that Alessandro had been instrumental in the destruction of the Colombian drug supply behind their backs, and were given the impression that this had been deliberate and part of a carefully planned strategy to ruin them, Alessandro's days were numbered.

Two weeks after Professor Stolzfus took up his appointment as the new Lucasian Professor of Mathematics at Cambridge, Alessandro decided to spend a week on the *Nike* with his girlfriend. Twenty minutes after the *Nike* left Fontvielle harbour, there was a huge explosion on board. The luxury yacht was obliterated and sank. There were no survivors. It was rumoured the Lombardos were behind it all, but no evidence to that effect was ever found, nor were the authorities particularly troubled by this.

Aladdin and Silvanus refused to talk and were eventually put on trial in Italy, convicted of Jack's abduction in Florence and sent to jail.

This had only been possible because of the evidence provided by Jack and Tristan, as the previous *Nike* crew had remained silent and refused to cooperate in any way.

Shortly after the trial, the Americans secured extradition arrangements with Italy. Both Aladdin and Silvanus would be extradited to the US after serving their sentences to face multiple terrorist-related charges in connection with the assassination of the US ambassador in Istanbul a few years earlier. It was almost certain they would spend the rest of their lives in jail.

Agabe's application for asylum in France was successful, and with the help of Countess Kuragin he was put in charge of the charity operating the *Caritas* out of Malta. Generously supported by the Isis Foundation and Rahima's money, the *Caritas* had been refitted and was one of the best-equipped hospital ships operating in Africa.

Staying discreetly in the background, Rahima directed a large network of charitable donations from Madame Petrova's apartment in the retirement home for aging celebrities and impecunious artists. She enjoyed her close proximity to Countess Kuragin, who became a close friend, and, of course, Jack when he was staying at the countess's chateau – which was quite often, especially when he was writing.

A Parting Note from the Author

Because a lot of cutting-edge science and medical subjects have been incorporated into the multi-layered storylines of this book, a few observations are definitely warranted to put that material into its proper context.

For me as a writer, authenticity and accuracy are paramount. Without that, it isn't possible to create a seamless storyline where the boundaries between fact and fiction are blurred, so that the reader is never quite sure where one ends, and the other begins. This is quite deliberate, as it creates the illusion of truth and reality in a work that is pure fiction. In my view, a successful work of fiction is a balancing act: reality must rub shoulders with imagination in a way that is both entertaining and plausible, and this can only be achieved through meticulous research and attention to detail.

All the material touching on physics, cosmology, technology and science generally, has been carefully researched and is, to the best of my knowledge, based on the latest findings and theories accepted by scientists today. The same can be said about the cutting-edge medical subjects, especially surgery, dealt with in the text. That said, please keep in mind that I am not a scientist, nor a doctor, but a fiction writer with a legal background whose aim is to entertain and tease your intellect and imagination with questions and scenarios that are both realistic and plausible, but are of course pure fiction.

The best way to illustrate this is by way of a few examples. Let's begin by examining Professor Fabry's cephalosomatic anastomosis (CSA), the controversial in vivo human head transplantation that is the centrepiece of the storyline. One could be forgiven for thinking that this is futuristic medical fantasy. Not so. Such an operation is definitely feasible and within reach, and is being contemplated right now. In fact, it may have already been carried out in China, where medical teams have been exploring the possibility of transplanting a human head for some time.

Only quite recently, Sergio Canavero – an Italian scientist – was in the news about planning such an operation on Valery Spiridonov, a patient with Werdnig-Hoffman disease. Canavero was working with Chinese surgeon Xiaoping Ren at Harbin Medical University to perfect the complex operation at the time. The surgical procedures described in the book are accurate, based on detailed research, and set out the main steps involved in such a complex, groundbreaking operation.

The extraordinary brain implant to facilitate communication with a computer via thought alone, is based on a recent technological breakthrough that has made this a reality. Technological advances to help incapacitated patients like Stolzfus have moved at a breathtaking pace, and Stolzfus's extraordinary wheelchair and his ability to speak and operate a computer assisted by technology and artificial intelligence software alone is not only feasible, but available today.

Another example is Professor Fabry's fictitious *Our Bodies* exhibition, which he used as a vehicle to raise money for his charity and clandestine work. The idea of such an exhibition is in fact anchored in real life. It does exist and features real bodies preserved in a unique, totally original way. It is based on a hugely successful travelling exhibition touring the world right now, called *Real Bodies*. I have seen this extraordinary, controversial exhibition just recently in Sydney.

Finally, all the concepts, theories and ideas relating to theoretical physics and cosmology featured in the book are based on the work of the late Professor Steven Hawking, who passed away in March 2018. I have followed the work of Professor Hawking for the past thirty years, and have admired his extraordinary insights and discoveries that have elevated theoretical physics to an entirely new level, and became the inspiration for this book.

MORE BOOKS BY THE AUTHOR

Jack Rogan Mysteries Starter Library
The Empress Holds the Key
The Disappearance of Anna Popov
The Hidden Genes of Professor K
Professor K: The Final Quest
Jack Rogan Mysteries Box Set Books 1-4

JACK ROGAN MYSTERIES STARTER LIBRARY

So, what exactly is a STARTER LIBRARY? I hear you ask. Well, it's a way to introduce myself and what I do, to new readers, and create interest in my writing. How? By providing little insights into my world, and the creative process involved in becoming an international thriller writer.

The Starter Library consists of four short books:
1. ***Letters from The Attic*** – a delightful collection of auto-biographical short stories;
2. ***The Forgotten Painting***– a multi-award-winning Jack Rogan novella;
3. ***The Kimberley Secret*** – a much-anticipated prequel to the Jack Rogan Mysteries series;
4. ***The Main Characters Profile*** – provides some exciting background stories and insights into the main characters featured in the series.

The Starter Library is available right now, and can be downloaded for FREE by following this link: https://gabrielfarago.com.au/starter-library2/

Please share this with your friends and encourage them to download the Starter Library.

In 2013, I released my first adventure thriller –
The Empress Holds the Key.

THE EMPRESS HOLDS THE KEY

A disturbing, edge-of-your-seat historical mystery thriller

Jack Rogan Mysteries Book 1

Dark secrets. A holy relic. An ancient quest reignited.
Jack Rogan's discovery of a disturbing old photograph in the ashes of a rural Australian cottage draws the journalist into a dangerous hunt with the ultimate stakes.

The tangled web of clues – including hoards of Nazi gold, hidden Swiss bank accounts, and a long-forgotten mass grave – implicate wealthy banker Sir Eric Newman and lead to a trial with shocking revelations.

A holy relic mysteriously erased from the pages of history is suddenly up for grabs to those willing to sacrifice everything to find it. Rogan and his companions must follow historical leads through ancient Egypt to the Crusades and the Knights Templar to uncover a secret that could destroy the foundations of the Catholic Church and challenge the history of Christianity itself.

Will Rogan succeed in bringing the dark mystery into the light, or will the powers desperately working against him ensure the ancient truths remain buried forever?

***The Empress Holds the Key* is now available on Amazon**

Encouraged by the reception of *The Empress Holds the Key*, I released my next thriller – *The Disappearance of Anna Popov* – in 2014.

THE DISAPPEARANCE OF ANNA POPOV

A dark, page-turning psychological thriller

Jack Rogan Mysteries Book 2

A mysterious disappearance. An outlaw biker gang. One dangerous investigation.

Journalist Jack Rogan cannot resist a good mystery. When he stumbles across a clue about the tragic disappearance of two girls from Alice Springs years earlier, he's determined to investigate.

Joining forces with his New York literary agent, a retired Aboriginal police officer, and Cassandra, an enigmatic psychic, Rogan enters the dangerous and dark world of an outlaw bikies gang ruled by an evil and enigmatic master.

Entangled in a web of violence, superstition and fear, Rogan and his friends follow the trail of the missing girls into the remote Dreamtime-wilderness of Outback Australia – where they must face even greater threats.

Cassandra hides a secret agenda and uses her occult powers to facilitate an epic showdown where the loser faces death and oblivion.

Will Rogan succeed in finding the truth, or will the forces of evil prevail, taking even more lives with them?

***The Disappearance of Anna Popov* is now available on Amazon**

My next book, *The Hidden Genes of Professor K*, was released in 2016. Here's a short sample to pique your interest:

THE HIDDEN GENES OF PROFESSOR K

A dark, disturbing and nail-biting medical thriller

Jack Rogan Mysteries Book 3

"Outstanding Thriller" of 2017
Independent Author Network Book of the Year Awards

A medical breakthrough. A greedy pharmaceutical magnate. A brutal double-murder. One tangled web of lies.
World-renowned scientist Professor K is close to a ground-breaking discovery. He's also dying. With his last breath, he anoints Dr Alexandra Delacroix his successor and pleads with her to carry on his work.

But powerful forces will stop at nothing to possess the research, unwittingly plunging Delacroix into a treacherous world of unbridled ambition and greed.

Desperate and alone, she turns to celebrated author and journalist Jack Rogan.

Rogan must help Delacroix while also assisting famous rock star Isis in the seemingly unrelated investigation into the brutal murder of her parents.

With the support of Isis's resourceful PA, a former police officer, a tireless campaigner for the destitute and forgotten, and a gifted boy with psychic powers, Rogan exposes a complex web of fiercely guarded secrets and heinous crimes of the past that can ruin them all and change history.

Will the dreams of a visionary scientist with the power to change the future of medicine fall into the wrong hands, or will his genius benefit mankind and prevent untold misery and suffering for generations to come?

***The Hidden Genes of Professor K* is now available on Amazon**

My next book, *Professor K: The Final Quest*, was released in October 2018. Here's a short sample to pique your interest.

PROFESSOR K: THE FINAL QUEST

An action-packed historical medical mystery

Jack Rogan Mysteries Book 4

Gold Medal Winner in the Fiction - Thriller - Medical genre!
2019 Readers' Favorite Annual Book Award Contest

A desperate plea from the Vatican. A kidnapped chef. An ambitious mob boss. One perilous game.

When Professor Alexandra Delacroix is called in to find a cure for the dying pope, she follows clues left by her mentor and friend, the late Professor K, which lead her on a breathtaking search through historical secrets, some of them deadly.

Her old friend Jack Rogan must step in to assist while also searching for kidnapped *Top Chef Europe* winner, Lorenza da Baggio.

He joins forces with his young friend and gifted psychic, Tristan, a dedicated mafia hunting prosecutor, a fearless young police officer, and an enigmatic Egyptian detective on a perilous hunt for a notorious IS terrorist.

Together, they stand off with the head of a powerful Mafia family in Florence and uncover a network of corruption and heinous crimes reaching to the very top.

Will Rogan and his friends succeed in finding Lorenza and curing the pope, or will the dark forces swirling around them prevail in their sinister plots?

***Professor K: The Final Quest* is now available on Amazon.**

JACK ROGAN MYSTERIES
BOX SET BOOKS 1-4

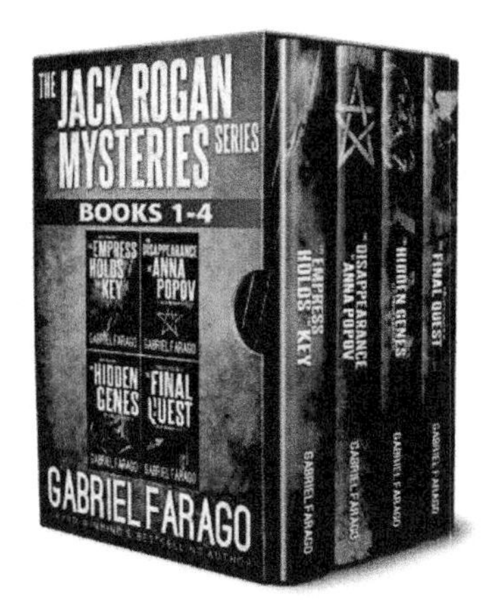

The Jack Rogan Mysteries Box Set **is now available on Amazon**

About the Author

Gabriel Farago is the international, best-selling and multi-award-winning Australian author of the Jack Rogan Mysteries series for the thinking reader.

As a lawyer with a passion for history and archaeology, Gabriel Farago had to wait for many years before being able to pursue another passion – writing – in earnest. However, his love of books and storytelling started long before that.

'I remember as a young boy reading biographies and history books with a torch under the bed covers,' he recalls, 'and then writing stories about archaeologists and explorers the next day, instead of doing homework. While I regularly got into trouble for this, I believe we can only do well in our endeavours if we are passionate about the things we love. For me, writing has become a passion.'

Born in Budapest, Gabriel grew up in post-war Europe and, after fleeing Hungary with his parents during the Revolution in 1956, he went to school in Austria before arriving in Australia as a teenager. This allowed him to become multi-lingual and feel 'at home' in different countries and diverse cultures.

Shaped by a long legal career and experiences spanning several decades and continents, his is a mature voice that speaks in many tongues. Gabriel holds degrees in literature and law, speaks several languages and takes research and authenticity very seriously. Inquisitive by nature, he studied Egyptology and learned to read the hieroglyphs. He travels extensively and visits all of the locations mentioned in his books.

'I try to weave fact and fiction into a seamless storyline,' he explains. 'By blurring the boundaries between the two, the reader is never quite sure where one ends, and the other begins. This is of course quite deliberate as it creates the illusion of authenticity and reality in a work that is pure fiction. A successful work of fiction is a balancing act: reality must rub shoulders with imagination in a way that is both entertaining and plausible.'

Gabriel lives just outside Sydney, Australia, in the Blue Mountains, surrounded by a World Heritage National Park. 'The beauty and solitude of this unique environment,' he points out, 'gives me the inspiration and energy to weave my thoughts and ideas into stories that in turn, I sincerely hope, will entertain and inspire my readers.'

Gabriel Farago

Author's Note

I hope you enjoyed reading this book as much as I enjoyed writing it. I'd be very grateful if you'd post a short review on Amazon. Your support really does make a difference.

Connect with the Author

Website
https://gabrielfarago.com.au/

Amazon
http://www.amazon.com/Gabriel-Farago/e/B00GUVY2UW/

Goodreads
https://www.goodreads.com/author/show/7435911.Gabriel_Farago

Facebook
https://www.facebook.com/GabrielFaragoAuthor

Signup for the author's New Releases mailing list and get a free copy of *The Forgotten Painting** Novella and find out where it all began ...

https://gabrielfarago.com.au/free-download-forgotten-painting/

* I'm delighted to tell you that *The Forgotten Painting* has just received two major literary awards in the US. It was awarded the Gold Medal by Readers' Favorite in the Short Stories and Novellas category and was named the 'Outstanding Novella' of 2018 by the IAN Book of the Year Awards.

Made in the USA
Monee, IL
25 June 2021